AMBASSADOR 12: THE UNFOLDING ARMY

PATTY JANSEN

GET FREE EBOOKS

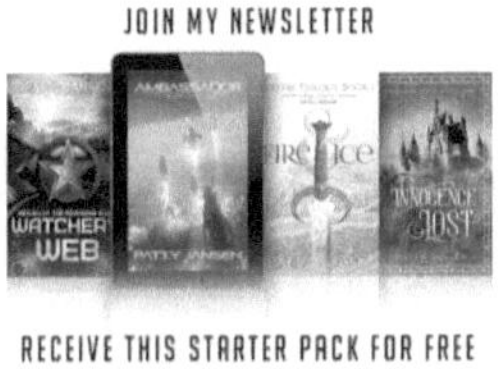

Visit pattyjansen.com
or scan the QR code below with your phone to get four series starter ebooks for free!

CHAPTER ONE

THE UPPER DECK of Asto's vast military command ship was not a place where I had come very often in the past three months.

It was the domain of personnel dressed in desert pink military uniforms who kept this ship running, nameless and faceless troops of which there were very many, and who considered me to be an oddity in this quiet, efficient and secretive place.

The civilians, including myself and my team, spent most of our time on the middle and lower decks of the habitat module, where, for one, there was more room than on this surprisingly cramped command deck.

After having declared for many years that Asto's military ships didn't do artificial gravity, I had found out that they, in fact, did. But only when stationed in orbit, because unfolding and setting up the habitat not only took energy from whatever military operations the ship was running, it also required a fair bit of time. It was, in fact, a mark of how comfortable the military had grown that they had the situation under control.

I know.

Famous last words.

When I entered the control room of this ship that had been my home for the past three months, the giant blue shape of my home planet occupied the top half of the view through the window. The half-orb was slowly rotating and sliding off to the side as both ship and planet moved independently. It was a beautiful sight, although not one I was used to seeing, and definitely not in such a dizzying, upside-down way. I had been to Earth's Space program's orbital station, but it hung out in much lower orbit. From up here, we could sometimes see that little unit whizz past, speeding like crazy on its endless quest to not fall back to the surface.

We were much further out, and moved slowly, and by stealth.

This giant and dangerous ship wasn't meant to be in this position. It had no authority to be here, certainly not for a period of three months. Nations of Earth had not acknowledged its presence and the *gamra* assembly was starting to make some very unhappy noises about it, and the attached military fleet. What were we doing? Was our presence warranted and, most importantly, had the local authorities asked for help from this ominous military fleet?

No. They had not.

Nations of Earth had barely been in contact with us since the drone attacks started, now more than three months ago.

They had definitely not agreed for the Asto military to hang out in orbit and although the fleet protected Earth, some shit was going to hit the fan over its unauthorised presence sooner rather than later.

But for now, the upper command room of this big and threatening war ship was a pleasant place, with the large circular bench rotated so that it faced the window, much like a tourist vessel for super-rich passengers.

There were, of course, the usual control workstations along the sides and the walls, but they were empty today. The ship wasn't doing very much, other than telling a fleet of smaller ships what to do, and to give commands to the many satellites that the military had launched.

One of the wall screens displayed a diagram of the locations of those satellites.

They kept Earth safe, all by themselves, because no one was watching them right now either. They did a good job.

There had been no successful drone attacks for three weeks now.

The atmosphere inside the ship exuded a sense of hope that we had begun to crack the code, that our tactics of waiting and observing were paying off and that it would be a matter of time before a slip-up by the nebulous and elusive enemy led us to the precise origin and control centre of these drones. Something that we could destroy that would stop the drones from coming, rather than react once they appeared.

Two men sat on this lush couch facing the window, and I knew both of them well. Ezhya Palayi, Chief Coordinator of Asto and his second, Asha Domiri, commander of the Asto military, and my father-in-law.

When I came around the front of the couch, I also saw a third man, even if he was not here in body.

The form of *gamra* Chief Delegate Marin Federza was projected onto a section of the couch in between the two others.

I nodded a greeting to him, which he acknowledged, a greeting which was relayed through satellites and the military's own Exchange node all the way to Barresh.

He said, "Well met, Delegate."

There was only a slight delay between image and sound. Somebody would be paying top money for this connection.

The presence of the projection left me with a kind of awkward decision: did I sit in between the two others in the middle of the projection, or did I take a much more awkward position on the end of the bench?

I decided neither was acceptable and remained standing, but Asha shifted sideways, making a spot for me so that I could sit at a proper spot at the end of the couch while being able to look Federza in his fake, projected eyes.

Asha's movement, in fact, caused the projection to shift as well.

Huh, a sentient projection. Yes, serious money was being spent here.

"Well then. It seems everyone is here. Let us start," Federza said. He met my eyes. His light, sand-coloured irises never failed to disturb me, not even when they weren't real. "And let me explain the reasons I need to speak with you. Although I'm confident that you probably know what this is about."

In typical Coldi style, neither Ezhya nor Asha said anything.

Ezhya held his arms crossed over his chest. He was wearing his red sash, which he only did when on official business.

Asha was in full uniform, the pink dress variety, with his jacket with shiny studs and decorations, with his weapon strapped to his arm and communication node blinking on his chest, with his two feeders and his hair tightly pulled back into the customary ponytail.

His face looked menacing at the best of times, but right now, his expression spelled thunder.

Right. They had called me up here to do the talking, because neither would score high marks on the *diplomacy* scorecard. Talking was, as everyone always reminded me, my job.

"The *gamra* assembly has debated your position and specifically the function and location of Asto's military forces," Federza began. "For quite some time now, we have understood that you were defending the planet from attacks, and we accommodate that view. But increasingly, the questions have grown louder about whether *defending the planet* is morphing into a more permanent situation, where you establish a permanent base in orbit. In order for us to keep approving and sanctioning your position, we will need to see that your defence of the planet is in fact necessary, and that the planet has, in fact, asked for your assistance."

They were well-chosen words that still didn't hide the underlying sentiment. There were a lot of parties in the *gamra* assembly that had said for a long time that Asto was trying to annex Earth by stealth, and that all the actions they took towards Earth had that underlying aim. These voices would be screaming murder right now.

"The planet is truly only safe because of the military's presence here," I said. "I can vouch for that."

"Oh yes, of course. So you would say. But there are those in the assembly who wonder whether your definition of *safe* is the same as that of people on the planet. They have, after all, signed up to begin the process of joining *gamra*, and member entities cannot occupy parts of territory that belongs to *other* member entities without their permission."

"They have not ratified those documents yet," Ezhya said, his arms still crossed over his chest.

And this was the usual problem. Because nobody understood, including myself really, why Earth, having signed to join *gamra* and having sent its first preliminary delegates, had stalled in the joining process. This had happened when Simon Dekker took over the presidency from Margarethe Ollund. There was no animosity, just a distinct feeling that Nations of Earth had other priorities.

Now, Earth and *gamra* operated in a kind of legal limbo and nobody was sure what laws applied.

The usual answer I gave to this question, which was *We haven't been able to contact them*, was fast outgrowing its usefulness.

Federza continued, "They are in the process of joining and have not given us reason to doubt their intent. They are, for the purpose of the current situation, a proper member of *gamra*. The assembly has debated and decided that the ability for us to give our continued approval of your presence in a member entity's orbital space without their specific agreement will be limited. To be blunt, you will need to show us proof that the authorities, namely Nations of Earth, sanctions your military presence, that you have communicated with them about what military actions you can undertake and what the limits of those actions are, and that you have agreed with them on a process whereby you return control of the orbital space to them once safety has been established."

And then I said the tired old words, anyway. "I have explained this to you many times, but we have not been able to establish any useful level of contact with them."

"And I remember you telling me this, and I have accepted your explanation. But as time wears on, I need to ask one thing: is the lack of your contact with them because you haven't tried, or is it because they don't want you there?"

"I believe it is neither."

"Don't you?"

Asha on the bench next to me made a small snorting noise. Ezhya pressed his lips together.

The three men had—how shall I say this—a bit of a history.

I remembered all too well one of those occasions where the three of them had been in the same room and Ezhya had pulled Federza up by the front of his well-tailored and expensive shirt.

Those were the days.

"I assume that the concept of democracy is strange to you, but I strongly believe that the vast majority of people on the planet object to being attacked from space—"

"—of course they do. There is no point being smart."

"No, I'm not being smart. Because the fact that we can't establish contact with the Nations of Earth assembly is irrelevant. The people on the planet, all four billion of them, object to being attacked by an agency they don't know and don't understand and never supported, even if that agency appears to be part of their own population."

I spread my hands, half-expecting arguments about the *part of the population* statement, because the attacks *did* come from some disenfranchised group who had split off from Earth's space colonisation effort and had wandered off into the void and people had forgotten about them until suddenly three months ago, they'd sent an army of drones.

I was even half-expecting the statement that if this was the case, neither *gamra* or the Asto military had a place in the conflict and we should let them sort it out and negotiate with whomever emerged as the victor.

And I would have something to say about that line of thinking because I flatly refused to deal with thugs.

But he said nothing, so I continued in a more measured voice, because holy crap, I suddenly hated his arrogant Aghyrian butt. He knew nothing, he did nothing except make up impractical and irrelevant rules for the sake of looking like he was doing something.

"I don't know why Nations of Earth are not engaging in meaningful discussion with us. I very strongly suspect that part of the reason is safety. In the past, the attacks have followed patterns of communication. They're in hiding, they don't want to be discovered, they don't want us to be unmasked, or worse, they simply don't have a functional assembly at the moment and can't debate replies to our communication. We have evidence that there have been attacks on the assembly, and I've heard rumours that certain parts of the bureaucracy have moved to underground shelters."

"But at the same time, the president has not spoken to you since that message where he supposedly asked you for help?"

"Not supposedly. He did ask for help. I can send you a recording of it if you want. I know the man, and he dislikes me so much that he would die before he asked me for help. Yet he did ask, and I believe him, so this is a strong reason why I am still here, and while I don't command the Asto military," I looked sideways at Asha. He smiled. I wasn't sure why because I was losing my patience with this man— deep breath. "While I don't command the Asto military, they are the only means available to stop my world of origin from falling into the hands of blatant thuggery. I object to innocent people being subjected to a regime of terror while we all sit around and debate the legalities of what we could potentially do to help them."

"You never cease to give good arguments."

"I'm a diplomat. That's what I do."

"Fair enough, and I have given you leniency for quite a while already. But this has now gone on for so long that people in the assembly, including me, are no longer willing to wait. We want to see some results or some justification for this continued situation. I strongly suggest that you address our concerns. At the next sitting, the assembly will debate this issue again. They are likely to withdraw their consent for your presence in a member's orbital space without seeing their express approval. This has gone on for long enough. You've had your time. Various members need to see better justification."

And with that, he disappeared off the couch.

He left a silence in which both Ezhya and Asha glared at me.

Then Ezhya said, in perfect Isla, "Fuck his bony arse."

I chuckled. "Who has been giving you lessons?"

But my mirth about Ezhya's remark didn't last long. He knew exactly what he'd said, and he meant it.

If I was rather unimpressed with this situation, I could only guess how these two men must feel about the bureaucratic incursion in their lives.

Asto did not do democracy.

They objected to being told what to do at the best of times.

"We need a plan for some quick action," I said.

"What we need is to send some well-chosen language to that arrogant prick," Asha said. "What does he think he is?"

"He is still the Chief Delegate of *gamra*. I think overall he has done a decent job. As a person, I don't really like him either. But overall, he has been quite fair, and we have expected this moment to come up sooner or later."

And then nobody said anything for a while, because we had debated this before, and we all knew that there was going to be an end to Asto's unchecked reign in Earth's orbital space, even if we were the only entity defending the planet.

Ezhya snorted. "So what? Do we try to reach another diplomat to sign an agreement that will take the *gamra* assembly all of a day to rip apart?"

Asha said, "They make it so very tempting to ignore the whole lot of them."

But while he was full of bluster, he would never do that. As much as Asto and *gamra* could seem at odds, both also needed each other for a wide variety of reasons.

"With your permission, we might try something different," I said into the silence.

They both gave me a sharp look.

I began, "The situation has been stable for a while with recent drone attacks that have penetrated our defences."

Asha gestured, *go on.*

"The communication chief has told me that the main networks are secure."

"Yes," Ezhya said. "There will be no problem talking to the Nations of Earth assembly this time."

There had been plenty of issues last time.

I continued, "But who will I be able to reach? President Simon Dekker sent us a garbled message asking for help three months ago and we still can't track where it came from. We know we have the situation under control, but do they know that?"

"I made sure that we told them," Asha said.

"Would they listen? Would they believe us? Their track record is not good."

He lifted his chin. "What are you saying? That they've become distrustful? That's hardly news."

"I'm saying that it's very hard to assess what's going on—and to get an agreement of the type that would satisfy *gamra*—from up here, so if the situation is stable, I propose to write up an agreement. There are excellent lawyers on board this ship. With this document, I shall travel to the Nations of Earth assembly and present it to them, explain the reasons for our presence, make amendments if they want, and get the highest authority in attendance to sign the agreement. That way, we can be certain that we'll get *gamra* off our backs."

"Hmmm," Ezhya said, but he clearly liked the idea. Doing something like this was totally his style. "Yes, we can probably do that now. If you could pull that off, it would save us a lot of trouble. Just for a small spearhead party. Do we have the security coverage for the area?"

"We do," Asha said, and he brought up another projection above the table in the middle of the circular couch. It showed areas where they had control and where they didn't, based on countless intercepted communications that had been analysed by the huge team downstairs. Europe was considered safe territory.

He continued, "I would still like to be cautious and send a well-shielded craft, and provide backup from orbit, and use an independent communication node, and make sure the group was well-prepared and well-armed."

"Do we ever go into anything unprepared?"

He chuckled. "You might do things less well-prepared than Sheydu would like."

"That's an impossible bar to clear," I said.

"Yeah." He let a short silence lapse in which an amused smile crossed his face. "Take Sheydu."

I guessed we had decided the trip was on. To be honest, it was a relief after so much time of being inactive. Of watching and waiting.

"Anyone else I need to consider taking?"

"A good lawyer, anyone who speaks a local language, anyone who has been there before and who has local knowledge. Don't worry about transport, defense and fighting. I will lend you an elite unit to do that for you."

"Well, I do have a few excellent fighters."

"Yes, take them. But you should be in and out quickly, and then we can get those off our backs and get on with the real job, like finding the command centre of these attacks."

He clapped me on the shoulder and for a moment, I felt we were getting on top of the situation.

But of course, reality was not as simple as that.

CHAPTER TWO

WHEN AMARRU HEARD of the impending expedition, she pleaded to be allowed to come. I was hesitant to make the party any bigger than necessary, because more people meant more danger and less flexibility.

I told her to ask Asha, in the hope that he would fob her off and tell her to wait, but he agreed.

Having an increased number of people at the Exchange to resume some of their operations would help our expedition, he said.

But of course she had another motive.

For the past three months, since shutting down the Exchange core and evacuating most of its workers, she had watched with anxiety from orbit as attacks raged and might hit or miss the building, and she would spend ages sending encrypted messages to her remaining staff on the ground to check whether they were all right.

In short, she was sorry she had abandoned her position and wanted to go back.

"If the Exchange dies, I will die with it," she told me. "I have nothing else. I can't go back to Asto. I wouldn't know what to do there. I never did any of the selection trials. My life is in Athens."

I heard on the rumour mill that the fact that her life partner had chosen to stay behind had a lot to do with this. There were even accounts that he had accused her of pandering to Ezhya—on whose orders she had closed the Exchange.

I knew very little about Amarru's partner, but suspected that he might belong to a rogue section of the Zhori clan and that he would rather die than put his life in the hands of Asto.

Deeply split loyalties had always characterised Amarru's life.

Personal motivations aside, Asha agreed with Amarru that it would be good to have some Exchange operations functioning and that it was probably safe to start ramping up the core.

In his words, worse than being discovered by the enemy was to not succeed in our mission and the Exchange was an important tool. Being discovered by the enemy didn't mean failure, he said. It just meant he'd have to dedicate *extra resources* to keeping us safe.

Resources with advanced weaponry, no doubt. Great.

So my hopes to keep our party small and nimble by telling Amarru to talk to Asha, and expecting him to tell her to wait, back-fired spectacularly.

Worse, instead of getting dropped closer to the Nations of Earth complex in Rotterdam, we would go to Athens and we would then have to make our way across several countries.

And this happened while we only had three weeks until the next *gamra* assembly sitting and we were going to spend a good deal of that time catching trains across Europe.

It was, Amarru assured me, an excellent way of assessing the situation on the ground.

Great, but she wasn't the one having to cross a continent using public transport systems that might or might not be functional.

"It might take us days or weeks to get to Rotterdam," I said.

"I don't know where you were expecting to be dropped off. We can't just fly a military craft over densely populated areas into Rotterdam. That would be certain to upset the Nations of Earth assembly and they have a whole raft of rules that they can use to punish us with."

"Those rules have never stopped us before."

"In remote areas, yes. Not anywhere near the Nations of Earth complex."

"We're in a war."

"The Exchange can lose its permission to operate. I'm not willing to risk that."

Her eyes were fierce.

Of course, she took a lot of pride in honouring these agreements. The situation was somewhat different now, but I let it go.

It wasn't worth the argument.

Besides, I was sure she was right.

And Amarru was a terrible stickler for rules, which she had to be, operating in the hostile environment in Athens for years.

I understood why, but it still annoyed me.

So, we were going to be dropped off near Athens, and would somehow have to make our way to Rotterdam.

What a stupid waste of time in the middle of a conflict where we had a deadline hanging over our heads, a deadline that would affect the local people much more than anyone. Bureaucratic rules versus the future of the planet.

The pinnacle of stupidity.

"Hey," Thayu said in the tiny cabin that we shared. "It's not that big a deal. Let her live with her rules. We'll be fine."

"This is about the future of the planet," I burst out. "About me, about my father and Erith, about Emi."

I gestured at Emi, out cold on the little mat in the corner of our cabin.

"This is about whether I can ever come back to the place of my birth, about whether billions of people live or die, and she is worried about *rules*."

"We'll be fine. The trains are running, Reida says, and after we've left the Exchange, we can do as we want. We need Amarru's cooperation, and she worries about the Exchange. We've all been worried about the Exchange. Now that the threat of attacks is less, it's important that we make sure it doesn't fall into the hands of people who shouldn't have control over it."

"Huh. Do you know anything I don't?"

She flicked her eyebrows. "The situation might be stable, but we shouldn't forget that we've discovered very little about where the threat is coming from and how much help they have from rogue groups like Zhori rogues and their sympathisers on the ground. It's important to get enough people back into the Exchange so that it can run again."

Thayu had been uncharacteristically diplomatic with her opinions recently. Where people would say opinions are like arseholes, everyone's got one, she would say opinions are like pimples, they draw attention to the wrong part of someone's face. It was, apparently, one of the proverbs commonly used at the spy academy.

Right. This was her way of telling me that there was something going on in her sphere of work, which involved secret meetings with high-ranking military people.

It was also a reminder to stick to my task, which was preparing my team.

I only needed to bring as many people as needed and then only the ones with skills we needed.

Veyada offered to look after the children. There were many people more useful in stealth and combat than he was, and Mereeni was much better at Earth law besides.

Everyone with an inkling of understanding of Isla would come. Nicha, Evi, Telaris. Then Thayu, Deyu and Reida, and Sheydu. Also Isharu and Zyana, whose skill as sharpshooter I'd not yet witnessed, but was said to be legendary.

Leisha would prepare my craft and would take my father and Erith and Veyada and the children to my father's farm. Now that it was safe enough, he was keen to return home to look after his llamas.

One or two from Sheydu's association would go with him, and the rest would stay on board the military ship to assist us and the military, especially Anyu, who would look after our communication with the ship.

I asked Ynggi if he wanted to go with Veyada, but he wouldn't have a bar of it. He was going to protect me, no matter what.

"I have promised Isharu that I would be available to her," he said.

I assumed this meant he wanted to stay on board the command vessel. What for, I had no idea.

"Isharu?"

I'd noticed that he'd gone off to do things, as we all had. I'd seen him with Isharu a few times, but hadn't noticed any particular relationship between the two.

During the three months we'd all been subjected to intense testing, as the military called it, personality tests and aptitude tests. They'd been voluntary, but most of us were bored and wanted to help, and the tests were kind of fun, little games, even if I knew Coldi didn't play games for fun.

No one in the military had ever come back to me about the tests and I'd assumed they wanted me to keep using the part of me for which they had little use: my mouth.

It hadn't dawned on me that *other* members of my team might have been found to possess far more useful skills.

Ynggi, apparently. And he was being tutored by prim and proper, military Isharu of the high-class Vonayi clan.

I didn't know how to feel about that. He was so much smaller than us and came with less physical strength as a result. He was fast and good at climbing things, but that wasn't much help in a fight. The tribe had trusted me with his wellbeing.

I told him, "This trip may be dangerous."

It was a lame argument and an utterly lame expression of feelings I had trouble voicing. I imagined having to go to Abri telling her that her trusted envoy hadn't made it out of a world that wasn't his, defending people who didn't care about people who looked like him, who called him a monkey.

"You came to my village, and that was dangerous. Now we have to save your world from the same people. The tribe would be upset if I didn't help."

Ah, that was the real issue: *karrit* points. Maybe he had cajoled Evi and Telaris or Deyu into maintaining the complicated accounting system for those points even while he was away from his home. I thought Ynggi's standing in the tribe was already good. What favour would he be able to negotiate for yet more points?

The tribe had already allowed him to have partners, and he couldn't aspire to become an elder. He wasn't old enough and the tribe elders were almost always female.

His motivations were a mystery, but throughout my objections about danger and this not being his world or his problem, he remained adamant.

He said, "If you are afraid that I'm small and not very strong because I'm small, and that I don't know how to handle modern weapons, I have been training on board this ship."

Over his shoulder, Sheydu watched our conversation, and she gestured her approval. She had probably conducted the training in the idle months that we had hung in orbit. Most people on board had gone through at least some training.

But for Sheydu to approve, it had to be something special.

So reluctantly I put Ynggi in the team as well.

We packed, we prepared. We said goodbye to my father, Erith, Veyada and the children. To Nicha's dismay, Ayshada was happy to go, but Emi made the most heart-rending scene in the—very military— departure hall.

Thayu was trying to hold it together, to appear professional, to keep up her madam spy persona, but she was struggling.

This was a dangerous mission, and in the moment that the group walked away, my father holding Emi, whose screams echoed around the departure hall, this really hit me. We were at war with an invisible enemy, and we might hit trouble and not come back.

My eternally over-active imagination saw Emi putting on her school uniform and carrying her bag on her way to the tiny school in White Bay, all alone without her parents. And it wasn't something I wanted to think about, or something that was halfway helpful for me to think about.

Thayu was still waving, although I doubted Emi could still see her. I had to pull myself together because there was a lot of work to be done.

When I turned around, I found Asha waiting to speak with me. He told me he was sending a full association of military guards with us. They came forward: seven people—men and women I guessed— but in all the years of dealing with Coldi I had come no closer to definitively being able to tell gender in these nameless, faceless mili- tary people who all wore armour and protective gear, their hair pulled back in an immaculate ponytail from their flat, emotionless faces.

The leader of the association performed a submissive greeting to me, and Asha told me that *mashara*, the Coldi collective and singular noun for a security unit, would look after our safety.

It had been a long time since I had last addressed security personnel with this term, and the memory of that time was not a pleasant one. We were not supposed to know their names, because that would distract them from doing their jobs.

I let my gaze roam over the similar outfits and similar hairstyles. Coldi faces typically confused Earth humans, but I'd spent enough time around Coldi people that I'd learned to recognise people.

Mashara, huh? We'd see about that.

Their presence increased the numbers in our group such that we needed a second shuttle. If necessary, Asha said, there would also be other craft on standby.

"You're really pulling out all resources," I said to him while standing in the lift foyer that would take us to the departure's docking hall.

I understood that once the civilians were all gone, including my father and Erith and the children, they would fold the rotating arm back up and the ship would return to weightlessness, so that they could react quickly to developing situations.

He gestured yes, his face disturbingly grim.

"We don't have the luxury of time. We can't negotiate with these rule-pushers. If we try, we'll be accused of annexing the planet. But we desperately need to stop these people. They tried to destabilise Barresh and failed, but that doesn't mean they won't try again. We have two options: either we find who they are, they start talking and negotiate a meaningful peace, or they won't do anything of the sort, in which case I will order the military sling to come within range and we will fire it at localities where sympathisers are known to be, and keep doing this until they show themselves and fight and they're defeated or they're all dead. Simply retreating and leaving them be is no option, because these people have the stealth and technology to create trouble for us in the future."

They would do that, too, if the Aghyrian experience was anything to go by.

He continued, "*Gamra* wouldn't be so wise as to foresee the danger and act accordingly. The assembly is hijacked by people who make it their first priority to hurt Asto without considering any of the other matters. Sadly, they do have the power to make us sing and dance. They can just exclude us from the Exchange network with the flick of a switch."

"More than that, Asto actually signed *gamra*'s conditions so it would be advised to keep to them."

"Yes."

That was a *yes* so full of meaning that each letter of the short word carried a dictionary of implications.

I didn't ask what "yes" meant.

Whether he implied that Asto was fed up with *gamra*'s restrictions, whether there was a risk that Asto would go it alone, much as the Tamer Collective had done, whether they would act in defiance of *gamra*'s rules.

One thing had been clear to me from the start: Ezhya and his extended association that controlled Asto's reactions were deeply concerned about a civilisation that could mount attacks of this technological level while also shielding itself from detection. Such a civilisation was by definition a large society and Asto had no appetite, like, absolutely none at all, to let this society stake out a spot on the already crowded dance floor of power.

They would negotiate with the Aghyrians and the Tamer Collective. They would even accept a second Exchange system. After the Exchange had gone down a number of years ago, they probably secretly wanted a backup system, anyway. But they would, under no circumstance, allow anyone at that table who had a halfway decent military power.

And they would bust apart the *gamra* agreements before they allowed that.

So it was up to me to come up with a solution before the next *gamra* assembly sitting. Preferably, while not letting four billion people on my planet of origin die in the process.

Seriously, no pressure at all.

CHAPTER THREE

SO I HAD to admit it was a fairly grim group making our way to the Athens Exchange.

The military did end up finding a craft big enough to take all of us. The vehicle was so basic inside that it didn't even provide us with connectivity.

We were officially silent, not allowed to use, or communicate with, devices that sensitive enemy equipment could pick up. Communications officers, assisted by Anyu who was going to stay at the ship, had provided us with safe encrypted devices but we couldn't use them until the local hub was operational. And that apparatus sat in the cargo nets with the other luggage. It was also only to be used for essential information, and not for the chatter I liked to listen to: the local news, the background conversations that went on in the communities of Nations of Earth and the Exchange enclave. So I had nothing better to do than stare out the window while others caught up on sleep.

The craft took us to the same farmhouse outside Athens where, a long time ago, I had met Asha when hunting down Romi Tanaqan.

The first glow of dawn radiated over the hills on the other side of the valley. Rows of olive trees poked out of the haze. A group of goats grazed in a stubble field.

The farmhouse looked less run down than I remembered. For one, a very schnazzy modern farm tractor stood in the yard.

I also didn't remember the large solid-looking shed with the metal doors next to the old farmhouse.

The doors were open, allowing the craft to move half into the entrance.

The pilot opened the door.

Asha's people unclipped the cargo netting, allowing us to collect our things and carry them into the hall.

The luggage grew into a big heap against the side wall.

While we were gathering our things, the craft did not turn off the engines, and when we had finished, two sections in the middle of the concrete floor dropped and then moved aside.

Bits of dirt and straw on the concrete, and a charging lead that a man hastily dragged aside, indicated that the tractor normally stood over the trapdoor.

When it was fully open, the aircraft moved forward and slowly disappeared into the ground. The pilot climbed out, and then the slabs of concrete moved back into position.

We put on our backpacks, shouldered our bags and carried everything into the yard.

A tall fence ran between the house and the shed, behind which two dogs barked and growled like crazy.

They poked their snouts through the gaps between the palings, showing teeth and pulled-up lips.

I remembered those dogs, although these were probably not the same ones. Thayu had been scared of them.

Ynggi snapped his tail with a crack.

The dogs stopped barking for a few seconds before starting to growl again.

He said something in Pengali. His tail went up into the air and wiggled.

The dogs fell quiet.

A bus waited in front of the house, a plain unmarked twenty-seater.

The driver, who sat waiting on the bottom step, greeted Amarru with a smile and a clap on her shoulder. Not a traditionally Coldi way of greeting someone of higher rank.

He shoved as much of our luggage as would fit into the luggage compartment underneath, and we carried the electronics and small bags up the stairs into the cabin.

I ended up somewhere halfway down the bus' aisle.

The driver got in last, shut the door and steered the bus down the bumpy and pothole-riddled driveway to the road that ran past the property.

Amarru remained at the front with the driver. He was from the local Coldi population, and they were exchanging news.

The bus made its way across the valley with its selection of active and abandoned olive orchards, past the dilapidated checkpoint shacks and fence lines that used to indicate the boundary of the Exchange enclave.

Nobody said much on the bus.

Deyu sat on the first bench behind the driver and Ynggi in the back. It was their task to look out for unusual things.

Deyu was in the full black battle gear given to her by the military, including the uncomfortable armour that I also wore, and that cut into the soft flesh under my arms.

She wore a headset that would normally go under the helmet, but this helmet lay on the seat next to her, together with an impressive military grade gun. That was not her normal gear.

Ynggi wore a shimmering protective suit that covered most of his body. The people in charge of outfits in the giant military ship had displayed levels of curiosity and skill to offer him an outfit that was the right size and that didn't include jamming his tail into the trouser legs. They had developed a flexible glove for it that only left the all-important white-haired tip uncovered and also allowed him to keep using his tail for climbing and communicating. The effect of the military attention on his confidence had been profound. He had shown me the suit after he got it, utterly pleased that snapping his tail in his new gear resulted in a resounding crack and whistle. Jamming his tail in the door apparently also didn't hurt him.

He also wore a pair of wraparound sunglasses that included a sensor that tracked eye movement and was paired to the short and stubby charge gun he carried on a bracket on his arm, a weapon also designed especially for him.

Sheydu and the others in the team were in discussion. She held one of the approved, fully shielded devices on her lap and was talking about something on the screen in jargon. Reida sat on his knees on the seat in front of her, leaning over the backrest.

Mereeni looked on from the seat behind.

Thayu and Zyana stood in the aisle hanging onto loops in the ceiling or the armrests.

Isharu sat on the floor in the back of the bus, surrounded by electronics. She was kitting out a few additional devices to be safe for local communication. Occasionally, she handed a device to one of Asha's people, seven silent, massive, highly armed men and women— I wasn't sure which and their abundance of armour made it hard to tell.

They sat in the seats between us and Ynggi in the back, silent, dark mountains of muscle, weapons and electronics.

It was customary that you didn't communicate with guards, calling them by the collective noun *mashara*, but I didn't like this and I wasn't alone in this opinion. Ezhya himself had two children with the former head of his guard association.

Right now, they were talking to Evi and Telaris, whom I had referred to as *mashara* long ago.

I sat next to Nicha, who was asleep because he also had little knowledge about this security operation.

The bus crested the saddle of the low ridge and we were now going down into the city, meandering between the abandoned buildings, shrubbery and whatever small farm plots and olive groves were still operational.

It was scarred country.

This area had always endured times of conflict, and once had harboured forested suburbs that were the home of the well to do in the city, until most of the hillside went up in flames one too many times and the rich abandoned their houses or never rebuilt them and packed up for the city or less flammable places like northern Scotland or Sweden.

The hospital on the hillside that used to serve those well-off people now housed the Exchange. It was a relic of that time.

It was still surrounded by forest groves, and they still battled fires most summers.

Apparently they had tried growing megon trees from Barresh as a protective ring around the building, because the oil was a strong fire retardant, but the climate was to dry so they resorted to spraying megon oil to make sure that the building didn't go up in flames.

I could see that familiar building from a distance, poking out of the haze.

The driver told us to get onto the floor of the bus, just in case there was any trouble. No, he didn't expect any, he said, but just in case.

We all got off the seats onto the dusty floor. Nicha got woken up and looked grumpy.

Ynggi got off his seat, but attached a small device to a strip to the end of the sleeve that covered his tail. He stuck it up over the edge of the window so that he could still see outside. His screen showed road-side shrubbery flashing past.

I looked at Thayu. She met my eyes, but her expression was empty.

It was hard to figure out what she was thinking, since we'd said goodbye to Emi on the military ship in orbit with my parents. Thayu would normally prefer to take our daughter, but this mission was truly too dangerous. I was glad that I hadn't needed to argue this case.

Mereeni had faced a similar dilemma. In debating who would come on this trip and who would look after Ileyu, Veyada had offered to come, but his mother had only wanted Mereeni on the trip, because of her experience in the Hedron guards and because she spoke Isla really well.

Deyu announced that she'd set up the local network, so we should test our devices.

I took mine out of my pocket where it had sat since we'd left the military ship—seriously I didn't think I'd ever not looked at my reader for so long—and turned it on. The logo of the local network scrolled over the screen.

"Mine works," I said.

Others confirmed the same.

I stuck the device back in my pocket, because we had agreed that we should keep use of electronics to a minimum, and certainly my obsession with checking news sources would be considered *frivolous use* by Sheydu, even if I liked checking the news and not having to rely on my team to let me know if something important happened.

Sheydu crawled through the aisle and picked up a reader that Isharu held out to her, which she then handed to Amarru. We were getting close to our destination and Amarru needed to disable the security locks to get into the compound.

Amarru brought the device to life with a touch of her thumb. It came up with a scan portal that required her to put her hand on the screen and then asked access to her feeder. But she wasn't wearing one, like all the rest of us, because we'd deemed them too risky. Feeders were designed to seek out and respond to the weakest transmitted signals.

Amarru put the reader on her lap and put her hand in her pocket.

"What are you doing?" Isharu asked.

"I can't access the Exchange's security codes without the feeder."

Her tone was brusque, condescending almost.

I'd noticed this brusqueness in her towards people with power in Athyl before. Amarru had strong relationships with the Zhori clan, and that clan had almost disappeared from Asto.

She located the feeder and had to untangle its long and spidery legs.

Reida was watching intently as she did this.

She lifted the feeder to the back of her head.

"Amarru, stop." I put my hand on her arm.

She gave me a surprised look. "I don't have access without it. I need to open the gate and the entrance."

"With the modifications Isharu has made, you shouldn't need the feeder."

Reida made a hand signal. He agreed.

Amarru lowered her hand.

Reida breathed out a relieved breath.

Sheydu, Isharu and Thayu stared at the reader with horrified looks. Had they missed something with their testing?

Amarru looked from the feeder in her hand to the screen. "I thought this device was safe?"

Reida said, "It probably still is. I don't think we should risk it."

"No." Sheydu reached out and took the reader back from Amarru. She flicked through the menus, but it didn't look like she found anything. Her face was set in a deep frown.

The military guards had figured that something was up. Sheydu gave the reader to one of them, a broad-shouldered young woman with a hard, determined face.

A colleague passed a scanner over it. He frowned at the screen, but said nothing.

"*Mashara*, do you think there is trouble?" I asked.

The man showed the screen to another in the group. Blue text scrolled across a black background. They both studied the screen for a good five minutes, ignoring my question.

Meanwhile, we arrived at our destination.

The gate in the tall wall that surrounded the compound was shut.

The bus stopped.

Well, that was kind of interesting. We had arrived at the Exchange but couldn't get in.

From what I understood, the few people who guarded the building never left it, living off the huge stocks of supplies stored in the extensive underground sections of the complex.

If this was an enemy structure, we would blast our way in, but we had an interest in keeping the Exchange safe.

And now that we doubted the safety of the feeder that Amarru needed to open the gate or communicate with the people inside, we were stuck out here on the road where no one was likely to see us.

Great.

What was worse, I really needed to pee.

The driver opened the door.

I was the second person to jump out, after Deyu, who checked the road before signalling it was safe for us to come out.

The wall that surrounded the complex lined one side of the road.

Across the gate was the entrance to a driveway that led to a sprawling residence that had once housed some sort of wellness commune, but that had lain empty for many years.

Stunted gum trees grew in the shrubbery, some with black marks on their trunks, relics of fires that had passed through.

I walked a little down the uneven flagstone paving and did my business in an area of shrubbery where pine saplings of a few metres tall grew amongst blackened tree trunks. In places, a vine with bright green leaves covered fallen branches. The air was thick with the smell of gum resin and smoke and the incessant racket made by cicadas.

I was on the way back and in view of the bus when I spotted movement in the undergrowth.

I called out, "Action!"

At first, a white and brown goat shot out of the bushes. It ran across the road, realised that the wall around the Exchange complex was in its way, then did a sharp left turn and ran off down the road.

Deyu lowered the weapon she had pulled out.

Reida came out of the bus laughing, but Deyu raised the weapon again, aimed to the left of where I was coming back up to the bus and discharged.

A discharge always made the hair on my arms stand up.

A split second of utter silence was followed by a heavy thump of something falling down in the bushes and dead wood.

Mereeni jumped from the bus and she and Reida ran across. I took my weapon from the bracket on my arm and ran to the bus.

Most of the others had come onto the road. Sheydu, Isharu, Nicha, Evi and Telaris, and Ynggi. They all stood around the vehicle protecting it like a wall of armour and weapons.

Asha's guards had dispersed across the closest section of the road. All had pulled on their helmets.

Reida stood in the bushes near the attacker, while Deyu and Mereeni crashed through the bushes. Another discharge chilled the air, followed by a man's shout and someone running away.

The guards fanned out through the narrow patch of shrubbery between the road and the messy remains of the lawn in front of the old commune building, dotted with thistles and tussocks of grass.

I joined Reida with the fallen attacker.

One side of his clothing and protective jacket had singed away, revealing raw and blistered skin. His neck was bent at an uncomfort- able angle, and his face set in an expression of permanent surprise.

His lifeless eyes were open. They were grey. His hair was dark blond and the stubble on his chin reddish.

"He's not going to run anywhere," I said.

Reida shook his head. "Nope. Deyu doesn't mess around." Said with a deep appreciation of Deyu's lethal force.

"Did you see what happened?"

"He must have been disturbed when you came too close to him. He scared the animal and when we saw him, he pointed a weapon at us."

This weapon now lay in the dead branches and pine needle litter. Reida picked it up and turned it over in his hands. I was no longer familiar with the makes of weapons on Earth, but Sheydu would no doubt have something to say about it.

Reida used the laser setting on his weapon to cut through a leather belt that the man wore around his waist. A pouch was attached to it, as well as an electronic device in a small box, square with rounded corners, with a few rubbery buttons and a small screen that was black.

"What is it?" I asked.

Reida shrugged. "We'll find out."

He yanked at the man's jacket and searched the pockets. He found another small device and some keys.

In the pockets of his trousers, he found a card and a European travel pass. We had a small stack of those ourselves.

A bit further into the shrubbery, Deyu, Mereeni and the guards had discovered the remains of a camp, with a crudely-dug fire pit and areas of flattened vegetation where people had slept. But those were the only signs that people had been here. For all I knew, these people could be squatters or refugees.

Would they shoot at us?

It'd be more likely that they'd ask us for money or food, right?

I didn't like this.

We returned to the bus. Asha's guards followed not long after. One had picked up a piece of fabric, like a ripped shirt.

They signalled they thought the threat had passed.

"Well," Thayu said. "That was interesting."

Interesting indeed.

At that moment, the door to the Exchange compound rolled aside a crack and someone said in Coldi, "Quick, come in."

CHAPTER FOUR

AS THE METAL door rolled further aside, we all ran across the road into the safety of the Exchange compound.

The bus followed when the opening was big enough.

Wow, the building looked... different after having been closed for three months.

Or maybe it was just because the lack of maintenance on the lawn and the oleander beds. The weather had evidently been quite wet and weeds had exploded everywhere.

The blinds were shut behind many of the windows on this side of the building, something I hadn't seen before either.

I walked next to the bus to make sure that everyone in our party had come in when the door started rolling shut again.

While we walked along the side of the bus, my reader pinged. That was strange. No one was supposed to be able to reach me, and the members of my team were all here. Except Veyada and Leisha with my father and Emi.

I took the device out of my pocket with a feeling of foreboding. They wouldn't message me if everything had gone to plan, right?

But it was not from Veyada, or Leisha, or my father.

Some text in Isla appeared on the screen. It said,

Don't worry. We will get you.

I stopped walking and stared at it, while the bus continued slowly down the driveway to the building and the Exchange's security people who had opened the gate for us ran to catch up.

All through the previous three months, I had gotten a few of these mysterious messages. They were always in Isla, and they always arrived after something significant had happened. Once that event had been a drone attack that we could only observe from orbit. Once had been when the Asto military identified and shot down a few problematic satellites.

The messages were short and appeared to goad me into replying.

Asha Domiri's military security personnel had been involved in trying to trace the origin.

And so far, they had been unsuccessful.

And now, after we'd been shot at, here was another one of these messages, sent through a system that was supposed to be secure.

I called Sheydu and showed her the screen.

She swore.

"This was exactly why I told you to leave the old device on the ship and take a new one."

"This is the new one. I did leave the other one on the ship."

She stared at me. "Then how did they find this one so quickly?"

We just stood there, staring at each other, while my mind cycled through all the possibilities about what this meant. For our safety. For the reasons we were here.

I asked, "Does this mean that they know where we are?"

Sheydu cast a brief glance at the entrance to the compound, where the gates were now fully shut, and the last few Exchange guards were now also walking back.

"Give that."

She held out her hand. I gave her the reader.

She put it on the grass, aimed her weapon at it, and fired before I could protest. Half my life was on that thing.

There was a brief burst of flames before the thing disintegrated into a heap of molten resin and blackened metal.

"There."

She stuck the gun back into its arm bracket and ran after the bus.

I stared at the remains of the device.

Well, great, Sheydu, but now what was I supposed to do about contacting people, drafting documents and making notes? What about accessing my pre-drafted agreement, getting into my Nations of Earth accounts and the lists of contact details of people I hadn't spoken to for years? What about all that? Those were the reasons we had come.

Bloody hell.

I ran to catch up with the bus.

I stumbled up the steps while Sheydu was explaining the situation to the rest of the team about what had just happened. Of course, I had spoken before about these mysterious messages, and people were rightly concerned about them. Asha's people, however, didn't know, and they were concerned. We were all concerned.

"If you hadn't destroyed the thing, I could have investigated," Reida said.

Sheydu snorted. "Young man, you have far too much to do already. We don't have the time to mess around with this dangerous fool who sends these messages angling for a response. I don't want that device to be part of our mission and it should not be sending out anyone any information from anywhere we go. So now we will severely limit our communication and filter everything."

As usual, it was hard to argue with Sheydu's logic.

"That's all very well, but I'll still need a device to access my accounts and information I've prepared," I said.

"We will fix something."

The bus had arrived at the building's entrance.

A metal grate spanned across the glass facade, blocking off the sliding glass doors where the public would normally enter. I didn't even know that this safety feature existed.

The local guards directed us to an entrance along the side. There was a kind of tunnel barely wide enough for the bus. It took us to an underground parking area, where a number of other buses sat in rows along the charging bay.

Our bus joined them, and we all got off.

From the car park, we went up the stairs into the main hall on the other side of the glass facade and the metal grate.

Amarru walked at the front, talking to an employee. A couple of others must have been alerted and came to meet us in the hall.

There were about twenty of them, and a few more people came running down the stairs.

Some performed proper Coldi greetings, with their heads bowed and arms by their sides, palms facing backwards, but a few others slapped the hand that Amarru held up.

Which of the men was her partner? She didn't act in a way I could tell. None of the employees wore clan earrings, and while it was Zhori custom not to wear any, it was also becoming less common amongst all other Coldi on Earth.

They were all happy to see her and asked when all the other employees would also be back.

"I'm going to have to disappoint you," Amarru said, after the greetings were done. "We're here to use some of the facilities and not to turn everything back on. The threat that made us leave is still present. Nothing has changed about that."

A man asked, "You mean you still don't know where the attacks come from and who these people are?"

"We do know some," I said. "Asha's deep space division has taken out the satellites that were steering the drone attacks, and that's why we could come here. The enemy has suffered because of it, but we're not confident that we got the source of the attacks."

I glanced aside, but the military people were not listening. They stood in a huddle a bit further down the hall. Two people sat on the floor, looking at our local communication hub.

Deyu was in that group, I realised, surrounded by military personnel.

"It's not simple to find out where these attacks come from," a man said. He was in middle age, old enough to be Amarru's partner.

"No, it's not," I said. "Machines leave a trail of their origin, but these drones appear out of nowhere, multiplying from a single point out of empty space. But we can now detect in advance if that's about to happen, so that we can destroy the drone army before it can do any damage. We're safe for now."

"Until they find a way around it," the man said.

Amarru said, "Let's go upstairs and continue our discussions in the canteen. By the way, for those who don't know, this is Jean-Pierre."

Really? He looked utterly unlike the way I imagined someone called Jean-Pierre to look.

Coldi. In sturdy workman's gear, as if he'd been performing maintenance. His bronzed skin betrayed that he spent a lot of time outside, possibly sailing, judging by his shirt that displayed the name of some yacht club.

Damn, and even that made sense. I knew there were good souls in Athens who sailed across the Mediterranean to pick up Coldi people in trouble, so they didn't get stuck in the huge refugee camps on the shores of northern Africa.

We followed Amarru up to the canteen, all the way up the stairs to the top of the building. The lift had broken, they told us, and they'd been too busy to fix it, and besides, the parts they needed were hard to get.

While we trudged up the stairs to the seventeenth floor, the Exchange employees came up to me one by one.

Communication between the Exchange building and the military ship that now performed the Exchange's function in connecting Earth up to the *gamra* network had been limited for reasons of limited personnel, priorities, limited bandwidth and security.

The people wanted to know whether family or friends had made it to safety.

I told them that everyone had been transferred to wherever they wanted to go and that the only people left in orbit were the military and those who still had roles to play in the conflict.

They asked if we could pass messages to friends and family.

I couldn't see why not, if and when it was safe.

We arrived at the canteen.

I had been here many times, but since this building was now the home of about fifty people, the canteen now resembled a living room more than a sterile office canteen. The staff had also moved the security monitoring screens here, those that used to sit in the security station downstairs. Those screens took up a section of the back wall and one of the people in the canteen would be monitoring the images, while an employee also appeared to be on duty, keeping an eye on the building's surroundings in front of the large window.

Funny how living with security people alerted my mind to these sorts of things.

A couple more people sat around a large table in the middle, made from a bunch of tables pushed together and surrounded by chairs so that all the people in the building would fit around the table at the same time.

Someone came out of the kitchen with a trolley full of cups, a large earthenware jar with a lid and a hot water urn. The jar was the only traditional Coldi thing in the room. It was for storing *manazhu* powder in optimal conditions. One needed to oil the inside of the jar regularly to keep the powder from sticking together.

Soon, the bitter scent of *manazhu* filled the room.

There was a lot of catching up and exchanging of information.

For the people at the Exchange, the destruction of the public facilities and the crippling of local authorities that began three months ago were starting to bite. Power supply was intermittent. Large parts of the city were without running water. The Exchange was fine because they had their own power supply and held considerable stockpiles of everything, plus the infrastructure to harvest and store water from occasional downpours. But because the inhabitants of the city were increasingly desperate, people wandered into the hills in search of food, water or transport elsewhere.

"Where do these people want to go?" I asked. The airport was in the other direction, and the station in town.

A woman said, "These are Coldi refugees, often from other countries in Africa or near Asia. They've lived here for years, don't have much and can't afford tickets. They're hoping we have a humanitarian refugee program, even if they have nowhere to go." Coldi skin was lightly coloured and didn't tan easily, but she was very dark, evidence of long days of sun exposure. Apart from the brightly coloured singlet that displayed heavily tattooed skin and form-fitting pants, she was wearing orange Zhori earrings. I was surprised to see them so openly on display. The Zhori clan eschewed Coldi customs.

"It wasn't a Coldi person who attacked us outside the gates," I said. "He looked like a local, and he was well supplied."

"I am not sure who you saw, but there are several groups that hang out in the forest. Some just appear to camp and hunt goats, but others..." She spread her hands. "We can't engage with them because we don't have enough people to try to drive them away."

"Have there been any direct attacks on the compound?"

"Just a few small scuffles. Nothing major. Those people hang around the main gate like they're waiting to get in. Maybe they hope we can offer them safety or food. Some people are really desperate."

"We recovered some gear and weaponry from one of these characters," I said.

"We would be happy to look at it. Some groups seem to be really well-supplied. Better than you'd expect a band of refugees to be. Any of the gear we've examined has been stolen from the authorities, the Nations of Earth border guards, or from warehouses illegally importing stuff from Asto."

We moved on to talk about world events. More *manazhu* and additional plates of snacks appeared at the table.

I hadn't realised how hungry I'd been.

In the middle of the talk and eating activity, Thayu came to sit next to me. I'd noticed her spending some time with the military group earlier.

"Everything all right?" I asked.

"Yes."

"We need to get someone onto booking us tickets to Rotterdam," I said.

"Yes," she said.

And that was one of those definitive yeses. I didn't think she liked being here, or being dependent on Amarru and people whose loyalties she didn't like.

And then she added, "That's not why I came to talk to you."

"Oh?"

I looked at her, realising that, of course, she rarely sought anyone out just for a chat, and that included me.

She had some news, and it didn't look like she liked this news.

"Come," I said. I got up from the table and walked to the window. Thayu followed me.

By now, it was almost dark. It struck me how few lights were on in the city.

Then she said, "Deyu got the communication specialist to check out the local hub to see what they could find out about this message you got."

"And?"

"It's not on there."

"What do you mean—it's not on there?"

"What I said: there is no evidence that this person used our local hub to reach you."

"But if they didn't, then how would that message have gotten to me?"

"I suspect we've been looking in the wrong place. They reached you through a system that is not related to the Exchange or any of our hubs."

"Why didn't anyone pick that up before?"

I felt sick.

Deyu and Reida *had* spent some time looking for unusual patterns. They hadn't found anything out of the ordinary, such as data coming in from unknown locations, not because that data was well-hidden and didn't trip any filters, but because the data they were looking for simply wasn't there at all.

But then how could they send me these messages?

Thayu couldn't suggest how this was possible. I didn't carry anything that connected to a network right now.

This was a distraction we couldn't use.

We finished eating.

Nicha had been checking the status of the trains and reported that some fast trains through Europe appeared to be running, though not as frequently as before. He'd booked tickets for tomorrow morning.

So it was time to clear up a few things before going to bed. One such thing was to see if we could contact Nations of Earth to let them know we were coming and request a meeting with the relevant people.

Thayu declared that she was tired and took our bags to the residential section on the floor below the canteen. Nicha and Sheydu helped her carry the packs belonging to the others. I thought Sheydu looked tired, but more likely, she was just annoyed by these people's looseness with what she considered important loyalty ties.

No, the Exchange was not solely loyal to Ezhya. They split their loyalty between Asto and the Zhori clan and other Coldi who lived permanently on Earth.

As I had already suspected, the Exchange's security staff were going to investigate the gear we had taken from the man outside.

Reida, Telaris, Ynggi and Isharu would check out what they were doing, while Amarru and I went to one of the lower floors of the building.

Of course, the lift wasn't working, so we used the stairs to go down.

Amarru had to unlock several solid metal doors.

It was amazing how quickly the building had assumed the abandoned look. Everywhere on the walls hung large screens that would normally display the status of various shuttles, their arrival and departure times and locations where people could meet passengers.

All those screens were now blank, turned off and lifeless. And dusty.

We walked through dark corridors where the normally smooth floor felt gritty and dusty underfoot.

We entered the Exchange corridor. I had been here a few times while it was in full operation, and there had always been people in the offices, seated behind workstations, walking in and out, talking to colleagues. People coming out to speak with Amarru because they heard her voice.

Today, the place was deserted. It was depressing. I'd never imagined I would see the place like this. I'd had so much hope after the referendum, and we had even celebrated the win here. It might all have been for nothing.

Most of us had a long history with this building and its extreme importance for *gamra* and Earth. It hurt to see it like this, as if the past twenty-five years had all been a waste of effort and time.

"This way," Amarru said a bit further down the hallway.

Her voice sounded loud in that very quiet place. She stood at the entrance to a side passage and then a set of open double doors that led to a huge room that was almost completely empty.

Holy crap.

The control centre of the Exchange lay deserted. All the equipment had been removed or disconnected if it couldn't be removed. The only sign that the workstations had ever occupied the room were the markings on the floor.

"What have you done with all this stuff that used to be here?" I asked, almost afraid to talk too loudly.

"There are safe localities," Amarru said. "Locked rooms under the building."

Of course, there were many reports of secret bunkers in the building, and it wouldn't surprise me at all if there were other warehouses in the city or in the mountains where are the Exchange would store back up equipment.

But they must have worked extremely quickly to get all the stuff moved out within such a short period of time.

If I knew anything about the layers of power in Coldi society, it was also that they always kept lots of options open.

This devastation could be reversed. I hoped. If we could stop the drone attacks.

CHAPTER FIVE

WE ENTERED the main Exchange hub, now empty, and with much of the equipment gone.

We walked through the room and then entered the second room where I had spent that legendary election night with Amarru and Margarethe. Back then, I'd thought the election victory would solve all these kinds of problems. How wrong I was.

Amarru needed to use her access key to get in. The door panel blinked briefly into life but went back out again soon afterwards.

"Temporary local power," she said in response to the question about power and traceable communication that I didn't ask, but either Sheydu or Reida would have asked had they been here.

It was pitch dark in the room beyond. A tiny light flickered on as we moved through.

A very basic workplace setup occupied the middle of the room. Three portable screens stood on an ordinary table, propped up with equipment boxes.

The screens lit up when Amarru sat down, and the projectors at the top of the screens projected a control module onto the table. Amarru used a stylus to touch the controls.

This was a mini-hub, even simpler than the one in my apartment in Barresh.

The projected control module was very schnazzy, though. I wouldn't mind one of those. When we inevitably would have to access both the Exchange and the Tamer Collective version, we could just switch while staying in the same room in the same chair.

Yeah, wishful thinking.

This super-secure connection was not very fast, though. I stood looking over Amarru's shoulder for quite some time while she cycled through the menus.

Or was it because the machine was trying to connect with local communication systems that were damaged? A bouncy dot tracked from one side of the screen to the other and back again while we waited.

But eventually, she achieved a link to Nations of Earth and vacated the chair for me.

Since the president's office had been dead to us for months, I started by trying to contact the people I knew in the Nations of Earth offices. But most of my messages bounced with warnings that the accounts were no longer active.

I could get no response from the head of the *gamra* relations office, and no response from the off-Earth department.

They seemed to have vanished.

I had no idea what was going on there.

Of course Amarru didn't know either.

She said that the offices might have moved because there had been a couple of drone attacks on the Nations of Earth complex, but I couldn't see how that would have compromised the accounts of the workers in those offices.

The official news sites were not helpful. I had already seen that while we were still on the ship, where our access to Earth media was very limited. Of course I had expected this. Nations of Earth would want to control what citizens saw through official channels to curb the level of rumour-mongering that was common amongst the sensationalist news outlets. We checked those outlets, like Flash Newspoint, anyway, but found little concrete evidence for what was going on inside the Nations of Earth compound.

A few of the buildings had taken damage, including the Assembly hall. But that was a while ago and public officials assured the populace that everything was still working as it should. The assembly meetings were slimmed down, held remotely as they had allowed many delegates to return to their countries of origin where they were safer. It all seemed very sensible and well-organised.

But in that case, I still couldn't see why the *gamra* relations office would not be reachable.

Then I had another thought: it was not unlikely that given the current crisis, the Emergency Council would have temporarily closed some of those departments and moved staff to offices where they were needed.

What were those areas likely to be?

I scrolled through the list of departments.

The Office of Commerce—nah.

The Office of Financial Relations—probably not.

The Office of Equal Opportunity—definitely not. Conflict and trouble were as unequal as hell, and afflicted the most heavily those who had contributed nothing to their creation. Fact of life.

The Office of War.

Yeah, Nations of Earth had an Office of War.

This was not a well-known fact. When I first learned about its existence, the lecturer at Mars University told me that the office occupied a tiny department in the building that held the Office of Country Relations.

The purpose of the Office of War was to coordinate armed responses to major conflicts.

Of course, Nations of Earth only had security forces and nothing resembling a formal army, so that was why the department was small. But the lecturer had also assured a bunch of very bored students that there were provisions for it to be expanded quickly when that was necessary.

And what else would trigger this expansion if not an invasion from an off-world entity? Even if the invasion, on the surface, appeared to have its roots in Earth's messy politics?

Yeah, the Office of War might be the one.

This wasn't a part of Nations of Earth I dealt with, ever, so I had to look up contact details. The last current directory of Nations of Earth contacts I had dated from Margarethe's time, so even some of those contacts were no longer valid.

But when I got frustrated and simply contacted the office's main desk as listed on their public information site, I got onto someone straight away. The young man sounded almost robotic.

"Good afternoon. You've reached the Nations of Earth Office of War. If you are contacting us because you want to sign up, please be advised that you need to apply at the Enlistment Office."

"No, I don't want to sign up. I would like to speak with the president."

There was a moment of stunned silence on the other side. "The president, you said?" He sounded like he was about to burst out in laughter.

"Yes, I thought I was clear."

"The president is busy and doesn't have time to just speak to anyone."

"I'm not just anyone, and I'm pretty sure he'd be interested to see me."

Another silence.

"And you said your name was?"

"Cory Wilson, speaking on behalf of *gamra*. I'm sorry if this is an unconventional way of requesting an audience, but the lines are down and none of my usual contacts appear to be working. I have important matters to discuss with the president and the assembly."

Another silence.

"Can you hang on a moment?"

Without waiting for my reply, he put me on hold.

I was blasted in the ear with loud trumpet music followed by a cheerful jingle about signing up to defend the planet and *stake out our territory in the face of a great threat.*

To be honest, the level of naked patriotism made me feel ill, and the suggestion that military boots on the ground could do anything against an endlessly self-replicating army of drones even more so. Just how many young people were they prepared to sacrifice?

Had they learned nothing from history?

He came back on the line. "I'm sorry about the delay. I needed to consult with colleagues. Of course the president's office would like to arrange a meeting. But you will need to show proof of who you are."

"Yes, I can provide it when we get there."

"I'm afraid the circumstances demand that I need it now. I will need your identity documents, your GenCode number and your travel information before we can authorise your entry into the compound. We take security seriously, as you will understand."

"I can provide all of that, except GenCode. I've never had implants. But I can provide my *gamra* pass."

"That will also do. Will you be bringing people?"

"Yes."

"They will also need to provide identity checks."

"You should already have my information and most of my team also has a standing approval to enter the assembly building. Normally, the guards at the gate will check all that information at the gate."

"This is not a normal time."

"Granted."

"I'm glad you understand. Before we can proceed with giving you permission to enter the compound, we need to collect this information. I will send you a document detailing everything we need to see before we can proceed."

"Thank you. But this doesn't answer my most important question: can I talk to the president?"

"I've just said that you need to—"

"No, that's not what I mean. What I mean is this: is the president in the compound?"

A small silence. "Why would he not be?"

"Because last time I spoke to him, he wasn't in the compound."

"How long ago was that?"

"Three months ago."

He chuckled. "You're not suggesting that—"

"I suggest nothing. He contacted me and asked for help. So I'm curious whether I misheard him or didn't understand the nature of his call."

"He... asked you for help."

"Yes, that's what I said."

"Why would he do that?"

"That's what I'm here to find out."

"You're talking about Simon Dekker."

"Yes. Is there another president?"

Another silence followed, longer than all the previous ones

combined. Then he said, "Well, if you submit all your details, we can check them, and you can come here and have your meeting."

"With the president."

"I assume so, unless he's too busy."

I told him we'd send the information he requested, signed off and faced Amarru.

She would have had no trouble following the conversation.

We said nothing for a while, but just frowned at each other.

"That was utterly weird," I said, eventually. Honestly, I didn't know what to think. It had been quite a while since I had dealt with Nations of Earth, seeing as that was Melissa's job in Barresh and what with Dekker avoiding us altogether.

I met Amarru's eyes. "Have you noticed that communication under Dekker has been full of this kind of rubbish bureaucracy?"

She sniffed. "Yes, that's been our experience on occasions that we have dealt with his administration. I can send all that stuff for you."

I opened the document that had arrived.

It included a long list of information they wanted. Contact details, alternate contacts, citizen numbers, place of residence and stuff none of us had, like the GenCode chip ID or other markers like our health designation codes.

Amarru looked over my shoulder so that she could see the list.

I changed my mind. "Actually, no. Don't send this stuff."

She frowned at me.

"I've never needed special permits to get into the Nations of Earth compound. Yes, you have to identify yourself at the gate, but they already know who I am and there shouldn't be a reason to ask for this. The GenCode chip is controversial and I don't have one, because they became mandatory only in some communities and only for short periods of time." Mars had been one of those communities, but fortunately, I'd left before the law requiring them was instated.

Over the many years I'd worked as a diplomat, the pendulum had swung back and forth about these issues. At first, they'd tried to classify people according to their health status and how much money they were likely to cost authorities based on their genetic health.

I'd squeaked into being classified in the right way, even if my mother had died of genetically transmissible brain cancer.

That deplorable system had led to the GenCode, a way to not only classify people but to identify them as well.

"Why are Nations of Earth messing with this garbage again?" I said, more to myself than Amarru.

Predictably, I got no response.

Amarru said, "You don't trust them." It was not a question.

I blew out a breath. "I don't know. I guess in the face of a technologically far superior enemy, they want to play all the cards they have, although I'm not sure what purpose this one serves. We'll see when we get there."

Amarru sighed. "I've never trusted Nations of Earth with these classification systems. I never understood why you put so much stock in them. I always found it a little..."

"Naïve?"

"I guess." She shrugged, looking at her hands. "I've often thought you were playing with fire, cosying up to the powerful people, like Ezhya."

"Ezhya is my *zhayma*."

She almost flinched. "You shouldn't be so flippant with Coldi customs."

"I'm not."

"Yes, you are. You're in their pockets and then some. In the place where Jean-Pierre grew up, that's where the hardship shows. The people in Africa are ignored by everyone. That's where we as Coldi on Earth get our strength. You will find the same strength in the Outer Circle in Athyl."

"I know. I've been there. Where do you think Reida and Deyu come from? My Athyl apartment is in Eighth Circle."

She gave me a sharp look.

"You didn't know that?"

She looked down again.

"Amarru?"

She half-raised her head.

"You're allowed to speak your opinions."

"I do this job for the benefit of all of *gamra*. It's not helpful to express opinions."

"What would Asto do to you? As part of the off-world Coldi, no one in Athyl can do anything against you."

"I wouldn't be so sure."

"I would be. I'm telling you. As Ezhya's *zhayma*, Asto's relationships with other entities are my responsibility. I'm telling you."

She shrugged again.

Then I had a thought so clear that I didn't understand why I hadn't seen this before. But Amarru's reactions to Ezhya had always been very uncomfortable, and I'd always wondered just where she stood in Asto's hierarchy, and I'd never seen that she just... didn't.

"You don't have the *sheya* instinct, do you?"

"No. Not at all. Why else do you think I'm here?"

There was so much pain in those words that I searched for something appropriate to say. I'd never found it easy to talk to Amarru. Oh, she was extremely competent at what she did, but she was one of those people where you were forever wondering whether you understood them.

Neither of us said anything for a while.

Then she said, "I was going to make a suggestion and hope I can trust you with the information. While we're here, we could find out where Dekker was when he sent us that message, even whether he sent it or it was the same joker who has been messing with your communication."

I met her eyes. I knew what she was talking about.

"You never destroyed that network?"

The ancient spy network that lay embedded in all the electronic chips inside Earth's electronic parts. In radios, phones, computers, cars, heck, vacuum cleaners and kettles that had been built and sold by the billions for over a hundred years before, finally, people caught up on the scheme and forbade further bugging.

There had a been an uproar about this, and Coldi had denied the existence of the network until the referendum.

"We can't destroy it. It's too widespread, and I didn't want to destroy the painstaking work of the first Coldi settlers. I agreed with Margarethe that I'd seal it off, and it's still sealed off. No one has used it for years. But it's still there. We can use it now. I can give you the data dump, because we can't turn it off, and it's still collecting data. It's not high quality stuff, but low-level data points about where people are. There's likely to be a lot, but you're welcome to have it. In the mess, we're likely to find information about Dekker's movements."

Another realisation hit me. "Is this the true reason you wanted to come back here?"

"One of the reasons. There is something going on. That man from the Office of War seemed surprised that Dekker had been in contact with us. Also, he never confirmed that you can definitely talk to the president. Or that the president is in the compound. Or, for that matter, alive."

CHAPTER SIX

AMARRU'S last argument swayed me.

We didn't know why Dekker had contacted me, where he had been when he did so, whether it was actually Dekker, and not some prankster, who had contacted me—although I doubted it.

But with the assurance by the Office of War that I could speak with the president, while the same president had asked me for help, something didn't add up.

And in that case, I could justify the use of a highly illegal form of spyware, right?

I told her to go ahead with a deep sense of dread. Throughout my career, I considered it a piece of my human, Earth-born pride that I hadn't "allowed" this system to be used. Although whether I could have prevented its use if Ezhya really wanted to use it was another question, of course.

Amarru got up from the workstation.

On the far side of the room, a panel sat in the wall with a film of tape stuck over it. A sign stuck to the tape, both in Coldi and Isla script. It said, in both languages, that the room beyond was off-limits, and could only be accessed by agreement from both the Exchange and Nations of Earth. Underneath a seal, unbroken, was a security panel with a warning that trying to access it would send messages to both authorities.

The controls to the secret Coldi network.

I knew this was here, but I had never seen the full extent of this secret network of Coldi technology on Earth in operation. Since electronic equipment included small microchips, and the Coldi had been involved with their development, especially in Japan and later in China, little Coldi routines had been embedded in many of those chips. Silently watching and waiting. Recording basic data about the equipments' owners. Linking up their communication devices, recording their voice. Registering who else lived in the house. After dismissing and downplaying it for years, I had been horrified by the extent of this network, even if I already knew that it existed and understood why those early Coldi settlers had built it.

Amarru had negotiated with Margarethe prior to Earth signing the final declaration for its intent to join *gamra*, that this network would be locked away only to be used with consent from both parties.

Amarru started peeling one side of the tape.

It was stuck down well and was hard to remove.

I offered to cut it with a laser setting on my gun, but Amarru didn't want that, because it might damage the electronics.

I didn't know what electronics these were until she pulled off a length of tape and a couple of bugs fell out of the space between the door and the door frame and rolled over the ground.

As more and more of the protective film came off, it became clear to me just how well the Exchange had sealed the door.

The adhesive was so well stuck down that she even pulled off sections of the paint. Gradually, the removal of the film revealed a door panel.

When all the film was in a heap on the floor, she pushed it together into a sticky heap with her boot.

She stood looking at the door, her hands planted at her sides.

"Well, in case someone is ever going to write about and analyse my life, I'll tell you now that this is the most outrageous thing I have done in my career. People accuse me of all kinds of wrongdoing all the time, but I do not go against the rules, and in normal situations, would never agree to break an important agreement. I'm doing this for the safety of this world that's my home."

Of course, the situation bore no relationships with normal agreements.

Once all the tape was off, Amarru held her reader to the lock in the door. There was no door handle, and no visible panel that kept the lock in place.

A simple menu came up on the screen. It reminded me of those very simple designs that my grandfather would have grown up with that displayed green text on a black screen. Nothing else. The beginning of the computer age.

The door clicked open. The room beyond was pitch dark. A musty smell wafted out.

When Amarru stepped in, a feeble light came on in the ceiling, revealing a small room crammed full of equipment of a type that belonged in the museum. Big boxy monitors such as people would use at the end of the 20th century. Big clunky keyboards. Whoever used these any more? There were electronic cords everywhere. Granted, we still use those on many occasions, but we did this for security and for fast operation. Most of the normal civilian people would never use a power cord in their lives.

Amarru walked into the room.

"Be careful where you put your feet," she said.

It was not an idle warning. There were bundles of cords all over the floor. They were tied together with tape and went to plugs that slotted into connector boxes.

In the middle of this spaghetti stood a couple of desks arranged in a square, with a chair in the middle. It was a modern chair, and on the table lay a couple of reasonably modern readers of the type that I also used to own when I was a boy. It was amazing to see how much technology moved on.

As soon as Amarru sat down, one of the workstations sprung into action. The light in the room so far had been quite sparse, but the added light from the screen revealed just how many old computers were here. Not just on the table, but also in racks along the walls.

"They're spares," Amarru said. "This stuff was built quite well, but a lot of the materials don't last. If something breaks, we can take the other machines apart and reconstruct it."

Now that she said this, I did notice how the computer on the corner furthest from me was attached to a Coldi keyboard made from two regular keyboards bolted together with a strip of a type of material that was common on Asto.

An Asto-made nozzle projector hung off the ceiling. Even it looked like it belonged in the last century.

This room could be a museum.

The projector started blinking and a moment later an image sprang in the air, shimmering lines that connected the different items of equipment in the room, even though many of the screens were still turned off.

Some of them now sprang into action and displayed text, because that was all they were designed to do. The text itself consisted of what Coldi people were so uniquely excellent at reading: solid blocks of hexadecimal characters that were impenetrable to most mortals.

Almost as if Coldi had designed the hexadecimal system. Every time I thought about that, it chilled me.

The hexadecimal code consisted of combinations of sixteen characters, and the number sixteen was the whole number four in the Coldi exponential way of counting. And then I would think about whether maybe Coldi people had helped design this code when people on Earth first started building computers, and I would wonder about why on earth no one had ever considered this a possibility before and that certainly I couldn't be the first one to ever have thought about that option. The people who designed the first computers were all dead, so we couldn't ask them whether any of them employed technicians from Eastern Asia, in particular people with the last name Oyama or Chan.

And that thought sent my mind into spirals of panic about what Nations of Earth would do with that information when it became part of the official history.

And what *gamra* would do with it, or Asto, after having strenuously denied that it was trying to settle Earth by stealth. Because despite the denials, that was *precisely* what they had been doing.

The whole thing made me cringe.

While the code scrolled over the screen, the projector in the ceiling warmed up and all of a sudden, a three-dimensional projection sprung into the air.

At first, it was hard to figure out what I was looking at. I recognised the type of image from the Exchange, where the interwoven web of blue-green lines that moved and shimmered represented a visual image of the locations that had connectivity. This network curved like a three-dimensional blanket hung over a ball, but only the top of it was visible. The lines followed the shape of continents.

"Hang on, this shows only part of the Earth's surface," I said.

Amarru flicked her finger across the screen and the image turned around. I could now see the outline of a continent. Africa.

To the north lay an incredibly bright spot that had to be Athens but from there on to the north and west, there were substantial holes in the network that cris-crossed through Europe and met the clearly recognisable shape of the shoreline of the North Sea.

There was a lot of coverage to the east, in Poland and Russia. Parts of eastern Asia also showed up very well. The technologically advanced parts of southern China formed great holes in the network, as did Japan, Thailand and Korea.

Indonesia was another bright spot on the map, but when the globe turned to America, coverage was very patchy. Mexico showed up as a couple of very bright few spots to the south, and other spots of coverage included the islands of the Bahamas and some parts of the southern tip of South America.

My country of birth, New Zealand, was also on the map only with a few bright spots, most clearly on the North Island. In Australia, there were only a few spots along the northern and eastern coastline.

Amarru breathed out heavily, her lips pressed together. She shook her head. "This is worse than I thought. Big parts of the network have gone offline. We used to have much better coverage."

"How long since you have last accessed this?"

"A few years ago. It looks like in between then and now, a lot of the old electronics have been upgraded."

Or, as I suspected, people knew that those old devices from the 20th century contained the chips that sent this data back to the Exchange and had disabled this function. They had been more successful at this in some places than in other places.

Judging from the projection, areas of the world that were both prosperous and that were suspicious of *gamra* had erased most of their coverage. The modern countries in Europe, and China and Japan.

Some, like North America, probably never had that much to begin with.

Amarru sighed. "We're going to have to work with what we have. I hope it's still going to do the job. Anyway, it's all we have."

She placed her own reader on the surface of the table and extracted a strangely old-fashioned device from a drawer.

It looked like one of those really old-fashioned telephone handsets that had a cradle for the receiver to charge. I had sometimes still seen these in some of the old human space technology that still relied on wired connections. When I flew on the *Endeavour* as a ten-year-old, many of the corridors still had emergency devices like these. They had a springy cord and kids used to love knocking the receiver off and making it jump around in the low gravity. That, of course, elicited a strong response from the flight deck, so we usually weren't so happy afterwards. Oh, those were the days.

Amarru put the device into the cradle and brought up the menu on the screen.

It took a good fifteen minutes to copy the data dump. She gave me a single data stick that contained all the movements of all people on Earth since the sealing off of this room.

I stuck it into my pocket where it felt like a heavy brick. I'd give it to Reida to analyse. It would be invaluable to use it as a reference against what people at Nations of Earth would tell us when we got there. When or if they let us in and when they let us talk to Dekker. If he was indeed there.

CHAPTER SEVEN

WE WENT two floors down into the residential section of the building, where I found the room where Thayu had dumped all our bags. She sat at the tiny desk in front of the window, working at something.

She looked up when I came in.

"How did it go?"

I told her of the strange conversation we had had with the man at the Office of War.

"Did they ask you for all those personal details? I thought most of those were already in their possession."

"That's the same thing I said. But he said they needed it for security." But as I said that, I knew it was odd, almost as if that part of the system no longer worked. Well, it was a war, so that could theoretically be possible.

"What is this GenCode thing, anyway?"

I explained it was an identification marker that was attached to a database that included people's genetic information.

"Like the human tree project?" she asked.

"A bit like that, but then for identification purposes. When they ask you to identify yourself, you can send a sample of your coded genetic material and they can see if their database record and the material you sent are the same."

"You mean actual genetic samples?"

"No, it's digital. It's on a chip that gets implanted in your arm that sends the information but checks it against your real genetic information all the time. So that you and only you can have access to certain information."

"Then it's not like the human tree project. That is only for research."

I agreed that GenCode was not like the human tree project, although it collected several same types of data.

"And you said that there was a chip involved?"

"Yes. It contains a digitised copy of your genetic material and was meant to keep track of all the citizens as they move around. It would eliminate the need for things like permissions and passwords and passports."

"Like the chips that people from Hedron carry in their earrings."

"Yes, a little bit like that, but more than that, because it would also allow the authorities to program the chip with certain things."

"What do you mean—certain things?"

"I don't know. Permissions, levels of caution for employing people in certain positions. Whatever security does. I don't know that much about this kind of stuff. That's your department. I never got one of those chips. They were going to introduce it as a mandatory thing when I was at Mars, but I left before I could get one."

"Would you have gotten one?"

I shrugged. It was a good question. "If I wanted to complete my studies, and it was mandatory, then probably yes."

"Can you remove a chip?"

"I'm sure you can, but it's probably not a good idea in their eyes."

"They? This is not standard Nations of Earth procedure?"

"They were talking about it, but it never went through as far as I know."

"So why are they asking for it now? Who controls this data?"

Good question. I shrugged. "This was the first time in about twenty years I've been asked about the chip. I have no idea."

Thayu, being Thayu, was intrigued. She did some searches on GenCode and started reading, while I went into the shower and got changed.

When I came out, she was still reading.

"Interesting?" I asked.

I opened the door into the corridor. This was a habit I'd picked up in the year I'd lived here. The former hospital rooms were small and not intended for people who could look after themselves, especially if they liked hot showers.

More than once I'd set off the fire alarm by having a hot shower and then failing to let the humid air out of the room.

"Yeah, I think this is interesting. Listen to this: the GenCode data chip was never fully implemented, although it is estimated to have been implanted in over ten million people. The chip was meant to be programmable with a wide variety of functions, including communication, which was to be linked to a secondary implanted device, and passes to access certain aspects of society, including things like finance and travel."

"Yes. It was something like that. I remember there was a lot of resistance to it."

"It sounds something like they will do at Hedron."

At that moment, Mereeni stuck her head in the room and said, "Like what?"

And we both explained the whole thing yet again.

Being a lawyer versed in *gamra* law as it related to Earth, she had heard about GenCode, but also said that the project was abandoned.

Mereeni was also not going to take the assessment of her home world lying down. "Something like that would never be allowed at Hedron. We may have an authoritarian system according to some, but this kind of thing can be used to keep people prisoner, and the chips at Hedron can be taken off, because they're only embedded in an earring which you can remove. You don't have to wear it either. There are plenty of people who don't. The chips are just a handy thing. They are an option and make life easier for you, but if you don't want it, you're free not to use one."

From what she said, I agreed with her.

I also didn't consider Hedron authoritarian. Hedron was a political enigma, a very rich world that nevertheless retained social structures that would be slagged with the *communism* tag on Earth. One day, when I was old and retired, I might write a political essay about it.

Mereeni said we should go to dinner and disappeared again.

Thayu asked, "So what are you going to do about this request for the chip?"

"I told him I don't have one, which is true. He didn't say that would be a problem. But I don't really want to send him all the information they asked for, because they should have it already."

"Yes." Said with heavy agreement.

"I take it you have an opinion about this?"

"Well, if they don't have the information, two things can be true. One, that it was destroyed in the drone attacks, and in my opinion, they would readily share that fact. The other possible reason is that they don't have access. There is an issue within the security systems. And they use bureaucracy to cover up some breach of trust or a failure of process."

"An issue?"

Of course I had considered something similar, but I liked to hear her opinion.

"There is something they're not telling us. It could be anything, from something that would embarrass the administration to their own people, or would lead to uncomfortable questions about an unrelated topic. Or it could be more sinister. Probably not. Probably they're just poorly organised after the relocation of their offices."

"But then, where is the president?"

"He's never wanted to talk to you since he started in the job, and we should entertain the thought that the request for help we got was a hoax and that he still maintains the position of not wanting to talk to us."

This was just a measure of how much Thayu had changed. When she first worked with me, she would never have said anything like this.

"You're probably right. He still doesn't want to talk to me. They're using excuses and bureaucracy to make sure we give up. I said I'd send them the documents they wanted, but think we should just go there and turn up. They can check out our documentation when we get to the gate and then they can decide whether to let us in, and if they don't, we'll find a way to get in, because there are plenty of people I know we can visit who can arrange permission or an invitation to let us inside. If the worst comes to the worst, I will contact some of my old colleagues."

Although I would dread having to do that. They would probably not appreciate being asked to do things they didn't like.

Thayu said, "So you're not going to tell this man that we are coming?"

"I don't think I will. I can't see the problem. I think this guy was just way out of his depth and making life far more difficult for us and himself than it needs to be."

"All right then, let's get something to eat."

"There is one more thing."

"Yes?" She turned around at the door. And shut it.

We so absolutely felt each other's concerns, even without working feeders.

"Amarru gave me a data dump from the old Coldi spy system."

"Good."

"Good?"

"I told her she should do that."

Riiiiiight.

"Amarru and Margarethe signed not to use it without permissions from both entities."

Thayu snorted. "Rules."

"They are important."

"Sometimes. They're for politics."

I could be made to disagree, but it was not why I mentioned this to her.

"What do you think should be our priority to do with the data? There is rather a lot."

"Give it to Reida. Tell him what you want to know. I've released him from his usual duties so he can do data processing."

Usual duties? This was a rare glimpse into the security operations of the team.

"Breaking into things. Organising transport. We have Riyala to deal with all that stuff."

Riyala? Ah. "*Mashara.*"

"Yes. He's the leader of that association. I don't like that term."

"You and me both."

"But come on, I'm hungry."

She opened the door again.

"Thay'."

"Yes?" In a *what now* tone.

I strode over to her and nosed the soft skin under her ear. Her beautiful scent filled me with a sense of belonging and desire.

"I love you."

She leaned back. "I don't mean that kind of hungry." But a smile played in her eyes.

"Yes, you do."

"Later, maybe."

Yes. Later was good.

Thayu and I followed Mereeni down to the canteen, which the remaining employees had turned into a living area, where many of the people in the building sat talking to some members of our team.

We sat with them at the table.

A few of my team members had not yet returned, including the group who had gone to investigate the weapons captured outside the gate.

Sheydu and her group were also not back from checking out the security situation for getting onto the train tomorrow. I hoped that was a good thing, and they had found a way to make it work.

The rest of the employees sat around the table with a surprising amount of food.

I asked them about what had been happening inside the building.

The Exchange had been very quiet recently.

Initially, they had catered for a lot of Coldi refugees, but gradually, both the refugees and the craft to pick them up had stopped coming.

Because they were meant to be silent, they communicated only if absolutely necessary, and then mostly with Coldi communities who were mostly within the Athens enclave.

Otherwise, they just continued going about their daily lives as normal as they could. They had fixed damage. They had fixed vehicles. Since it was turned off, they had cleaned out and completed maintenance on the core and recalibrated it. They were ready to resume service once the situation was stable.

I asked the local employees around the table what they thought about the goings on at Nations of Earth.

Not all of them had an opinion. Some didn't care.

Others said there had been talk in the news about meetings of the Emergency Council. They hadn't seen any recent public appearances of Simon Dekker, but announcements were usually read out by the Speaker of the assembly and she had definitely made public appearances.

Dekker was media shy, people said, and that was true. He was a bureaucrat and rather awkward in public. People often wondered why he had been elected.

Also, after there had been a drone attack during a sitting of the assembly, Nations of Earth had decided to send most of their members home, and rely on remote plenary meetings and only hold Emergency Council meetings in person at the complex.

Then someone in the room said, "I understand that people at the assembly are also worried about local help that these drone attacks may be getting. I've read reports that they are pretty sure that some of the attacks are linked to groups on the ground, especially in North America."

"We suspect the same, but I would love it if someone could find me solid evidence for this," I said. "Who these groups are, how big they are, what sort of contact they have with the space-based people behind the attacks. Because I want to know where those people are. Unless we tackle the source of the drone attacks, we're not making much progress. Unless we get the source, we're likely to need to stay in orbit to fend off increasingly smart attempts to evade our defences. Given enough time, everything can be broken down. They *will* break through, because the drones are machines and they just keep trying until they're successful. And the enemy seems to have an endless supply of drones."

A woman said, "I am sure the Nations of Earth security forces know more about the organisers behind the attacks, but they're not talking, because they don't want to give anyone the idea that they're onto something."

That was another thing I'd heard before. And the thought behind this was that some elements in Nations of Earth remained suspicious of *gamra* and didn't want to share information with us. I had no idea where this rumour came from, but I'd seen no evidence to prove or disprove it.

There were so many conspiracy theories doing the rounds.

And so it all came down to the fact few people knew anything, and that there was a lot of baseless speculation.

CHAPTER EIGHT

WHILE WE SAT TALKING around the table, the lift doors opened in the hallway and a group of people came out. From my position—where I couldn't see the lift—I already heard Sheydu's voice.

Sure enough, a moment later the complete group came into the canteen, including Reida, Deyu and Ynggi, Evi and Telaris, even including the seven nameless military guards Asha had lent me. Riyala, huh? That had to be the association's leader, identifiable by the way he walked, quite casually, but distinctly, at the front of the group.

As I understood, they'd held a security meeting and checked out the weapons and other items we had confiscated from the man who had attacked us outside the gate.

Sheydu was now carrying a couple of these items in a see-through satchel.

I suspected they were about to go into a storage system of some kind.

"And? What did you find out?" I asked her as she sat down next to me.

"The weapon is locally made, but it contains elements of *gamra* technology and also some innovative technology that *could* have been developed locally, or not. We're not sure where the owner would have acquired the weapon. Like most things about this enemy, it's infuriatingly inconclusive. I suspect I'm not really telling you anything new there."

No, she wasn't. Because the problem was that the technology from the drones was so enmeshed with our own—both from Earth and *gamra*—it was hard to tell where one began and the other one finished.

She continued. "It could be a purpose-built weapon. Or he could have just acquired the weapon on the street. People tell me that a lot of illegal and sometimes highly modified weaponry gets sold on the street by people who have no business selling it to people who are not allowed to have it."

"Yes. That has always been a problem for as long as I can remember."

Even Asto made weaponry made its way through illegal channels that often converged on Athens, simply because that was where many people of Coldi origin resided, and Coldi people would not look out of place, not even when illegally selling weapons. From Athens on, the stuff was usually taken either to South America or to Africa and it entered the underworld at that point. Sometimes, it resurfaced in crime busts, but more often than not, it didn't.

It just left a trail of dead bodies that looked like they'd been attacked with off-Earth weaponry.

That had been a problem for as long as I remembered.

With Earth becoming part of *gamra*, processes were supposed to be introduced with the aim of stemming this illegal flow of technology, but I guessed that the current hostilities had pushed those issues into the background.

In past years, I would have said *remember Kazakhstan*, but even the conflict in Kazakhstan and its first-ever reported use of Asto-made weapons was a cakewalk compared to what we were facing now.

Sheydu showed me the report, which found the weapon to be an aggregate of technology from different places. The body had been manufactured in Russia, the electronics came from some place in Sudan and used Asto-developed technology, and the whole thing had been assembled in America Free State.

I didn't like that last bit of information, because I wasn't aware that America Free State traded much with the rest of the world, but I supposed criminal elements traded wherever they could make money and surveillance was lax.

As Sheydu had said, the report was infuriatingly vague and non-conclusive.

This was the story that had repeated itself over the past few months. There was nothing that definitively pinpointed where the people in control of the drones currently were, whether they were even our enemies or only Nations of Earth's enemies, and where their command centre was.

Asha's people talked about their meeting, which had included Amarru, Isharu, Zyana, Ynggi, and people in charge of the Exchange's security systems.

Amarru described the precarious situation in which the Exchange found itself, surrounded by rogue bands of refugees, some of whom might have hoped that the Exchange might be their ticket to safety. Many of these people were also unregistered illegals. The Exchange had done work on trying to trace these people for troublesome backgrounds, but there were only fifty people in the building and there was a lot of other work to do.

They had passed all their information about these people to us, in the hope it might be of use.

It was now fully dark outside. The canteen's windows offered a view of the lawn in the moonlight. Normally there would be outdoor lighting along the driveway, but those lights were off today.

Jean-Pierre said that the refugees outside constantly hijacked the building's external power supply, and people were sick of fending them off as a distraction for other people to sneak into the compound. I presumed he spoke from experience.

Even if none of the local employees said so, life here had to have been miserable for the past three months. I must remind the appropriate person—who? Ezhya? Marin Federza?—to give these people a reward.

It was getting late and people left to go to bed.

The employees used the rooms in the corridor below the control rooms, and we were on the floor underneath.

The long, linoleum-lined hallway had about thirty rooms, some small, some big enough for two people and other dorms suited to sleep several people. After all those years, the walls still bore the markings where the emergency call buttons, oxygen tanks and other equipment had been.

Thayu and I shared a room and Deyu and Reida were next to us.

We were about to go into our room when I held Reida back.

"Can I talk to you for a moment?" I asked him.

He raised his eyebrows.

I dug in my pocket and took out the data stick Amarru had given me.

"I'd like you to look at this."

"What is it?"

I explained to him. While I spoke, his eyes widened like a kid getting a present.

"When do you want me to do this?"

"As soon as you can. I want you to find Simon Dekker in all these records. It may give us a clue about what Dekker was doing when he made the call for help that no one else here seems to realise he made."

He frowned. "What do you mean?"

"Exactly what I'm saying. Dekker ignored me for months and when he finally contacted me, he asked for help. When I mentioned that to Nations of Earth, they didn't seem to know about this call. They're acting like nothing has happened. But something must have happened to make him ask me for help."

"Or it wasn't really him."

"Maybe. We don't know. But when I talked to Nations of Earth, the man avoided answering my question about whether we can see Dekker. If the call for help was a fake message designed to confuse us, then they would have told us that the president was fine and we could join the line of hundreds of people wanting to see him."

"I guess..."

"So here is data that may answer questions about Dekker."

He took the data stick, looked at it, went into his room and came back a moment later with his reader and a data port.

He inserted the stick in the data port and waited for the content to come up on the screen.

He whistled. "There is a *lot* of stuff here."

His eyes moved as he observed the scrolling text. He repeated, "A *lot* of stuff."

"I know. I believe the best way of searching it is to feed in an example of what you want to search, like an image, a message tag or a sound. I can provide samples of images and recordings of Dekker's voice."

He blew out a breath. "I know. But this is going to take a lot of time. As soon as possible, you said?"

He put his finger on the screen to stop it scrolling and read, blue light reflecting in his eyes.

"Holy crap, this has even got movement records of huge numbers of people."

"Yup."

"And you want me to find out what Dekker has been up to?"

"Yes. The records for the Nations of Earth complex are not as complete as they could be—"

"There is more than enough here to get a good picture."

I thought of the incomplete coverage the network had shown upstairs. "Wait until you analyse it."

Reida was looking at the screen again.

"There is far too much here for me to do this quickly. Unless..."

"Unless what?"

"Unless I can enlist help. I could do it quickly, if that is possible."

And here I stopped and looked at him, realising what he was saying.

"Just tell me honestly, are you proposing to send the entire database of this world with all these people their identification and their movements off to a bunch of teenagers in the Outer Circle of Athyl?"

"Well, we could do it."

His cheeks had coloured red.

From the time I had met Reida for the first time, he had always skirted the boundaries of what was legal. He used to sneak into warehouses and into the houses of the rich keihu people in Barresh, and I had deemed it an innocent pastime, because he liked to show off to the councillor's daughters. It had gotten him into a number of scrapes, and the Barresh guards had only recently deleted his long list of petty criminal records.

Recently, though, Reida had been capable, and had done very well in his studies. He would know that what he proposed was highly illegal.

"This is why I'm asking you," he said. "Because I am saying that we could do it quickly. Not saying it's legal, but that we could do it. We have all the systems and the processing in place. These people have already done a lot of work for us recently. They've been scanning all the military's star systems data to look for enemy activity. I've reported on their work many times. They work for me and I pay them out of the project allocation that Asha gives us. Of course, I can't be sure that I can trust all of them fully and that there won't ever be anyone who will find out something they're not supposed to see, but these people are not from influential families. They won't know about all the different ways they can misuse the data, because they simply wouldn't realise what it was and what to do with it. They would be running the scans for whatever I tell them to compare against. If you're concerned, I can select the people I trust most."

"Could you also do something that de-identifies the data?"

"Of course I could. If I put all this in a big table, then split the identification records from the data content, send my people the data and rejoin it again when they've run the analysis."

I looked at him, and he looked at me. This was a devil of a choice. There would be a lot of trouble if someone found out that we had done this.

If they found out I'd used Amarru's secret network, if they found out I'd passed the data off-world. If they found out we'd handed it to private individuals.

But on the other hand, we had been spectacularly unsuccessful in finding out exactly who the enemy was, where they were, how they had dispersed and, most importantly, from where they controlled their drones.

And there was only a short time left to act.

I took in a deep breath and let it out again.

"All right. Do it. Anything that can help us. Just... don't tell me what you've done. I don't want to know about it. Tell me the results."

CHAPTER NINE

I FINALLY FOLLOWED Thayu into our room, where she was unpacking her bag onto one of the single beds in preparation for the shower.

"Did he have any trouble?" she asked, referring to Reida.

I explained to her what Reida had told me.

She didn't hesitate. "Let them do that. Those kids can come up with a lot of good stuff that we don't have the time to look at."

"But we'll be breaching a raft of confidentiality clauses."

"It's war. They won't mind." She peeled off her jacket. "If Reida finds anything, they'll be grateful. If not, there is no need to tell them we did this."

"I hope you're right." If this had happened a few years ago, I wouldn't have hesitated twice, but dealing with Margarethe had softened my viewpoint against the slightly archaic stance of Earth's administrations about privacy. At least I understood the concept. The Coldi didn't understand.

And part of me was still trying to make amends for letting Asha destroy Romi Tanaqan's base from orbit, which was literally a violation of sovereignty and hence an act of war by definition, even if it had also solved a pressing problem. I was keenly aware that I *could* have lost my citizenship over that, and it was due to Danziger that I hadn't. Probably Dekker had wanted to lock me up and throw away the key?

Heck, I wanted to keep my relationship with the Nations of Earth assembly healthy and had tiptoed around Dekker much more than my team thought was warranted.

But we really were getting desperate. And now that the Asto military felt they had at least neutralised the attacks by taking out the satellites, and because the enemy wasn't interested in talking, they were getting ready to withdraw and wanted to hand the defense of the planet over to Nations of Earth, under pressure from *gamra*.

And Nations of Earth wasn't cooperating.

I was afraid that there were elements on Earth who were cheering the invaders on. There had always been that element who didn't want to have anything to do with "aliens".

Thayu disappeared into the room's tiny shower.

I took my shoes off and sat on the bed.

I thought of Emi, now possibly safely on my father's farm in New Zealand.

I thought of Ezhya, who said he was going to return to Asto but was involved in all top level military meetings.

I stared at the wall. I didn't even have a reader anymore, and in order to use Thayu's, I needed her face recognition.

Life without it felt strange, boring, as if I'd never noticed how the paint on the walls was starting to peel. I wondered if the roof needed repairing. This building was old and tired.

Sitting here, feeling out of sorts with my lack of communication, scared about what it could mean that the mysterious messages had followed me even here, I noticed the effects of the passage of time on this building and the need to change. Perhaps, when all this was over, it was time to modernise the building, or even to move the Exchange, since no one needed to keep its presence a secret anymore.

"Hey," Thayu said, her voice soft.

Her skin was red from the shower and her hair was wet.

"Don't worry so much. Something will sort itself out."

I got up from the bed, crossed the room, and closed her in my arms. She was very warm and smelled of soap.

"I'm worried that all this means that the agreement of Earth to join *gamra* is off the table. I'm worried that they're not up to defending themselves. Even Asha, with the most powerful military with the most resources, has had trouble. I'm worried about what this will mean for my family."

I didn't know if I could live with the thought of not being able to visit my father anymore.

Could I convince him to come to Barresh?

No, I didn't think he would ever give up his farm. And I didn't think Erith would be too happy to return to the world of *gamra*.

We went to bed, but as usual in a new place and with a lot of stuff to worry about, I didn't sleep very well.

I felt the absence of Emi in our room, her soft breathing, the little cute noises she made while she dreamed. Every time I heard a noise, I thought it was her waking up, only to realise that she was hopefully safe in New Zealand.

Twice, I woke up because I'd had some sort of dream about Dekker, but each time, I'd already forgotten the content of the dream by the time I was fully awake.

I fell asleep briefly, but woke up again. Through a crack between the curtains, I could already see the brightening of the sky over the hills in the east. We would soon have to get up, and we would have to start planning our next move.

I lay dozing for a bit while Thayu was still asleep.

I wouldn't mind checking the news, even if only to check up on insanely trivial things like sports and dog trials in New Zealand. I needed this bit of normality.

Before we went to sleep, Thayu had set up her reader so that I could also use it, but it lay on the bedside table next to her and I couldn't reach it from where I lay.

Then I became aware of a low rumble. It sounded like thunder, but as far as I knew, there were no clouds in the sky.

Thayu sat bolt upright.

"What's that?"

But I couldn't answer that for her.

We both listened. I peeked out the window to check the sky and found there were indeed no clouds.

I lay back down because it was too early to get up.

Someone ran through the corridor and banged on each of the doors.

Whoever it was—and it sounded like Sheydu—shouted muffled words I couldn't make out.

I jumped out of bed and put on my clothes. Thayu was doing the same. We threw everything into our bags and went into the hallway, where other people were also streaming out of their rooms.

"What's going on?" Nicha asked. He stumbled into the corridor.

He had a habit of sleeping deeply, and might not even have heard the thunder-like sound.

"Impending attack!" Someone yelled at the end of the corridor.

I looked at Evi, who had come out of the room opposite ours, looking annoyingly awake and scrolling through information on his encrypted reader. "What? You mean a drone attack?"

He replied without looking up from his device. "I'm not sure. Seems unlikely, since Asha has told us that this area is safe."

Meanwhile, Asha's military guards were checking each room, making sure that everyone was up.

Deyu came out of the room next to ours, carrying her big gun. With her was Ynggi, dressed in his camouflage gear. The broad canvas belt he wore blinked with several devices, and included his glass-stone knife, loops for the gun he carried, a satchel with recharges, two power packs and a strip of adhesive explosives. Reida called those sticky bombs. When you threw them against a structure, they stuck until they exploded.

He wore the surveillance camera on his tail, which he held over his head like a periscope.

One of Asha's guards gave him a wide berth, even if Ynggi was at least two heads smaller.

Despite the early hour, several people had been at breakfast.

Reida was one of those. He came into the hallway still eating with one hand, and carrying all the electronics in the other. I suspected that he'd been working on my data for most of the night.

We all filed into the hallway and took the emergency stairs down. The narrow staircase only let through one person at a time. The first people were already several floors down before the last ones entered.

There were twenty floors above the ground, and a further four or five below ground.

On the ninth floor, an alarm started wailing.

Someone at the back of the drawn-out group shouted, "Hurry up!"

Amarru stood on the landing at the first underground level, directing the Exchange staff into a side door.

A sound like thunder grumbled in the distance.

"Do you know what's happening?" I asked her.

"Drone attack."

"But Asha said…"

"I don't care what he said. This is what's happening. Asha was wrong. He doesn't rule the world. If you're still keen on trying to get to Rotterdam, take all your people to the next level where the vehicles are. You'll find instructions on how to open the doors on a plaque on the back wall."

"What about you?"

"We protect the building. This is our underground operational centre—"

The ground shook with a nearby explosion. Dust rained from the ceiling.

"Quick, get out of the stairwell. The car park is a fortified space. There is a shelter room in the storage area. Wait there. You will find some of my staff in there. The attacks never last long."

Most of my team had now come past. I followed Evi's broad back down a few sets of stairs.

We came out in the car park where the buses still waited at their charging stations and ran in a line across the underground space. A couple of heavy thuds hit nearby, one powerful enough to make the ground shudder.

We ran into a bare corridor, passed room after room full of stored equipment, and finally came to a meeting room with tables and chairs and a small kitchen. Three Exchange staff sat at the table with cups and a bevy of electronics between them.

We joined in silence and listened. Some hits seemed quite close. On one occasion, some plaster fell down from the ceiling. I watched over a man's shoulder as his screen showed a fast-moving object come closer and leave again. Was that one of Asha's military defence craft? I thought so. At any rate, Asto's military people were thoroughly caught on the back foot. What was this about a safe zone?

Drone attacks usually lasted less than ten minutes, one of the Exchange staff told us. By that time, the drones had discarded all their explosives and had blown themselves up or they had been shot out of the sky.

We waited and watched the situation for some time after that, as the Exchange staff told us. There might be secondary attacks. Those usually happened without warning, they said, because the first attack took out the warning systems.

An Exchange employee offered to have a look. Ynggi wanted to go with him. Isharu tossed him a device that he caught with one hand and his tail and stuck it to the front of his suit. Even if he was more than a head shorter than the Exchange employee, he looked infinitely more menacing. And what was up with that thing Isharu had given him? What was the deal between those two, anyway?

We waited in the safe room. Isharu sat at the corner of the table with a screen that displayed a three-dimensional representation of something with dots and lines. I was too far away to read any of the text except for the military code in the top corner.

Asha's guards sat at the other end of the table and appeared to be busy scanning local Coldi communication. I didn't *think* they were both undertaking the same task. Their screens lacked the military code.

Reida, in the middle of the table, held several devices in front of him where he scrolled through rows and rows of data, occasionally inspecting something closer.

He was working on the material I'd given him last night, which had nothing to do with whatever Isharu and Ynggi were up to, either.

In the middle of all this, Evi and Telaris sat on either side of a screen playing an Indrahui game, which would normally be played with flat wooden chips.

We waited.

The scouts came back not much later and reported that the building had taken some hits, that the glass in the foyer had been blown out and the awning over the entrance was damaged. But the building was safe.

We all went back with them to see the damage for ourselves.

The scouts had understated the damage. I couldn't see one glass panel in the foyer that was still intact. The glass all lay in millions and millions of little pieces scattered over the normally smooth floor. Bits of ceiling plaster had also come down. One of the arrival and departure screens had come off its brackets and dangled perilously.

The perimeter fence must have been breached, because some people were walking on the lawn. I wondered what they were picking up from the grass.

One of the posts that supported the awning over the entrance stood at an odd angle. On closer inspection, the awning roof had peeled off and taken the post off its anchoring block.

A group of Exchange employees were outside the entrance, trying to wrench open the protective metal grate.

Amarru walked around taking pictures.

I went up to her.

"Do you want us to help to secure the building?"

"We're secure. Those people on the lawn can't come in here and they'll leave once our people manage to open the grate. You can go if you want."

"Is it safe?"

"I don't think it's ever going to be safe from now on."

"Have you heard from Asha?"

"Too busy. I first have to check if everyone in town is all right. That can be your department."

Of course, Asha's military guards already had contacted the ship. I found them in a huddle on the floor in front of the ticketing desk, where normally long lines of people would wait.

I called for a meeting of our group in the area behind the ticketing desk that would normally be the domain of cheerful employees in uniform directing travellers to their flights.

Some of us sat on abandoned and dusty chairs, but there were not enough chairs for everyone.

"We need to figure out what we are going to do. Has any of you heard anything from the ship?"

The guard leader, Riyala, said, "We have, if you will allow us to give a report."

How formal.

"Of course, *mashara*. Go ahead."

I met Thayu's eyes. She flicked up her eyebrows.

He began, "The command on board the ship was unpleasantly surprised by this latest attack. According to our report, the attack started in orbit and didn't have a point of origin outside."

In the past, we had often observed that the attacks would originate from somewhere else, like those first attacks had come from probes that had been sent from outside the solar system, but later ones were exactly like this: they started in orbit with a fast-moving point that self-replicated into a swarm of drones in the space of minutes. Usually it was far too late, and they appeared at too low an altitude for the military to use serious firepower on them.

"Where else were they attacking?" I asked.

"Nowhere else. Just here."

"I take it that means they know where we are." I thought of the mysterious message. Damn. Had I unwittingly endangered our entire mission?

"Asha is trying very hard to find out how they got through. The satellites should have stopped the attacks." He didn't meet my eyes. I could only imagine the level of embarrassment for the military. They had vouched for our safety.

And obviously, the satellites were not the only way that the drones operated.

"I'm not interested in who is at fault. I want to know what we're going to do now. Are we going ahead with our plan? I vote that we do, because we are out of time."

Riyala spoke again. "We assume they know where we are, also because they sent a message to you. All they need to do is watch us."

I looked around my team, all those serious faces. No one objected. Ynggi's tail waved gently, swinging the camera attached to the tip back and fro.

"I just want to make sure that everyone understands that this is the case," I said. "If we proceed with our mission, we may become the target of attacks until we find out how they track us."

"It is more important to consider what would happen if we don't consider this mission," Mereeni said. "Because legally, if we can't get permission from Nations of Earth to continue, we no longer have permission to be in orbit, which means that we would cede control of this world to the enemy. And we're not even too sure about who the enemy is and what they want."

"That's not for the lack of trying to find out," I said.

"So I would urge to continue with this mission, because abandoning it would create a lot more trouble," Sheydu said.

Evi signalled that he and Telaris agreed. So did Thayu.

I agreed as well. "Right. I just wanted to make sure that you understood our position. We are still going to the Nations of Earth compound. We'll travel on the train as planned. We will get our orders and details and all communication up to speed before we leave this building, and from there on, we won't use any electronic communication until we get to Rotterdam. We will see the president or the Vice President. We will find out how much the assembly is still in control. We'll leave as soon as possible."

CHAPTER TEN

WE MADE a list of all the things we needed to do before getting on the train.

We had to break our silence temporarily.

I spoke to Leisha, who was with my aircraft at my father's farm in New Zealand.

Part of me had trouble believing it. I'd spent a career trying to justify why we could only have one entry point from *gamra* to Earth—the Athens Exchange. It had never been *gamra*'s rule either, but a restriction placed by Nations of Earth to control what some said would be a *wave of aliens* coming to take away Earth's riches.

I had defended the single entry point, worked with it—whatever spin you wanted to give on my position—because we needed to work together, which meant accepting some foibles of the other party, and this utter anachronism was one of them. Most other jurisdictions had only a single Exchange—sometimes two—but only Earth controlled where craft could fly and land *after* having passed through the Exchange.

And after years of sticking to it, and a few years of pretending to stick to it only for as long as it didn't involve an emergency, we were now openly flouting this rule left, right and centre.

So I tried to imagine my aircraft moored on the same buoy as my father's boat in the bay where the locals got into their dinghies and checked the crab pots every day, and just could not.

But they were there.

Veyada had unloaded an entire truck of hay into the hayloft. Apparently, he never even bothered with the ladder, but just tossed the heavy bales up.

"He finished the job in fifteen minutes," my father said, and his voice sounded indignant in a *why-don't-we-employ-someone-like-that* kind of way.

The kids were enjoying the animals.

Ayshada had attempted to ride a sheep with the predictable result that it had bucked him into a tangle of blackberries.

Ileyu had escaped from the house and after frantically searching the beach in fear she might have gone into the water, they had found her in Diana's tea shop eating cakes.

Emi had been so fascinated by the fire that she had singed the front of her jumper.

In other words: the normal things.

They had heard about the attack on Athens, but there had been no other drone attacks.

I told Leisha about our plans, and I told him I wanted him to find a safe location relatively near the Nations of Earth compound from where he could rescue us if that was necessary, and wait there.

He said he and Veyada would come, because they felt guilty that they were having a holiday while we were being shot at.

I had asked Nicha to check the train timetables and to make sure that all the train routes were still operational.

Most of them were, even if some services were cancelled, and the train booking system was very diplomatic about when the trains would actually arrive. The timetable was subject to conditions, it said.

But it also seemed that after there had been an attack, there often wouldn't be another one for at least a couple of days.

We considered all the things that we needed to bring. Since we wouldn't use our own vehicle, there was a limit to what we could carry. And since we also wanted to defend ourselves, weaponry was part of the load. Quite a significant part.

And because it was getting towards the end of summer, we needed to be prepared for all kinds of weather.

Travelling with Coldi people who weren't used to bad weather was always interesting. Asha's guards liked travelling light—they always had backup, right?

They didn't want to bring jackets and rain gear, besides wearing their temperature retaining suits. The suits were enough, they said.

I protested. "I don't think so."

A woman said, "Some of us have worked in Barresh, and we know about rain. Our suits will cope with these types of conditions."

"This is not Barresh. Please, take the extra gear."

They said they would consider it.

I didn't like the weather forecast one bit. A big rain area was imminent. There would be little sunlight. I hoped we wouldn't need to spend much time away from buildings.

I tried to book my usual accommodation in a hotel just outside the Nations of Earth complex, but they didn't reply.

Then I tried the rather basic option inside the compound, but they also hard to get onto.

After about an hour of trying, I spoke to a junior employee at the gate, who told me that accommodation in the entire complex was closed because of safety concerns, and that most of the assembly members met each other in different parts of the city, which could not be disclosed to anyone.

Since I also didn't disclose my identity, for fear of these calls being tapped, I couldn't tell him who we were, and hoped that something would shake out by the time we arrived there.

I asked him how to go about applying to meet some delegates, hoping I might learn something from a different perspective. But I didn't even want to name names of who I wanted to meet, also for fear of someone listening in.

It was a very odd conversation.

Twice thwarted, I booked a hotel much further away.

Amarru told us that her responsibility was with the Exchange, and that she preferred to stay and help the employees get back on their feet.

People were still assessing the damage and trying to salvage items from the collapsed parts of the building. Apparently, the foundations of the main tower displayed worrying cracks. A builder needed to assess it properly.

This would be a rather long process. I didn't think that the Exchange would be up again soon. There would be no more meetings in the canteen on the top floor looking out over the city for a while, if not forever. Another building might rise in its stead, but it would almost certainly look very different.

Amarru took us to an underground room which contained a lot of Asto's military provisions. I got jackets for the guards, who had shown no interest in taking on extra gear.

We tested our communication hub. It was only a compact unit strong enough for local coverage, rather than a unit that could communicate with traffic in orbit.

Deyu joked that she should have known that she was going to be carrying a communication unit again.

"I would prefer that someone else carry it," I said. "I want to keep you and your hands free for fighting, in case that is necessary."

So she gave the unit to Nicha.

Then we had a sparse meal and divided up the rest of our supplies.

In the middle of this, Sheydu got up, and got her reader. She placed it on the table screen up.

"I just got this package from orbit," she said. "It's probably the last communication we're going to get from them. We should all watch it."

She activated the projection, and Asha's face sprung into the air. He was seated in the control chair in his command module.

"I am more than glad that all of you survived. This attack was not meant to have happened, and it was a major failure on our part. We have also taken some damage, and all our operations have retreated to the main ship for now. We cannot continue to give coverage in the way we plan. I'm afraid you're on your own, and if you end up in trouble, I'm not sure how quickly we can be there to help you, or even if we can do that at all. We have sent all civilians to safe places, either to their homes on the planet or on their way to Asto or Barresh. We have become the focus of their attacks, and it looks like the way we developed to predict their actions has been breached already."

It was the most sombre speech he had ever given in my presence.

I looked at Isharu. They would know what sort of damage the fleet had taken. The Asto military was not used to being defeated.

He continued, "We can only conclude that in addition to the communication point that we already knew about, and we are guarding, there has to be another one. If there is another one, there is likely to be a third one and a fourth one. Somewhere there has to be a nerve centre where all these infernal machines get their orders. We thought we knew where it was, but it turns out we were wrong. And *gamra* is breathing down our necks, so if we can't get permission to stay, we will have no option but to withdraw."

I looked at the solemn faces around the table. If we didn't succeed in this mission, then we might not get home at all.

"We have already decided to go ahead with our expedition," I said. "Leisha will back us up with my craft. We'll be silent. If you need to contact us as a matter of urgency, you can do that through the usual channels."

Meaning the Coldi register.

"I see."

He sounded strangely subdued.

"I'm very, very sorry for having put you in this difficult situation."

"Knowing that *gamra* has an ultimatum, I might have attempted this expedition, anyway."

He didn't reply to that.

"Are my children both there?"

"They are. Would you like to speak with them?"

"I just wanted to know that they're safe. And Nicha's boy and your daughter?"

"They are with my father." I was tempted to tell him about the blackberries and shirt-singing incident, but his mood seemed too intense for that.

"Your father is a good man. If possible, I'd like to see him again in a less stressful situation."

"I'm sure he'd welcome that."

Heck, this was the weirdest conversation I remembered having with him for... well, maybe not forever, but certainly for a long time.

Usually, this meant he was deeply worried.

I said, "I'm committed to striking at the heart of this enemy and I may not command a lot of weapons, but I'll do my best to play my part."

"Weapons are not terribly useful, anyway. We can shoot installations to bits, and they just send a new drone, open it up, and a new installation unfolds quicker than we can shoot it down. You have our best weapons: your mouth and the ingenious members of your team."

"Well... thank you." I didn't know what else to say, and then I realised there was only one thing that was appropriate to say.

"*Iyamichu ata.*"

Soldiers off to war.

He repeated, "*Iyamichu ata.*"

I signed off and looked around at the solemn faces of the members of my team.

"Let's go."

We turned off all our communication, extracted all feeders and put them away, made sure that all devices were powered down.

Then we went down to the car park.

Amarru lent us a bus and driver to take us to the station.

The bus took us down the hill through the streets of the suburbs where the signs of damage were everywhere. Apartment complexes where all windows had blown in, a community hall that had lost a roof. A car stood abandoned on the road. Bikes and scooters stood randomly propped up against walls when the owners had fled.

There was almost no one on the streets.

Some shops were open, and a long line stood outside one of them, but many other shops had been boarded over.

Many people had left, especially the Coldi people, and this was a part of town where many poorer Coldi families lived.

I only imagined the level of confusion and fear for these people, if not even we understood exactly why we were under attack.

The train station was quite busy. A train had just arrived and people streamed onto the platform.

Harassed looking Coldi families with children, groups of young people in *gamra* clothing, people travelling by themselves or in mixed groups with people from other worlds. Many spoke Coldi, but I also heard some other languages.

Almost no one was waiting to get on.

The employee who checked us for the ticket was surprised and asked if we were absolutely certain that we wanted to leave.

"We have some business to undertake," I said.

"Just as long as you realise we can't extract people from areas outside the enclave as well as we used to."

"Don't worry, we are prepared."

But as we walked across the platform to the train, I wondered if these were to be our famous last words.

CHAPTER ELEVEN

THE TRAIN SET off across the track where I had travelled many times before. Through further suburbs with highrise buildings, past the back of yards to commercial premises, along major roads, picking up speed all the way.

But the landscape was no longer familiar to me. Most of the outer suburbs of the city lay abandoned. In one place, there was obvious damage, and the drone strike had led to a fire which had gone into the hills, colouring the ground black.

The haze of fire still hung over the horizon.

The train gathered speed. The surrounding landscape became utterly desolate. Many of the towns we passed looked abandoned. Not all of them had taken damage, although a patchwork of fires had travelled through and turned the sparse gum tree and pine forest or grassland into a patchwork of black markings.

We didn't seem to go as fast as I had expected, and indeed, when I checked the timetable on the screen next to the door, it turned out that the train would not travel at top speed. The journey would take almost 2 hours longer than it usually did. I didn't ask why this was because I doubted my team would know, but I presumed it was as a precaution, because there might be damage to the tracks, or because there might be extra stops needed.

There were very few other people on the train. Just a group of young men with big packs. I suspected they were going to join a military base somewhere.

They kept a close eye on Ynggi, who stared out the window. He didn't ask questions, but his expression looked disturbed.

"Anything the matter?" I asked.

"You said other parts of this world were different," he said, and sounded disappointed.

At the ship, we'd had many discussions about our trip to America Free State and I'd assured him that not every part of the countryside was a desert in which rivers turned green and fish floated on the surface—I didn't think Ynggi would ever get over that sight.

I said, "There are many different parts of this world. You've already seen some."

"Just the towns are different. I don't care about towns. In the landscape, I'm still seeing the same thing: dead trees and dry rivers and not much fish."

"I promise, there are places where fishing is really good."

"Are we going there?"

"Not right now, but later, maybe."

"Why are the trees dead?"

"Because of fires and because there isn't enough rain."

"But it takes many seasons for a tree to grow. There must have been enough rain for the tree to grow to that size."

"Yes, once, there was, but these trees have been dead for a long time."

Old images would show the tree-covered hillsides. This area had always been dry, but it was now little more than a rock-covered desert with a lot of tree skeletons.

People had done so much damage. I'd tried to explain it to Ynggi, but he failed to understand, because according to him, it was impossible to take all the fish out of the ocean. It was not moral to catch that much fish, because you couldn't possibly eat that much.

The same with forests. There were always more trees, especially if you were careful with only cutting down certain trees and making sure that you planted new ones.

Pengali tribes attached special *karrit* points to looking after trees.

What about the animals? he wanted to know. *They* could go somewhere else, so why did they stay to eat prickly plants in dry paddocks?

The concept of farming livestock was not entirely new to him, but he didn't understand at a very deep level how one could own a sentient animal.

Especially when we got to the part where I had to tell him that unhappy animals couldn't just leave if they didn't like a farm because in the first place there were fences and they belonged to a person, and in the second place, there were few places that were within walking distance of a large animal where it could survive on its own without running into farms or villages, or where there was enough food for the animal to eat.

And then he looked at me with his large, deep brown eyes and said, "You must understand. I know you left this world as a boy and this..." He waved his tail at the landscape that whizzed past at high speed outside the train's window. "... Is not *your* fault."

At that, I had to look out the window while emotions raged inside me.

Ynggi had this uncanny ability to dole out emotional king punches to the gut.

Of course, it was my fault. It was everyone's fault, and I was absolutely part of that society that had created this world as it was, a world in which large areas of continents were barely liveable, where a disease raged through a camp in Djibouti and killed hundreds of thousands, so many that not even international forces could burn them all in time, a world in which Nations of Earth security squads had gone into refugee camps in Morocco under cover and actively *murdered* thousands of people sleeping in rickety tents to relieve the desperate pressure on the settlement camps in South Spain, itself a country dangling at the top of the economic cliff by the grace of oranges and almonds and some very strong fingernails.

Of course it was my fault.

And also, I was a coward for fleeing the planet, and for returning to one of the very few places that had seen benefits from the upheavals, and that was only because New Zealand had slammed shut the borders during the wars in the second half of the last century and had never fully opened them again.

It was my fault, all right.

The spacefaring expat community pretended that settlement elsewhere was an option, but for the vast majority of people, going to space was not an option, nor was retreating to a comfortable city or hiding behind a diplomatic pass, or enjoying holidays in New Zealand, while people who had lost everything they owned died of hunger and disease.

And *those* people were the ones that Amarru supported. The Zhori clan were the only ones who had improved the lot of countries in Africa so poor that any semblance of a government had evaporated with the last water supplies.

It was absolutely my fault.

It was comforting that it grew dark, because the landscape was too depressing. All those abandoned villages and the scars of wildfires that had torn through the landscape unchecked, crops abandoned and animals turned loose. Bridges lay destroyed and roads blocked with debris or with fallen trees.

It was truly dystopian. Worse than I'd ever seen it. The drone attacks had pushed a lot of smaller towns over the edge. People had packed up, left their houses and travelled to the cities. Or they had... died.

At least when darkness enclosed us in the comfortable little cabin travelling across the utterly alien landscape, life seemed normal.

We folded out the benches.

The bench was narrow and hard, and during the night I woke up a few times disturbed by the smell of fire.

I would check that my bag still stood next to the bench, that Thayu was still asleep on the bunk below me, check that Sheydu's reader wasn't flashing any warnings before being happy enough to lie back down. I didn't think the others were getting a lot of sleep, either.

But I must have drifted off because suddenly, a violent lurch pushed me into the back wall of the cabin. There was a big thump as someone who had been sleeping on the bench facing the other direction fell on the floor. The person cursed in Coldi.

Sheydu.

The train was still slowing down, and was now almost at a standstill. This was not the normal station. I thought we weren't supposed to stop until Salzburg. It was too early for that. It was still pitch black outside.

But slowly, as the train hummed, slowed down, and the brakes hissed, I registered that roughly-hewn rock and sections of concrete passed the window: we were in a tunnel.

"What's going on?" I asked, not expecting anyone to have the answers.

I peered out into the darkness, but apart from vapour hissing from under the train, presumably from water cooling the brakes, I saw nothing beyond the rock wall.

From memory, there was a long tunnel, in fact several of them, where the tracks crossed the Alps. I presumed we were in one of those tunnels and also that the train had encountered something unexpected on the tracks, triggering the emergency brakes.

The notification screen in the cabin remained blank.

Deyu wrenched open the window. It only opened enough to let out her hand, but she stuck out the reader and tried to use her camera to see if she could figure out what was going on at the front.

From memory, our carriage was the second or third one in the train.

Her screen showed an area of lights so bright that was impossible to make out detail. Shapes moved in the bright spot.

There were people in the tunnel.

"Is that the driver?" she asked.

"As far as I know, there are no drivers on these trains."

"No one at all?" Coming from someone who had been a train driver, the horrified expression disturbed me.

"There might be someone in attendance, but these trains drive themselves."

Yes, there probably would be people in attendance. It was unlikely that the staff numbered more than one or two people, not a handful, as I could see on her screen.

The people now moved out of the train's headlights and walked along the side of the engine.

We had stopped in a slight bend where there was a bit of extra space. A box with blinking lights hung on the rock wall, with a metal door with a voltage warning sign next to it.

The people were coming in our direction. The sound of their voices echoed through the tunnel.

When I pressed the side of my head against the window and looked out, I could even see them.

They were definitely not railway employees or military. They were families with children, people dressed in civilian clothing carrying bags.

They called out to passengers in the carriage in front of us.

Someone climbed onto the section in between the carriages, but the flexible tunnel that allowed passengers to walk to the next carriage—marked "Emergency Exit"—was locked to those not holding a valid ticket.

When they saw us, a woman came to the window and knocked on it. She wore a coat and headscarf as if they were sheltering from the weather. Peeking out from the dark fabric, her face was pale and her cheeks bright red from the cold. She yelled something through the glass.

"Who are these people?" I asked.

But of course, my companions would not know the answer.

A couple of children joined her. They were carrying bags and wearing lots of jumpers over the top of each other. These people looked like refugees.

Thayu had gone to the entrance to the carriage and prised a bigger window open. Voices drifted through the opening.

"I have no idea what they're saying," she said. "Should we open the door?"

"Let me talk to them," I said.

She stepped aside.

I breathed in the scent of hot metal from the train's brakes, mixed with the scent of stone.

"What is going on?" I asked.

The woman at the front squinted against the light in the cabin. Who knew how long she had been sheltering in this tunnel?

"Help," she said. "We need help. Children, sick. No food. You have money?" She held up a dirty hand, palm up.

She said a few other things, but her dialect was so thick but I didn't understand her. In many smaller villages and farming communities, they were so isolated that they didn't speak Isla as their first language.

"We can give you a lift to the next station. Salzburg?"

"No-no-no. No Salzburg. Money. You have money."

Beggars? Living in the tunnels?

At this moment, the door opened to the flexible *Emergency Exit* tunnel to the next carriage, and a man came out who was definitely a railway employee. He shouted something really unfriendly at the woman and she retreated away from the window.

"What is going on?" I asked him.

"They're squatters, building camps in the tunnels. The idiots. They don't realise how dangerous that is."

"They're refugees. They are sheltering here against drone attacks."

"I don't know where you're from, but these people are no refugees. They are gypsies. Thieves."

He meant these people had always lived here, and I'd blissfully travelled past them and not known about them for years?

That was... disturbing.

I asked, "So why have we stopped? Is the track blocked?"

"That's what I'm here to investigate. Why we've stopped. Some idiot must have pressed the emergency stop. Ignore the rabble. We'll be on our way again soon. I just need to reset the brakes. Sit down and grab some hot chocolate from the dispenser. It's very good stuff. No points needed."

He winked at me, before continuing his way down the carriage.

"Idiot," Nicha mumbled after him.

But he crossed the cabin to the dispenser against the back wall of the carriage, pulled out a cup and filled it with hot chocolate, anyway.

Of course, being *gamra* citizens, we had never needed to subject to the ridiculous points system that forced the eating habits that governments considered healthy—and hot chocolate was sure to rate poorly.

I frowned at him. "I didn't know you liked hot chocolate."

"I don't." Coldi people didn't usually go for sweet things.

He carried the cup to the window and carefully manoeuvred his hand through. Two skinny teenage girls outside tried to reach it, but they weren't tall enough. Then one lifted the other up, and the top girl grabbed the cup with pale-skinned, red-knuckled hands.

"Wait," I said.

I went to the dispenser to get a second cup.

As soon as word went around that there was food being handed out, many people came back to our window. They all crowded along the side of the carriage while we handed hot chocolate out to them.

I wondered how long it would be before the train got going again.

Already, heavy clangs made the carriage shudder. And still more people lined up for hot chocolate.

"It's almost empty," Nicha said, coming back with yet another cup.

"You will need to move back. The train is about to start moving again," I said to the sea of heads and outstretched hands as I tried to hand them the cup without spilling.

Then I heard another sound: that of the doors to the carriage moving aside, and then footsteps, and the sound of adolescent male voices. Crap, someone had worked out how to open the doors.

I said softly to my team, "Action."

Weapons came out.

Deyu, Isharu and Sheydu moved to the door of our train compartment, forming a protective barrier between the door and me and my team.

A male voice called out, "Stop, stop, stop, sir. You do *not* have permission to enter this train. Get out immediately. You, too, sir."

But more people came in. Their footsteps thudded on the floor. I could see them in the reflection in the window. A scruffy man looked into our cabin. His eyes widened when he saw Deyu and Sheydu. He retreated. He was followed by two young men, who did the same.

The train attendant was still yelling at people to get out, or he'd call the authorities. Then he came into our cabin, flinched at the sight of the guns, and yelled, "This is your fault. I'm going to call ahead to Salzburg, and they'll take this rabble off the train. I'm going to lock this carriage and you can deal with them for the journey—"

"Oh, shut up, man," a male voice said behind him. "These people are not dangerous."

The man who came to the doorway wore an oversized coat with a hood pulled over his eyes. He wore sunglasses and an unruly beard. His clothes were sturdy, black—Coldi military gear? But his beard was blond, and he wasn't broad-shouldered enough to be Coldi.

The train attendant turned to him. "What, sir? Who are you? Can I see your ticket?"

"No, you cannot. You can go back to your cabin and get this train moving before the next service arrives and hits us at full speed. I cannot guarantee that the warning beacon still works."

The man's throat worked. "But... sir!"

"Stop complaining and do it."

The owner of the voice pushed the attendant aside, ignored Deyu, Isharu and Sheydu, came into the cabin and sat down opposite me.

He lowered his hood and took off his sunglasses.

It was Klaus Messner.

Ah. That explained *everything*.

CHAPTER TWELVE

"THIS IS AN UNEXPECTED... ENCOUNTER," I said.

I couldn't bring myself to say *pleasure*. Seeing his face brought a lot of feelings, not all of them good.

Memories rushed back to me of how smug he was, and how he had basically abandoned us in the middle of dangerous territory in South Africa.

This man might work for Amarru, but he was not necessarily my friend.

His grey eyes took in every member of my team.

"Amarru not here?" he asked.

"She chose to stay in Athens. Too much to do there."

"Good. Someone with their head screwed on right."

I ignored that barb.

He and I were not always on the same page. All right, he didn't like that we invaded his territory.

"So you stopped the train. What about those people?"

"They're just a cover. They'll get off at the next station and find their way back."

"Do they live in the tunnel?"

"Usually. But you've probably never noticed them."

No, I hadn't, and the thought horrified me, but the patronising way he said it annoyed me.

He was openly wearing his Zhori earrings, and he looked at my Domiri ones. "You have changed a bit since I last saw you."

If he was angling for a response, I wasn't going to elaborate.

"You might tell me why you're here and why we were important enough to mess with the train's automatic piloting system to intercept us."

"Ah. Is it going to be one of those days?"

"One of what days?"

If he was going to play this game, then so could I.

Thayu was also watching this conversation. She liked Klaus even less than I did. After he had abandoned us in South Africa, she had been scathing about his motives. She also didn't like Amarru very much and called the entire section of Coldi on Earth a bunch of corrupted traitors.

I didn't think either Klaus or Amarru had deliberately abandoned us, but had judged us capable enough to use the resources to escape on our own. But that was a discussion we'd had many times and I couldn't win, because I agreed with her on the lack of basic decency. He could have told us what he was going to do.

He peeled off his coat, dropped it on the seat next to him and went to the back of the cabin, only to find out there was no hot water left, because we'd given all the hot chocolate to the people in the tunnel.

He sat down again, clearly annoyed.

"They'll refill it at the next station," I said.

"No, they won't. You really don't understand what's going on, do you?"

"I think I have a decent grasp, but I'm always open to hearing other viewpoints."

He snorted and said nothing. Then he rummaged through the pockets of his coat, but came up with nothing.

"Look, I'm sorry you missed Amarru, and she's not here. Meanwhile, I've said before that I don't think we're enemies. We're actually on the same side."

"Yeah. Only you're about to ruin everything we've worked at for the past few years."

"We're going to Rotterdam. I need Nations of Earth to sign a declaration that sanctions the presence of Asto's military in orbit for defensive purposes."

"Just like that, huh?"

"In a nutshell, yes."

"And you and your overlords are naïve enough to believe that the only reason you've been unable to speak to Nations of Earth from orbit is failure of technology?"

"I said nothing about that, and I have my own motives. I'm trying to protect Nations of Earth, because if I don't get this agreement, the Asto military will have to withdraw and they are Earth's only protection against relentless drone attacks. The agreement is important because *gamra* insists that we act according to the laws, because they consider Earth a full member and treat it as such."

"Except Dekker never continued with it, did he?"

"The people voted in favour. The bureaucracy rolls on regardless of who sits in the president's chair."

"The one thing…" He breathed out a sigh. "The one thing I can't get over is how you are so in their pockets that you believe all this holier-than-thou bullshit that comes out of *gamra*. A lot of people have questions. Yes, I think a lot of them are rubbish, too. I agree with you that whatever *gamra* is, it's better than the alternatives, but Earth is a democratic society and that means people ask questions and questions need to be answered. And because of these questions, Dekker is stalling."

"I have noticed that."

"But you don't seem to understand why."

"If he has questions, why doesn't he ask them? I'm happy to hear them. Melissa is happy to answer them. Anything better than this stupid game of chicken."

"Because—and I want you to understand this, *really* listen to this: Nations of Earth is rotten to the core."

He let a silence lapse as if for effect.

"Well, that's a very radical opinion—"

"It's rotten to the core. Get off this train. Don't go there."

"I have to. That's my mission, and that's what I will do."

"Why? For the sake of an organisation we haven't even yet properly joined?"

"For the sake of avoiding a major war, and for the sake of maintaining the only form of defence in orbit that Earth currently has, yes."

"The danger is not in orbit."

"People who have suffered drone attacks might beg to differ."

"Those attacks have to be coordinated from somewhere, right?"

I met his grey eyes.

Someone in my team—one of Asha's guards, I thought—had made a trip to another cabin to get us drinks. He came by with a tray. I was sure this was not an accident. He wanted to hear what was going on.

We both took a cup of hot chocolate and sipped in silence. From across the cabin, Thayu also listened to every word we said.

"Are you telling me you know where their coordination centre is?"

"No. But I have a decent idea who these people are."

"The Southern California Aerospace Force."

"That's who they *were*, once, maybe a hundred years ago."

"Less than that. About fifty."

He looked at me in a *suit yourself* way. Seriously, this man rubbed me up the wrong way with every word he said. Yet I knew he was not an enemy. I had to keep repeating this to myself all the time. He was probably highly knowledgeable and capable, but did he have to be such a dick about it?

Take a deep breath, Mr Wilson.

He continued, "There are lots of sympathising organisations on Earth, in countries other than just America Free State. People who are unhappy with their lot. People who don't like the governments, people who don't like *aliens*."

"Yes, I know. I've met some of those people. A few months ago, at the time of the first attacks, we were actually in America Free State to investigate their old bases."

Now it was his turn to look surprised. "You did what? Why?"

"Because we found one of their ships in the rainforest near Barresh. They had also passed technology to a Pengali tribe that had reason to be unhappy. They wanted to stoke a Pengali war to destabilise Barresh."

For the first time, the smug expression left his face.

"Shit. Are you serious?"

"Yes. This is the angle I'm coming from. It's not just an Earth problem."

He breathed out heavily and dragged a hand over his face.

I continued, "Factions within *gamra* are livid. They say if this had happened before the referendum, *gamra* could have isolated Earth, closed the Athens Exchange and given the military forces the mandate to attack anything that comes out of the sector, but now any military action requires permission from Nations of Earth. The military ships in orbit are there without permission."

"But you won't get that permission from the current lot."

"Why are you so certain? Do you know what's happening at Nations of Earth? Where is Dekker?"

"Nations of Earth has put out statements that they're under attack and in hiding. There has been a serious drone attack on Rotterdam and the complex and there are very strong rumours that assembly members were killed."

"How many?"

He spread his hands.

"Any names?"

"No, sorry. The news has kept quiet for security reasons."

"That seems an odd reason, to say the least. I lived in the compound during the attacks of 2099, and I remember distinctly that all the names and photos of the victims were published."

Holy crap. That attack back then was carried out by the same type of people: those who despised *gamra* and its people.

"I didn't think you were that old."

"I was nine. I went to the school for diplomat children. My father was director of Midway Space Station. The children of these people were in my class."

He took in a whistling breath. "There are many groups. They're well-organised. They're all over Nations of Earth. Very limited information comes out of the complex anymore. Nations of Earth is damaged, deeply compromised. These groups, the anti-*gamra* elements and violent cells and other rabble are supported by a group of influential people."

"Governor Patterson of America Free State."

"That's one of them we know of. There is also an Egyptian mining baron, and the president of Kazakhstan, media empires and communication companies."

"The Pretoria Cartel?"

"No. They know they can get much further by selling stuff to us than going to war with us."

"Yeah, I didn't think so. Minke Kluysters' outlook on life holds as much ideology as a sieve holds sand."

"Oh, I don't know about that. You say anything bad about any African, poor or rich, black or white, and he gets real shirty."

"True." That defensiveness about his origin gave me a sliver of respect for him. Minke Kluysters was an arrogant piece of shit, but he was true to his word. "Huh. If you're right, that's probably the first time that he and I are on the same side."

I finished the last of my hot chocolate and put the empty cup in the holder.

"But what we've been looking for is: how are these people tied up with an attack from deep space? The first drone attack must have taken years of planning. We followed the approaching probe for months. It never communicated with us and we never found out where it came from."

He shook his head. "Neither have we."

"We've obviously been looking in the wrong place."

"This is where it gets weird, but I've heard several theories. Some people say that the groups on Earth are a vanguard or naïve fringe. They know little about the organisation that gave birth to their movement, but they create chaos in their name. They join under the banner Independence Force. The off-Earth attackers hide themselves behind their facade, but the Earth-based and space-based groups may not have that much in common. Much like what happened with the Asto-based Aghyrians when the original Aghyrians returned. This space-based group may be a large society or a smaller one. There is evidence that people disappeared years ago, mainly from North America."

Wonder who provided that evidence? Still, it was good to hear that at least some people had taken my reports seriously.

I said, "Ezhya says that in order to create advanced technologies that can build self-replicating drones, you need a large population."

"I've heard that pyramid theory, too. The higher the tip of the pyramid, the broader the base needs to be. But I'm not so sure. It only applies if there are no other technologically advanced societies, and you need to create everything from scratch. But there is plenty of technology to borrow from and frankenstein into something that adds up to more than the sum of the parts."

"The children climb the cliff from the shoulders of the parents."

"I see you know your proverbs."

"So, where would this shadow society be? They were unsuccessful in Barresh. They were also unsuccessful in taking one of the Nations of Earth craft to New Taurus when I was a kid. That must have been thirty years after the attempt to settle in Barresh." We had already investigated Taurus and New Taurus ourselves, but had not found evidence of a large population.

They had also been unsuccessful in joining with the Pretoria Cartel, if they'd ever tried. Even criminals like Robert Davidson had warned about dangerous people lurking south of Barresh.

I couldn't imagine that they'd joined with the Aghyrians, because the Aghyrians had a deep disdain for anyone not Aghyrian.

Klaus said, "I'm actually considering the option that the drone attacks might be a smokescreen. Have you noticed how quickly people are to blame *gamra*? They want *gamra* to be the main accused."

"Like way back with Amoro Renkati and Sirkonen's murder."

"Yeah."

"So you think Dekker is under the influence of these people and that's why he's been playing hard to get?"

"Not under the influence. He *is* one of them. It's his mission to be the last president of Nations of Earth. Just look at how these people have chipped away at the confidence that Nations of Earth is effective. They despise international organisations."

Dekker's behaviour suited that theory, but on the other hand, he *had* called me for help. I still believed that call was genuine.

Klaus continued, "It's pointless for you to go there to make them sign some document. They won't. The best you'll do is waste time. But you could also risk your life and that of others, including your people here."

"We have plenty of eyes. Plenty of weapons, plenty of experience."

"You're not taking my warning seriously."

"I do, but I've dealt with these people and the rat's nest that's Nations of Earth almost all my life. There have always been many political influences in the assembly. I don't need to deal with the assembly. They meet remotely these days, anyway. We simply *need* the declaration because we need to stop further drone attacks, and we need Dekker to sign for it."

And I didn't believe that Dekker would have been electable had he openly held the opinion that Nations of Earth was irrelevant. I considered Eva's father as one of the most conservative people I knew. He thought little of people from different worlds and had told me so many times, but he was deeply loyal to Nations of Earth.

"Don't go," he repeated.

"I have to, and we're going to. We'll be careful, but we'll be fine. I know many people there from all sides of the political divide."

The train slowed down. We were about to stop in Salzburg.

It was still dark. The only thing I could see outside the window were a few sparse lights behind windows. Governments liked to force residents to keep their windows obscured at night. Street lamps were off, advertising screens and other notifications were off.

A group of people we'd picked up in the tunnel were arguing near the entrance. Men spoke in loud voices. The children crammed in front of the windows looking out.

Klaus held his head turned to listen.

"What are they arguing about?" I asked.

"The young guys want to get off so that they can catch the train back. The old guy says that they're better off going to the next station, because the police are going to be waiting for them here."

The train stopped, and the doors opened. A group of people got off, but others remained on the train.

With the dimmed lights on the platform, it was hard to make out anything.

A tiny light above the door to an office highlighted the heads of many people.

Some came onto the train. Others remained on the platform.

Voices shouted in the dark.

A couple of people pushed their way through the crowd.

Someone jumped into our carriage and ran into the corridor.

Klaus said, "Uh-oh."

A couple of additional people jumped into the carriage.

A woman shouted.

Men's voices joined her.

"What's all that about?" I asked.

"Police. These people are not welcome here."

A shouting match broke out in the next cabin. Something heavy thumped against the wall. More people came into the carriage. Their silhouettes were broad, and they wore helmets with lights.

A tussle broke out in the next cabin. Three women ran past the entrance to our cabin.

A moment later, the helmeted figures—I could just make out the word *police* on one of their jackets—frogmarched a few of the tunnel youths out of the carriage.

I looked out the door. The three women stood huddled together in front of the toilet door in our carriage.

"The police officers are gone," I said to them.

They gave me blank looks. I had no idea if they understood me.

I retreated into the cabin while the train doors closed.

Someone had replenished the hot water supply. We needed to wait until it heated up. The cabin was also on its last satchels of hot chocolate, but my team would carry supplies of tea.

While the train pulled out of the station, the first glow of daylight peeped over the horizon.

CHAPTER THIRTEEN

KLAUS GOT off the train when we arrived in Munich. A haze of smoke hung over the station and when the train stopped and the doors opened, the faint wailing of sirens drifted in, evidence of another recent attack.

By now, it was dawn, and I watched him slink into the crowd with the remaining people we had picked up in the tunnel. Klaus said most of them would stay with friends or family before travelling on to other places in whichever way they could without paying.

Klaus hadn't told me what he was doing in the tunnel and where he was going. His family lived in Munich, and maybe he had travelled overland from South Africa. Flying would require him to declare his identity, but most of the land borders ranged from porous to non-existent. Except the one that required crossing the Mediterranean. That one was a nightmare of refugee camps devoid of hope, places where poor, nameless and faceless desperate people came in search of a better place to live and died while waiting or trying to escape the horrendous conditions in the camps.

Almost every part of the world had a shadow society of people who lived off the offcuts discarded by the rich and powerful. Those people lived in abandoned buildings. They rarely had money, much less official identification. They were to be found in places where charities provided free food, and many were illegals, people down on their luck or people whose history and temperament made it hard for them to find or keep a job. There were many of these people on Earth, but Barresh had them, too.

A very small number of people actively chose to live like this, carefree and unburdened by any possessions other than those they could carry, hitching rides on various modes of transport, or begging for tickets outside the entrance of stations or airports.

I could see Klaus pretending to be part of that world.

But he was more than that.

He was too smart to have just accidentally stopped the train we were on, but even when I considered the stuff he told me, I couldn't pick up how my visit to Rotterdam was important enough to want to meet with me because a lot of what he said was not news to me, anyway. Except he had confirmed my suspicion that the Pretoria Cartel was not involved.

"I don't like him," Thayu said when the train had started moving again. "He acts like he has all the answers."

"That's just Klaus. He's an arrogant bastard."

"He identifies as Zhori and the Zhori clan has a long history of being troublesome. When you have access to news again, read up on what made the Zhori clan leave Athyl. They love to accuse Misha Palayi of being a tyrant who chased them out of their homes and who sought to colonise Earth."

"He did that. He drew up proposals for Coldi settlements in the Sahara and years later, we were still dealing with the fallout. He was hoping to use the chaotic times before the inception of Nations of Earth as a cover for a low-key invasion of Earth. I read all that. I argued with Ezhya about it, back in the time I was still terrified of him, remember?"

"You are not nearly terrified enough of him." Her voice was low.

"I don't need to be terrified of him anymore. He's kind of my *zhayma* now." Also, how did we get here from discussing Klaus Messner?

"Never take your eyes off Ezhya, or anyone in power, but especially Ezhya or whoever takes his position. You absolutely need to be terrified of what he can do when he feels that his power over the settled worlds is at stake. Officially *gamra* controls settled space. Of course, they don't really do this because *gamra* is a gutless, toothless administrative organisation. It has always been about Asto's grip on settled space, using *gamra* as cover. When this Pretoria Cartel and the stuff at Tamer came up, Ezhya was concerned, but he's neatly made the Tamer Collective your problem. This new, nebulous enemy, however, strikes at the heart of Coldi power in a way not even the Aghyrians and their captain did. Because they're in space and we have little idea where. And because they're also on the planet and we don't know where. We have some ideas, but we can't be certain because they don't look or act any differently from the rest of this chaotic planet with its chaotic people and jumbled-up leadership. And that leadership is not helping us identify the enemy and therefore, they may well *be* the enemy."

Her dark eyes met mine. The pale dawn light made only a few of her peacock eyelashes sparkle.

She continued. "If the enemy are spread throughout Nations of Earth, as Klaus says they are, then can we even prove Nations of Earth is not the enemy? That's the version of the truth Ezhya and my father are interested in. If it's clear that this enemy is so enmeshed in this world it's impossible to extricate them, and what is more, that Nations of Earth is not interested in doing this, then they may well conclude this world in its entirety is the enemy and take drastic action before submitting to *gamra* bureaucracy. Because ultimately, Asto has by far the most to lose from admitting this world to full *gamra* membership."

Well, *that* was disturbing, even if also a thought that had crossed my mind before. Asha could do that, absolutely, agree to withdraw as per *gamra* regulations, but utterly destroy the Athens Exchange before they left, plus a few strategic localities, and then use any unidentified movement in space as extended target practice for the military sling until all of Earth's space communities were destroyed.

"I think Klaus is bluffing about the unreliability of Nations of Earth. He doesn't want us to talk to Nations of Earth for some other reason. Look, he may well have been setting up some plan for doing... something, who knows what... that we're now upsetting. Clearly, the plan involves us keeping away from Nations of Earth. I've known these people for most of my life. I was involved with Nations of Earth before I became involved with *gamra*. Each country sends their delegates who are elected. Klaus is never going to convince me that a good proportion of over one hundred and fifty countries supports the abolition of the very institution that gives them their power. Nationalistic, anti-*gamra* types have always been part of Nations of Earth. I've had many discussions with some of them." Like Eva's father, like Danziger. "Klaus is not even on that spectrum."

"I agree, but I still don't like him."

"You've said that before."

"Because I don't. We shouldn't trust him."

"I'm not trusting him. I'm not listening to him and haven't told him anything he wouldn't already be aware of. But also, I do believe he's on our side and has always been on our side. But I'd never tell him that, and I'd change my opinion about this in a split second."

Thayu glanced at the door to the cabin, where Isharu stood guard and Nicha had just left, presumably to visit the toilet at the end of the passage.

She said in a low voice, "Before we left the ship, Ezhya asked me something."

"Yes?"

"He asked me to tell you he's considering expanding our team's intelligence function."

"We already tell him everything we find out."

"Officially expand it. For you, it would mean going through the military spy academy, because you'd need to be familiar with all the protocols."

What the heck. "He hasn't asked me?"

"No, because he knows you might feel hesitant. It might mean reporting on your own world."

"As long as it would be to the benefit of everyone."

"When you gather information, you don't usually know what it's for."

That remark was full of implications I didn't want to think about.

"Would you want me to do this? I thought intelligence would be your responsibility."

"I don't think you should keep it a step away from your control. Especially since you often get people to talk and you're good at getting information. It should be made official."

"You want me to do it?" I asked her directly.

"Yes. We need to help Ezhya. We need to make sure that when someone replaces him, the new person will be a step forward. We need to make sure that there are no needless conflicts that cost lives and resources that people in the Inner and First Circle feel could have been avoided. We need to work hard to make sure this doesn't happen."

I had never seen her more dead serious in our entire relationship.

Ezhya felt that his leadership was under threat. He wouldn't rest until this drone army and their operators were thoroughly defeated. And he might be prepared to sacrifice this world I cared about for this aim.

That meant it was up to me to pull them into line. And we didn't yet know who or where they were. And worse, we needed the help of Asto's military—the very body that wanted to annihilate these people—to discover this.

I spent most of the rest of the train journey thinking, weighing up all the options and their consequences.

Specifically, the suggestion that Asto might hit out much harder than I had expected disturbed me.

In the past, I had defied established rules by Nations of Earth plenty of times. Even the fact that Dekker was upset with me attested to that.

It might be time for me to adhere less to Asto's rules.

Specifically those about who I spoke to.

I went to talk to Sheydu.

She was talking to Reida and Isharu, holding one of their super-secret devices between them. Ynggi also sat in the bay of seats. He was working on a row of bugs lined up on the little table near the window and was so deep in concentration that he didn't look up.

"I want you to give me a reader," I said to Sheydu.

"We're meant to be silent."

"I know. I still want a reader."

"I can't give you access to the security codes."

"I'm not asking for that. I want a reader, unsecured. I don't ask for access to anything you consider sensitive. I want to check the news and I want to be able to send local messages."

She frowned at me. "We agreed to keep silent so they don't know where we are."

"Over the past three months, have they ever acted like they didn't know where we were?"

She gave me a sharp glance. She wasn't used to being challenged, least of all by me.

I continued. "Give me a device you consider safely sheltered from all the stuff you're doing. I don't want to be involved in any of that and don't need to know. But I do want to be able to contact people in society, not just others in our team. Hiding and cutting ourselves off hasn't worked. Everyone knows where we are. I'm going to angle for this mysterious person who has been sending me messages. I'm going to talk to him and see if I can get him to say something that gives away how or where to find him. We're going to the Nations of Earth compound, which is not a super-secret locality. Given that I asked to speak to the president, Nations of Earth is probably waiting for us to turn up. If we need to go back to being silent, I will abandon the device."

She met my eyes. I could see in her expression that she might have argued had I not outranked her. Ultimately, even if she now had her own association, she still worked for me.

She made a hand signal *it will be done* and added *a few days*.

"Thank you, Sheydu."

She snorted.

"I do appreciate this is not the way you would choose to go about our business. But, as everyone keeps reminding me, my best strength is my mouth. I want to use it."

She snorted again.

I returned to my seat opposite Thayu, who had watched the exchange from her position. She said nothing, but I presumed she had heard everything, and had filled in the bits she missed.

The train slowed down, coming into another station.

From memory, the train didn't usually stop this often, but I guessed the extra stops were what accounted for the longer travel time.

The station was very busy, with a lot of people coming out of a train that had stopped on the opposite platform.

The section in the middle of the platform was occupied by stalls where vendors sold their wares. They had fruit for sale, and tomatoes, lots of those. Also second hand clothing and there was even a stall with electronics.

Our train stopped for a few minutes, long enough to let passengers with bags get on. It got busier in the cabins, and my team members were forced to gather some of their possessions that had been spread out. Ynggi got some strange looks.

On a notice board, I saw Rotterdam would be the next stop.

The doors shut.

Sheydu came back a moment later and handed me a simple electronic reading device. It still had a protective cover over the screen.

"Did you just buy that?"

"You said you wanted a simple device. I didn't think we'd be able to get one until we arrived at our destination, but the opportunity presented itself."

"Yes, this will do." I guessed the electronics stall holder would have had a good day.

"I'll ask Reida to set it up for you."

CHAPTER FOURTEEN

REIDA DIDN'T TAKE LONG to do whatever needed doing. I was unsure what needed setting up, because these types of readers were usually good to go out of the box, but I presumed he checked for obvious security flaws.

I spent the rest of the trip looking at the various news sites.

The attack on Athens was not an isolated incident. Drone attacks on other cities, including on London, Munich—as I already knew—and also Johannesburg, Los Angeles and Mexico City all involved places with vibrant Coldi communities.

The victims numbered over three thousand. It said something about the state of the world that none of the news channels made a big issue out of this. These latest actions followed much worse attacks. People were numb to death and destruction.

I found limited information about the damage to Asto's interests at a news channel run by a Coldi group in Los Angeles, who must know Clay and Vanessa and might even be part of the same community. They reported the destruction of several military strike craft. The main ship suffered minor damage. They had retreated to a higher orbit and had evacuated any non-essential personnel.

Where to, they didn't say. Fortunately, my father and Erith were already in New Zealand with my own aircraft.

I tried to contact him to see if he could tell me more, but the communication wouldn't go through.

I was sure that if an attack on the main military ship involved casualties, that would also have been in the news report, right? The destroyed strike craft were drones.

Of course, I couldn't speak to Asha in orbit, but I pieced together, through comments made by Sheydu and her team, that there were some very angry people up there. Who was angry and what they were angry with, I was left to figure out for myself.

Asha's military guards did what security did best: they sat with their noses in their devices and ignored everything.

Thayu was right that there was a whole security world out there that seemed to operate on a different, needs-to-know level. Did I want to be part of it? Would it be beneficial for me?

The train arrived in Rotterdam at the end of the afternoon.

It was summer, the trees were green, the grass was green and flowers bloomed in the garden beds. From the peaceful scene, you would never guess that a war raged in orbit.

But the road verges were messy, bins unemptied, street lights sported broken covers, an abandoned truck stood on a road verge and the street-facing windows of many buildings had been boarded over.

A tree lay by the side of the road, the largest branches cut off, neatly stacked next to a pile of debris containing splintered wood, broken sheets of plasterboard, and broken and half-burned furniture.

The whiff of stale smoke still lingered.

The road seemed undamaged, but Klaus had told me that the high-speed train tracks into the city had been repaired more than once in the last few months.

It was also surprising to see how few people were in the streets.

The bus station that was normally very busy lay almost deserted, and only a few trams were running, and several tracks were out of action. This included the track to the Nations of Earth complex.

So we tried to catch one of the driverless cabs to get there.

Our party was too big for a single vehicle.

The cabs were busy, and it took quite some time to corral two cabs, both with an available time slot long enough to take us to the complex.

I didn't feel it was a very common destination.

I got into the first vehicle with my team, minus Isharu and Telaris, who went with Asha's guards.

Ynggi was most interested in all the ways things had changed. I pointed out to him that when he came here with us to attend the court—that now seemed ages ago—we had not come to the Nations of Earth complex.

He had, he said, studied the location extensively. He noticed that the tram line—which we followed in places—was damaged, but restoration work, while underway, displayed little urgency.

"People are meeting in secret localities and remotely," I said.

"It says there is damage to the main halls of the complex," Mereeni said. "I guess we'll see it when we get closer." Having worked for Amarru, she would be familiar with it.

In the past few hours on the train, I had read about the attacks on Nations of Earth and seen some aerial photos. The Assembly wouldn't be using the hall because the building no longer possessed a roof. Strangely enough, I couldn't find references about these attacks, except one on an unofficial news channel which suggested the attacks had come from inside the building. The rest of that report had a strong political bent. The author was highly scathing of Dekker and the assembly, and I filed it as less reliable, even if the author said that he worked inside the compound. So many people did. They couldn't all know what was going on. In fact, most of them wouldn't.

Activists made up theories, twisting and mis-interpreting events and data. People were looking for answers. They were nervous.

Military personnel stood on every street corner. Many of them wore Nations of Earth uniforms. The guards displayed an enormous variety in age: from kids barely old enough to order a drink to people who should have retired years ago.

The entire city had been mobilised.

The members of my team were looking around with wide eyes. Most buildings we passed were still intact, but the atmosphere was so different. Guards were out on the street everywhere. They wore helmets and bristled with technology as they stood, looking miserable, in the drizzling rain.

We soon found that the self driving car network no longer covered the whole city, so we had to continue with a regular taxi. The driver was a local who took great care of his vehicle. The battered old van was painted bright green.

He assured me it used to be yellow, but that he didn't like being a target. You never knew whether the drones saw colour, but he wasn't going to tempt them.

He warned us he couldn't enter the Nations of Earth complex.

"The gates are closed," he said. "They don't let anyone in. There are so many guards at the gates. I don't think the assembly meets there anymore."

"They don't," I said.

He glanced at me as if wondering why we needed to go there.

Only when we got to the entrance of the complex, did I fully understand the level of security protection that Nations of Earth had instated.

Not only were the gates closed for traffic, but a barrier of steel and concrete blocked the road.

A group of heavily armed guards stood at a gate that was only wide enough to let through pedestrians, not vehicles.

After the taxis dropped us off, we crossed the intersection in front of the main gate on foot.

The road wasn't busy, and the intersection riddled with potholes, filled with brown water from the rain. The tram tracks that would lead into the complex lay twisted on the ground. A bus picked its way across, avoiding the puddles.

The hotel where I would normally stay lay across the gates. It was part of a strip of buildings containing short-term accommodation for visitors to the complex. The whole row was reduced to a heap of rubble. No wonder they never replied to my calls about booking rooms.

When we came closer, the guards left their shelter. There were four, but more men still stood out of the rain under the awning and in a tent next to the shelter and the old guard house itself. That structure consisted of a boom gate with an awning where vehicles would stop to show their permits, and a small cabin with glass windows—all of them broken. The panels of the old metalwork fence lay twisted on the ground.

The four men met us in the drizzling rain and directed us into a white tent, where a further three colleagues waited, one with a computer on a desk.

My team members needed to take off their weapons and submit them for inspection.

The guards wanted all our names spelled out in Isla.

They wanted to see my identity papers, not once, but twice.

They didn't like that some in my team didn't have formal identities registered with Nations of Earth. This applied to Isharu, Zyana and Ynggi. The latter elicited a lot of comments and communicating back and forth with their supervisors.

I told them Ynggi visited a few years ago and he should be known to the systems because he had been our unofficial interpreter at the court. It turned out they only registered Jetari's name.

Ynggi... didn't count because he was just a monkey with a long tail. Jetari turned out not to be a real person. That old story again. Tiresome.

Of course, they asked—and we needed to explain in detail—what we planned to do at the complex. I said I wanted to speak with the President or Vice President and I had it on good authority that he used the bunker underneath the main building as his office.

How did I know about the bunker?

Of course, I had been there before.

Then that had to be checked.

Frankly, I started to wonder whether it might be better to find our accommodation and something to eat and come back tomorrow, because it was getting late.

But I had also heard that, like at the Exchange, the dedicated officials lived and worked onsite, so someone would work after office hours.

Finally, we got permission to go in. This happened in batches because the gate only let in so many people at a time. We first let through Sheydu and some of her people.

I stood waiting at the guard station when my new throwaway reader pinged. The device I hadn't told anyone about.

When I took it out of my pocket, a message appeared on the screen: *I know where you are. You can't hide.*

Thayu had gone through the gate with Sheydu, so I showed it to Reida. Bingo. Not only had I just proven that these people didn't use any of our regular networks to contact me, they had now replied to me on a device where I could respond without risking access to our systems.

When I showed her, Sheydu said, "If they found you so quickly through a device that contains none of our information, then we can search our network for all we want for a breach, but we won't find it, because they come in through another way."

"And they have a way of recognising me. I don't understand how they do this, because I've left all my devices at the Exchange and turned everything off and have kept it that way."

And annoyingly, I'd have to deal with this after we came back out of the compound, because I wasn't carrying that cursed reader on me while it could listen in on what I said.

I handed it to one of Asha's guards with the message to stick it in a safe place.

Then, finally, we walked into the complex.

CHAPTER FIFTEEN

I DIDN'T RECOGNISE the place where I came out. I mean—I should recognise it, because I'd been here so many times before, but none of the familiar landmarks were in the places where I remembered them to be.

The broad avenue that ran through the complex looked like a military barracks. Two walls of concrete and metal stood along the sides. An array of tents and container-based accommodation lined the road.

Some pieces of rubble poked over the top of the barrier, the remains of... whatever building used to be there. I didn't remember. The building on the other corner was also gone.

The normally bustling footpaths lay deserted. A couple of ducks sat with their heads tucked in their wings in the spot where a cheerful young man in a yellow outfit would offer tours of the complex from a tent booth. The signs advertising tour prices and times of departure lay in the grass, broken and discoloured by the rain.

The main thoroughfare was barricaded off for vehicles with yellow and black signs erected across the road and an office-container in the median strip. A man came to the entrance and watched us walk over the footpath, which was not covered by the barricade. Another man came to the door. They briefly spoke to each other, but neither spoke to us.

We walked on through the wasteland. I wracked my brain to

remember what buildings used to be here, but they had to be administrative buildings that I had never needed to visit. They were all reduced to rubble, as were the mature trees that lined the road. Broken and dead branches lay stacked in a heap.

The tram tracks that used to run along this road lay twisted and tangled on the grass.

There was even a tram carriage, toppled over, with all the windows broken and the side smashed in.

I walked through with a surreal feeling.

Throughout my youth, Nations of Earth had been a pinnacle of justice and hope. The organisation was only young, but it was a beacon of a shining future and a past the world wanted to forget. These gracious modern and faux-historic buildings carried the hopes of many. Peace in times of upheaval. Fairness when life was exceedingly unfair. Restoration of civilisation where civilisation and decency were lost.

All those beautiful buildings were gone. The road cut through the residential section of the compound, and at least I could still see the roofs of the townhouses over the little hill that ran along the road. We lived there for two years, while my father received training. The school was on the other side, surrounded by parkland.

Here, the trees were still standing, but the complex where people could get accommodation when working at the assembly looked deserted. Rubbish had blown into corners, houses sported broken windows, and although there was no visible damage to much of the housing, there were no people to be seen.

Where was everyone?

We came to the quadrangle, the inner sanctum of the compound. The faux-Roman marketplace with its cobblestone paving normally bustled with journalists and tourists, but now also resembled a scene from a dystopian movie.

The administrative buildings that housed the delegations of each of the member countries still stood, but plywood boards covered many windows. A light burned in one window, and I spotted movement. Behind another window, a woman—not in military uniform— watched the activity outside while holding a cup.

Military personnel stood in groups along the perimeter of the quadrangle.

They kept a close eye on us, but their colleagues at the gate must have briefed them well, because none of them disturbed us.

Most of them wore Peacekeeper uniforms, but I also spotted some from the secretive Special Services division.

The president's office's majestic entrance was unscathed, although a lot of military officers stood on the sweeping staircase.

The windows above the entrance were intact and clean. Those were the windows of the foyer in front of the president's office. The office itself was on the other side, and its windows overlooked a small courtyard and another park.

The guards stopped us at the bottom of the stairs.

They wanted to know who we were and what we were doing here. We'd already told them and their colleagues should know, but this was all part of the bureaucratic game, so I answered all the questions for a second time.

"I'm Cory Wilson, representative of *gamra*. I'm here to see the president or a representative."

"The president?" His voice carried an amused tone, like he was about to burst into laughter. "Just like that?"

"I've told you who I am. I haven't been able to make arrangements via the usual channels. This is an unusual request, I understand, but it's also an unusual time. We have an urgent matter to discuss. I spoke to an officer at the Office of War who assured me I'd be able to arrange a meeting if we could provide the correct identification. We have just done that at the gate. The assembly knows that I'm coming, and will understand that the unusual process is a result of security issues."

He didn't question me any further, which told me his superiors had briefed him, he knew who I was, and that the assembly wanted to hear what I had to say.

He eyed the various members of my team. "Do you want all of them to come in as well?"

"If possible. But they don't understand Isla, so some of them can wait outside the room."

"We need to do security checks for those who don't have prior records."

"I understand." There was no escaping bureaucracy. It was part of the game.

He accompanied us into the foyer of the building. It was a lot busier here. The guards had set up a security station where each of us had to walk through a bay of scanners. They found an old and no-longer-used feeder in my pocket, so I had to go through twice, standing still for a few seconds while the security guard looked at the screen. Experience told me they studied an X-ray image, and also scanned for electronics. I couldn't see his screen.

Then he got up, presumably to speak with a supervisor. I stood, awkwardly, in the machine. Was it all right to walk out?

He came back with a stern-looking woman who asked me lots of additional questions.

They asked me for references of people I knew who could vouch for who I was and what I was doing here.

All the names I mentioned, even the name of Eva's father, met with blank looks. These guards and employees were usually not the most cooperative, but this lot seemed to have put the bureaucratic obfuscation into overdrive.

I guessed Piotr Zbrowski had retired in the years since I'd last seen him and had gone back to Poland. And since I heard on the grapevine that Eva had divorced her husband and now lived with Alma Savage, I could see that her highly conservative father was less than impressed with this situation.

I had to explain several times who I was, what I was doing here, and that it was important for somebody with the correct authority to sign my document.

They were vague and didn't answer any of my questions.

In their discussions with superiors, I picked up phrases like *He's here to talk about aliens in orbit* and other expressions that made me uncomfortable. When I first started my job, I'd vowed to fight the discrimination and proliferation of unhelpful language that dominated the public discourse back then. I thought we'd made progress, but things had regressed a lot, if these men were anything to go by.

We were told to wait in an office.

Sit and wait. Be quiet. The same things they had told me all these years ago. It was difficult not to get angry. I'd been at this point before. Had nobody really learned anything?

It was getting late. Everyone was tired. We had a very long day. Our accommodation was not exactly close to the assembly hall, and I had no idea as yet how we were going to get there. For all I knew, the city operated on a curfew, and no traffic was allowed on the streets at night.

But the members of my team were much better than I was at waiting. Waiting was what they did when I went somewhere they couldn't or didn't need to come. But I stood in front of the window looking out into the quadrangle at the abandoned and damaged buildings, with my hands in my pockets, thinking of just how vulnerable we were, and how little had gone to plan in this mission so far and how Ezhya had *gamra* breathing down his neck.

I also wanted to get back to that message that I had received on the throwaway reader. Who this person was and how did he get in contact with me? I wanted to know if this was just a prank or whether we were really talking to one of the enemy.

Eventually, an employee came to get us. He took us through a long corridor and into a door on the left, through a security checkpoint into the basement of the building. I had been here before, years ago, when Dekker had tried to bluff me.

The guards at the bunker decreed that Nicha and I could come, probably because Nicha had a fairly extensive record at Nations of Earth. The others had to wait in a room next to the security station.

The bunker was a well kitted out apartment, with comfortable couches, a kitchen and bedrooms for several people. There was a door to what I assumed to be an official meeting room where I would have seen Dekker all these years ago. My memory was hazy on the details.

We entered a small office.

In the seat on the other side of the desk, facing the door, sat a man I had never seen before. It was the president's desk, but he was not the president, or even the vice president.

He had an open, friendly face with freckles and a short beard. His hair was red.

He got up as Nicha and I followed the guard in.

"Mr Wilson, it's a pleasure to see you. My name is Glenn MacArthur." He spoke with a pronounced Gaelic accent.

"I'm glad to find someone here. I was hoping to meet the president or vice president."

"The president or vice president are unable to see you at the moment, I'm afraid. I'll explain later."

We sat down. His face was really familiar to me.

"I have to ask you. Have we met before?"

He smiled. "We have indeed. Pavona? Mars University. I didn't have the beard then. I remember you well. There was always a lot of talk about you."

I squinted at him, trying to remember what he would have looked like without a beard and twenty years younger. "I hope it was good talk."

"You honestly don't remember, do you?"

"I'm afraid not."

"I was two years above you."

I really didn't remember. What had I been doing back then? I had a powerful group of friends. We were highly politically active. It was in the early days of the Coldi on Earth coming out of hiding. There was a lot of hostility towards them. My father had married Erith when I was ten. I had seen how she got treated for no good reason. I got angry when seeing this type of injustice.

We advocated the same rights for everyone. People got furious at me for holding those opinions. As young people do, we all got hot under the collar, but I still held those opinions today. There had been arguments. Once, a dissenter had attacked me on my way home late at night, needing attention at the hospital.

If he remembered me from university, I wondered what side of the argument he supported. Unless he volunteered the information, I had better not ask him, *especially* if he worked for Dekker, who was hostile to *gamra*.

"It was a bit of a wild time," I said, faking a smile.

"Yes, it was indeed."

Then the smile faded from his face.

He placed his hands on the table. "It's a different world today. You will have seen that we're hamstrung in our operations."

"I would appreciate if you could tell me where the president is or if you're in contact with him."

"You can't contact him. It's a matter of safety. You're aware that we have suffered several attacks on the assembly."

"If the president is in hiding, why has he contacted me asking for help?"

He frowned. "He did?"

"Yes. As I just said."

His frown deepened. "When was this?"

"Three months ago. I've been in orbit all that time, partially because of it. We were ready to bail on the situation, and evacuate everyone to Barresh, but Dekker contacted me asking for help. He never told me why, because the connection failed. I expected additional communication, but it never came. I expected to read news about events that allowed us to put together what happened, but nothing ever made the bulletins. We've tried to trace the message, but we couldn't."

"A message asking for help." His voice sounded flat, puzzled.

"Yes."

"And you're sure it came from the president himself?"

"We ran voice comparison scans on the recording, and the confidence level that this was Dekker was high enough that we believe so, yes. I was in orbit, but the call got cut off. We've been trying to find out where he is to reestablish contact."

"He is in a safe location. That's all I can say. You can't meet him."

"Then I need to see the vice president."

"You can't see him either. I am the administrator of the president's office and currently acting president. Vice president Yoon Ha was, sadly, killed in the latest attack on the assembly."

What? I glanced at Nicha, who I knew had been studying the Earth news channels even more than I had. He signalled, *That's a lie.*

I asked, "Why wasn't that all over the news?"

"Security and safety. We are extremely vulnerable. Nations of Earth is relatively young and the attacks have exposed weak spots in our laws and processes. I know you'll find this hard to believe, but I'll show you some highly classified information."

He activated a projector at the corner of his desk, and cycled through a progression of horrific images showing the aftermath of the attack that had destroyed much of the assembly hall during a sitting.

"The vice president was standing right there." He pointed to an area of destruction that might have been a speaker's dais, with splintered wood covered in splatters of blood. A body lay face down on the floor, missing a leg and an arm. A dark stain had seeped into the grey carpet underneath. "We felt that the publication of these images—and there is also video footage—did not help our cause, because it would show the enemy that we were weakened."

I felt sick.

MacArthur continued, "And we are weakened. For a new vice president to be appointed, a majority of the assembly needs to vote in person. To give the assembly the power to vote remotely, we need to audit the voting process to a similar standard as we can do this in the hall and, frankly, it has been impossible to make these arrangements, as you might appreciate. The hall is unusable, and the remote links are not secure enough."

"How long ago did this happen?" My mind was racing. I'd expected some difficulties here, but nothing remotely like this.

"Three weeks ago. We haven't been able to hold a service for him yet. We've had Office of War meetings back to back to organise a force to fight back. It's not easy to herd the military forces of two hundred countries together."

"I can imagine."

And I could, and he was an administrator, and not a politician. He had never signed up for a job like this. Accepting that he was third in line for the top job when things went wrong would have been one of those *yeah, like that will ever happen* clauses buried in his contract of employment.

"I think we can help. The reason I'm here is that I have an important message from *gamra* and the ships in orbit."

I explained the situation where *gamra* required that the assembly sign for the continued presence of Asto's military in orbit.

He wanted to know if they wanted the assembly to vote on it or the president to sign for it. I assumed that those two options were the same in *gamra*'s eyes, but he said they weren't. Because the president had the discretion to make certain limited decisions, but he wasn't sure if those rules covered matters related to *gamra* and therefore he might not be able to sign on behalf of the assembly, or as he put it, "I could sign the document, but my signature might not be worth anything because I'm not an elected representative. We'd have to check it legally, because there isn't much point in me signing the document if it turns out that my signature is not valid."

"Yes. No. I see." Well, crap.

He gave me a stern look.

"We have a lawyer in our team," I said. "I'd need to consult with her."

Mereeni was very good at this. She would know where to find out.

Part of me wanted to scream, *We're in the middle of a war, why do we even care about this?* but sadly, this stuff was important. The mess that poorly followed processes created had the potential to linger and disrupt for years.

"I need to consult with my lawyers, too," he said. "It's getting late and realistically, I won't be able to get onto them until tomorrow, so why don't you stay here in the bunker? Because that's what we are doing. It's one of the safest places in this city."

"Thank you."

"Let the staff know about your dietary requirements and the kitchen should be able to accommodate for it."

"I had booked rooms for us in a hotel."

"I wouldn't trust much of the local accommodation. They just don't have the security features we need. Their buildings are compromised, their networks are insecure. They were never set up for security, anyway. It's much safer here, and we can continue to solve the legal issues. We can give you access to whatever you need."

"Thank you. I think I will accept that offer. So what do you think you'll need to do? And what is the predicted time frame? We have a few days, but the *gamra* deadline for signing this agreement can't be moved."

He blew out a breath. "We're in unchartered waters. I suspect that the Emergency Council has the authority to delegate someone with a binding signature, whether mine or someone else's. But I think you'll find that several countries in the assembly have reservations about the rules and there will be questions that need to be answered. Questions I would prefer to have answered before we proceed."

"I'll answer them and address all the problems they can bring up."

"I'm not sure you understand the depth of the issue. It's their argument that we are a sovereign world and this power struggle is ours to solve."

"And yet, it isn't. This enemy group has also been active in *gamra* space and tried to destabilise Barresh, the home of our assembly.

There will be a lot of benefit in working together and treating this as a *gamra* issue."

"The assembly will have to decide about that."

I sensed hesitation in his voice. What was the bet that some strong conservative voices had spoken up in the assembly?

"Let me make one thing extremely clear. We are not here to threaten you. We are looking for the cooperation of Nations of Earth to solve what is going on. Regardless of what members of the assembly may say or believe, Asto's military has been protecting you from attacks. Apart from the fact that their mandate is running out, they lack enough data to locate the enemy's control centre. The enemy attack with armies of drones first unfolded from a single deep space probe using a technology unknown to us. The probe brought the technology into the solar system. Right now, every drone attack starts in orbit with a similar single data point that expands into hundreds or thousands of attack drones. We can disable satellites that steer these attacks, but we can't stop them from forming unless we know who directs them. It could be someone off the planet, but more likely, it is someone locally. Someone in a hidden location where we can't trace them or identify them or their motives. Based on our data, we can guess. But we need your help in finding them. Because otherwise we will continue to fight the symptoms and not the cause. And once *gamra* tells the Asto military to leave, you're on your own. But more than that, *gamra* is taking an interest, because we've had a brush with this enemy already. Asto's leader is worried about this, and he won't hesitate to use shall I say more crude methods to solve this issue. I would much rather have this solved without the loss of life that would entail."

He looked at me and gave me an intense gaze.

"That sounds like a threat."

I could hear the soft voices of my team in the corridor and also the voices of unfamiliar people.

"You could see it as a threat, but only if you fail to grasp the serious and time-sensitive nature of the situation. You say that this is a problem for Earth to solve and I say it absolutely is not. Because these people are active off-world, and the *gamra* agreement that you signed clearly states that any matter that has off-world components is by definition a *gamra* matter and will entitle you to *gamra* protection.

That is worth a lot and could make this conflict very short. But I do need your authorisation."

"I won't be able to call the full assembly."

"But you mentioned the Emergency Council. They should be able to sign."

He nodded, while staring at the desk. "We're still checking the powers of the Emergency Council. What if we can't get enough people together to agree on this?"

"Then you step down from full member to associate member. That is a serious matter and I want to avoid that. It leads to a position like that occupied by the world of Indrahui and it's a permanent naughty corner that is hard to escape."

Whether Earth was a full member was up for debate anyway, but I desperately wanted to avoid the bureaucratic mess and double standards that applied to Indrahui.

I met his eyes.

He shook his head. "I'm honestly not in a position to make any of those decisions. At the moment, we're barely surviving."

My team in the corridor was still speaking. I was wondering what was going on there and whether I needed to check on them.

But now I understood at least some of the cageyness.

These people were nervous and very much out of their depth. They had a drastic shortage of trustworthy workers.

CHAPTER SIXTEEN

HE TOLD me to stay around and he'd call in some legal people to prepare for a preliminary meeting. The rest of my team was also welcome to attend. We would hold a meeting in a larger room down the hall. He would make electronic communication and overnight facilities available to us.

I met the others in my team in a dorm room in a different part of the bunker, along a narrow passage with rooms on either side. We dumped our unimportant luggage there. We had been allocated two of these dorm rooms on either side of the main passage.

This looked like a place where members of the president's security force or military officers could stay during an emergency.

The dorm was next to the kitchen and storerooms full of non-perishable food and other supplies.

Laughter drifted in from the kitchen, and the scent of hearty food wafted in through the door.

People walked back and forth through the corridor, and because the door was open, our team only communicated in hand signals. *Be careful* and *Record everything* and other things that were beyond my level of comprehension. Hey, I had gotten much better at sign language after learning that there were two different dialects of sign language that my team used interchangeably. There was the Inner Circle code and the Military code. Mixing of the two was a deliberate strategy to throw off people who possibly wanted to make sense of the signals.

Deyu had climbed onto a top bunk and was setting up the local hub. Apparently, she had found a small window to transfer a data dump off a satellite. These data dumps contained concentrated messages from whoever wanted to correspond with us in orbit. They'd have to look at it tonight because there was no time now.

I did, however, ask for my replacement cheap reader back. I figured that since I'd already decided to reply, this was the safest location for doing so.

I wrote, *I know where you are, too.* Pressed *send*.

There. Let's see what came back.

This person might say that he knew where I was, but I wasn't so sure. My disposable device would use the local communication networks, which were run by companies with an interest in hiding information. People liked to call it *privacy*, but it was a draw card for illegal activity. Not that any of the information transmitted through their network was actually secret, it was just being kept out of the hands of ordinary people with legitimate questions, but in the possession of people with the means to blackmail or sell important information.

If the person truly knew where I was, this would mean he was in cahoots with these companies, a government, or working for someone with deep pockets.

We'd find out *something* through this exercise.

The meeting room where we congregated a bit later held a square of tables with enough chairs for about twenty people.

A young man and older woman turned up with a trolley laden with food. They told us to grab whatever we wanted. I had to ask on behalf of the members of my team about the ingredients. Evi and Telaris were familiar enough with the offerings that they could look after themselves, but Asha's guards were not sure.

Ynggi wanted to know if there was any fish, which there wasn't, but there were eggs, and eggs were also good. He then explained the menu choices to Isharu and Zyana and Riyala and the other guards. They asked him questions, and he replied with confidence. Hunter, fisherman, climber of walls, tour guide. I wondered what other qualities the military had discovered in him. He seemed to like the attention they gave him.

Several of the guards, including from Sheydu's association, took black coffee and dropped their red-coded supplements into the fluid. I could smell the distinctive scent of this stuff—highly poisonous to anyone not Coldi.

Reida had brought in all his devices, which he spread out over the table and proceeded to connect everything up, test it, and hand it out to my team members. Thayu settled in the corner with a plate and a cup. She had opened the events database on her screen. I assumed she would make observations, like taking photos and making notes about people's behaviour.

While this was going on, more and more people filed into the room. They came in small groups of two or three and sat around the table.

Glenn MacArthur came in from wherever he had gone. He carried an old-fashioned notebook, the paper kind, which he put on the table and went back to the door, where a woman in military uniform had come in. She was half a head shorter than MacArthur, but when she spoke to him, she raised her hand and pointed at him in a frankly disturbingly aggressive manner. He replied, and she raised her chin and strode into the room, leaving MacArthur looking helpless at the door. Two male uniformed officers followed her like ducklings. She stopped at the table. Her lively, jet-black eyes surveyed the gathering. Her gaze found me—she nodded—then Isharu and lingered on Ynggi. She said something to one of her officers before taking the empty seat next to Isharu. The two officers went to stand behind her, the tallest one next to Ynggi.

"You must be Cory Wilson," she said.

"That's right."

"I'm General Gracelyn Sebaya, Liaison Officer for the Nations of Earth forces."

"Nice to meet you." I wasn't sure what to make of that interaction I'd witnessed between her and MacArthur.

Another three people entered the room and introduced themselves. They were representatives of the European countries, South America and China. I was used to seeing delegates come to the assembly hall in traditional dress, but these people were administrators and didn't play those dress-up games.

They all sat at the table. Some people acted like they knew each other well. Others looked around as if it was their first time coming here.

Some people asked me how things were in orbit and the rest of *gamra*. Those were such all-encompassing questions I didn't even know how to reply. Were they just being polite but clumsy or were they truly interested? I didn't think so.

Then Glenn MacArthur started the meeting by formally introducing all the attendees. They were mostly administrative staff, people who took influential positions within departments but who always remained behind the scenes.

I wondered why so few elected members of the assembly were still in Rotterdam. Certainly elected delegates wouldn't have *all* left their affairs to their staff, especially in the middle of a war.

Then a thought: just how many people had been killed in the drone attack on the assembly hall?

MacArthur said, "I also have to point out that this is not an official meeting of the Emergency Council, because there are people here who aren't in the Emergency Council. If this applies to you, and you're wondering why I called you here at this hour, I will explain. This is a meeting between Nations of Earth and representatives of *gamra* to establish the rationale for the presence of a military ship of off-world origin in orbit. Mr Wilson can explain why he thinks this presence is necessary."

Whoa, that was rather a different tone from the one he had taken with me earlier.

But I outlined the situation in the clearest possible terms. And it wasn't a complicated situation. Sign here and we can keep protecting you.

When I finished, there was a rather long silence. I noticed that the tall military officer next to Ynggi was still looking at Ynggi's outfit. If he was well-versed in security, he might realise that the bump at the end of Ynggi's tail sleeve, just above where the hairy white tip protruded, contained a camera.

A man said, "According to the law, this group doesn't have the authority to make decisions of this importance. That can only be done by holding a plenary meeting."

I said, "I thought this is the reason we're holding this meeting now. We have little time to get this document signed. This is why we've come here in person, because it's an important decision and it needs to be made quickly."

"You mean the document needs to be sent quickly?" the same man said. The card on the table in front of him said, *Office of International Law*.

"Isn't that the same thing?"

"No, it isn't. It assumes that we sign that agreement. That is for the assembly to debate. I'm fairly certain that many people will consider this a domestic matter and not one an off-world military will need to be involved in. You might have noticed we're recruiting our own forces."

"And the assembly has agreed on a framework for such a force?"

Setting up a military force had always been a major issue when I was at Nations of Earth. There were security forces and peacekeepers. There was an effective but very small air strike force that was bound by strict rules about where they could or couldn't engage. Some factions *wanted* a larger force, but no one had ever gotten that through the assembly.

"We resolved the issues about a general force under Dekker."

"Did you? I haven't seen it mentioned in the plenary meeting summaries."

I always read those, because I didn't want to rely on Melissa Heyworth to remember to tell me about important decisions.

"It was an Emergency Council decision," MacArthur said. "The proceedings of those meetings are not public. President Dekker believes in bringing our own house in order before engaging with outside entities to solve problems that are ours to solve."

"I've explained that it's not that simple and *gamra* doesn't consider this an Earth-only issue."

"No, but that is the view of many in the assembly."

"That still doesn't help our current situation. All I need is a formal agreement that the ships in orbit are there with Nations of Earth permission. That is all. That level of authority would be coming up with the next round of joining agreements, anyway. All we will do is bring that agreement forward by a few months."

"Our lawyers are still looking at that agreement." He looked at the man from international law who had spoken before. This man had put his fingertips together and nodded sagely.

So what? "Does this mean there are issues with the agreement?"

"We are looking at it in more detail. That is all I'm saying. We want to be fully aware of what we're signing and what the previous administration agreed to. We may want to change a few lines in the agreement."

"Could you bring this process forward so that we can ensure your protection?"

"I am not entirely sure what the benefit would be for us."

"The fact that you don't get attacked daily by drones from orbit? I thought I had explained it clearly that if we don't get this agreement, we will have to withdraw and you will have to fend for yourself."

"And you may have noticed that we are recruiting our own force. We have already expanded the deep space units a lot, and will be getting more people and hardware into those units."

"That's all good and well, but it takes a long time to get a force organised. Even at the highest priority, it won't be a fast process. Why not collaborate with the force that's already there?"

"Finally, someone who can see the problem the armed forces have with the current situation," Gracelyn Sebaya said. "The process is a shambles. We won't have a useful force by the end of the year, let alone within a few weeks. If only the Office of War would send us the protocols, or release the supplies we've been promised. We've got recruits walking around in old uniforms, without any gear—"

"We are dealing with those problems. Mr Wilson hasn't come to hear about our internal issues. Of course, there are going to be teething issues, but we have everything under control."

The two glared at each other. The other people in the room either watched intently or pretended to be busy with their devices.

I met MacArthur's eyes. "Do you honestly want to tell me you don't need any help?" Heck, they might be recruiting a force, but in the three months we'd hung in orbit, we'd seen no evidence that Nations of Earth had remotely enough spacefaring capacity to defend itself.

"We will accept help, but not without due process and without the approval by the assembly."

"Why don't you call an assembly meeting then and we can deal with it? Get the Emergency Council to come here and use their full powers. Don't you agree that this is an emergency?"

"We can't rush this process and then be stuck with bad decisions for the next fifty years or more. I have already said that the assembly is rather limited in its operations, and we need to wait for things to quieten down a bit until we can hold a proper election, recall all our delegates, and have discussions about this. There is no point in rushing through decisions that we will later regret."

"But if you don't do anything now, it won't quieten down. The military ships in orbit will leave. They won't be back, and then you will truly see how they have protected you over the past few months."

"I understand. But the Emergency Council will have to make that decision. I can't decide that on their behalf."

And so we were going around in circles.

MacArthur insisted that the Emergency Council needed to be called. He was probably right, but why were these people so enamoured with their bureaucracy? And if he wanted the assembly to be called, why didn't he just call the Emergency Council instead of sitting there talking about having to call the Emergency Council?

He said he was going to send out a call for a general meeting. He said he would ask his staff to draft the call and it would be sent tomorrow. Why not today? I didn't know, but by that time, I had no more energy to argue. I was so tired I had trouble concentrating.

It was well past midnight when we came back to the room, and having slept poorly for the previous night, I so badly wanted to go to sleep, but Sheydu gestured at me to talk to Reida.

He was sitting on the bottom bunk, his screen out of view of where my team assumed listening devices to be. I assumed that in the time we had been in the meeting, Asha's guards would have scanned the room thoroughly to find out where the listening devices were, because there were certain to be some.

I sat cross-legged on the bed opposite him, and he put his reader in between us, angling the screen so that we both had to lean against the wall to see it.

"I got this from the people who were doing work for me," he said, while being deliberately vague.

His boys and girls in the Outer Circle.

"They worked this hard?"

"They have set up a fairly extensive analysis process. Here is the material we used to check."

He brought up a map of Earth. A superimposed box over the top displayed a list of fragments and images they had searched and matched.

All the text was in Coldi, which was rather surreal.

Reida selected the fragments one by one. A picture of Dekker in the assembly hall, a picture of him in his office, an interview held in the foyer to the assembly building, two snatches of a voice recording.

But while I sat there, I could feel myself nodding off. I didn't know the hand symbol for *tired*, so I gestured to him, *anything important?*

He replied in the same manner. *It's interesting.*

I wished people wouldn't keep using the word interesting in the way Thayu did.

CHAPTER SEVENTEEN

A moment later, a voice sounded in the room. I recognised it. It was the voice of Simon Dekker, president of Nations of Earth.

"Just checking with you that these are the correct references," Reida said.

The clip was only short and had Dekker talking about some sort of agreement that would make everything better. He sounded like a typical politician: he said a lot of words but with very little content.

Reida had probably pulled the clip from a news service.

"I didn't use the one you gave me, because the sound quality is better in this one, and the voice recording has more depth. We needed to get rid of as much background noise as possible for the reference clip, because the data dump contains recordings by older equipment and the sound, picture quality or lighting may be poor."

He flicked to another screen. Dekker's voice fell silent.

"When we check this clip against the database and we search for voice signatures, we get a pattern of his most recent movements."

A map had come to the screen that showed the localities where the database had detected Dekker's presence. Most of those were local records, but there was a visit to Germany.

When Reida enlarged the map, you could see all the buildings in the Nations of Earth complex Dekker visited, and the places where he had lunch, the club he attended and even where he lived, because apparently, security had removed all compromised equipment from the house, but nobody had thought to remove the old chips from the power connection itself.

Much of the data was useless, Reida said, too short or garbled, but he also discovered there was a lot of data because Dekker's GenCode chip triggered the activation of the recording.

Reida continued, "All right, so now we know where he went for the period we're interested in."

He flicked to a different menu showing a time bar with both Earth and *gamra* notation.

A second time bar at the top of the screen only displayed *gamra* notation. This represented ship time in the large command ship in orbit. A bright dot on that bar indicated the time Dekker had contacted us.

All the activity Reida had detected based on the first clip fell at least a week before Dekker had contacted us and asked for help.

Reida flipped to a second clip, which was sound only, a very good quality recording, probably made for an interview in a studio.

It had brought up matches in a few additional places, which included a garbled recording with a lot of background sound from the checkout of a clothing store. The cashier asked if he was interested in buying a membership and rattling through his spiel before Dekker said tersely that he wasn't.

I wondered if that poor young cashier had recognised the man before her.

"Why is there a sound recording of this and not of the other data points?" asked Thayu, looking at the screen with us while lying on her stomach on the bed above us and hanging over the side.

I said, "Likely, the store is using older equipment—the type that still contained the full spy modules."

"But that would have to be quite old."

"Yes. There are devices that are over a hundred years old that still work. It's most common for the smaller businesses to still be using those. This stuff is expensive, because they would also have to rip out all the wiring and power sockets and connections, and we can see— with Dekker's house—that to try to save money and leave some of the infrastructure intact is not an option. You have to take all of it out for all the spyware to be gone. Since Margarethe signed the agreement with Amarru that this network would not be accessed anymore, many people no longer saw the need to replace their equipment unless they had other reasons. It's expensive."

Although it was disturbing that an electronic device over twenty years old could still be making full recordings of your data if you used it or came near it. Especially, apparently, if you had a GenCode chip. I wondered why that was and whether Asto was secretly monitoring these people already, or whether this was a thing they'd started doing when Nations of Earth appeared to be serious with introducing those chips, and had let it run like so many forgotten processes.

Reida walked us through the results for a few extra reference recordings, but they all showed the same: none of them had a single data point after that bright red dot in the top timeline, where Dekker had asked us for help.

I wondered aloud. "Shit, is he even still alive? He seems to have vanished off the face of the planet."

"Well, that's what we thought, so I asked my kids to collect everything they could find about Dekker and dump the lot into the entire database."

"The whole lot? Doesn't that require a lot of processing power?"

"Yes. The Eight Circle Energy Board may have something to say about this when they discover the reason for the power outage."

"We were meant to do this secretly."

"Huh. They wouldn't have a clue where to start finding out about it."

Well—pffft—I hoped so.

Reida pulled a portable projector into the middle of the bed. He was clearly enjoying himself. He switched it on. The nozzles emitted a faint glow of white light.

"Now watch this. I'm going to show you this how it appeared to us in real time."

His screen displayed a long list of places which I assumed had produced matches for Dekker's voice, his face and the equipment he carried, and his GenCode chip. The data were all latitude and longitude notations in the Coldi system. He fed the list into the projector and pulled up the keyboard, projected on the blanket that covered the bed. Text scrolled over the projected screen.

The characters were not in Coldi but in hexadecimal notation. Reida's fingers moved in the light while he typed.

This aspect of the Coldi ability never ceased to amaze me. How could one type in hexadecimal code? How could one read it when there were no words? But Coldi people used hexadecimal code like no other.

The projection that hovered in the space between the two bunk beds showed the part of Earth that included Europe.

As the data scrolled over Reida's screen, light dots appeared on the map and the timeline which hung in the top of the projection, with that bright dot when Dekker had asked us for help as a looming deadline.

The matched dots grew closer and closer. The locations jumped all over Europe.

Closer and closer...

And then the deadline passed, and two spots appeared on the timeline *after* Dekker had contacted us.

I squinted at the map. The most recent addition should be green.

But I couldn't see any green dots.

Thayu said, "What?"

But Evi near the door said, "Over there, across the water."

He was right. Two green spots had sprung up across the ocean in Atlantia.

Well.

Shit.

Those were definitely recorded after Dekker had contacted us. A day after, in fact. No further dots came up.

"So, what does that mean?" I asked. "That he went to New York?"

"According to this, yes," Reida said.

He enlarged the area.

One of the dots was in New York, and the other was to the south long the coast. A town surrounded by fields and forest and a beach.

He enlarged it again. The small town dissolved into a pattern of streets.

The locality dot was not in any of the streets, but a peninsula that jutted into a larger bay. On one side lay a beach, on the other the mouth of a river.

"What is that?" I asked. "Dig here and find the body?"

I'd meant to say this as a lighthearted comment, but of course it could be true.

"Why did he go there?" I asked, not expecting answers. "Or could it be that someone took his devices?"

"One of these recordings was triggered by the GenCode chip, so no, unless they cut the chip out of him."

"There are three options," Thayu said. "One is that he's dead, and this is where we'll find the body. One is that he got the GenCode chip and everything else removed and disappeared elsewhere. The last one is that he's still there."

"I just don't understand why he would have gone there?" Deyu said.

"He has a partner from New York," I said.

"Then why ask us for help?"

"Because he feared for his safety and no longer trusted the people around him."

The people who were now around *us*. Great.

"Do you know anything else about these two data points?" I asked Reida.

"The first one has a short audio recording."

He played it back, a short piece of garbled conversation where you could barely make out Dekker's voice in amongst busy foot traffic. Locality data showed it was recorded in the airport hall.

The second was only a locality ping triggered through his GenCode chip.

"That's it? There are no further records of him?"

"That's all there is after the time that he contacted us."

By now, the entire team had gathered in the room. They stood around the bed, sat on the floor, and leaned against the walls.

"Doodle time?" asked Deyu.

"I think so."

One of Asha's guards gave me a strange look.

"Doodle?"

"This is what we do with our association when we need to make decisions and need everyone's input."

"But don't you…"

"No. I don't tell them what to do. That way, we would miss many good ideas."

Everyone gathered around in the narrow room, on the top and bottom bunks, on the floor.

"How secure is this room?" I asked Sheydu.

Which, when you came to think of it, was a strange question to ask when talking about the bunker where the president would shelter.

"There were some bugs. We disabled them," Isharu said.

"There might be external listening devices," Telaris said.

I agreed. "There would be many external listening devices, except the walls of this bunker are probably too thick for listening in to soft conversations."

"That's just as well, because there are no useful bathrooms in this place," Sheydu said.

"I can turn up the disrupting signal," Deyu said.

"Do that, because we wouldn't want to use electronic devices to communicate, anyway. That would be asking for uninvited listeners."

Normally, we would meet in the bathroom, but there were only toilets and a shower cubicle.

Deyu grabbed the communication hub off her bed and fiddled with the settings. Reida's screen turned to grey fuzz.

"The president is not in the complex and not even on the continent," I began. "His records stop three months ago. There is no evidence that he ever came back to Rotterdam. We can ask many questions about this. MacArthur tells me I can't see the president for safety reasons. But is that really the case?"

"Is he even still alive?" Thayu asked.

"I don't know. I couldn't tell from this."

"I would guess that he is," Mereeni said. "The *president* has a lot more power than anyone else in the same position. If the *president* needs to step back from the job for a limited time, he would officially transfer those powers to the vice president. Regardless of whether Dekker did this, the vice president is dead. MacArthur occupies the position by default, but he can only be granted these powers—and they include powers to sign a type of agreement that we are asking him to sign—for a month, and that is if he actually got those powers. Whether he did doesn't matter, because more than a month has passed, so he doesn't have the powers. Presuming he had the powers, the law says he had to call an election within a month. Presuming you can't hold elections when an enemy is bombarding your planet, the power would pass to the Emergency Council who would decide based on an absolute majority, meaning every member has to agree. If they can't agree, they also have to call an election. The constitution is actually a little vague on the timing of this election, probably because if the Emergency Council is sitting, there is actually an emergency. So the Emergency Council could stall the need for an election by saying that it's not safe to hold one. But apart from the fact that decisions need to be unanimous, they also need an attendance quorum of eighty percent, and certain important members of the council cannot be absent."

She looked around with a fighting expression on her face. This was Mereeni's field of knowledge.

"So. Dekker disappears without passing his powers to the vice president, and the vice president dies in an attack. The acting president, not an elected official who doesn't have full presidential powers, says he can't hold the election because it's not safe, but it's no less safe than it has been since the start of the conflict. The second, major reason he wouldn't be able to hold elections is if the president is still alive and hasn't officially transferred or relinquished his powers."

I didn't miss Sheydu's appreciative look at Mereeni. Sheydu had no patience for legal stuff.

"Does MacArthur know where Dekker is?" Nicha asked.

I said, "That's the big question, isn't it? If he knows, then I cannot see why he needs to go to a safe place in a location that's considered less safe in the conflict. The assembly is scattered over town since the attack on the hall, but all those delegates are safe in Rotterdam or close by. Atlantia is not considered safe. But if MacArthur doesn't know where Dekker is, then that raises even more questions."

"Can you simply ask whether he knows where the president is?"

"I've already asked. He isn't answering the question. He says it's for the president's safety."

"But in that case, why wouldn't he offer to put us into contact with him, especially if the president can make decisions he can't?"

No one could answer that question. I didn't like some of the possibilities that crossed my mind, and my earlier discussion with Klaus came back to haunt me.

Klaus had warned me that Nations of Earth was deeply compromised. Klaus hadn't said which part was affected. I'd brushed it off as Klaus being paranoid because he had always been paranoid.

Deyu had taken out her reader and was drawing circles and arrows on the surface.

She drew us in the middle, then Nations of Earth on one side and *gamra* on another, with the Exchange and the military both related to *gamra*, but not exactly overlapping.

Then she drew a small circle.

"This is Dekker," she said. Then she drew an arrow from him to Nations of Earth. "We want to know if he is still related to Nations of Earth, if the relationship is damaged…" She wiped out a few parts of the arrow. "Or if he's no longer alive." She wiped the circle altogether.

"He's alive," Mereeni said.

I could see that some in my team questioned that, most notably Nicha, but since no one knew for sure, no one said anything.

"Everyone here is nervous," Thayu continued into the silence. "MacArthur sits in the *president*'s seat, but he knows he is keeping it warm. One good thing about these silly *elections* is that the vote of the people forms a safeguard against people grabbing power. Leaders who go against the vote have traditionally not ended well. MacArthur is smart and knows this. I suspect he doesn't see himself as a rightful candidate. I would classify his administration as *incompetent*. They're not in control. Given the circumstances, that is not unexpected. I suggest MacArthur is speaking the truth about Dekker's safety, but I think we need to consider the possibility that there has been a disagreement between the two and Dekker felt he had no option but to leave. Which leaves him here."

She took Deyu's stylus, drew Dekker's circle back where it was before Deyu erased it, but further erased the arrow leading to Nations of Earth.

Hmmm. There was something to be said for her argument.

"That's all very well, but where does that leave us?" Sheydu asked. She didn't have much patience with doodles.

I said, "It means that rather than try to engage in MacArthur's bureaucracy what we really need to do is to locate Dekker and get him to sign, because MacArthur can't make any binding decisions without having the full Emergency Council and maybe not even then."

MacArthur had warned us about this, but had presented the Emergency Council as solution... and had then brought together a group of people who were not the Emergency Council.

Mereeni said, "And I wonder what he's going to think of us trying to reach Dekker."

"My guess: he won't like it."

CHAPTER EIGHTEEN

AFTER THE OVERNIGHT TRAIN JOURNEY, I was extremely tired. Normally when arriving in a strange place, I had trouble sleeping, but I was ashamed to say that I slept like a log, even if I probably should have been more vigilant. I was just that tired. There is a special age when working through the night is no longer an option.

I woke up when people started rummaging in the dorm room. There were no windows, so I couldn't see whether it was light already. The clock said 5am so I guessed it would be, being summer.

"Is anything going on?" I asked Thayu, who was already up.

"Sheydu got some news from Asha that you might want to hear."

She sounded far too awake. This was all wrong. Usually I was the one who got up early.

I pushed myself up and got changed.

Thayu went into the corridor, leaving her overnight packs on the bed in case we needed to get out quickly.

She hadn't said how my team had managed to get news from Asha. We were meant to be silent, and this was a secure facility. Something to do with Reida and the secret hub, and the hacking of communication lines and other stuff I didn't want to know about.

I stuffed all my things in my bag to at least pretend I was similarly prepared, and went back into the large meeting room, where the members of my team had a veritable array of electronics laid out on the tables, the chairs and the floor. There was also a tray with cups of tea and a selection of toast and cereal with fruit and a bowl of eggs for Ynggi.

Ynggi himself was crawling under the table. His tail stuck out above the tabletop and the white-tufted tip waved back and forth, which it did when he was busy. Sheydu must be somewhere in this chaos, but I couldn't see her.

Deyu also sat under the table, doing whatever they were doing.

I grabbed some tea and toast, since once I started working, I was likely to forget. Although I had slept so well that my brain was still foggy and I had trouble remembering what we were supposed to be doing today.

MacArthur had not given a plan beyond *contacting the Emergency Council.* We had four days to get this agreement signed and either he got on with calling the assembly or enough members of the Emergency Council to sign the agreement, or I got onto Dekker.

In Atlantia. Who hadn't communicated with anyone since he had asked us for help.

That knowledge disturbed me deep down. A lot. Now I was less tired and could properly think about it.

Ynggi's tail stuck out on the other side of the table where I was sitting. It would be funny if it wasn't for the camera at the tip of the tail sleeve. I doubted MacArthur's people knew it was there, although Sebaya's military officers definitely did.

"Does any of that stuff work down there?" I asked.

"We're only using this to communicate to each other," Reida said, his voice muffled from under the table. "We need to make a record of the meeting so that we can check what's been said."

"I thought we were going to involve Asha."

"Not right now. Maybe later."

Deyu was testing whatever they were setting up.

I sat on a chair that had been shifted out of the way into the corner of the room and watched them work while I ate. As things went in the Coldi world of power, security devices and recording installations often served more than one purpose.

There was also a Nations of Earth technician in the room. He sat in the other corner, attempting to explain something to Isharu. I didn't *think* Isharu understood Isla—she was wearing a feeder that would connect with her reader to translate what he said—but I also noticed that he attempted a few Coldi words.

Voices sounded in the hallway, and a moment later, Sheydu came in with Glenn MacArthur following closely behind.

He stopped at the door, his eyes roaming over the tangle of equipment my team had created.

"We're almost ready," I said. "Do we have a list of attendants yet?"

"Not yet. A few still need to confirm."

"We will have the required quota?"

"That seems likely at this stage."

At this moment, a group of Nations of Earth people came in and MacArthur diverted his attention elsewhere, because people needed seats and needed to set up equipment to connect with their off-site teams.

Sheydu spotted me on my chair in the corner, and came in my direction.

She jerked her head.

I abandoned the last bit of my tea and joined her in the hallway. A couple of Nations of Earth people walked past, all very busy.

She didn't speak until they had gone into the large meeting room.

Her voice was soft. "I received some news from Asha this morning."

"So I heard." Not good news, I understood.

"There was another drone attack. This time, all the fury was directed at our ships, not the planet."

"And?" The situation was slipping away from us. There were a lot of important people in that ship in orbit and many people would get very angry if anything happened to them.

On the other hand, Asha would never flee while his association perished. He'd be the last off the ship.

"They've retreated even further. They took some damage and need to wait for repairs. The disturbing thing was that the drones knew exactly where the ships were."

"Even when they're always shifting?"

"They knew. It's highly likely the intelligence for the drone attacks has a local component. They can't physically get enough detail about where we're constantly moving ships are if they're using an Exchange process from a distance. If they had that capacity and were using it, we'd be able to detect it. They're detecting us visually and reprogramming the attacks."

"Do we need to change what we're doing here today?" I asked. While this was important news, I doubted it affected us directly.

"Asha said not yet, but he said that we won't have the backup if we need it. We're on our own."

"We always operated with that understanding. I don't want the military to intervene." I was still dealing with the fallout from the last time that had happened.

"No, but it's a good feeling to have the option."

No doubt.

She continued, "I just want to say that these people here are playing bureaucratic games. I think it would be wise to cut through those games and get that agreement so that Asha can call in additional ships. The situation is developing quickly. They're going to have to either retreat or strike back and unless we get the agreement, either of those is going to get us into trouble. And also, retreating and conceding defeat is not Asha's style."

No, it wasn't. "I'm trying my best. But it's like..." Coldi had no equivalent of *herding cats*. Their society had no cats, both the animal and the human kind. "I'll try the hardest I can. That's all I can do."

I was about to go back into the room when she held me back.

"Be careful. I don't like that man at all. Don't trust him."

"MacArthur? He's a bureaucrat. He never thought he'd be doing this job. Of course, he's not experienced and is really bad at it."

"Ask him why doesn't he involve the *president* in this meeting, if the *president* is indeed still alive? If they can involve other people remotely, why can't they include him? As a leader, don't you think he should be involved? Because otherwise, what's the point of having a leader? He could be just some person, but it's the fact that he's the leader that makes him valuable. Leaders should lead because otherwise, they're just a person."

Coldi *did* have a word for this. It was *manayi*, a collective noun for those in the lower ranks in associations.

And even within Earth's society, she was absolutely right.

And I *had* asked the question in different ways.

Was it really about security and did MacArthur trust us so little? Or was there something else?

Sheydu spread her hands. "This world is so illogical. I don't know what to think anymore."

We went back into the main room, where more people had turned up. Some of the same people who had attended yesterday's preliminary meeting were there, including Gracelyn Sebaya and her two military guards.

A projection screen on the back wall showed the faces of at least another twenty men and women. New ones popped up all the time.

I searched the images for familiar faces, like Eva's father, but I didn't see him. On the other hand, I'd think it unlikely that he'd agree to hold remote meetings, old-fashioned and traditional as he was. He'd probably send a lackey.

Mereeni had told me that the quota for decision-making at the assembly was seventy-five people and I counted seventy-six.

MacArthur opened the meeting and did a reasonably decent job of summarising the issue, after which I explained it in detail one more time.

People asked questions about the duration of the mandate and how the actions of Asto's military would interact with their own and the new force that was being mobilised.

Gracelyn Sebaya commented that the Nations of Earth mobilisation was nowhere near operational level. MacArthur tried to argue otherwise.

But she said, "It takes a long time to set up and kit out an effective force. We welcome any cooperation with established defensive forces, especially those that have operational capacity in orbit."

I told her we were happy to hold discussions with Asha and outlined Asto's motivation for their involvement. It seemed that, despite my report to Nations of Earth, most delegates didn't know about the SCAC ship we had found in Barresh and didn't realise that this was not just a conflict fought on Earth.

And because they didn't know, I had to go into the details about our trip to America Free State and how we'd determined that the driving force behind the attacks was the rogue group that had split off from the Earth space program.

An off-site delegate who looked barely old enough to be in university then asked how this related to a group he called the Exo-terrorists.

I gave him a look as blank as I could make it through the connection.

"I have never heard that term. Just what exactly do you mean? The group we have identified were those who were members of or sympathisers with the Southern California Aerospace Corps."

"I'm talking about alien evil forces who want our world."

"I don't know what the enemy wants." His use of the word *alien* disturbed me. I hadn't heard that word for so long and it didn't have a favourable history. When I had worked for Nations of Earth, people who were anti-*gamra* would use it. Aliens, ethies, chans. People who used those words were not usually on our side.

Another young man, also off-site, chimed in. "They want our planet, our resources. They want to kill us all or take us prisoner."

"We don't know what they want," I repeated, feeling ill. This was not going in the direction I expected.

I glanced sideways at MacArthur, who had a mildly disturbed look on his face.

I wondered how often he had led meetings. Not a lot, I didn't think.

Several attendees in the room were looking at their devices, no longer listening. This included one of Gracelyn Sebaya's guards, who held up a reader. Did he realise that Ynggi stood next to him, holding his tail up, recording for all the world to see that he was playing games, or looking at nudes?

I said, "We're coordinating our efforts with the aim to drive the enemy into a corner, into a position that they will have to talk to us."

"You can't talk to aliens," the first young man said.

Someone else added, "They don't even *want* to talk to us."

"Who do you think these people are, then?" I asked.

The first man replied, "They're lying and cheating aliens. We tried to warn the assembly. Never took us seriously. They just wanted our planet, the same as they've done for years. Only now they're hiding behind an army of drones. I challenge them to show their faces, because we're ready to fight."

Several people, also off-site, cheered at this.

I protested. "But we don't know who we're fighting and where they are."

"We know that exactly."

"The Asto military is protecting you in orbit."

"I see that you've been brainwashed. It's all by alien design that we're supposed to believe that we're attacked by fellow humans. What are these people drinking? It's been the aliens doing it all along."

Damn it, not that nonsense again. "You have no evidence for that whatsoever."

"We don't need evidence. Your so-called evidence is all doctored. We *know* this is true."

"Young man, we know it's true that your boss abrogated his responsibility by not presenting to this meeting and sending you in his stead. That doesn't mean you and your friends can peddle your crackpot ideas. Matters of war and peace get decided in this meeting. You have no legal authority to speak."

"My boss—or should I say, my former boss—is not my boss anymore. He went home and left his vacant seat to me."

Sebaya snorted and turned to MacArthur.

"That's true," he said.

Sebaya snorted again. "That still doesn't give you licence to tell outright lies."

"The aliens want our planet," the young man repeated. "We have to fight."

"Shut up, man!" a male delegate said. "You're not helping the cause."

"We won't be silenced. We've been silent for far too long and look where it's brought us."

He looked straight at me.

Another off-site delegate accused him of disrupting the meeting, to which the young man and his friends replied that meetings needed to be disturbed for people to see the truth. After this, several heated arguments broke out between attendants. I couldn't believe this. We'd spent years fighting this *evil aliens* rubbish and now that Earth had voted to join *gamra*, it again reared its ugly head right here in the assembly? It was as if we'd gone ten years back in time.

"Are you just going to sit there?" Sebaya said to MacArthur. "Who is in charge of this meeting?"

"Everyone, please be quiet," MacArthur said.

He had to repeat it a few times before the words had the desired effect.

"Good," Gracelyn Sebaya said into the silence. "I call on people to stop wasting our time with unproven nonsense. If you make a statement here—"

"Being quiet applies to everyone." MacArthur gave her a hard look.

The expression she returned to him would have set his hair on fire had he been sitting closer to her.

She opened her mouth to reply, but then the power flickered. The projection screen turned off and reconnected, but it only displayed the Nations of Earth logo. It had lost the connection to all the off-site participants in the meeting.

The lights in the ceiling flickered.

Everyone fell silent as we listened for the sounds of a drone attack. I didn't think the enemy was after me specifically, but they knew where I was.

My heart raced.

But all remained quiet.

"Go and figure out what's going on," MacArthur said.

A Nations of Earth staff member got up from the table and left the room.

We sat in silence.

It was surreal that the power had chosen this moment to get cut off.

I looked at the employees at the other side of the table, the ones who had been keeping the meeting running.

"I'm sorry. This happens quite often," a man said. His tone was apologetic.

"They'll fix it soon enough," another said.

To be honest, I didn't consider the power outage our main problem. "What the young delegate said, do you all believe those things, too?"

A deep silence followed my question.

Then a man said, "We don't believe either way. That's the problem many people have. It's all happening in space and no one can see what's going on."

MacArthur met my eyes. "This is precisely what many people in the assembly are saying. Who am I to think I know better than them? We have to allow them a voice and reply to their concerns."

I was highly tempted to say that he was the president, so why wasn't he replying to those concerns.

No, Nations of Earth hadn't gone back ten years. It was more like twenty years.

CHAPTER NINETEEN

MacArthur spoke to the tech people who came into the bunker, but they weren't sure what was going on. Meanwhile, time was slipping away from us. The delegates across town and elsewhere might not wait until the connection came back, thinking that the meeting would be rescheduled for another day.

But we didn't have another day. Not if we needed to get back to the ship to formally report to *gamra*, with the Exchange being out of action. Not if the military ships were in higher orbit. Not if there was a heightened danger of drone attacks.

It was time to do something drastic.

"We have a local hub and can re-establish connection if you give us the details," I said to MacArthur. "Time is running out for this agreement to be signed. We need to keep talking. General Sebaya needs to outline the military's perspective and we need to respond as to how Asto's military can fulfil the task of protecting Earth and will step back once the Nations of Earth forces are ready."

"That is a huge topic. It's unlikely that those negotiations can be completed today. But it shouldn't be too long. We get a fair few outages."

"It's been too long already. We need to get moving on this. We can use our network."

His eyebrows flicked up. "Really? You're proposing to bring this untested network and connect it to all the delegates who have gone through great pains to keep themselves safe?"

There was a hardness to MacArthur's voice.

"We can share the security protocols with you. It's purely a local network."

"And who else has access to it?"

"No one. I can show your technical people. It wouldn't take very long and then we can resume our meeting—"

"Put up a dazzling show of technology to woo them over? They would need much more time than fifteen minutes to check it all."

"We don't *have* that much time."

"Mr Wilson, this time limit seems constructed purely to put pressure on us."

"Attacks on your cities don't put pressure on you?"

He didn't reply. His mouth worked.

"Look, if you're that concerned, let's just leave it. I have another proposal. We can send a small mission to go to Dekker and get his approval in person."

"I don't know where he is, so I can't tell you. You may not believe me, but it's the truth."

"To protect him, right?"

He met my eyes, as he seemed to sense that I might like to ask him whether it was because Dekker had fled. Whether there had been a disagreement, whether he and Dekker were on the same side. Whether Dekker was, in fact, dead.

And the moment where the truth broke through all the obfuscating and possibly downright lies was barrelling down at us at the speed of a fast-moving train. Equally immutable.

It might be a diplomat's job to keep people talking no matter what, but there was also a point where talking was no longer useful.

"As I said, Dekker contacted me three months ago, asking for my help. He didn't say what it was about. Dekker might have thought he had everything under control until he contacted me. I'll be honest with you and admit that I have thought all kinds of unkind things about him and he and I have not been on friends' terms, but that message sounded awfully genuine. I find it really strange that there has been so little effort undertaken to ascertain his whereabouts or his welfare. That no one here can tell me whether he is alive or dead."

The expression on his face closed. His lips formed a thin line.

"We've been very busy and simply trying to survive here. We've been under attack for all of that time. President Dekker is in hiding precisely because of the danger to his life. You can make your own interpretation of what I'm saying."

"Considering his absence, there are several questions I would want to see answered. One of them is why everyone at Nations of Earth has been so scared of making the hard calls. I know, safety, but has no one asked why people were pushing the safety line so much? Was it that certain parties wanted Nations of Earth to stay quiet? Why, when you could have reached out to us, and we could have worked together?"

"I don't know what you believe, but we're an organisation made up of bureaucrats who have no jurisdiction over any of our member countries without a vote. In case you forgot, we don't command armies."

"The Office of War's recruiting drive is not happening?"

"That's recent. Because we had to do *something* and couldn't just sit and watch the world burn."

"And you didn't want to accept help either."

"What would you want us to do? We're severely restrained. We don't have the staff to undertake big risky missions."

"No, that's why we are here. This is what *gamra* is about. Dekker's predecessor signed to join. I'm offering you help. We'll need to get this signed. We will take this document to Dekker so that we don't need to hold this meeting that seems to be so difficult to organise."

"I cannot risk any of my personnel on such a dangerous mission."

"We can do it without help. Our way."

"I would not authorise that."

"You couldn't, because you don't know where he is."

"My God, man, I can see why Dekker called you an arrogant prick."

"As always, I'm happy to oblige. Anyway, think about it. It's something we could do if you think it solves a problem. Let me know if you change your mind."

I turned around and left the room, before I said anything I might regret later. I was half-expecting him to start yelling at my back, but he didn't.

Holy, holy batshit. What the actual fuck was going on here?

I met Thayu in the hallway, and she met my eyes with a concerned expression.

"What's up?"

We weren't wearing feeders, but she had an excellent sense of when I was disturbed.

We walked into our dorm, where I told her of my conversation with MacArthur.

"I don't even know what the man wants anymore. Everything I suggest, he says he can't do. It's like..." I spread my hands. I wanted to talk about my increasing sense of discomfort, the gnawing suspicion that Nations of Earth was caught in an impasse between factions that they couldn't overcome, but I was well aware of the possibility that people were listening in.

And at that moment, Ynggi came out of the communication room that MacArthur's staff had made available for us. He had gone in there presumably to save the recording from his tail camera.

He was still wearing all his gear. "I got something I think you should look at."

Thayu pointed at our dorm. *Let's go in there.*

Most of the other team members were already in the room, sitting on the bunks or the floor. Reida was the last one to come in, also from the communication room, I guessed.

Ynggi sat on the bed with us and spoke in a low voice. They had left the door open, presumably so as not to alert the Nations of Earth people to any unusual activity.

"When we were in the meeting, I was using my tail camera to record details of people's outfits and their notes. This man who was standing next to me was a companion of the military woman. When she got angry at those people who were asking silly questions, he opened a document on his screen that was close enough for me to record, so I moved the camera so that I could see it while he was reading. It was in your language, but I translated it. It's for us. They knew I would be looking at their screens."

Yes, I had gathered as much.

He pulled out his reader and drew the document up on the screen.

It was a simple image of plain text, one page, unsigned and unaddressed, but it was clearly readable.

"He was just holding it up so that I would see it."

I picked up the reader and read.

A lot of the things you will hear today are complete nonsense. You will have been told that Dekker is in hiding for his safety. He is, but he did not leave voluntarily, and he is not as incompetent, shy or scared as they want you to believe. The attack on the assembly where the vice president was killed was not a drone attack, but it was a raid by Independence Force soldiers from within the building. They entered because a number of them were employed in the compound. They killed the vice president so that they could instate their own administration. The rebels instated MacArthur in the position of acting president. MacArthur is a stooge for the enemy. He can't make decisions, because many in the assembly have also fled and no matter what he has told you, there is no quorum. Several of the young stooges he invited are not official elected members and were there only to sow confusion. He can't give you an agreement, because he does not have the authority and he knows it. He can also not call an election, because Dekker holds that authority and he is not in the complex and he never formally transferred his powers either to Yoon Ha or to MacArthur. MacArthur does not know where Dekker is and cannot contact him. The fledgling Nations of Earth defensive forces do not have the capability to defend our planet against drone attacks, and this is not the aim of the current administration, anyway. They are holding you here to thwart your attempts to resolve this peacefully. They want you gone. Your lives are in danger. Get out as soon as you can. Contact me when you've left the complex.

Well, crap.

This came from Gracelyn Sebaya, I was pretty sure of that.

I now understood why the gatherings last evening and today had been such a strange collection of people and not the proper Emergency Council. He couldn't call the Emergency Council together, because they didn't all support him. He could call part of the Emergency Council, but needed to make up numbers with his sympathisers, who wanted nothing to do with *gamra* because they supported the Independence Force.

The very bottom of the message consisted of a line of code. I pointed at it.

Reida gestured, *I don't know.*

Sheydu gestured, *Save it. Erase it.*

Thayu had been reading over my shoulder, using a translation device.

She took the reader and passed it around the others until everyone had read it. Nobody spoke, because there were sure to be listening devices in the room.

Ynggi got his reader back. He conversed in sign language with Isharu. I picked up that they should keep this information away from my devices.

I gestured, *What now?*

Thayu gestured, *I want to get out of here.*

Yes, she had been antsy all along. Spending significant amounts of time trailing and spying on outcasts in the underground tunnels of Athyl's Outer Circle had made her nervous about dark, confined spaces, especially where someone else controlled access.

"Do you think we would get help?" Nicha asked, gesturing at the reader.

Sheydu gestured, *No.*

I agreed. If Gracelyn Sebaya was sympathetic to *gamra*, she already took an enormous risk by coming here. Whatever the structure of the fledgeling Nations of Earth military forces, they were likely to be separated from the political body, but of course that didn't mean they could do as they pleased. Whenever military forces did as they pleased, no matter their motivation, words like "coup" were never far away. The military did as politicians told them to. End of. We might get additional support from her, but not while we were still here.

Which meant that yes, we needed to get out of here, because MacArthur was deliberately stalling. He didn't *want* Asto's ships in orbit.

Mereeni signalled, *How?*

Yes, how were we going to get out?

Evi mimicked an explosion.

I gestured, *No way*.

Then Sheydu replied, *It's your job. Use your mouth.*

Right.

What excuse could I come up with that was going to sound halfway plausible, that was going to convince MacArthur to let us leave? MacArthur, who was already unhappy about having us here?

But also, how could we still avoid a situation where Asto's ships would have to leave, ceding Earth to a secretive, restrictive and erratic enemy?

Damn.

No pressure at all.

I could just go up to MacArthur and tell him we were leaving, and that further discussions would be held remotely.

But since we made the effort to come here, he would rightly question our motives. And he was already suspicious of us.

I got up from the bunk bed where I was sitting and finally closed the door, because I couldn't stand it being open any longer.

I noticed a piece of tape stuck to the wall in a strange position. I presumed this was where the members of my team had detected security cameras and listening bugs.

"We need to consider our next actions," I said in a low voice. "I can think up some excuses, but we need to know what our next steps should be. Should we leave and let *gamra*'s ultimatum expire and accept that this world is lost to us? I don't want to give up. I've spent most of my life trying Earth to join *gamra*. I'm not walking away now."

"We could still try to get the *president*'s signature," Reida said, equally in a low voice.

"I've thought about that, but it would be dangerous. We'd be going into dangerous territory. Nations of Earth had to rescue us from there last time."

Sheydu snorted. "We would have gotten out by ourselves."

Yes, I had no doubt, but it might have taken longer and with a few more dead bodies.

"I've made a few additional discoveries in Amarru's database," Reida said, his voice even softer. "After showing you the previous results, I asked them to feed those sound clips they found back into the database as basis material for a search. The voice profile can change according to the person's emotions or the recording device. We call those second-grade results and they're likely to bring up results you have to dismiss unless they're confirmed by additional data that you already have."

Here was another sneak peek into the meticulous methodology of the Asto spy academy.

If there was anything I understood about spying on Asto, it was that since his brush with getting ousted from the job, Ezhya had embraced spying as an extension of the biological limits of his loyalty network and a lot of resources had gone into the spy academy— which they now wanted me to attend.

"We've been able to trace that Dekker went to talk to Celia Braddock," Reida continued in an even lower voice. "The two have a long history and they hoped to get their entities closer to collaboration. Patterson of America Free State objected. One thing about that part of the world is that the hardware is quite old-fashioned and Amarru's data contains some very unexpected interesting items, if you have the time to follow data trails. Like this."

He held a reader out to me.

On the screen was a transcript of an intercepted message, from Governor Patterson to someone only mentioned by the first name Joe, asking for help, telling him that he was losing control of the situation. He said, *If she joins up with those traitors, then I don't hold out much hope that any of them will ever see sense.*

Joe wanted to know what Patterson had done so far.

Patterson replied that he had *made life very uncomfortable* for both of them. This was followed by a crude and unrepeatable joke about Dekker's partner and their orientation. Seriously, did some people still think that kind of garbage was funny?

And then Joe said, *We're just about ready and could start something now. We'll need a fairly long lead time, because the stuff needs to come in from out-system, but once it's here, we'll have a limitless self-replicating supply to direct wherever we want.*

I stared at this sentence.

Was I imagining it, or did this one casual sentence explain the war in one fell swoop?

"Who is this *Joe*?" I asked Reida.

"He's not registered with any authority that we can track. He appears to be, or represent, the attackers."

Well... that was shocking. In trying to find Dekker and scouring through a network that should have been taken down years ago, we found the first ever proper communication from the enemy. It wasn't much, and of course Reida didn't know who Joe was, but this at last proved we were fighting people, and not solely drones.

"What are the dates on these items?"

The message to Patterson was two years ago, long before I'd set foot in America Free State. The communication between Dekker and Braddock was much more recent, right up to the time Dekker went over there.

Not only that, but Reida and his kids had found two messages from Braddock to Dekker *after* he had arrived in Atlantia, asking him if he was safe, and to one of them, he had replied, *Yes*.

Mereeni was looking over my shoulder. I turned around to face her.

"I said he was alive," she said, grinning.

"Yes, I think so, too. And if we can get him out of there, we have a chance to..."

And there I stopped. Chance to do what?

It was plain ridiculous that we should risk ourselves and whoever chose to help us to rescue a man who might not need rescuing, who despised me, for the sake of a bureaucratic process.

But Gracelyn Sebaya supported him.

And he was the legal president.

And *gamra* recognised him as such.

And if we were lucky, he had ties with other organisations that could help us fight this hostile takeover by "Joe" and his cronies, both in space and on Earth, and all those people who wanted to relegate Earth to a world in which they remained isolated from the rest of settled space. And an enemy to all of us.

Something Asto would never tolerate.

So... the unlikely allies were Dekker, Sebaya, Atlantia—maybe—, definitely PanAf, the Exchange, The Pretoria Cartel and Tamer Collective, *gamra* and the Asto military. An odd assortment of people and organisations.

Dekker could… sign for the Asto military to remain in orbit, and for it to assume a more aggressively defensive stance.

He could also formally sanction Sebaya to be involved, even if only on the ground.

It was further likely that PanAf had armed resources to help, since much of Africa was already heavily militarised, especially the northern half. They'd sunk years of Nations of Earth subsidies into creating military forces and militias to defend borders and shorelines against the human tide trying to enter Europe. Most of them refugees, but far too many also with nefarious purposes.

Atlantia was no friend of Patterson or his friend Joe. Could I make them work with Nations of Earth and *gamra*? That remained to be seen, but was worth a try. Their military seemed highly alert and competent.

Right.

I gestured for my team to gather around me.

Reida exchanged hand signals with Isharu. A moment later, the reader on the bed made a buzzing noise. Thayu switched it off.

"Jamming the signals?" I asked.

Reida grinned. "Yup. Everything. As much as we can. Hurry up, because this won't last."

"All right. This is the plan so far, although we'll probably change it along the way."

It felt good to speak freely.

"We're going to get him." Him meaning Dekker. "We're going to take him to a safe locality. He's going to sign that document. Then we're going to get everyone else together. We'll join our resources to defeat this enemy. Ask Leisha to be on standby."

"We can organise transport," said Riyala, the head of Asha's guard association.

"Good. Do that. Contact anyone you need off the register. Anyone who doesn't need to do anything right now, please rest. Who knows when we can next sleep?"

"That also applies to you," Thayu said.

"I'm busy."

"Busy at giving us an excellent excuse to get out of here."

Yeah, that.

Reida turned the buzzing signal off. Evi, Telaris and a couple of Asha's guards went to the other dorm room to have a nap.

The Nations of Earth technicians were still doing network stuff at the far end of the corridor.

I grabbed Thayu's reader and sat on my bunk to make some notes.

"I was actually serious about having some rest," Thayu said, her voice soft. "You tend to run yourself into the ground."

"I can't sleep when stuff is happening."

"No one benefits when you're collapsing with exhaustion, like you did yesterday. We need to be alert and ready for what we're best at."

She gave me a penetrating look.

Right.

There were two things I was good at that my team continued to remind me of: using my mouth and my hyped-up, magical ability to deliver a deadly accurate shot when any of our lives were in danger.

I wondered which of those two she referred to.

No prizes for guessing.

I lay down anyway, but of course my mind was churning, mainly about what I would say to MacArthur. What was a good excuse to leave?

We needed to consult with Amarru.

The ship was calling us back. That was good. Blame someone else. Politicians loved that.

But it was still a rather lame excuse.

Something had come up, maybe. But what?

I didn't know. Despite telling Thayu I was fine, I did feel rather tired, but also anxious. Was MacArthur going to resume the meeting today?

"Did you pull something out down there?" Isharu asked Deyu, who sat on the ground.

"No, what do you mean?"

"I've lost network access."

"Me, too," Reida said.

"So have I," Thayu said.

Well, sleep wasn't going to happen. I sat up. "I'll ask MacArthur what's going on."

CHAPTER TWENTY

BUT BEFORE I could leave the room, there was a clang at the end of the corridor and the sound of heavy booted footsteps in the hallway.

The members of my team looked at each other. I gestured *It's OK. Relax.* But Sheydu didn't seem to think so. She made a couple of quick gestures to the team. *Prepare, Caution* and a few I didn't catch.

Deyu unplugged and gathered up her hub and shoved it in her pack.

Reida shut down his work and put his screens away.

"What about the others?" Nicha asked.

He was referring to the rest of the team who had gone into the other dorm to catch up on sleep.

"I'll check." Sheydu got up from her bunk and went into the corridor. All of a sudden, everyone was frantically scrambling to get their things together, and I wasn't sure what had triggered it.

A moment later, Sheydu came back walking backwards into the room, facing a large and heavily armed man. Several others remained in the doorway. I could only see two of them, but could hear the voices of at least two others.

The man held a weapon in the crook of his arm, pointed at the ground. His reflective visor and body armour made for an intimidating picture, and for all of Sheydu's bluster, she had enough experience that she would never seek violence where she could avoid it.

He and his two fellows wore the Special Forces badge on their chest.

"What is this about? Is anything the matter?" I asked.

"There was a disturbance in this room," one man said, his voice with a curious accent.

"Not that I know," I said. "We were in here talking and resting, and waiting for the meeting to continu—"

"An electronic disturbance."

Oh. He was talking about Reida's jamming buzzer. They didn't like it that they couldn't listen into what we said.

"I'm not sure what you're talking about."

"*He* does." He turned to Reida, who retreated on the bottom bunk, a reaction that painfully reminded me of the shy and skittish youth Reida used to be. It made me angry to see it, actually.

I said to the man's back, "He can't understand you, so can you please address me?"

I faced him in the middle of the room. He was half a head taller than me. Deep inside his helmet, his eyes were brown.

"He's been messing with our systems."

"We were given access to communication lines. I'm sorry if in the process my people affected systems they shouldn't have touched, but they are not familiar with the equipment and protocols, and no one was available to help them."

He sniffed. "We have orders to search this room."

"Why? Who issued that order? We're a delegation from *gamra*. If you want us to show you our equipment, you only need to ask."

"I'm not here to debate our orders."

"This is not acceptable. We're here by invitation of Nations of Earth."

Was MacArthur aware that this was happening? Did he perhaps *agree* with this action, trying to intimidate us into… what exactly?

"Excuse me, I'm going to check this with MacArthur." I turned away from him and walked past the bunk where Reida and Mereeni sat and went to the door. The man who stood there did not step aside, so I had to worm past him.

There were two more men in the corridor. An additional man came to the door of the room we'd been using for communication—

there was no one in there as far as I knew—and two more emerged out of a storeroom.

I faced a wall of reflective visors. It could be that these soldiers weren't trying to be threatening to us, but they sure as hell gave me that impression. I addressed the man with the most patches on his chest.

"What is going on? What is this about? Can I speak with MacArthur?"

I had to do my best not to sound alarmed, but my heart was hammering. What in all of the seven hells was going on here?

The leader jerked his head. The other men came closer to me and dispersed along the walls, blocking my way back into the dorm room where Thayu and the others were.

All of them wore armour and carried heavy duty guns, which they kept pointed at the floor.

They were all Special Services.

One of them gestured at me. "Come. You only."

"What for?"

"Safety."

That was their standard reply to any question. What safety? We were supposedly in the safest place in town. Whose safety? Probably not mine.

Sheydu always called me out for having a big mouth, but I was dumbfounded. Sure, I could understand some hostility. The position Nations of Earth held towards me had always been ambivalent, full of curly questions and accusations of *siding with the other team* or *abandoning our values* and stuff like that.

But guards with guns wanting to separate me from my team?

There was no way—just *no way*—that was going to happen. I'd moved past allowing that treatment after Sirkonen was killed—at which point, admittedly, Nations of Earth had treated me very badly.

But even so, they had always *wanted* to talk, negotiate so that we would be, essentially, on the same side.

I heard Klaus' warning that *sections of Nations of Earth were deeply compromised*, and a sense of dread crept over me that I hadn't understood what this meant. Not compromised as in holding quaint and old-fashioned opinions, which was standard for Nations of Earth and which I expected. But truly compromised: being stooges of our new invisible enemy.

The men ignored my questions.

If I didn't know any better, I might have thought that they were here to apprehend us.

No, scratch that.

They *were* here to apprehend us.

Me in particular, while they did goodness-knew-what with my team.

This was not a friendly administration. Klaus Messner had warned me. Gracelyn Sebaya had warned me a second time. Perhaps I could have seen it earlier, but I had so much wanted to trust Nations of Earth.

Well, damn it, that was a realisation. We'd been looking for the enemy, and they were staring us in the face, with blue-tinged reflective visors.

The men forced me back into the dorm room.

I glanced at the members of my team past the soldier who blocked the door. They had all been misguided as well. Not just about not worrying that certain people at Nations of Earth had strange opinions —they had always held those—but about the deep extent to which the people here now sided *with the enemy*.

That was why MacArthur couldn't muster a full assembly or Emergency Council, or pretty much anything. Because a significant percentage of delegates were refusing to cooperate with him. Rightly so. And we'd blundered straight into that standoff.

Deyu still sat on the floor. Isharu and Reida faced the dark screens, which stared like blank eyes.

They were plotting, doing what they did best. Trying to get us out of here.

I didn't miss Sheydu twitching her little finger. Reida sniffed. Thayu picked up her cup and shifted it forward. Ynggi swung his tail in the darkness between the two bunk beds.

All these things meant something.

They were planning action.

It was my task to keep playing my role. Be the diplomat. Make a fuss.

"I demand to speak with MacArthur. I don't understand what

happened. We were in the middle of a meeting when we got cut off. We were waiting for the connection to come back and we'd resume our meeting. I don't understand why this extra security is necessary."

"We are going to search this room for unauthorised equipment," the group's leader said.

"I don't understand. You checked everything we brought in here at the gate and the security station. I demand an explanation for this behaviour. We're a diplomatic mission. MacArthur invited us to stay, and you can't just—"

"We can do whatever we please. You're in our territory. The Independence Force decides what happens in the compound. You have been spying on us, disabling our surveillance, making threats—"

There was a noise in the corridor, followed by a stifled shout.

A moment later, someone else came into the doorway: MacArthur, with an enormous black-skinned hand over his mouth.

Telaris. His intense moss-green eyes met mine over the top of MacArthur's head.

Telaris said, "This character seems to have ordered in a bunch of thugs to justify apprehending us."

MacArthur's gaze darted from one guard to the other, the whites in his eyes showing on all sides.

"Get out," Telaris said, in heavily accented Isla, to the soldiers in the room. His resonant, deep voice made it sound even more threatening.

In the split second that the Special Operations thugs hesitated to consider whether they were going to comply, Deyu rose from the ground and picked up the table that was in front of her. This was where Isharu was sitting. There was some equipment on the table which flew through the room as she hefted it to shoulder height.

She charged forward, using the table as a shield, and pushed aside one of the guards while Sheydu—good old Sheydu—produced something from inside her jacket that she threw in the direction of the door. It exploded with a bang, followed by a hiss and a lot of smoke. The guards retreated to the hallway, coughing. Whatever was in the smoke bomb smelled terrible.

Part of Sheydu's readiness kit was a breather mask made of a sheet of breathable rubbery material that stuck to your face like a sucker cup. It folded up into a small packet the size of a marble. All around me, I heard the pops of the masks unfolding. I popped mine by pressing the button and slapped the sheet against my lower face. You had to breathe in first so that the material sat snugly on your skin. It filled your mouth with a rubbery bubble.

Urgh.

But at least the air that filtered through was clean.

A fire alarm started blaring.

"Do you want me to shut that thing up?" Reida said. His voice sounded muffled through the mask and his exhaling while speaking made the mask look like the throat sac of a frog.

Sheydu called, "No point. It will be wired to their security hub. We need to get out of here quickly or we're going to have to deal with the rest of the security force." Her mask bulged a lot before sucking back in.

MacArthur was trying to shout and breathe and cough through Telaris' hand. His skin had taken on a blueish tinge. The whites of his eyes were showing.

Three guards charged back into the room. They had all put on their own masks. One pointed his gun at me and shouted, in a muffled voice, "You are going to come—"

Deyu barrelled into him with the flat side of the table, cutting off the rest of his sentence. He hit the wall with a bone-breaking thud and collapsed sideways on the floor. Knowing Deyu's strength, I didn't think he'd be getting up again. Deyu yanked the weapon out of his hands and swung it by the barrel so that the handgrip landed on the head of another guard who was struggling with one of Asha's military guards.

The man fell, blood pouring over his face. Deyu crouched to take his weapon, too.

The third man struggled in Reida's grip. He shouted in a language I didn't understand. Thayu casually flicked him on the side of his head with her elbow. His eyes rolled in his head and he, too, fell to the floor.

At some point, Evi and the guards who had been in the room with Telaris had overwhelmed the two men in the hallway.

That left MacArthur, still in Telaris' grip.

His expression was positively terrified. His face was blue from lack of air.

I faced him. "I don't know what sort of trick you were trying to pull on me, but you got the wrong people."

I gestured for Telaris to take the hand from his mouth.

He coughed. "You filthy alien fucker. Betraying your own people, huh?" He coughed again.

He spat, but the wad dribbled uselessly over his chin and fell on the ground because he didn't have enough breath.

"As far as I see it, between the two of us, there is only one betrayer, and it isn't me." And I continued in Coldi, "Come. Let's go."

My team collected their things at record speed.

"Good luck getting out of here!" MacArthur shouted. "The entire force is on high alert. This planet belongs to us, and we will determine who comes here. We will hound you alien scum to hell—"

"Deyu, shut him up, please."

I turned away while she brought down the handgrip of the gun on his head.

He fell to the ground with a thud.

"It's not that end of the weapon you're supposed to use," Reida said, in a dry tone.

"Oh. How does this thing work, anyway?"

She faced the weapon in the right direction, aimed and pulled the trigger.

A loud pop echoed in the room.

"Ah, like that."

A red patch spread over the back of MacArthur's jacket.

Deyu slung the weapon over her shoulder and picked up her pack.

Remind me to never, ever, mess with this woman.

Asha's guards rummaged through the gear worn by the Special Forces thugs, collecting further weapons, communication devices and other electronics.

We gathered all our things and also some things that MacArthur had given us. She tossed the notebooks in a bag and collected the electronic devices. The latter, Sheydu put in a pile in the corridor and set fire to it with another device out of her jacket.

The fire alarm was still ringing. We ran out of the corridor, where Telaris and Ynggi at the front overwhelmed two more guards who came in from the other direction. They were on the ground before I could even see what was happening.

Shouts down the hallway suggested that people were calling for reinforcements, but for all the bravado they displayed, I didn't think the group of occupiers was very large.

We ran past the staircase into the building's main foyer. The sound of yelling male voices drifted through the glass that cut off access to the stairs. The corridor ended in a solid security door that looked much more substantial than the glass door.

Reida dropped to his knees. He inserted a few metal strips in the slit between the door and the door frame.

Meanwhile, the smoke from Sheydu's smoke bomb was creeping in our direction. It was hard to see what was happening behind us.

A blast of cooler air sucked the smoke away.

"We're in," Reida said. He had opened the door.

I followed him and Isharu and Ynggi into an underground car park. Rows of vehicles sat in parking bays, all of them with the Nations of Earth emblem engraved in the corner of the side window.

A row of white mini buses stood at a charging station.

Reida ran to the first. He used his gun at the low setting to fry the lock's electronics and then had no trouble opening the door. It was incredible how fast he had become.

We all piled in, with Reida at the wheel. Deyu and Evi ran in front. They destroyed the security door so that we could get out.

The bus roared out the alley and onto the road that ended up in the central square of the compound where often people held demonstrations, politicians gave speeches and tourists took photos. Today the square was empty. I guessed this would be the last time I ever came here for a while.

A fire truck was coming the other way, followed by another one and a security vehicle.

"Quick!" I called out to Reida.

The broad leafy avenue led to the main gate with its heavy security presence. Already, the officers were coming out of their guard house.

One stopped to aim a weapon—

Reida steered the bus off the road onto the grass, in between the trees and over the footpath that ran along the hedge.

A shot rang out. A siren started wailing.

The bus barrelled across a side road, barely missing a vehicle that came out. The driver blasted the horn.

I was just about to shout that we might have a better chance climbing the gate at one of the less frequented parts of the perimeter when Reida brought the bus to a screeching halt and opened the door. Evi and Telaris jumped into the grass, both carrying the familiar long shapes.

"Get down on the floor!" Reida called out.

The door swung shut again.

I dropped next to Thayu between the seats. Nicha huddled next to me, with Isharu, with all her equipment in the aisle. She was busy talking to people in amidst all this chaos. Deyu, Riyala and two of Asha's guards and Ynggi sat on the bus steps and the forward facing part of the aisle, all clutching weapons.

Ynggi had taken so well to being the frontline of our defense. It was his choice. I had not forced him to do this.

The bus bumped back across the tree roots and the grass, down the curb—

Something hard and metallic slammed into the side, not too far from where I was sitting.

They were shooting at us, and also: how had Reida known the side of the bus was armoured?

Reida himself wasn't sitting in the driver's seat anymore. He crouched in the aisle, his head below the bottom of the windscreen, one hand on the wheel, the other on the accelerator. He was using his reader to see where he was going—using the image recorded by the camera on the end of Ynggi's tail, which he stuck out above the bus' side panels.

The bus made a kind of drunken, lumbering progression down the avenue, hitting the curb a few times, and venturing into the median strip. Bushes scratched along the sides.

Then the window popped. Something metallic ricocheted around the bus before coming to a rest on one of the seats. A bullet.

Reida opened the doors.

In quick succession, Deyu, Riyala and Asha's guards, Sheydu and Mereeni all left the bus.

Reida continued slowly, leaving the door open.

People shouted outside. I thought I could hear a charge gun discharging. The siren was still going. People ran past.

A few more bullets hit the windscreen. Most left the bus again through the back window.

Then a heavy explosion made the vehicle wobble, followed by a cloud of acrid smoke. Sirens were blaring in the distance.

Then Sheydu came running back, followed closely by Mereeni. A moment later, the others also returned.

"Everyone in? Go!" Sheydu called.

Reida resumed his position at the wheel and the bus started moving again.

As we came past the guard house, I could see smoke and flames in the limited view from my position on the floor.

The bus turned into the intersection at the entrance and sped away from the scene.

For a while, no one said anything.

I peeled the mask off my face and handed it to Sheydu, who sprayed to clean it and inserted it into a device that turned it back into a little marble. I took it back from her and dropped it back into the emergency kit, still warm.

Everyone was exhausted, dusty, sweaty, and in the case of Deyu and at least one of Asha's guards, covered in dark splatters that might be blood.

Meanwhile, Isharu was busily communicating with someone. Hopefully there were people from the Coldi register that could render quick assistance. But I'd take military assistance if it was on offer.

It had been stupid to come here. Yes, this place was deeply compromised.

If I hadn't disliked Klaus Messner so much, would I have believed him and saved us from having wasted this time and put my team at risk?

CHAPTER TWENTY-ONE

FOR A WHILE, no one said anything.

Reida drove, and the rest of us sat on the floor. Deyu, Isharu, Ynggi and Thayu were listening.

Deyu had turned her hub back on. Of course, its reach was not as limited as they had told me, or MacArthur. Deyu carried an attachment that boosted the reach of the network. They had installed this and were busy finding out who they could contact.

I got out of the way by not distracting them with needless questions.

Sheydu repeated the mask-folding action with the masks of the other team members.

Asha's guards busied themselves with checking the charge level on their weapons. They also wanted to check mine. I hadn't used it yet.

Meanwhile, the bus made its way through the streets and later along back roads. The light turned deep golden when the low sun peeped underneath the clouds, but that lasted only a minute or two before dusk set in.

Some time later, Reida stopped the bus, and opened the door. A person came in with the cool evening air. A man, I thought, judging by the silhouette. He said something in Coldi and sat in the seat behind Reida. They spoke in quiet voices.

The bus turned around a sharp corner, and another one and then stopped.

I figured it was safe to look out the window. At least Sheydu had also raised herself off the floor.

We were in the paved yard of a warehouse. Outside a closed metal shutter sat a small truck.

Reida opened the door.

The Coldi man got out, walked over to the truck, and lifted the flap at the back.

We all scrambled out of the bus, into the opening he had made.

Reida came with us, because the Coldi man was going to drive.

"Where are we going?" I asked him when I climbed into the back of the truck after him.

"We're meeting up with some people who can help us."

"From the Coldi register?"

"No. Through Gracelyn Sebaya."

"You managed to contact her?"

"That's what the code was for. The last line in the message."

Finally, we had found an ally.

We all crammed into the back of the truck. It was smaller than the bus, so we all had to pull up our knees and some of us had to sit on the packs.

The man closed the back flap and got into the cabin.

The only light in the cramped cabin was the glow from Isharu's reader.

While the truck made its way to wherever we were going, the members of my team caught up on some sleep. I sat with my knees pulled up against my chest and stared into the darkness, with bad thoughts whirling through my head.

We'd crossed a threshold, and I wasn't sure we could return to normal relations with Nations of Earth after this.

There was a line between pointing out the mis-steps made by Nations of Earth—and there were plenty—and blatantly supporting the other side.

I'd walked this line since I started working for Nations of Earth.

Many old-school diplomats would argue that I'd crossed it—in accepting work from Ezhya, in remaining in Barresh after losing my position, in letting the Asto military violate Earth's sovereignty by attacking Romi Tanaqan from orbit, in all the thousands of little ways that I had become more Coldi and less human.

But today might finally mean that I'd no longer be welcome at Nations of Earth, even if sense prevailed and they got rid of these traitors.

Even if our actions were in self-defense, and it was clear that the assembly was—and had been for a while—deeply compromised.

What we did next was vital. For me, for Earth, for *gamra*.

Find Dekker. Get him to sign that document to keep *gamra* off our backs. Then find help from as many people as possible.

There was a small window in the front-facing side of the cargo compartment. It provided a view of the driver's cabin—with only the Coldi driver inside—and out through the front window.

Judging by the hint of orange glow on the horizon, we had gone west from the city, and were driving along narrow dikes hemmed in by water on both sides. I'd often flown over this landscape, a patchwork of green fields walled off by dikes with stretches of water in between.

Moonlight cast its glittering glow over the water.

We were on a long stretch of road with a wide expanse of water on both sides. To the left, reed beds extended from the bank. A dark patch of land lay ahead. This had to be an artificial island, because it stuck out too far above the water, was too tidy and quite large. The moonlight cast little flickers of glinting light above the piece of land. I couldn't figure what caused this.

Where the road met the island, a solid metal gate barred the way.

The driver stopped the truck.

Well, what now?

Thayu came to stand next to me so that she could also peek out.

A little red light blinked at the control panel next to the road. A moment later, the gate rolled aside.

The truck continued through, first up an incline. At the top, we could see over the field on the other side. Huge windmills stood in rows. Their moving blades had caused the glinting I had noticed. The field underneath contained a crop, probably potatoes, but it was too dark to see. Even though we sat in a closed cabin, I could hear the soft humming from the windmills.

"What are all these things?" Thayu asked.

Ynggi said, "These are machines that use the wind to pump water from one end to the other, for power generation. Did you notice how the water level was higher on one side of the road than on the other?"

I wondered how he could see out, but he'd wormed his tail in between the cover and the frame.

Of course. And no, I hadn't noticed, but he was absolutely right.

There were many of these windmill parks. You could see them when coming into Rotterdam by air. Some were in the middle of the ocean, although I'd been told that some of those had to be relocated all the time. Some were for direct power generation, others were for creating a water reservoir that generated power when there was no wind.

I'd never visited a windmill park on the ground. You didn't realise how many windmills they contained.

As we progressed through the field, losing sight of the gate behind us, it was eerie to be enveloped by their constant hum. Deyu complained about the lack of reception.

On the other side of the field, we went up the surrounding dike again. The water loomed before us, dark and with only a few lights, from ships, I presumed.

The driver stopped the vehicle and turned off the lights. Then he jumped from the cabin, came around the back and opened the flap.

"Your contact is going to meet you here," he said.

We collected all our gear and got out into the warm night. The Coldi man climbed back behind the wheel.

While we walked along a service road towards the water, Reida told me he was going back and would abandon the bus we'd taken from the Nations of Earth complex in a place that would mislead pursuers. This man was a mechanic who knew everything about servicing these vehicles, and would also upload false data to the module that had recorded where we had taken the bus. He might even set fire to the vehicle.

The road ended in a small parking lot next to a low building that probably contained the control centre for the power generation plant.

Next to it was a fenced-off piece of land filled with ten or so square boxes the size of a small shed. Signs on the fence warned about high voltage. You could hear the electricity hum.

"We need to wait for our ride," Nicha said when we had all gathered under the awning of the building, where an outdoor picnic table was probably a place where the plant's workers would have a break.

Reida sat at the table, the screen lighting his face from below. He checked the location of our contact—a moving dot on the water—and then switched to another process. Communicating with the ship so that they could send messages to his band of workers in Athyl. He was using the power plant's connection.

I wondered if I should do something, like letting my father know we were all right, because he might have heard news about the mess we had made at Nations of Earth. Were we still meant to be silent?

I didn't think we had been silent for a while now. I doubted it was still possible to be silent.

I could also check the news on my throwaway reader, but I was still quite rattled by the fact that this mysterious person had so quickly identified which device I was using. My appetite for engaging with him was less, because we had so many other problems, so I left the device in my bag.

After a while, Reida said that the transport was on its way. We walked from the building to the water through waist high grass. Crickets chirped in the grass and the smell of flowers hung over the ground. This was not the right time and setting to go to war. This was a night to walk with a dog or a lover.

A flexible walkway extended over the water, bobbing up and down with the very gentle waves.

At the end of the walkway lay a boat.

I was surprised that I hadn't heard it arrive. Did that mean it had been here all the time? I didn't think so.

There was someone on the jetty.

I had expected to see Leisha. But of course he would be with my craft and if he was in the area—and I'd asked him to come—he probably didn't want to come this close to the shore. We would also need to bring more people than my shuttle could carry, so there might even be a second ship.

The boat lay low in the water, a big chunky thing, dark and menacing.

A narrow gangplank led up to the boat, and on the deck we found a familiar face. One of the two military officers who had come to the bunker with Gracelyn Sebaya.

He nodded at me. "I'm glad you made it out, Mr Wilson."

"Not without some damage, I'm afraid."

"If you have any injured team members, see my mate in the cabin. Make sure everyone comes on board quickly. We need to get out."

I understood.

We descended into a dimly lit cabin and sat on benches in rows. The seats were really basic—it looked like they could be removed—and had seatbelts.

The cabin was barely big enough for all of us, with some people, including Evi and Telaris, having to sit on the steps. Both of them carried their rocket launchers over their shoulders.

Sounds on the deck indicated that the ropes were pulled in.

The light in the cabin finally allowed me to see all the members of my team.

Not all of them had come through without damage.

Reida had a scratch across his face, and Deyu's uniform was ripped.

She also had several dark spots on her uniform that might be blood. Sheydu's face looked pale. One of Asha's guards had sticks in his hair and another was covered in mud. I probably looked similarly bedraggled.

One of the men came into the cabin and took up position in the tiny cubicle that held the controls.

"I'm sorry about the lack of space. Please come in here as much as possible. You won't need to sit in here for very long. You might want to do up the seatbelts, because it could get rough."

So we all crammed in the cabin as much as we could, but Asha's guards stayed outside. They wanted to, and it was probably a good idea to have someone on the lookout for any visual signs that people were following us.

Isharu also stayed outside, where she was fiddling with her reader and picking up signals from orbit, judging by the information scrolling over the screen. I didn't ask what she was doing, and nobody else seemed to question it.

Was it safe? Was she talking to super-secret military satellites? Did she use a very high level of encryption? Probably yes to all those things.

Thumps on the deck above me suggested that the second crew member was pulling the gangplank onto the deck.

With that done, the man came down the steps into the cabin and asked who of us needed first aid. I pointed to Deyu and Reida, and one of Asha's guards pulled up her sleeve to show a nasty row of blisters on her arm.

The boat turned away from the jetty and gathered speed and the crew member attended to their injuries.

The engine was very quiet.

I recognised the signs: the basic interior, the advanced technology. This vessel was likely to be part of a military force. Not Asto's, I was pretty sure.

The man at the controls peered at a radar screen.

I asked if we were meeting up with someone else. I had an insane desire to see my own aircraft and Leisha.

"Not this close to the shore," he said. "I'm looking out for rogue vessels that haven't declared their presence. We can't afford to run into anyone."

I had thought that fishing in the North Sea was highly regulated, but apparently you could still buy licenses, and not all of them were legal, and those vessels operated at night. At low tide, the sea was treacherous, with sand banks and channels full of fast-flowing water.

He explained this while steering the boat through the shallow channels and around sand banks. At one point, he needed to cut the engine to avoid a group of seals.

"There are the big fleets that travel around the Atlantic and fish wherever they are allowed to at that particular time of the year. And then there's the small time fishermen who change their operations during the year. They go further north and south as they are allowed, but some stay in this region, don't fish all of the year, so the rest of the time they take freight and people to places where they want to go."

"Sounds like you have experience."

"I used to work for the coast guard."

Ynggi asked about fishing. I translated for him.

I sat on the hard bench in the cabin, and watched over Ynggi's shoulder how the man deftly steered the boat through the narrow channels. He said the large shipping channels were kept open by dredging barges, but only on the approved routes that freight ships used.

Those were wide channels, closely patrolled, and used by the very large container vessels, some of them operating without any human crew.

It was dangerous territory, he said, for a small boat like this, and he also said that there were a lot of authorities patrolling.

Smaller companies also had a tourist license, which meant that they would take people on day trips or camping trips around the sand bars that would be used for sailing or hiking or sand boarding or any of the action sports.

It was a very strange world.

After a while, we came into deeper water and we picked up speed.

The waves also grew bigger, so it grew rather rough.

"Listen, everyone," he then said.

The sound of his voice jolted Thayu out of dozing. She looked cranky.

"I want to make sure everyone comes into the cabin, does up their seatbelts, because the next few minutes are going to get rough."

While we all fished for and did up our seatbelts and the other team members came into the cabin and the crew shut the door to the deck, the boat went faster and faster. A jolt went through the craft and we were tossed about in our seats each time we slammed into a wave. Still, the boat increased speed until it bumped over the top of the waves with big jolts. Wings folded out from the sides. The bumping stopped, and we became airborne.

Well, that was... interesting, to speak with Thayu.

The craft kept at very low altitude, skimming the surface of the waves.

To the right lay a patch of blinking lights on the horizon.

Those belonged to the windmill park, and receded fast into the distance.

I was wondering whether he was going to take us all the way across the Atlantic, which would seem ridiculous, since this vessel didn't even have enough room for us to sit.

But he was busy, and the members of my team were trying to

catch up on sleep, and I tried to do the same, with poor results, as usual.

I sat and dozed, but just as I fell asleep, the craft landed on the surface again. My head banged against the side wall. Ouch.

Someone said, "There they are."

CHAPTER TWENTY-TWO

WE ALL WENT UP onto the deck. The sea was a bit rough, but not badly so. Having been sailing in all kinds of weather on my father's boat in New Zealand, I had experienced much worse, but I couldn't say that it was a calm night either. A humid squally breeze hinted at a change of weather, and whipped the waves into little foam heads that would splash and spray over the deck.

There was not that much room up the top, so half my team waited on the stairs into the cabin. The younger crew member was working in the dark, rolling out some kind of floating walkway that attached to a darker shape that lay on the waves ahead.

This was a much bigger vehicle, another ship, for as far as I could see, but it didn't look familiar.

"Okay, we are ready. Go," the crew member yelled.

Deyu was the first one across. Normally in Barresh, when we went into an unknown place, they would walk next to me or slightly behind me, but nobody cared about that protocol and there was not enough room for it besides.

Evi was the next across and after he disappeared onto the wobbly gangplank, I followed him. The sea pitched and rolled the flexible surface. There were two handrails along the side of the floating walkway, but they offered only limited stability. The surface of the thing was rough with knobs or spikes, and I couldn't make up my mind whether this helped or hindered in the rolling sea. I reached the other craft, which was also a seaplane of some kind. It was much bigger than the one we had just travelled in, but of similar design.

Not an Asto-made craft—that was all I could tell about it.

A crew member was waiting on the wing, holding himself on a handhold clipped into the surface. He had extended a rope into the cabin, visible only as a dimly lit door.

I followed the rope and joined Deyu in the semidarkness of the cabin.

This was clearly also a military craft, with sparse furnishings and plain seats, but it was equipped to carry a lot more people than the previous one.

There were some people inside, including, I saw, someone with a crate of refreshments and blankets.

"I am glad you made it," said a familiar female voice. I had to search the semidarkness of the cabin to find Gracelyn Sebaya.

I went to join her on the bench where she sat.

"I'm sorry. I'm not trying to be rude. I didn't see you. One of the characteristics of the Coldi is that they are night blind."

In fact, I had never appreciated how much I would hate being night blind.

"You're human," she said.

"Not as much as you think I am."

I sensed that this reply puzzled her, but she said nothing, probably considering it too personal and not important right now.

She said, "We will turn up the light for you guys, once we've taken off. There will be some hot drinks as well."

"Thank you very much. I won't pretend that we don't need it."

Even though a lot of Coldi blood now coursed through my veins, I had never developed the ability to vary my body temperature.

I leaned back in my seat, and let the crew go through the motions of checking all our harnesses. Someone gave me a packet of food items and a blanket. The small box contained a bread roll, a packet of juice, something that looked like cheese, and some jam or similar spread. I couldn't see anything that would cause problems with any of my team.

The cabin member who had been on the wing came back inside with the rope and shut the door.

It turned out to be a young woman, not a man, and she sat down in the seat next to the door, after having made sure it was properly closed, and pressed some buttons on the panel next to it.

Then she gave the thumbs up to another crew member at the front of the cabin.

The floor started vibrating.

Gracelyn Sebaya asked, "What happened in Rotterdam? How did you get out?"

"How much of the news has gotten out yet?" I asked.

"We know there has been an altercation. We don't know exactly what has happened, because nobody has been in contact with us yet. Once I left with my guard, we had no operatives left in the bunker. I don't know how likely it is that we will hear precisely what has happened."

"Oh, you will hear, in one way or another."

I still thought about the devastation we'd left behind.

"Was it that bad?"

"Believe me, it was."

I leaned back and sipped from my tea.

She continued, "So, we need to talk urgently, because we don't have that much time. I presume you're tired and want a rest."

"You're not wrong there. Most of us are exhausted. But yes, we need to talk, and we need coordination."

On the other side of the aisle, Nicha and Telaris unpacked their food parcels. Nicha tried the bread. On the seat behind them, Ynggi seemed to have remembered the concept of cheese. He had unwrapped the parcel first and had almost finished eating the—I thought—unappetising-looking pale yellow squishy block.

Next to him, Deyu had wrapped her hands around a steaming mug. Her face was pale.

They were all tired and hungry and cold.

I began, "You know why we came to Rotterdam, and that reason still applies. Our first task is to find Dekker and get his signature."

"I've not known you to be such a stickler for bureaucracy."

"It's not about the bureaucracy. The reason I am pushing for this agreement is this: *if* the Asto military are forced to leave, they are likely to deliver a parting salvo that no one on Earth is likely to forget in a hurry. They have intelligence to tell them where the enemy is likely to be active, and they will leave those places in ruins and to hell with the consequences. If there is one thing they won't tolerate, it is to allow a force to exist that will live in the sanctity of a world where they can't reach and that is likely to challenge their rule over settled space in the future. They made the mistake of playing soft with the Aghyrians. They won't repeat that mistake."

"So?"

"So it's vitally important that they be allowed to stay in orbit."

"It's not actually *that* part of your activity I'm questioning. It's the *find Dekker* part."

"We know where Dekker is."

"His exact location?"

"Yes."

"How?"

I eyed her. "It's a long process, and not all of it is conventional. I presume you know where he is as well?"

"More or less."

"Do you think he is safe or imprisoned?"

"A bit of both. I suspect Atlantia holds him as safeguard. He's a valuable person, but if it's too clear that he's a prisoner, they might provoke demands for his release. So instead, the line is that he fled, which is not entirely untrue."

"He went there of his own accord?"

"Yes, he did, against my advice, to tell you the truth. I told him we could protect him, and that the enemy elements in the assembly were just loudmouths, same as they'd always been. He disagreed very strongly. It turned out he was right."

She blew out a breath.

"Our intelligence did *not* see the attack on Yoon Ha coming. But at the time Dekker told me he wanted to go to Atlantia to negotiate a stronger alliance with Braddock, and then let it shine through that he feared for his life, I told him I doubted this was the right time for negotiations and that we could protect him. He said he'd go, anyway. I was unhappy. I believed Braddock wanted to lure him into making concessions to the long-running sanctions against Atlantia. Basically, they're tired of being a country with limited resources. Who wouldn't be?"

She shrugged.

"I've changed my mind about Braddock. She had a much better

appreciation of the threat posed by the Independence Force than any of us. I believe she wanted to ally herself with Dekker, to stand against Patterson. She's been trying for years to reunite the north American states and to get them to become members of Nations of Earth."

I thought back to my visit to Braddock's residence. How the house at the lake was a bastion of security. How she had made public statements that *gamra* was to blame for the attacks. Was that all a game, or had she actually looked at the information I had brought her, and concluded that she'd been wrong?

That was a disturbing thought.

In my experience, leaders on Earth rarely admitted publicly that they were wrong. Especially not when the rest of the country might think differently.

I said, "Whatever Dekker's doing there, he needs to get out. I want to get everyone together to coordinate our knowledge so that we can strike hard at Patterson, the Independence Force, the remnants of SCAC, and destroy their most important localities."

"They'll probably retreat to New Taurus."

"We can deal with that. That's outside *gamra* space. We just need them gone from Earth. If Earth is to join *gamra*."

She nodded.

"We can take you most of the way. You'll be meeting up with some of your people a bit closer, because obviously, we can't come close to the coast and you seem to have intelligence that we don't. We have to stay over international waters."

The seaplane had taken off and was again flying very low over the water. I had heard that these craft could evade radar detection.

Now that I was warm and dry, fatigue swept over me. But there was still more territory to cover.

I said, "I have a proposal to make. We get one chance at striking at their bases. We need to be certain that we hit them as hard as we can. We need to be as certain as possible about where to hit them. We have some guesses, but we don't have enough information at the moment. If we can coordinate, extrapolate, and join our efforts, we will have a better chance."

"We can definitely help. We may not have great numbers, especially because I can only rely on people known to be loyal to me."

"Is anyone inside Nations of Earth still on our side?"

"There are a few, but they're outnumbered and lying low. Whatever passes for a military force is also split, but the Independence Force has been trying to recruit young people to support their cause."

I knew. I had seen them on the train to Rotterdam. I had heard the patriotic jingles when I tried to reach the Office of War.

I met her eyes. "What about you?"

"The force hasn't officially declared war on itself. We are officially still in the stage of investigation into the origin of the drone attacks. We officially don't know where the enemy is, except a good percentage of us do know, and a good percentage should support the enemy. On the surface of it, everyone is in the force to fight the invasion, only there are two different opinions on what that invasion is."

"That sounds like a mess."

"It is, and it's the enemy's full intention. The forces that are loyal to us and to the original agreement between Earth and *gamra* are small, but we have a fairly high level of integrity and can give you assistance, such as this."

I wondered who her superior was. She was probably directly answerable to Dekker.

"I take it you're also in contact with the people in orbit?"

"We are, and they impressed on us how important it was that you be allowed to do your work. I understand the basics of Asto's dilemma, and also how Earth is tied up with it, much as I also dislike the fact that Asto has that influence. But we can live with it, because I like the alternative less. And I understand why you had to be allowed to come in order to stop Asto's forced retreat."

"And I have failed dismally."

"We're not done yet," she said.

"No, we're not out of the game until we are all dead."

She nodded, her expression grim.

If she was Coldi, I might have said *Iyamichu ata*, but she wasn't, so I didn't. But it was the type of situation where Coldi would say that.

So I said, "We'll fight in the best way I know to fight, and that is to join forces and ally ourselves with groups that have the same aim, even if only on this same subject. I'd be willing to speak with the Atlantian forces who brought down the first drones, and with those who feel that they need to hold out against Patterson. I'm going to be calling in representatives from the Asto military and also the Pretoria Cartel."

"The Pretoria Cartel? Are you serious?"

"Dead serious. They are a member of the Tamer Collective, who have resources we can use. Minke Kluysters is not allied with these Independence Force people at all. He wants to sell stuff and wants to use the new Tamer Collective Exchange to do that. Right now, he can't sell if the Athens Exchange remains closed. He wants to further the fortunes of Africa. As I see it, the Independence Force has already carried out attacks on Africa, because countries like Ethiopia and Sudan are full of Zhori clan people and those people have set up businesses—some of them illegal, but businesses nevertheless—that bring life back to these ravaged lands. None of Nations of Earth *or* anyone else ever did that. That's solidly Pretoria Cartel and Tamer Collective territory."

She interjected, "And PanAf. They're part of Nations of Earth."

"In name only. I don't think too many people at Nations of Earth care too much about what happens south of the Mediterranean. And the Independence Force people are even worse."

She nodded. "Most of Africa is already dead to them. Believe me, I have seen their grandiose plans, which include building floating islands where the right kind of people can live blissfully glamorous lives, unburdened with such things as a refugee crisis of desperately poor people no one cares about, and annoying aliens."

With a chill, I thought back to my youth at Midway Space Station, at Arcadia, and New Taurus where this new young idealistic frontier feeling was just what described the society. Where people who were my friends, like the *gamra* observers to the settlements, were very much out of place and unwanted.

"Oh, those communities are really suffused with this kind of crap, aren't they?"

She nodded, looking at the darkness outside the window. "Part of my family's heritage is Malaysian, and I grew up hearing the stories. We were fortunate because my parents had access to good education. But my husband... he was from Senegal. He worked himself up into the Nations of Earth security forces. As a fifteen-year-old, he went to the camps, he rode the illegal boats across the Mediterranean, he was shot at, sprayed with poison—that's what killed him, years later, the cancer he got from the poison. He was an *angry* man, and he never stopped fighting."

"I'm sorry."

She shrugged in a *don't be* kind of way.

After a silence, I continued, "Anyway, I was going to get all the interested parties together to coordinate our knowledge about the enemy. Nations of Earth representatives, the leadership of the Asto military, Minke Kluysters, PanAf, because they're great at surface-based warfare. We'd be signing some sort of agreement that would hold us to a standard that satisfies the principles of *gamra* and basic human principles of decency and respect."

"I'm guessing you want me to be there?"

"If you could, yes, that would be great."

"It will depend on where it is. Obviously, there are parts of the world where it's going to be a bit of a logistical nightmare for me to attend in person."

"I'm pretty sure that the location I have in mind is freely accessible to anyone."

"Then let me know, and I will make sure I am there in one way or another, if not in person, then remotely."

I opened my bread roll and started eating, before I fainted from hunger. We had a lot of work to do.

CHAPTER TWENTY-THREE

FIRST, of course, I needed to communicate with *gamra*. Thankfully, Marin Federza was not as unreasonable as his manners suggested. He said that he could delay the subject of Asto's military in Earth orbit due to a technicality. This sort of bureaucratic crap usually annoyed the shit out of me. I knew it was part of the bureaucratic chess game and people used "procedural delays" to wear out, intimidate or distract the other party. In this case, it bought us a few valuable days.

I couldn't believe anyone at *gamra* wanted to see Asto put under so much pressure that they would lash out, never mind they also disliked the stranglehold Asto had over the assembly.

A few days, Federza said, no more. The assembly was sitting, and this needed to be on the agenda before the delegates took a study break. I calculated the time we had as best as I could. I thought it gave us an extra five days of Earth time, although time through the Exchange was a surprisingly rubbery concept.

I spoke to Ezhya. He was very blunt, even more so than usual. He said he was tired of Nations of Earth and if I judged that the current leaders were compromised, he would be happy to meet any people who didn't consider themselves part of the establishment to talk, but that he wasn't going to hang around and play softly for much longer. These Independence Force people were a threat to all of *gamra* and he wanted them gone.

I tried to explain how much they were integrated with Nations of

Earth, but to be honest, I don't know that he ever understood the principles of Nations of Earth, and he was much more worried about risks to his own people. If he placed Asto in the way of a significant threat, the threat may well come after Asto. After dealing with the Aghyrian ship and ceding control of Tamer to the Tamer Collective, he was not in the mood for compromises, especially not with people in possession of significant technology that we didn't yet fully understand. Where did all those drones come from and why had we observed the initial attack craft coming from the outer solar system while most of the enemy cells were on Earth? He wanted answers to those questions. Any of my attempts to explain that much of the problem came from Earth, caused him to reply with, *Just shut them up.* If not with words, then with weapons. Like we'd done with MacArthur. He very much approved of that.

It was up to me to do the talking and get people together.

If we couldn't do that, he said he'd send in the military sling to deal with the problem and keep it there for as long as these attacks kept happening.

I'd seen the power of the military sling and was sure I didn't want to see it used on the places where I'd spent my youth. It might well result in all the things we'd been talking about for centuries, like nuclear winter and dystopia.

I also said to him that he might use the sling, but unless we could locate where the attacks originated and where the home base of this group was, it would only be a temporary solution.

I was afraid that didn't improve his mood.

Every time I thought I knew Ezhya, I found another perplexing corner of him.

If he was as much of an iron-fisted ruler as people wanted to point out that he was, why did I get the feeling that he felt under pressure from people in Athyl who had gotten wind of this violent invading force to do something about it?

Yes, if I really wanted it, he'd be at a meeting, but it had better be relevant.

Boy, he was cranky.

I also spoke with Asha, and to be honest, that was a relief. He was, as usual, very practical. He didn't dwell on failures and didn't appear to get angry about them, either. My experience was that his temper could be short, but only with people who stood in the way of reason.

He reported that his intelligence people had gleaned information about the drones and he was sure they could do a better job in preventing an attack next time.

Their communication was secure, encrypted and backwards-encrypted, whatever that meant. The military satellites were operational. He gave me codes to use these for non-military communication.

The first thing I did with the codes was contact my father.

It was dinner time in New Zealand, and his answering the call—on the reader I'd given him years ago—was accompanied by the chatter and laughter of children and the barking of a dog. Good old Fred.

Emi was fine, and asking about us. She had been adding words to her babbling vocabulary, and made sure that people around her heard those words.

I told him that we planned to come, and that it wouldn't be a holiday.

I wanted to hire the town hall, the little rectangular shoebox at the beachfront where the town would hold craft fairs of crocheted blankets made out of camel hair and markets to sell locally grown vegetables and stuff like that. I wanted people with boats for hire, and people who could provide accommodation. I needed certain protocols inserted into the town's communication hub. I needed someone from town who knew what they were doing to send Reida a dump of all the recent travel and communication data. My father, having been a station director, didn't miss a beat.

He said he'd get all that sorted.

And then he said, "You know, I've not told anyone about this recently, and you might have been too young to remember, but when we were at Midway and there was the kerfuffle about the group who wanted to make off with one of our ships, I'd been monitoring the staff for a while. When I left, I took all the data I got, because I expected to be slapped with legal action in the future. That never happened, but I still have that data. Do you think you could use it?"

Hell, yeah.

So he said he'd send me the material later.

Reida sent messages to his army of workers and got several progress reports back. He hoped to be able to look at them soon.

I then sent a message to Minke Kluysters asking for him to be involved.

I was still apprehensive about this. He was such a skilled smooth-talker that if you got too close to him, he was likely to draw you in with feelings of sympathy.

These days, he was all about putting forward the cause of Africa. There was no denying that scandalous things had happened to Africa and African people, and he was using the fact that decent people at Nations of Earth felt terrible when faced with reports about these events.

To gain sympathy for poor forgotten Africa.

To further his own cause.

The Pretoria Cartel would do business with anyone, as long as there was money to be made. They didn't care terribly much about background and ideology, as long as there was something to sell. And over the past years, I had come to understand that the reason the Cartel had been against Earth joining *gamra* was about rules that would apply to their exports. It wasn't about the people. Also, the Pretoria Cartel was fundamentally uninterested in getting involved in war. Wars were expensive, unpopular and required strong ideology. They didn't have any.

For some reason, while I psyched myself up to resist being manipulated by this man, I thought about the trophy room in his house, where he had taken me and shown me the photos of his showjumping and the Olympic medal he had won. This was a man who would not take no for an answer.

Minke Kluysters had begged me for a meeting with Ezhya for years. I had tried to fob him off, but now I used this meeting to lure him into committing to come to the gathering I was planning.

If I could pull this off, this was going to be one hell of a strange meeting. It would be the last chance to defeat this enemy, which had its claws all over Nations of Earth.

"It's Dekker's fault," Minke Kluysters said. "The idiot never wanted to talk to people who could sway things."

"Dekker is a victim. He contacted me for help. I hope he'll be there."

"If he is, I will have a few things to say to him." His potato-in-mouth South African accent made the statement sound threatening.

Say a few words to Dekker?

Didn't we all want to do that?

I asked him about resources he could bring.

No, don't worry about PanAf, he said, they'll be there. They commanded a sizeable fleet of gyrocopters to help mop up messes and *get the idiots out of places they shouldn't occupy.*

Phew.

I was glad he wasn't going to argue with me.

I then sent off some additional messages to people, notifying them of the impending meeting and giving them the opportunity to respond. Margarethe Ollund, Joyelin Akhtari, Sigobert Danziger, although I'd heard he was very frail these days.

After I finished all those tasks, I found some time to rest. I didn't want to go a second night without proper sleep. If, at the end of this flight, we had to fight to defend ourselves, that would not end well.

Thayu was asleep on the floor at the back of the cabin.

I lay down next to her, using my jacket as mattress, but the floor was still uncomfortable. Even if she was asleep, Thayu rolled over and draped a warm arm over me.

For a brief moment, and for as long as my poor back tolerated the hard floor, I slipped into a world of bliss. Strangely enough, the last thought I had before nodding off was whether, when I accepted suggestions to go through the spy academy in Athyl, I would be doing much sleeping in uncomfortable places.

It seemed less than five minutes later when the craft landed on the water with a lot of bumping and splashing that sounded like it was happening right inside the cabin. We were in the tail end of the craft and evidently, the cargo hold and battery didn't extend that far underneath the craft.

The members of my team were up and sitting in a circle around Reida with his reader. It was still dark, and the light lit their faces from below.

Thayu smiled at me, but they were so deep in discussion that I didn't want to disturb them, so I grabbed some tea and an energy bar and looked out the window.

Distant lights blinked on the horizon. I decided that at least some belonged to boats, and the glow in the distance would be the shore.

The meeting was finished, and the members of my team dispersed, some to collect their gear, others also poured some tea.

In the middle of all this, Gracelyn Sebaya entered the cabin and went first to the drink dispenser.

The craft slowed down.

A crew member opened the door, letting fresh air and salty spray into the cabin.

A moment later, the sound of voices drifted in, accompanied by the thudding of footsteps on the wing. Asha's guards came forward, all dressed in black, wearing armour and with their weapons ready.

Through the open door, I caught glimpses of another craft—someone standing on a wing holding a rope.

A voice yelled out in Coldi.

"This is as far as we can take you," Gracelyn Sebaya said, clutching an anti-spill cup. "We're still inside international waters. The other craft is here illegally, but they'll take you the rest of the way. Good luck."

"Thank you for your help, and we'll hopefully see each other soon."

I followed Telaris out the door and into the weather. A stiff breeze whipped salty spray into my face.

The other craft was an Asto-made vehicle. It used the reduced-visibility current running through the surface, but as I'd seen previously, this didn't work well when half of the craft touched water, and the resulting effect was that some parts of the craft—the open door, the wing and bottom half of the main fuselage—were visible, while the top half shimmered in and out of visibility like a malfunctioning projection device.

A straight-faced Coldi military person—a woman, I thought—stood on the wing, supervising all of us stumble over the bobbing flexible walkway. I was one of the last people across, and she pulled the construction loose after Evi had crossed.

She tossed it back in the direction of the Nations of Earth ship. A voice shouted, "All clear," in the dark.

I'd never seen any military of the two entities work this closely together.

Gracelyn Sebaya had come to the door of the other craft.

I waved to her before descending into the Asto-made vehicle, embracing the familiar smell, the adequate lighting level and familiar faces.

Amarru.

Heavens, Veyada.

I dropped into the seat next to him.

"What are you doing here?"

"Your father was happy to look after the children," he said. "He was anxious when we didn't hear from you. You made a bit of a mess."

"You can say that again, but I don't know how much of it came out in the worldwide news."

"Not that much, and that worried me as well. I could tell something had happened, but it was hard to find out what."

While the crew shut the door and the craft took to the air, Amarru explained that when they had received a request for help from Nations of Earth, they had figured something was up.

I told them what had happened to us since we parted in Athens.

Veyada and Amarru were surprised to hear how compromised the office of the President was. Three months ago, we had tried for weeks to identify the origin and veracity of Dekker's message, but it seemed just as I felt, he had fled, and contacted me as a last resort. That had been my first suspicion, later overtaken with other suspicions, but when hearing his voice three months ago, that was my first thought.

At the time, it made little sense, but it made a lot of sense now.

As to how these Independence Force people had been able to infiltrate the assembly, that was another question. To be honest, I suspected the sympathisers had always been there. I knew that there was always an element in Nations of Earth that wanted all these nasty aliens to just go away so that everyone could return to the good times.

Even Eva's father had been taken in with it, although I didn't think he would go as far as MacArthur had when the opportunity to act presented itself.

I liked to think that Piotr Zbrowksi still retained that level of integrity.

I wondered where Eva's parents were, but suspected that, like most other delegates, they had returned to their home country. Postings at Nations of Earth were always temporary, and delegates expected to return to cushy jobs in their home countries.

They'd be in Poland, for sure.

I ended with, "So, anything that's happening at Nations of Earth is out of our control. We can trust Gracelyn Sebaya, but we shouldn't trust anything anyone else says. Any data they have given us in the past was probably given with the intention of deceiving us. MacArthur was in power for most of three months, and he could have done untold damage in that time. We don't know what he passed on to the enemy. We need to work as hard as we can to make an agreement to make sure that Asha sees no need to come and unleash a total war on the planet."

The rest of the team joined us. We then spoke about the locality where Dekker was hiding. This was in a sparsely populated area along the coast. The locality was a holiday house set on the edge of a woodland that surrounded an inlet. A forest formed the boundary of one side of the grounds, and a rocky ocean shore with a shallow inlet on the other side. A river led into the inlet and it also cut across a small town.

The suspicion was that the house belonged to a top government official in America Free State. The owner might even be Patterson himself.

Sheydu spoke about the practicalities.

The craft would land on the water and approach the coast as much as possible. The river would be best for this, because there was a marina upstream and recreational boats used it a lot. No one would question the presence of an extra boat.

To my question whether we would fall foul of airspace regulations, the pilot said that we wouldn't go that high.

The craft would drop us at a spot from where we could cut across a bit of woodland and a few streets to the back of the property. There were fences, and there might be security cameras, and there were also likely to be dogs.

Deyu and Ynggi glanced at each other, because they were the experts on all dog-related things.

Once we'd broken through the fence, there was a large sprawling house on the hill that overlooked the bay.

It also looked out over the main entrance to the property, which included a guard house that was likely to be occupied by at least some people sympathetic to the enemy. We were to keep out of view of those.

According to Reida's data, Dekker's presence had been recorded three times in a room in the guest wing of the house.

The aim was—Sheydu said—to avoid armed altercations, and leave the property in the same place we'd entered, where then the craft would pick us up at the same spot and we'd be gone before anyone realised what had happened.

A lot of the expedition hinged on electronics. Shielding, encryption, whatever. Reida, Isharu, Sheydu and Ynggi, and two of Asha's guards went into a frenzy setting up devices and distributing them to us.

The ship landed on the water and motored over the surface like a boat. The pilot turned off all lights inside the craft and out.

The lights on the shore came closer and then appeared on both sides of the craft as—according to Reida's map—we travelled up the river mouth.

After a while, we slowed down so much that we were going at a walking pace. Then the engine cut out, and the craft drifted to the river bank.

A crew member opened the door to the cabin, letting in cool humid air.

We all scrambled out into the darkness onto the craft's wing and from there made our way across the wobbly inflatable walkway to a jetty. A walking path lit by the occasional lamp wound along the grassy riverbank, now deserted in the pre-dawn. We waited there until everyone had come out. This was a spearhead party, consisting of just myself and my association. Asha's guards would stay on board the ship, ready to pick us up and assist if things went off the rails.

When Evi, the last of our group, was on the bank, the door to the craft shut and the pilot let the craft drift down the river before engaging the engine and steering it out to sea.

We turned into the forest.

From now on, we were on our own.

CHAPTER TWENTY-FOUR

WE ALL TOOK off through the forest in single file. I was following the broad back of Deyu, and Thayu followed me.

The path was paved, like a well-maintained walking or bike track. The forest turned out to be not as big and dark as it had looked. It was more like a recreation park. On the other side, we reached a quiet road. A couple of modern vehicles sat around a charging hub. The roof of a sleepy suburb poked out from well-established, leafy gardens. Huge trees cast dark shadows that made it hard to see with my night-blind eyes.

Thayu behind me had the same problem. I knew there would be a road edge, but I forgot to warn her and she tripped and almost fell.

We followed Deyu as we ran in a line through a pedestrian or bike path between two houses, then through another bit of parkland with a playground, and after we crossed through a patch of bushes, we reached a tall fence with barbed wire on top. Two security cameras sat atop long poles inside the grounds.

The land on the other side of the fence sloped up. From Sheydu's briefing, I knew there was a sprawling residence up there, but I couldn't see it.

The area had been cleared of trees, and light from a distant lamp cast long shadows over the grass.

Reida put his pack in the grass, which was wet from the dew. He unclipped his weapon from the arm bracket, slapped a small device to the side of the barrel, aimed at the closest camera and fired.

The charge gun went off with a small *zoom*. He did the same with the camera on the other side. Then he took the device back off, dropped it in his pack, and put the pack back on his shoulders.

Isharu had dialled her weapon down to the laser setting and cut a neat hole in the fence.

Deyu rolled up the fence and held it open to let us through.

When we were on the other side, Deyu rolled the fence back so that it was hard to see where the opening was without coming close.

While we stood there, the tall grass rustled, and a dark shape rushed towards us.

"Careful, dog!" I hissed, trying not to shout but hoping my team could hear me.

The animal came to a screeching halt, followed by a second one and a third one.

One of them growled a low rumble.

Not friendly at all.

They were powerful tall dogs, their ears pointed up and their coats dark and sleek.

Ynggi faced the animals, his knife glittering in the moonlight. He could overwhelm one dog, but I doubted he could tackle three of them almost his size. His tail waved above his head.

The dogs watched. They did not have tails, only short stumps on their backsides.

Sheydu had taken her weapon out of its arm bracket.

So we stood for a while. Ynggi in front, facing the dogs, Sheydu with her gun ready. Ynggi flicked the tip of his tail from side to side. The dogs watched intently. Every now and then, one grumbled.

Sheydu made an impatient gesture. *Hurry up.*

Ynggi stepped forward. He waved his tail high in the air. Two of the dogs grumbled and retreated. The third one remained. It barked, once, and its whole body shook with the barking.

"Look at how skinny these animals are," Deyu said. "You can see their ribs."

I had to admit I was looking at the other end, but yes, I agreed with her.

Deyu dug in her pocket. She pulled out something that she unwrapped and ripped. She held it out.

The dog stretched out its neck without coming closer. One of the other two animals abandoned its position and joined its fellow.

"Give that," Ynggi said.

Deyu handed the package to him, and Ynggi unwrapped the parcel further, while all three dogs now came forward. Two of them were wagging their stumps. Ynggi broke the content of the parcel in three pieces and handed them out to each dog. He was still waving his tail. Pengali tails were much longer and more solid than dog tails, especially because he wore the tail sleeve that was part of his body armour.

But the dogs responded to him. The morsels were gone in seconds, but each of the animals sat down.

"These animals have been neglected," Deyu said.

One of the dogs nosed Deyu's pockets for more. Deyu patted its back and sides. "The hair is full of sticky seeds."

Deyu took another packet out of her pocket and divided it between the three animals. One even sat neatly on its haunches waiting for her to dole out the pieces. These were trained animals.

"Aren't these supposed to be guard dogs?" I asked.

Ynggi said, "If people want the animals to do something, they should feed them better."

I knew little about dogs, but I was fairly certain that highly trained dogs would not let themselves be bribed so easily. So what did that mean? Nobody was expecting people to break in?

With the danger averted, Sheydu stuck her gun back in her belt. "Let's go."

Reida went first because he had studied the layout of the place. The dogs kept close to Deyu and Ynggi.

We walked across a grassy area to the cover of a shed. From the front of the shed, in the shadow of the awning and next to a mowing machine, we had a view to the other side of the ridge. This included the bay and the rocky point. The water was quite calm and reflected the light of a fat-crescent moon. It was an hour or so before dawn, and there was no light in the main building, a low sprawling house that stood at the top of the hill to our left.

I couldn't see a sign of the gatehouse that was supposed to be at the bottom of the hill at the entrance of the property, nor of any vehicles.

We made our way across the terrain, moving from tree shadow to tree shadow while trying to keep under cover. It was sometimes hard to see where I put my feet, and I had to make sure not to trip.

The dogs followed us, still quiet and curious, and keen for more food.

At some point, these animals might cause an issue.

The night was still and peaceful.

We reached the immediate surrounding of the house. There was a rose garden at the front. The faint scent of roses hung in the air, a homely smell that reminded me of my grandfather.

Thayu checked the veranda for bugs and, finding none, we followed her in the shadow of the overhang.

We walked past several windows, and at each, we stopped. Reida scanned through the glass, looking for any inhabitants, and then continued on.

After we had checked three windows, Reida pointed at the next one.

He gestured.

That one.

Reida took one more scan, and pointed at the room.

Mereeni grabbed her weapon and carefully opened the veranda door. She went inside, but came back a moment later. "There's no one here. It's just a sitting room with some tables and chairs."

One of the dogs let out a low rumble.

"Shhh," Deyu said. She pointed at the ground and the dog sat down. One dog came to stick a wet nose in my pocket.

I had no idea where Deyu got this ability to handle otherwise dangerous animals. It couldn't be just the food. These types of dogs could be vicious. Even if they were not highly trained, it was unlikely that they would just follow us like little ducklings. It had to do with Ynggi and his tail.

Reida stopped again and pointed at another room. It only had a window, and blinds covered the inside.

Reida moved the scanner while studying his screen. He gestured *Yes.* Sheydu pushed the fly screen that covered the window. It didn't budge.

Reida grabbed a sticky pad while Sheydu used the laser setting on her gun to cut through first the insect screen and then the window.

He lifted out the glass and put it carefully on the ground without making a single noise. Then Thayu and Mereeni jumped in through the hole she made and disappeared in between the curtains.

They were sounds of a scuffle inside the room. A male voice protested, but was cut off.

One of the dogs whined, but Deyu said, "Shhhh."

A moment later, the curtain moved, and the two women came out with a third person, with a cloth over his mouth and his hands bound to his sides.

Sheydu and Telaris lifted him out.

The feeble light of a street lamp showed that it was Simon Dekker. Thin, lanky, with short-cropped grey hair and dark skin. His eyes widened. He wore a loose tracksuit that was too big for him, and old sneakers.

He blinked against the light Evi shone into his face to confirm we had the right person.

We did.

Like this, there was nothing important or presidential about him. He looked like a frightened rabbit in a spotlight.

"Is this him?" Sheydu asked.

"It is," I said, and I continued in Isla, "Mr President, can you confirm that you're prepared to go with us if we can take you to safety?"

His eyes widened as he recognised me. At least I thought he recognised me, because it was really still too dark to tell.

Sheydu let go of the cloth around his mouth.

"There is no safety." His voice sounded hoarse. "There is only endless running, only to find that your destination has been compromised."

"Not *our* destination."

He shook his head. "I have been in this hell for weeks. I've had too much hope." He looked tired and old.

"Come. You asked us for help, and here we are. We'll take you out. Do you have anything to bring?"

"There is a small bag in the cupboard," he said.

I climbed over the windowsill into the room, and looked around, using the light on my reader.

The room was quite large and contained a bed, two cane chairs with cushions, a desk, and a cupboard. The door into the hallway was closed. I tried the handle. It wouldn't open.

I found the bag in the bottom of the cupboard. There were soft items inside, probably clothes. Was there more? A fluffy dressing gown hung in the cupboard, but I doubted Dekker had taken it.

I needed to make sure we got all his electronic equipment.

But there was none on the desk, and in fact, the room didn't even seem to have a power connection.

There did seem to be some hard items in the bottom of the bag. I put my hand in. My fingers met the smooth casing of a reader. I pulled it out. A second hard object was the cradle of the charging dock.

A notebook lay open on the desk, with an old-fashioned pen in the fold between the pages.

Dekker had written notes in barely legible spindly handwriting.

I closed the book and put it in the bag.

I checked the drawers of the desk, but they were empty.

On second thoughts, I went back to the cupboard and collected the dressing gown and stuffed it in the bag. Then I looked on the bedside table and under the bed, but found nothing else I needed to take.

I handed the bag to my team outside before climbing back out.

In the time I'd been inside, a light had come on in the gatehouse at the bottom of the road. The sky was also getting alarmingly lighter over the ocean. I could see the road that ran along the ocean shore and ended at the gatehouse. The rocky point held a viewing tower or disused lighthouse.

The forms of Evi, Telaris and I thought Nicha were silhouetted against the light.

"There he is. Let's get out of here," Sheydu said. She sounded nervous.

We took off around the side of the house, but ran into Deyu and Mereeni around the corner, who held us back.

Mereeni said, "Someone is out there."

There was, too. The headlights of a vehicle lit sections of grass.

"That's the caretaker," came Dekker's voice from somewhere in the distance.

"Is he likely to be armed?" I asked.

"In this country, everyone is armed."

"But dangerous?"

"He works for Patterson, if that's what you're asking. He's a mean bastard."

Best not to risk it. And also, Dekker would have quite a story to tell once we got out of here.

Reida knelt on the ground, next to Deyu with the hub. I could see text scrolling over his screen.

"All right, change of plan," he said, his voice low. "People have discovered the hole in the fence. Also, the dogs are gone."

"They ran off while you were inside," Ynggi said.

So, we'd been discovered.

"We're going down to the beach," Reida said. "The pilot says they can come up close, and the people guarding this place will expect us to go back into the forest. But they'll come to the house soon."

"The house is empty and has been for a long time," Dekker said. "This is Patterson's beach residence, but he hasn't been welcome in Atlantia for a few years now, ever since this mess started."

A few of my team gathered around Reida and his map. They spoke in low voices about how to get to the beach. Reida said his data wasn't detailed enough to tell him whether there were any fences, but it would be safe to assume that there were some.

Evi shouldered his rocket launcher.

"Come, follow as close as you can behind us," Telaris said.

They set off along the edge of the lawn.

Deyu accompanied both of them, then Reida and we followed behind. I kept an eye on Dekker, both because he was the oldest of all of us, but also I wanted to make sure he didn't do anything that would bring attention to us. I *thought* he was happy to get out, but exactly what he'd been doing here would need to be discussed once we were safe.

Dekker's earlier words about the house being empty rang true. The grass was short but full of thistles and uneven clumps. We crossed a path almost hidden by leaves.

As we came closer to the beach, I became aware of a foul smell, like a cloth that had been sitting in water for too long.

We stopped at the high water mark. I presumed the beach was normally sandy, but it was now covered in a thick mat of rotting vegetation. I could see it in the glow of Sheydu's light.

Long, blackened strands of what looked like algae, all stuck together into a hard mat.

Reida put his foot on it. The dried vegetation held his weight.

But the smell was something different altogether.

"Oh God, this stink is insufferable," Dekker muttered behind me. "I thought it was bad up at the house."

"Be quiet!" Sheydu said in Coldi.

I doubted Dekker understood what she said, but her tone was clear enough.

There were signs of activity at the end of the beach, where we could just see the roof of the gatehouse poke over the top of a row of bushes.

Voices. The sound of a vehicle. An alarm going off.

"The guards are onto us," Dekker said. "If you have a way of escape, use it now."

At that moment, an aircraft rose over the tops of the rocks at the tip of the inlet, glinting in the dawn light.

It was an Asto-built craft and would belong to the military. Not the one that we had flown on.

The invisibility current that allowed the ship to be near-invisible took engine power, so the pilot had switched off that capability, but the effects of it still lingered in the glimmers that edged the wings.

This was an attack craft belonging to the giant fleet I had seen in the shuttle bays at the military ship.

The craft barely cleared the tops of the rocks, glided over the beach and splashed in the water. Then it engaged the reverse thrust engines with a roar. No way those were going to keep quiet.

Several floodlights came on at the gatehouse.

People shouted.

Dogs barked.

"Quick!" Sheydu shouted.

The craft drifted across the inlet.

Sheydu ran across the algae mat and the others followed behind. I ran after Deyu.

In the middle of the frantic scramble for the water's edge, my right foot cracked through the hardened layer and slid up to my ankle into a slippery mush underneath. I just managed to stay upright and warn Thayu behind me.

But my shoe was covered in muck and I could feel the water seep into my socks.

Ew.

The first of our group had reached the water's edge. The craft had floated much closer and had turned the concealing current back on, which made most of the craft hard to see, but produced a weird effect where the metal touched the water.

Someone had opened a door, which made a brightly-lit rectangle that floated in the air like a portal to paradise.

A silhouetted person stood in the doorway, shouting to Sheydu on the beach.

Sheydu waded into the water. Someone tall and broad followed. Evi, I thought.

They grabbed the craft's wing and pulled it closer.

"Quick! Get in!" Sheydu called.

We all had to wade through the water, which came to just above the knee. Deyu balanced her communication hub on top of her head. The person at the door helped everyone in.

The water was lukewarm and walking through it brought up a disgusting wet sock smell. When the crew member pulled me up into the cabin, threads of vile green algae covered the bottom half of my legs. The others were no less dirty. Reida had stepped in a deeper patch.

The pilot shouted over her shoulder, "Hurry up! Get in your seats!"

The last of the group clambered into the open door. Ynggi, Nicha. Thayu already sat next to me. Sheydu was the last, and she pulled the door shut behind her.

She dropped into the nearest seat, completely wet and covered in algae.

Through the window in the side of the craft, I could see bobbing lights on the shore.

People were running in our direction.

The engines roared. The craft shot forward. The force pushed me into my seat. Next to me, Thayu was still doing up her safety belt.

For the next couple of minutes, the craft climbed so steeply that speaking or moving around was impossible.

In a sliver between the row of seats in front, I had a view of the pilot's controls. There were other craft in the area. I could see that from being familiar with the display.

Not long after, the craft evened out. I heaved a sigh of relief. That was one part of the plan completed.

"Huh, it seems you can actually do what you promise," Dekker said.

"I don't promise anything unless I have a decent chance of delivering it, regardless of whether or not I'm dealing with thugs."

He gave me a pointed look. Oh, he had an elephant's memory.

CHAPTER TWENTY-FIVE

WHEN IT WAS safe to do so, Sheydu got out of her seat. She took off her jacket and shoes and then her trousers.

The pale skin on her upper and lower legs was red with angry welts.

"Sheydu, what did you do to your legs?" Reida asked.

"I don't know, but it's uncomfortable. Do we have something for this?"

Mereeni dropped to her knees. "That looks horrible. Does it hurt?"

"It itches like mad."

"Did you spill something over yourself?"

"No. I just walked through the water."

"I think it's the slimy stuff in the water," I said. Something about contamination with algae stirred in the back of my mind. There was a small lagoon out the back of my father's farm that would go green with foamy algae that smelled bad and made your skin itch. But I'd never seen it this bad.

I took off my very wet shoes and found that my skin, too, had gone red with little raised lumps. Now that I thought about it, it did feel itchy. I'd just had so many other things to worry about.

Nicha lifted his trouser legs and his lumps had progressed into thousands of little blisters. "Well, damn."

Almost everyone's skin had a red rash where the water had

touched it. Now I fully understood why the house had been abandoned as a holiday destination.

Mereeni produced a bottle of lotion, which she used to wet a packet of little towels. She gave us each one to wipe the skin. Except Sheydu got two because she was by far the worst affected. I tried not to notice how she winced when putting the towel against her leg.

She was trying very hard not to show her discomfort, but to those who knew her, it was obvious that she was very unhappy. Ironically, Dekker had suffered the least because people had carried him part of the way.

My team was exhausted.

They didn't say this, but I could tell. And we weren't done yet. We had a long way still to go, and we would need to do more clambering from one craft to another. This craft was a fighter, not a transport vehicle and much too small for us for a long distance.

The pilot turned in a sharp circle over the ocean that glittered in the moonlight. I couldn't see any sign of life down there.

You could land Asto-built craft on the water, but it required a lot of skill. They were nowhere near as stable and manoeuvrable as my own craft.

But the military pilots all had excellent skills. We touched down on the surface not much later. It was not until we had turned around and motored along for a while that I could see another ship, dark and menacing, floating on the surface of the ocean.

When we got close, one of the crew members opened the door. He stepped into the dark, where I could hear voices.

"All secure," he called into the cabin a moment later.

I desperately didn't feel like getting up, but we had to.

We had to balance over both wings to get to the second, larger craft, which was the same one that had taken us here.

The waves washed over the wings and my shoes were still wet from the last time, and probably contained residue of algae. My skin burned like fire. I could only imagine what Sheydu must feel like.

I shivered.

Inside the cabin waited Veyada and Amarru, handing out blankets to us.

We found places in our seats and strapped in.

"Where are we going?" Dekker asked. I noticed his face looked weary, with bags under his eyes and deep creases in his skin.

"Somewhere safe," I said.

And because I figured I sounded terse, I added, "I'm going to bring together everyone who can help us defend Earth. We're meeting in a safe locality that's out of the way and that we can protect."

He nodded and gratefully accepted the cup Veyada held out to him.

The crew pushed the two craft apart. Veyada told me that the fighter craft would return to orbit.

The pilot engaged the primary engine, making it too noisy to continue talking. I sat in my seat as the craft gathered speed over the waves and then disengaged from the water. We climbed straight up into the air.

By the time the craft evened out, Nicha had procured some food, which he was handing out. I was starving. The encounter with the algae and the rash on my legs made me feel feverish. I glanced at Sheydu, who was much worse off than I was. She was eating, but her face looked pale and she kept rubbing her legs.

She gestured *I'll be fine* when she noticed me looking at her.

"Just make sure you get some rest," I said.

She didn't protest, and with Sheydu, that was probably a sign of how worn out she was.

We'd been on the road constantly since leaving Athens, and the fight at Nations of Earth had probably taken more out of all of us than we wanted to admit. Sheydu was not the youngest.

Amarru looked after Dekker with food, dry clothing and blankets.

He looked more relaxed, although also haggard and tired. But I thought he looked grateful, and before I headed off to bed, I needed to speak to him.

So I pushed myself from my seat—oh damn, the rubbing of my trousers against my legs made me itchy—and kneeled on the floor next to Dekker's seat.

"You're recovering?" I asked.

"Yes. Thank you," Dekker said. "I'm sorry."

"No need to apologise."

"Yet, there is. I seem to recall that we've had certain run-ins in the past and I honestly thought that you'd ignored me as I probably deserved, but thank you. I mean it. My honest colleagues and family will thank you, too."

Was it just me, or did he have the slightest North American accent?

I had never noticed this before.

"I'm afraid contacting your family will be out of the question for a while."

"I understand. Jayde should be fairly safe. Sara is with him."

"Sara?"

"Our daughter." His mouth curved up. "She's twenty-eight and doesn't normally live with us, but thankfully, she decided she was better off at home than in Denver."

"At home, in Rotterdam?"

"At Jayde's apartment in New York."

"You have a lot of connections with Atlantia?"

"I do. Celia and I have been working towards repairing the broken relationships with Nations of Earth. But we've all been taken for a ride by Patterson, not that he ever had more than a passing interest. But unleashing this force on us…" He spread his hands.

"So he is behind the attacks?"

"Yes, and no. America Free State is a pretty ineffectual, hopeless kind of place. But as you rightly identified, it gave rise to some ultra-conservative, purist groups that also contained dedicated military personnel who made their way into the space program."

I completed the thought. "Who then went their own way? Let me guess. They failed to stop Nations of Earth taking full control of the program. They failed to take one of the few shuttles the program operated at that time to their secret locality, but they did misappropriate another shuttle and hid in deep space. They emerged occasionally to buy technology, mostly in places with poor rules and lax supervision, such as the Pengali lands to the south of Barresh. They cobbled together technology and developed some of their own. They tried and failed to create havoc in Barresh. But at that time, their unfolding probe was already underway with their grand aim to re-take Earth."

"Something like that. Patterson hasn't played a major role so far. His task appears to be to make it look like they're also victims, and also to destabilise Nations of Earth, which they have done over the past few years. They got many people into the assembly who were sympathetic to their cause, even if those people rarely realised that they were being used. Then you pulled off a victory for the referendum. They hadn't expected that, and it made them very angry."

And here I was, having thought that the Pretoria Cartel had been responsible for the near-defeat of the referendum.

"Why didn't you ask for help from us, or at least notify us what was going on?"

"I'm sure you would understand how bad that would have looked. We also didn't appreciate how precarious the situation was. Nobody saw the drone attacks coming."

"Not even Patterson?"

"He might have, but I still don't think he had any say in it. He just sees the opportunity to further his agenda."

"Which is: to get the evil aliens out."

"Something like that."

He met my eyes.

Even when I'd met him for the first time, he'd been much older than I was. His close-cropped hair was salt and pepper-grey and the rims of his dark irises were slightly cloudy. Heavens knew how he'd seen me at the time of our first meeting: *an arrogant upstart with questionable alliances* was a popular assessment of me back then. While I felt like the same person, a lot had changed since that time. People who would never give me any time were forced to take me seriously, or wanted to take me seriously, because I was the bridge to things they wanted. People like Minke Kluysters.

Well, damn it.

I thought Dekker and I came to that conclusion at the same time.

He nodded, leaning forward with his elbows on his knees.

Forced to take me seriously.

I was tempted to say, *Enough with the games*, but that would hardly be appropriate, at least not while we needed each other. He needed us, but we also needed him.

So I began, "Maybe we should start at the beginning. What was going on when you contacted me? Why was the communication cut off?"

"It's a long story that goes back months—years, even."

"We've got time. We've got a long way to travel."

"Where are we going?"

"Right now—somewhere it will be hard for people to track us."

"Into space?"

"The military is being shot at regularly. Would you join them?"

"I thought you said somewhere safe."

"There are safe places on Earth."

He glanced out the window. The sun had come up and cast an orange glow over the clouds underneath us.

Dekker started, "I don't even know where to begin. The resistance to the agenda that Margarethe Ollund had set for joining *gamra* was always there. It became stronger when her retirement from the presidency neared. I needed some of these people to form a stable bloc if I wanted to get any of our agenda through the assembly. I'm not sure what you know about the process."

"Quite a lot."

He told me how from the moment he took the position, certain groups of delegates demanded special concessions because Dekker needed their support. They wanted their supporters in key positions in important departments and agencies. They'd seen their opportunity to do this when Margarethe stepped down and a power vacuum emerged because a new president usually employed all new staff and the administration's grip on the situation loosened.

"The trouble first started out of a small group in America Free State," Dekker said. "But the free world movement existed when America Free State was formed. They existed during the Second Civil War. They've always existed in some form. Most of the time, they were embedded in our society and we didn't notice them."

"Such as Midway space station," I said.

His face grew dark. "Don Sullivan. He was one of their leaders."

Yes, I remembered him.

"They operated out of America Free State?"

"Most of the time, yes, especially after Midway, when their plans to take one of the shuttles to a secret location were discovered."

"I was there and involved in that."

"I have said before that you are a cocky, arrogant bastard."

"It's true. If I actually *was* a cocky, arrogant bastard, I wouldn't have missed, for all those years since the Midway Incident, that obviously these people didn't just go and behave nicely after their attempts came to nothing. They couldn't misappropriate a shuttle, so they built their own. They'd been building prototypes for years, and some of those had come to grief on various worlds. They'd attempted to set up groups against *gamra*, against Nations of Earth. It's been going on for a while."

He nodded. "For years."

"We travelled to America Free State especially to look for them," I said. "We couldn't find any recent trace of the organisation."

"How did you search?"

"We knew some of the research facilities where they had been building spaceships. Most of them are abandoned, and we spoke to locals and asked them if they knew what happened to the people who worked for these organisations. None of them knew. One of them even gave me a long list of people who went missing."

Dekker said, "Yeah. That was what they called the great leap. Many of them went into space."

It was as I had suspected. "But they said they knew nothing about any sympathisers remaining."

"Did you talk to the churches?"

I frowned at him. Were we meant to have talked to the churches? Of course, with our very Coldi sensibilities, we tended to ignore institutes of religion, because Coldi didn't like or understand religion and I was uncomfortable engaging with it for fear of upsetting old relationships made between churches and Nations of Earth, relationships and agreements that were between two groups on Earth and nothing to do with me or my work.

He met my eyes in a sage expression and nodded. "The churches. That's where you should have looked, especially those churches that were founded less than a century ago. Although I must stress that not all churches are involved, and some are involved, but not knowingly or willingly. But they preach the notion that all these aliens..." He looked around the craft a little self-consciously. "... Need to get out of here, and that we can manage space exploration and settlement just as well by ourselves."

"Is that something you believe?"

"To a point. But I am also willing to accept the reality that it's probably easier to just cooperate with the devil."

"So, I'm the devil."

"You work for the devil."

"Just so that we are level. I don't work for him. He is my business partner."

"Great. Two devils."

"We are also in contact with a few other devils, and I might as well point them out to you before we get started."

He gave me a wary glance.

"Anyway, the election was a tumultuous time. Fredrickson was a very good and popular candidate and when he had to withdraw and I had to carry the flag, I never thought I'd win. I was up against a really popular candidate who was outspoken and colourful, all the things I'm not. So I campaigned on a rational platform: being careful about what we signed. The conservative forces flocked around me. I consider myself only a moderate conservative."

I raised my eyebrows.

He continued, "That may surprise you, but it's true. Many people gathered around me who were far more conservative. In the end, I didn't win the election. The other party lost it. But having won, I needed to work with the people who had promised me allegiance. And that proved hard. We descended into a blazing argument about the rejoining of the American states. I didn't understand why the ultra-conservatives wanted to pick a fight about that. Celia Braddock is a long-standing friend and she and Governor Sukar of Prairie were very much for rejoining Nations of Earth. Sukar has been trying for years to revitalise his country's devastated agriculture industry. He'd make deals with Nations of Earth and *gamra*. But the ultra-conservatives wanted me to stop doing that. The arguments they used were ridiculous and made no sense. I often thought they *wanted* Nations of Earth to remain separate from the American states. When I continued talking to Braddock and Sukar, the conservatives sent people to talk to me, sometimes a couple. They were usually junior members or staff members of the assembly, so they could always come to me without profiling by security. I objected to the pressure or the bullying they were trying to apply to me and to the things they wanted me to do. Me breaking off contact with Braddock or Sukar wasn't in the pre-election agreements between me and the conservative factions, and I wasn't going to agree. The threats grew worse. Celia offered me a reason for a brief trip away as a circuit breaker. But when I got to New York, Celia was there to meet me, but soon it was obvious she hadn't come of her own volition and I was, in fact, under siege."

He sipped from his drink.

Dekker continued, "Once they got me, they took me to Patterson's beach house where you found me. I managed to get onto your people for a short moment before they shut the connection. After that, they tried to re-educate me, and when that didn't work, ignore me. But Yoon Ha had more guts than I gave him credit for. When Patterson's militia broke into the assembly, he wouldn't step aside, as they expected him to do. That's why he was killed."

"And the fact that this wasn't big news means that the killers are still in power?"

"You got it. MacArthur and his cronies."

Well, about that... "When we came here, we attempted to deal with Nations of Earth and came to Rotterdam first."

"God. You walked right into the trap."

"You can say that again. I thought you might still be there. I'm afraid we left a bit of a mess. It involves MacArthur."

His dark eyes met mine. "Is he dead?"

"As a doornail. Him and a bunch of his staff."

"Hmm. Anyway. That's no great loss. He's one of the moles, but unfortunately, I only realised that after you gave us the data connecting the old Southern Californian Aerospace Corps with the recent events and we passed it around the entire assembly."

"Including to the traitors."

"Yeah. We were perhaps naïve and misled. We had no sign that we should distrust a good chunk of the Emergency Council. The fact that many people distrusted 'aliens' and didn't believe you was not out of character. But all their pieces were in the right place and they played us like a fiddle. It's a mess and I'm not sure that we can get out the other end safely."

"I'm convinced that if we get everyone together, we can find a way. Where we're going, we are going to be talking to the Pretoria Cartel and the Tamer Collective. Most of these are devils and you can't trust them. This is where we stand. We want to defend our home, and we want to make sure that there is a planet left at the end of this, where everyone who abides the law can come and be fairly treated."

Just as I said this, I realised it would make Earth just about the only entire world where that could be said. Earth was going to be a powerhouse, just as Asto was a powerhouse. If only Nations of Earth would understand the importance of that position. On the other hand, I figured that one day they would have a president who understood, and would misuse every aspect of it. That was only a matter of time.

"All this brings me to the reason I came to Rotterdam. I need someone in authority to sign the next stage of the *gamra* agreement that spells out the right of *gamra* to defend member entities with military force."

"I know your visit is about that rule, and debating it got us into this trouble in the first place. I would need to study the document."

"It's part of the original agreement, signed two years ago."

He gave me a pointed look. "I was under the understanding that aspects of that document were in draft mode and subject to change."

"All *gamra* entities have signed the same document."

"Let me read it again. We can't rush this sort of thing. Trouble erupts when you try that. We tried and failed before."

I gave him the document, and also impressed upon him that the *gamra* deadline would soon expire, but he wouldn't be hurried.

Why did I still suspect he didn't want to sign this at all?

CHAPTER TWENTY-SIX

DEKKER FURTHER TOLD me other things about North American history I was not aware of, or was likely to have misunderstood, as he put it. I sensed that seeing this part of the world in a "proper" light was important to him.

He wanted me to understand that the split of the former United States into four semi-independent nations was because of differences in philosophy, and not because of riots and street protests. That the four nations were all upset with Nations of Earth for being excluded from membership. That Governor Patterson was privately prepared to talk about a truce with Nations of Earth because although America Free State was large, it was also mostly desert and had little export opportunities since agriculture was marginal at best, the tourism industry was non-existent and oil exploration ceased being profitable a long time ago, and trade boycotts had done the rest.

He was at pains to point out that Atlantia was by far the most progressive of the North American states, and that Prairie was so poor they'd go along with everything Atlantia did. Celia Braddock had tried for most of her career to bring all the states together to give a unified response to Nations of Earth.

"But he just doesn't want any public part in it." *He*, being governor Patterson, who had the temerity to call himself president, and Dekker pointed out that a strong line of thought was that there was only one president—and no, it wasn't Simon Dekker or Celia Braddock—but

President Alaina Sherbourg, whose deposing and later murder late last century had been the final trigger that started the Second Civil War and the irretrievable split of the North American states into four countries.

It was all stuff I'd heard about long ago in school and had, rightly or wrongly, banished to the part of my mind where quaint, Earth-based facts lived.

Dekker got really fired up. "Those interested in reconciliation in north America don't subsume the word president and he who does so seeks to impose his will over the other countries. They did not stand up for their fellow poor and outcast citizens to have to accept his bull-shit years later."

And I also thought about my travels to America Free State and wondered whether Dekker had been there recently and whether he or Celia Braddock knew who those poor and outcast citizens actually were. Because I'd met them. Sage and Junco both seemed decent men to me. They'd even continued sending me occasional messages. They didn't dwell on injustices and carried on with their lives. The militia we had grappled with, they probably considered themselves outcasts with an interest in maintaining the current state of outraged status quo.

But heads had rolled over arguments less contentious than this, and if I gave my opinion, Dekker would probably—rightly—shout me down.

I was no expert.

It mattered less to find someone to blame for their current misery than that we had at least one North American person who was happy to talk.

Dekker said that Celia Braddock had *always* been happy to talk to Nations of Earth, but "authoritarian" people like Margarethe Ollund imposed impossible conditions.

I did not question his characterisation of Margarethe, since we had also invited her to the upcoming meeting, and she indicated she might come. Let's see whether Dekker was up to facing that particular devil. Or Braddock, for that matter.

Because I wanted Braddock to attend. Probably not in person, but remotely.

Simon Dekker told me, "Patterson is a man with a deep sense of betrayal. Do or say something he doesn't like once, and he will forever consider you an enemy."

That was funny, coming out of his mouth. But I chose not to bring up the *nuke from orbit* incident.

The crew member brought us drinks and a packet of food, and I retreated to an alcove at the back of the craft to make notes and gather my thoughts.

I needed to catch some sleep, or I would fall over in the middle of a discussion.

But as I went into the back of the craft where the cabins were, Isharu came to see me.

"We got a response. We're still tracking the origin."

Whoa. Total change of subject.

She was talking about my mysterious stalker.

We went into one of the cabins, where she handed me the cheap reader. The screen said, *Your futile actions will all come to nothing. We can easily defeat your puppet army. Your arrogance won't help you this time.*

Just bluff. I'd have to craft another response aimed at keeping the mudslinging feast going so my team could continue its tracking.

But it was the first time that anyone from the enemy directly communicated with us in a meaningful way.

Isharu said that she and Reida had monitored the device at all times and picked up an incoming signal from a communications company called Fayu. I recognised the name as one of the major personal telecommunications services people used worldwide.

At the time of the referendum a few years back, the Exchange ordered an audit of all these companies for their trustworthiness, but I had to admit to not having taken much interest in the results.

"Are you investigating the company or asking for records?" I asked.

"Investigating, yes, but to get the records for this user, we need to convince the law enforcement authorities to ask for them. It might take a long time for them to respond, and you have to prove that the operator was acting outside the law."

Yeah, like that was going to happen. Plus, who knew how compromised those authorities would be?

Not like the Exchange where you could just ask for this data. Then again, the company was probably nothing more than a vehicle used by the person at the other end of the message. These large companies owned networks and satellites and drowned in their own bureaucracy.

Then another thought. "Technically, for them to have obtained my contact details is a breach of trust." Especially since I hadn't given out those details to anyone, let alone attached my name or identity to this device. How *had* they known that I owned it?

"Could be, if this is what they used." Her expression showed she was working hard to grasp the concept of "breach of trust", which I'd roughly translated as *breach of loyalty*, except I'd never held any loyalty ties with any of these people. So that confused the heck out of her.

Ah, the fun of dealing with different cultures.

It was a mystery that could probably be solved by following the message trail.

Whenever we'd have time to do that.

Not now anyway.

I wrote a snarky response and sent it while Reida and Isharu were scanning the device, and then left the thing with them. It knew where I was and posed a security risk.

Of course, this conversation between me and my mysterious stalker was bluff and bluster designed only for the purpose of creating messages for my team to track, but the last sentence of their response gave me pause.

The words *this time* suggested prior involvement.

I was never much good with the whole *going with your gut* advice. I didn't trust my judgement to be right unless backed up by additional data.

But somehow I couldn't escape the feeling that these messages came from someone I knew. Or at least someone I'd been involved with in the past. That included an incredible number of people and was a rather meaningless realisation. When I started in the job, I'd consider almost all of Nations of Earth hostile to *gamra*. Did I think that someone like Eva's father would support attacks like this? Of course not, but stranger things had happened.

Not Piotr Zbrowski, but Jarek Malicki, Eva's ex-husband. Yeah, he might do something like this.

After giving the device back, I found a quiet corner. Most other people in the team were also asleep.

Thayu came to sit with me.

Of course, she had been listening in on my conversation with Dekker, and wanted to voice her own opinions.

She said, "This world of yours has more dark corners than the Aghyrian political labyrinths."

Probably an apt comparison.

"As with the Aghyrian labyrinth and the Aghyrian situation, ignoring any of those corners can cost us dearly. We have ignored this North America part of the Earth population, written them off as a quaint old-fashioned minority, and they have developed into a formidable enemy who wants to see us gone."

"That's what enemies do in dark corners," she said. "They multiply. So, you can do two things: eradicate them, or negotiate them into backing down."

"It's the second I'm interested in." Also, because I was no longer sure we could do the first, since they'd spread to other parts of the galaxy, and because they possessed technology to replicate drones out of nothing and hide their point of origin so well that not even the Asto military could locate it. Those were technologies we would understand, given time, but we didn't have that time.

Thayu sniffed. "I would be much happier with the first. I know Ezhya and my father would, too."

I bet they would.

"I'm still going to try talking."

But negotiating required a position of relative strength in an area the enemy wanted. We were weak in the negotiating stakes and about to become weaker. They wanted nothing we were in a position to give them. They just wanted us to go away. Closing the Exchange was our capitulation in their view.

When *gamra* maintained their deadline for the Asto military to withdraw and they complied, we would have nothing. *Gamra* would score an own goal, from the enemy's viewpoint.

And I wasn't sure that Asto would comply. They had more to lose than the enemy sought to gain.

And Asto might talk about more serious attacks using the military, but I suspected they would never take things that far because it would rip *gamra* apart, and they wanted that even less than they wanted to let a dangerous enemy live.

So again I came back to the fact that we knew so little about them.

If we threatened them with something that would affect them deeply, like destroy their Earth base or their communications or pull their collaborators away from them, then they might feel compelled to negotiate.

And it would be really great if we could do that before Asha engaged the military sling to randomly start attacking locations we knew were in the hands of sympathisers, like America Free State, and now, Rotterdam.

My plan to get people on our side together was a desperate quest for ideas and, more than that, data to allow us to determine, or even guess, where these people were.

So that if it came to pass that Asha would authorise the sling to be used, I could give him a better set of potential localities than we currently had, so that as few civilians as possible got killed.

Thayu said she was going to sleep, but I simply had too much to do.

This meeting required a lot of organisation.

Asha said that following the upheaval in Rotterdam, and now that our expedition to get Dekker had been successful, surveillance had increased. So far, the ship hadn't observed activity from any unexpected places.

I contacted Minke Kluysters to say that the meeting was on. I contacted others I had invited, such as Margarethe Ollund, who indicated she would be happy to chair the meeting. I contacted Celia Braddock, but it was night in New York, so I didn't get a response.

Sheydu informed me that the team decided to use way stations. We'd get important people in locations from where we could quickly take them to the meeting and move them out again.

Sheydu and Anyu—who was still at the ship—worked hard at securing safe communication to White Bay, where my father lived. It helped that they established these protocols before and had left many of them in place from our previous visit.

We'd drawn a circle on the map to describe the area from where we could get participants to the talks within twelve hours. I didn't want obvious movement of people in White Bay in the days prior to the meeting. I wanted everyone to get in and out quickly.

The circle was surprisingly big—taking into account the very fast Asto-made craft.

Amarru had a vast network of contacts within that area that were safe, like the Coldi enclave in Los Angeles, who also functioned as safe haven for the Asto military.

I sent the craft to collect Margarethe Ollund to wait there.

Minke Kluysters travelled to the coast near Durban where the craft had picked us up a few years back. I hoped for his sake that the weather was better than when we had been there.

For us, Amarru arranged another location to park Dekker for a few days while we travelled ahead. It was with a family who weren't Coldi but were sympathetic and loyal to the Exchange and provided services to them.

They owned a farm in Australia.

In New Zealand, people joked about Australia being a place where you flew over when you were underway to another place. You would stare out the window at endless brown dusty desert and hear stories of hellishly hot places and wonder why anyone lived there.

So to my—admittedly biased—mind, the words "farm" and "Australia" were two words that didn't belong in the same sentence.

It wasn't actually a farm in the usual sense of the word, but it was apparently one of the largest privately owned properties in the world, larger than some entire European countries.

It was, of course, in inland Australia.

CHAPTER TWENTY-SEVEN

DESPITE HAVING GROWN up in New Zealand, I had been to Australia only once, and that was on a trip somewhere else.

To my mind, and the views of the people in power at Nations of Earth, Australia was a blow-with-the-wind kind of country, opportunistic, but not terribly loyal or influential on the international stage. They would jump in to sell things, or take advantage in different ways, but I had learned in school that at various times in history, they had betrayed deals, or sold to enemies, just for the sake of getting some advantage, often monetary.

The local authorities were too far in bed with big companies to go against this, even if they might sometimes have wished differently.

A few people were insanely rich and lived in mansions in the cities and towns that hugged the coastline, and that was if they lived in the country at all, because many were also in Rotterdam.

These were the families of the agriculture barons, the media barons and the mining barons, although the influence of mining had decreased a lot. These days, the biggest commodity Australia sold was space.

After the compounded crises at the end of the twenty-first century, the wars, the desertification and resulting refugee crisis, the reduction of more than half the world's population through hunger, war, disease and the relentless decline in fertility, Nations of Earth countries had decreed that they each needed to dedicate a portion of their industrial capacity to produce and run plants to take harmful components out of the air. Since a lot of the areas that produced the most harmful emissions were also the most densely populated, they traded this obligation with countries that had space. For money, sometimes a lot of money.

Current estimations said that Australia currently housed about forty percent of those filtering plants. Another good twenty percent were in the Sahara, with a few outlying efforts by other countries.

In short, Amarru's contact in inland Australia owned a property the size of a small European country that was full of these filters. Rows and rows upon rows and more rows of light-coloured boxes that reflected the light as our craft came down.

It was desolate, dusty country, where skeletons of trees clung to the remains of creeks that had once flowed across the land. But even then, I understood only occasionally.

The air fans stood about a house's width apart, and the land in between was dusty and red, with rocks and whatever vegetation still adhered to life. Most of it was brown. A herd of animals ambled between the installations. Were they llamas or antelope?

The property had an airstrip, surrounded by lines of white-painted rocks like bright dots in the red dust.

Next to me, Thayu was looking out the window. Something had evidently captured her interest.

Ynggi, across the aisle, had stuck his tail right up, a sign that he also noticed something that interested him.

When the craft had landed, Dekker came ambling out of one of the cabins at the back. His face was drawn and a crease from the pillow was still impressed across his cheek. He carried his small bag and the fluffy dressing gown over his arm. I reminded myself to ask him about the garment, because I'd almost left it behind when we collected him.

"I'm ready," he said.

Good.

The crew opened the door, and with the already hot morning air came a tang of dust and a scent I found hard to describe that reminded me so much of New Zealand, especially those areas that were hot and dry.

I'd smelled it in South Africa, too. I'd say *gum leaves*, but I couldn't see any trees.

There were indeed trees, I saw when I walked down the ramp. A couple of weathered gum trees with a lot of dead branches grew in a gully to the left.

A vehicle was making its way towards us.

It was a strange contraption, a broad, low and flat thing, with a large sheet on top that contained a solar cell, and which formed the roof to a little shelter in the tray of the vehicle, encased in a cubicle of fly screen.

The thing stopped at the bottom of the ramp, and the driver got out.

The man was quite tall and of sturdy build. He wore a dust-caked grey shirt and khaki pants. His round face hid in the shadow of a felt hat that sported a few oil stains and some holes in the rim.

He greeted Amarru. "Had a safe trip?"

Amarru said that it had been uneventful, and he asked about the Exchange. He was not Coldi, but was clearly familiar with *gamra* people.

He spoke Isla with a familiar accent.

Although it was not exactly the same dialect that my grandparents had spoken, hearing the distinctive tone in his voice took me back to my childhood.

It was such a perfect encapsulation for what was at stake that I choked up for a moment. This wasn't just any world we were trying to protect. It was my home, no matter how Coldi I had become.

"Thank you for helping us out," Amarru said.

"Always a pleasure. I presume you're the legendary Cory Wilson?" He looked at me.

"I don't know about legendary, but yeah, that's me. I have to apologise because we'll be moving on soon, but most of the party will stay here for a few days. We don't know how long yet."

"I'm Jack Fossey. I—wait, is that...?"

The rest of our party had also come out of the aircraft, Dekker squinting against the harsh light.

"Yes. It is. Not a word in public about who he is."

"Understood." He faced the rest of the group. "I present my mobile tea room, the only vehicle big enough to carry everyone. It's a bit of a distance, so I don't want to leave anyone here in case we have trouble coming back for a second load. Hop in and we'll get going."

I wasn't sure how much everyone understood what he said. My team probably understood most of it, but Asha's guards... probably not. They had their own briefs and plans. We all climbed into the back of the vehicle. Underneath the canopy and within the cubicle of fly screen stood a table—bolted to the floor—with a bench around it. A row of depressions in the middle of the table represented charging docks for devices. There was also a display screen hanging from the ceiling. The text *display disconnected* scrolled over the black background.

I ended up at the very front of the cabin, behind the driver's seat. Most in the team were quiet, still groggy from sleep or cranky from the lack of sleep.

Except Ynggi, because he was still very alert.

"What's going on?" I asked him.

"Large creatures," he said. "I don't know what they are."

"Whatever it is, around here, it's the small creatures you have to fear. Snakes..." Coldi didn't have a word for *snake* but it did have a word for worm. "Insects." Again, the insects in Barresh were mostly a type of crustacean, but they occupied the same niche.

Ynggi wiggled his tail. "No. Really big creatures. Taller than me."

Jack was closing the cabin door now everyone was in. He jumped into the driver's seat.

Only the crew stayed with the craft, keeping it running for when we came back for the last leg of the trip.

The pilot had already engaged the concealing mechanism, and the craft was barely visible.

It disappeared completely when the other crew member shut the door.

They would wait here until I came back with a smaller party after I had made sure that Dekker was comfortable and looked after.

The vehicle started moving, quite slowly because the road was rough.

Deyu pointed. "There."

Yes, now I saw them, too, because a group of emus came out of a gully onto the road.

"These are part of our livestock," Jack said. "We have thousands of them."

I translated for Ynggi.

"Does he mean these are imprisoned animals? Does he own them, too?" He sounded defensive.

I translated the question.

Jack laughed. "I wish. No, they roam around wherever they please. No fence will keep them in. We round them up once a year and harvest the nice-looking animals. We use them for leather and meat and their feathers."

I translated for Ynggi.

He mildly approved of this type of farming.

Despite his opposition to *imprisoned animals*, he'd mentioned that it would be good for the tribe if they fed the right kind of fish so that they could catch more and sell more fish to the Misty Forest tribe.

I doubted the Thousand Island tribe would change, but Ynggi was changing a lot, especially since he'd started spending so much time with Isharu and Zyana.

We followed the group of emus up a small hill, in between outcrops of red rock. At the crest, the birds went off to the side, and we had a view over a huge spread out area occupied by air scrubbers.

"Wow," I said.

"It's quite impressive, isn't it?" Jack said. "We operate the largest carbon capturing property in the world. We take care of the carbon removal commitments of half of England, a third of Germany. Up north, we've got another property that is under contracts from Thailand and we're buying a big piece of land to look after China. These babies here are powerful machines, developed by my sister's company in Auckland. You're from New Zealand, right?"

"Originally. My father lives there, but I haven't lived there for a long time."

"She gets them custom made by a place down south. They export them all over the world. We're a kind of testing area as well. I can give you a tour tomorrow."

"We will be going on, but the group who stays here might be interested."

Keen to sell his business to world leaders.

People were the same everywhere.

The carbon removal economy was huge, especially on an international scale. Jack obviously did very well out of it. Even if this landscape was also kind of ugly.

The dirt road led through field after field of these white, boxy machines. Some scrubby vegetation grew in the shade of the machines—some even looked like it had been planted—and groups of animals were resting there. Cattle, antelope, large kangaroos, emus, ostriches, goats, camels even.

I asked Jack which animals he liked best and he said he thought the emus did the best. They were not destructive or aggressive, and they kept insect pests down. And they didn't destroy the machines.

"They're good eating," he said. "And the leather is excellent."

In a fenced-off area surrounded by straggly bushes stood a collection of single-storey white buildings. The vehicle bumped over a cattle grid to enter this tiny village.

A paved road snaked between the buildings. A group of primary school-aged children and their bikes had congregated under a tree and greeted Jack as we came past. The grass between the buildings was marginally green. A few small kangaroos lazed under a bush and looked annoyed that they had to get up and hop towards the fence. From the top of a low hill, where a kind of communal hall stood, the land sloped down to a creek that contained a couple of still puddles of water surrounded by white-trunked trees. The far corner of the fenced compound contained greenhouses made from shade cloth, where I could see the pipes of hydroponic installations, as well as water tanks, a bunch of windmills and the solar array.

It was very peaceful.

Jack stopped the vehicle in front of a building at the furthest point in the village.

"This one will be yours for the time being. We normally use these houses for our contract workers, because it's too far to travel to town every day. My people have been in here to tidy everything up and make sure you have all you need. The cook's got dinner going. It will be served in the canteen that we just passed. You can't miss it. Just follow your nose. If you're looking for something to do, just go to the greenhouse. Jess, my daughter, will be happy to give you something to pick, prune or plant."

A good proportion of our group got out and collected their bags.

Amarru was going to prepare for what was going to happen during the short meeting that everyone would be together. Probably something very different from what Dekker assumed about high-level talks. He'd be ready to talk about cooperation and empty promises. He wasn't going to expect to have to turn over his digital history.

The closer we came to this meeting, the more anxious I felt about it.

Other than Amarru, I left Mereeni with Dekker, as well as Isharu and half of Asha's guards and their weapons.

I re-boarded the craft with the rest of my team—Thayu, Nicha, Sheydu, Veyada, Reida, Deyu, Evi and Telaris and Ynggi—and in the gathering dusk, we took the short trip across the ocean.

If I'd been impressed with the pilot's ability to land this powerful but fickle craft on the ocean's surface, I was even more impressed that he could do this in the dark.

My father came to meet us with the dinghy and took myself, Thayu, Nicha and Veyada back to the land. The others had work to do and would come later. Deyu was keen to see my father's animals, but for the time being we needed to concentrate on the meeting.

On the way through the bay, I thought I spotted the familiar shape of my aircraft on the water.

I knew Leisha was at the farm because my father didn't stop talking about him.

I hadn't yet found the opportunity to talk informally to Leisha about his personal history. I'd trusted Sheydu's judgement to add him —a former Third Circle guard—to her association. He was quiet and observing, but evidently had hidden qualities.

Leisha was, apparently, also really good at fixing the community's hay baling machine, which needed a new part that had been impossible to get but Leisha had fashioned one by running a modelling tool and then using the community's 3D printer to produce it.

Erith had come to the beach to meet us. She carried Emi, while Ayshada, being Ayshada, had to demonstrate to Ileyu that he really could climb a tree in the dark.

Emi silently accepted Thayu's cuddles. I held her briefly and kissed the top of her head. She smelled familiar.

"Daddy," she said, in Isla.

"I see you've been teaching her," I said to my father as we walked up the beach.

"What else are grandparents supposed to do?" He laughed. "It's so good to see you, son. I had to admit we were worried for a bit."

"We're fine. Where is Fred?"

"He's home by the fire, the lazy sod."

There was so much that we left out of this conversation. No doubt the story would come out about how close to disaster we had come. And Fred's advanced age was symbolic of how much our lives were likely to change soon.

CHAPTER TWENTY-EIGHT

WALKING up to the house from the beach, I asked my father about the news.

The night was quiet and the familiar smell of sand and salty water, and of New Zealand Flax—a scent you'd only know if you'd been to New Zealand—enveloped us. The flax grew along the beach in big and dense clumps that hid the lights of the small town from view.

That scent of flax was as essential to New Zealand as the scent of megon nut trees was to Barresh, and if I was unsuccessful in my mission, Emi would grow up not knowing what flax smelled like, and my father and Erith would never know what megon nut trees smelled like.

That fact suddenly seemed weirdly, deeply emotionally, important to me.

Man, I was tired.

Talking about the shocking events of the last few days with my father seemed surreal.

White Bay had been quiet and safe, and neither my father nor Erith, nor Leisha or Veyada, had noticed any suspicious activity locally that suggested anyone knew what we were planning.

As for the world news...

We'd been shut off from the world news while we were travelling, but if I'd expected a huge furore to have hit about the events at Nations of Earth, I would have been disappointed.

But I didn't know what to expect anymore from this administration.

When I started to work for Nations of Earth, this would have been big news. The attack on Sirkonen certainly had been. Huge headlines. News services had reported on little else for at least the month following the attack.

But not now.

"There was disturbingly little news," my father said, while we crossed the road that ran in between the house and the beach. "In fact, the only reason I knew something was up was because Leisha told me. You remember the tsunami of alarmist news that came out after the attack on Sirkonen? Even when Asto performed the precision strike from orbit on Romi Tanaqan's base. The news never stopped talking about it for days."

"So what has the news been covering instead? Surely they would need to mention a new acting president. They would have to..."

"The news has been very strange," my father said. "I'll show you."

We entered the house, where it smelled of cooking.

Fred was also there, as was Leisha. He had ditched his Coldi-made clothing for local garb—a long-sleeved shirt and sturdy pants—and had even cut his hair short.

There wasn't much time for banter.

While Thayu put Emi to bed, I watched the news coverage my father had collected about recent world events.

No, there wasn't much about the destruction we'd wrought. Instead, the news channels fed people news clips in which Simon Dekker announced that recruiting efforts had resulted in record sign-ups for the army to protect the planet.

I wondered how these bits of imagery had been faked so well, since it was physically impossible that Dekker had made those speeches, since he'd been semi-imprisoned in Atlantia at the time.

But people lapped it up.

Young people talked excitedly about their duty. Older people were keen to bring their experience. Rich people provided money and resources. Poor people were happy to provide labour.

Right, I drew the line at that one. In my experience, on Earth and off, people on the margins of society were unlikely to either trust authorities or to volunteer their own scarce resources to the greater good, especially if that greater good was determined by a government that those people didn't trust.

The prevailing narrative was that poor people were poor because they were stupid. In fact, they were one of the least stupid in society. They were poor because, for good or ill, they refused to dance to the tune of the ruling class.

This was advertising garbage.

Why did no one report on MacArthur's death and our escape? It would make an excellent piece of propaganda that could effectively be used against us.

After all, this time around, off-earth people really had killed the acting president.

I also noticed how one of the most trusted news channels, World Newspoint, was not broadcasting at all, and when I tried to look for them, they stated that due to an attack on their head office, news services were temporarily suspended.

That could be true.

But it could also mask a different truth.

World Newspoint was generally considered impartial. It was a large organisation. Surely they had more than one office.

The lamentable Flash Newspoint—which I knew had only one office—had not suffered a similar fate.

This particular rat was getting to the stage of decomposition, and the smell was getting rather overpowering. Someone was messing with news reporting. There simply was no free world in which the deaths—violent or otherwise—of an acting and Vice President were not big news, regardless of the reason or manner of their demise.

We spent the next day organising and shoring up security.

I borrowed one of the community's vehicles and travelled up and down the single coastal road to the resort at the end of the road and to town to book accommodation and to arrange supplies of food.

It started raining during the day. Since it was late winter, it got cold and then it got misty, because the ocean was warmer than the air.

While I travelled in my warm and dry car—even if I had a few unpleasant encounters with road rules, but the less said about that, the better—others in my team spent the day traipsing through the countryside dotted with shoulder-high gorse, blackberries and the ubiquitous flax setting up perimeters and other security stuff.

At dinner, they returned to the farm, wet and muddy from stringing perimeter wiring at strategic locations, where it would warn us if anyone came into the area who didn't belong there.

The talk at dinner was all about security. About extending the perimeter to the bay, and putting bugs in the rooms I'd hired.

Thayu hated rain, so she was grumpy.

In our room after dinner, I said, "I'm thinking we should perhaps invite Melissa Heyworth to listen in. After all, she is the local delegate for *gamra*."

"She is not here. She should be here, if she cared about being a delegate."

Whoa, Thay', you really are grumpy. "Then we can perhaps invite some others."

"We can't even guarantee the safety of everyone we've currently invited."

"Anything wrong, specifically?"

"How about: everything. The people here are trying their best, but we cannot guarantee the safety of this gathering."

"I never asked you to make it watertight."

"Yes, you do."

"When?"

"Nobody ever asks for a guarantee, but when something goes wrong, you're supposed to have given one anyway."

"I know this is risky and not your standard location, but—"

"You're kidding, right?"

"—we've have done stuff like this before. You remember we went into the Aghyrian ship with no idea whether we'd get back out?"

"That was different."

"How?"

"We didn't have Emi. I worry about her. She's right here with us."

"I thought you wanted that."

"Only when we control the situation. When I can defend her. I can't defend her against an attack by unmanned drones. Our security is leaky. Ask Sheydu about it. It would take the enemy only a short time to send some drones and they could destroy us all as we sit here talking."

"How long?"

"What do you mean—how long?"

"How long would it take the drones to discover us and be on their way?"

"What sort of question is that?"

"Just answer it."

She spread her hands. Emi was asleep in her crib in the corner. She stirred and would probably wake up when we kept talking like this.

"Come." I grabbed her hand, and we walked through the dark house to the back veranda.

Somewhere in the house, I could hear the tinkling of Fred's collar as he shook himself, then the clacking of his nails on the floor.

We sat on the bench at the back door.

Fred came out. He sniffed me and because he could no longer jump onto the bench, he let his legs slide with a kind of doggie groan and lay down against my feet.

"I don't like the way we're going," Thayu said. "Ask Sheydu. She doesn't like it either. This area is fairly safe, but we can't seal it off completely."

"We never intended it to become completely safe. I just want it safe for half a day, no more."

"That's pushing things."

"What would I need to do to extend that time?"

"Honestly? You'd need to tell my father to keep some craft ready in orbit to deal with the drones."

And since the drones usually appeared in the stratosphere, that would be breaking the *gamra* guidelines and the agreement that— damn it—Dekker still hadn't signed.

"Yes," I said. "We will do that. If we have to make the choice between keeping *gamra* happy and protecting Earth from isolation, then there really is no choice."

"I'm glad we agree on that." And that remark let shine through all the worries Asto had about this enemy and their presence in deep space.

It was a slightly hopeful tone to go to sleep on, although I doubted I'd needed any more incentive to sleep well.

We had a work discussion over breakfast, in which all the team joined, including Amarru, who was still with Dekker, and the rest of the team who were floating in the aircraft offshore. They were going to join us later in the day.

I asked those in the team with military connections to brief Asha as much as possible.

For security reasons, we would have all the guests in town for less than a day. I'd get the least visible people here first and make sure that they didn't stay in the town. Then we'd get everyone together for a short period so that Reida could get what he needed.

And I'd talk to Asha to keep a defense unit ready in orbit.

Just in case things went pear-shaped.

It was my task to look after local operations.

My father had booked the hall, as I had asked him, but now we needed to set it all up. Of course, my team had set up security protocols for the bay, but now they had to bug the hall and set up defence stations. Asha's guards communicated with the ship, which would give us backup in case something went wrong.

Fred came with us and lay on the floor in the middle of the hall, moving only when someone with a vacuum cleaner came to get rid of the eternal beach sand people traipsed into the building.

My father and Erith's friends set up a square of tables and covered them with clean tablecloths—which Thayu used to stick further bugs onto.

Diana—bustling with plates and cups—warned her she had to be careful that the bugs didn't end up in the laundry and Thayu replied they'd survived much worse things.

Which pretty much said everything about the events that we were about to unleash on this sleepy and peaceful community. I felt guilty about that, but Diana and Mick and Ngaio and Tamati and the other community members told me they were glad to help.

"It's just horrible what's happened to all those cities," Tamati said. He was a huge, dark-skinned man, with his arms and even his face covered in tattoos. He lived in the house next to my father's and Ayshada followed him around everywhere.

In the afternoon, we held a community meeting in my father's shed, with all the townsfolk and my team members—watched by the non-plussed llamas—where I outlined what was going to happen. I also discussed the subject of payment. I suggested I had the means to compensate the community, and to pay for upgrades to their infrastructure or anything else they wanted.

If we were successful, the name of this community might become famous worldwide and maybe even beyond.

I inspected the accommodation. People wanted to show their efforts to me, even if the quality of the accommodation was not very high on my list.

I also explained that some people might be bringing accommodation in the form of ships that doubled as boats, and that we needed a couple of dinghies. Preferably ones that were not open to the elements.

The next day, I travelled again to the resort at the end of the road, and spoke to them about the very large reservation we had made, booking out the entire complex. I explained they were not tourists, but to treat the people as such.

Thayu spent half a day bugging that building as well.

On the surface, this gathering was to be about agreeing to work against the enemy. Behind the scenes, it was about data. And about finding out where we could hit the enemy hardest.

In the afternoon, Thayu and I drove to town, and we completed the same process with the hotels where we had booked rooms. A few thousand people lived here, so keeping out of the way was going to be both harder and easier.

Thayu, Reida, Deyu and Isharu then spent some time connecting all the bugs up to my aircraft, where Deyu ran the local hub through Anyu in orbit. Reida had his kids in Athyl on standby, and Asha had readied a dedicated satellite for us. We probably had a short window where we could communicate vast amounts of data before the enemy discovered the satellite and destroyed it, but once Athyl had the data, there were other ways they could contact us about what they found.

Then we were all done. We spent a quiet evening with Emi and my father and Erith sitting by the fire. It was winter, and the air was rather chilly.

I had sent messages that we were ready. All we could do was wait.

CHAPTER TWENTY-NINE

THE FIRST OF our preparations started to come together the next day.

Several groups arrived in the area as my team reported to me, because of course we couldn't see any of this. An Asto military aircraft landed on the bay, met a sailing boat and transferred a group of secret military passengers. Some took up position in a guesthouse in town strategically located on the only road to White Bay. A smaller group caught the bus to the conference centre at the end of the road. This meant they travelled through White Bay, but I didn't notice them. I didn't know who these people were, but they provided a lot of work for Thayu and Sheydu.

We also got word that a private solar jet arrived in Auckland from Cape Town. The owner hired a private driver to take him and his entourage to a beautiful house on the point that overlooked the bay. It was an old farmhouse that belonged to Diana and her husband. They had recently fixed the place up and hired it out to corporate customers with lots of money.

A little track led from the house to the beach and in the afternoon, I spotted two young women walking down who were definitely not part of the White Bay community. Both wore colourful dresses, one yellow, one red, and wore headbands and coloured beads in their hair that stood out against their dark skin.

They were proudly African. Part of Minke Kluysters' admin team? Spies? Guards in disguise? I had no idea.

Leisha and Veyada took my aircraft and made the three-hour trip to collect the people we'd left at Jack's carbon farm. When they came back after dark, he stayed further out in the bay, and two local yacht owners sailed out to meet the group.

A couple of minibuses came to the beach. They took Dekker to the conference centre where they would stay in comfortable luxury but were under the strict surveillance of the Asto military and would not be sending any messages anywhere.

Amarru came to stay in my father's shed with the security personnel.

While all this was happening, some of my team members turned my father's back room into technology central, where Reida, Sheydu and Isharu—connecting with Anyu in orbit—worked constantly to monitor every guest. They used the pool table as a prop, increasingly vanishing under the sheer weight of technology.

Fred acted as floor rug in this room, occasionally turning around in front of the heater.

Thayu presided over hourly meetings in this room that were so full of jargon that it made my head hurt.

I was well aware that I'd seen only fractions of her capabilities in full flight, but this was something on another level altogether.

The idea, she explained in a *you-should-really-learn-about-this-stuff* kind of way, that spies followed people around, chatted them up in bars and fed them poison to loosen their tongue was about two hundred years out of date.

Spies monitored data. Vast quantities of it.

What we were doing here was essentially a giant spying operation.

Spies knew where to insert their hacks to gather data that was useful and where their presence was least likely to be noticed. Because, as she said, all contacts and insertion points are disposable. The idea was to get as much data as possible before the hack was discovered. Because every hack would be discovered.

"Except when they're not," I said, thinking about Amarru's age-old network which was still partially functional.

"Those dumb systems that are completely open or have major security flaws that everyone knows about are also useless. The successful spy gets data that no one else can get. Because that data is the most valuable."

This upcoming meeting was not so much about my efforts to bring all these people together—although it could add to the importance. It was that my team were hoping to mine vast amounts of data, especially from Dekker and Braddock—who would attend remotely—and that they could send all this to people in orbit and Reida's kids in Athyl, to extract patterns that could tell us where we might find and target the enemy.

Later in the evening, another couple of craft arrived, bringing Ezhya, and Asha and his team.

Ezhya and Asha both arrived on Ezhya's aircraft that landed on the ocean and met up with my father's boat in the middle of the night.

I didn't go out with the boat, but met up with them once they'd clambered out of the dinghy and walked across the beach to the house.

We put up umbrellas because it was pouring.

Ezhya was wearing a wind jacket that belonged to my father.

Asha wore his black military gear. He looked utterly menacing.

They brought—on a different aircraft—a contingent of guards armed to the teeth. The men and women—equal numbers of both—did not want to come inside.

Sheydu informed them that there was a shed where they could set up.

That was, if they didn't mind sharing the shed with my father's ever-expanding herd of llamas.

They tromped off to the side of the house to do whatever security did. I reminded myself to send Deyu after them to check on the llama situation, because those animals were not well-behaved.

Ezhya and Asha came into the kitchen.

Fred grumbled a bit, but these days he was too old to get out of his dog basket and make a decent show out of keeping strangers out of his domain. Even if he usually found the scent of Coldi people objectionable.

Poor Fred.

Ezhya crouched to look at him.

He continued to growl a bit, while giving Ezhya a dubious look.

"This is what you call a *dog*?" Ezhya said.

He would know what dogs were. He'd been to Earth before.

"This is Fred," my father said. "He is very old. If you'd come a few years earlier, he would have been barking his head off and jumping all around."

Ezhya stroked his head and Fred leaned into his hand, because, being Coldi and having come from Asto, Ezhya's hand would be very warm.

We all sat at the table, where my father brought the tea.

Erith had retreated to the corner.

I'd never gotten a good measure of what she felt about the world she had left behind. I knew she thought little of the stodgy society in Damarq where her family lived, but she never talked much about *gamra*, much less about Asto.

Ezhya greeted her with a hand signal, and she returned the greeting. Then she got up to help my father with the tea.

We spoke about the situation in orbit. Devices came out and maps were projected on the old kitchen table. Asha detailed positions of the military ships. He didn't say as much, but I could tell they didn't expect the conflict to go away without a confrontation.

After the incident at Nations of Earth, I agreed with them, but still hoped to keep armed confrontation to a minimum.

Our strike should be targeted and hard. The enemy was dangerous, but there were unlikely to be very many of them. Or as Asha said in military speak, the defense line is hard but it's shallow.

The sound of a vehicle arriving in the driveway drifted from outside. There were footsteps in the hall, the door opened and a moment later Reida entered in the company of a vaguely familiar man, even if I didn't remember his name. He was in charge of the Nations of Earth security.

He introduced himself as Sandeep Mookherjee. He spoke with a Scandinavian accent.

He nodded to me. With him was someone I did recognise: Gracelyn Sebaya. She introduced her companion as the head of Special Services branch.

I said to Mookherjee, half-jokingly, that there were times I would have killed to have his ear about security situations.

He laughed. "We're both less and more powerful than you think. We don't control policy. But you wondered how you managed to get out of the Nations of Earth complex alive? We had everything to do with that. In fact, we were building a plan to do exactly what you did, maybe without the loss of life, but definitely not without sidelining a lot of people."

They both joined us at the table, where we had gone from tea to my father's supply of excellent gin.

Neither of them batted an eyelid when I introduced them to Ezhya and Asha.

Yeah.

They already knew each other.

They continued talking, assisted by—of all people—Reida, whom I spotted presenting some of his own material and explaining what he was doing.

It got very late.

Emi had woken up, and Thayu went to get her. With her came Ayshada and Ileyu, looking wide-eyed at all those important people.

Emi remembered Ezhya as someone who played games with her and demanded to sit on his knee, and so my little toddler girl sat there as a princess in the middle of projections and readers and talk of serious war. It was surreal.

We retired to bed for a few hours of sleep. I was so tired that I didn't even worry about what was coming.

In the morning, Ynggi and a local fisherman came to the house early to deliver a great variety of fish and scallops.

Diana came in to take some of it to her cafe and Erith accompanied her to prepare breakfast.

We took an early walk on the beach. It was strange to see Ezhya throw sticks for Fred to retrieve. An animal that brings back what you've thrown away, how fascinating. I could see his mind whirl.

When we arrived at the community hall still before sunrise, Minke Kluysters had already arrived.

He held his long-awaited face-to-face meeting with Ezhya, although I didn't doubt that the two had spoken in other ways. Minke Kluysters was not the type of person who would ask for my permission to contact Ezhya. And Ezhya, being Ezhya, was eternally curious.

I was also glad that there were plenty of other people and distractions, which meant that the two had little time to talk. I offered myself as translator.

The talk lasted only ten minutes and covered a couple of broad topics. Minke was most interested in commerce, making it easier to sell things to Asto and import things from there.

Ezhya was most interested in Tamerians and whether armies of them were still being produced. The Coldi mindset had interesting unexpected corners and one such was their absolute abhorrence for the concept of artificial people. Was the Tamer Collective still in bed with the Aghyrians, he wanted to know.

It was quite amusing to see the two of them walk on the beach, in the company of Fred, still carrying his stick, hoping that Ezhya would throw it one more time.

Since that meeting had gone off well, I could concentrate on the other important guests, which included Margarethe Ollund, who had arrived when I was on the beach. She would lead the discussion and needed to know about the logistics.

Diana came in to deliver breakfast: fish and eggs and fried cheese, beans and toast.

Other than the people I had already met, the group in the hall also included a brightly dressed, loud-voiced African woman who had to have come with Minke Kluysters but was clearly not a security person.

I met my father at the food table and asked if he knew who she was.

"Don't you know? That's Rika Verve. She's a delegate for PanAf."

I had heard that name before. "Minke's wife?"

Damn, stuff started to make sense now. The name Rika Verve came up in the news a lot. She was a politician who was active and very vocal in PanAf. And I also realised: those two young women I'd seen on the beach were their daughters. They were also in the hall, one of them talking to Margarethe Ollund.

Everyone mingled around the breakfast table, while the sun came up over the ocean.

This had to be the strangest thing I'd ever done. And much of it was totally out of my control, because I'd given Margarethe instructions to chair and plan the meeting. She'd called it an exploratory meeting.

Because there had to be a journalist covering these events, and we couldn't get any of the official news channels, I'd asked the townsfolk to provide me with someone.

So wandering around the hall with a camera was a young lad called Brad. He was Diana's son, eighteen years of age, with bright cheeks and shining eyes.

The townsfolk performed extremely well. The hall was comfortable, the food was fresh, and all of this was coordinated by Erith as if she had done this all her life. In fact, I often wondered what her career had been before she married my father. It had to have been something like this, organising meetings or going to gatherings, because otherwise, how would he have met her?

And then, when we were completely ready, we brought the last attendee over from his virtual prison.

I sent a driver to get Dekker with the minibus while we waited. I did last-minute checks.

We had everything in the hall set up. Screens along the walls, where people elsewhere dialled in and appeared on the screens, including Celia Braddock.

Word came that the bus had arrived.

Behind the scenes, Reida and the team opened the satellite links. We were now exposed. Time was of the essence.

The next few hours would be the most important ones of my life.

When coming into the doorway, a hint of surprise flickered over Dekker's face.

"My, you really do have everyone together here," he said.

"Today we will talk," I said. "Whether you like it or not, we will reach some agreement. This is the one last chance to sit down and talk before all hell breaks loose."

All the delegates found their places.

I gave a brief welcome, thanked the residents of White Bay, and gave the floor to Margarethe Ollund. She started out by outlining all the different things that we knew about the enemy and the different places where we had been able to stop them, and the places where we had not.

Each of the major attendees then got fifteen minutes to present their situation, attacks they had suffered, data they had on enemy actions or whatever else they wanted to talk about.

Dekker spoke openly about the tense situation at Nations of Earth that had sent him fleeing.

Celia Braddock was more coy, but confessed that she had spoken to Governor Patterson and knew that he had something to do with the enemy, even if she didn't think he was directly allied with them.

Asha spoke about how the military had developed a system for determining where the next attack was going to be, that this system wasn't foolproof—as our experience in Athens had shown—but that they knew there was a local component and couldn't determine through the usual means where these people were hiding because of the amount of noise generated by everyone on the planet.

Minke Kluysters said that the newly developed network of the Tamer Collective was also badly affected by the attacks. The enemy had taken out three of their four satellites in Earth orbit. The planned second Exchange network had taken damage and would now take longer to set up. He was happy for us to use data from the attacks. He was polite about it, but I could see he was really angry about having lost so much work.

General Mookherjee spoke about the recruitment drive of Nations of Earth. He said that while he had to maintain a non-political position, he was deeply concerned about some aspects of the program which benefited those in the compound, and those had shown themselves as sympathisers with the enemy.

I asked him if he could tell us about what had happened following our escape from the bunker. He told us that on that day, he had found his accounts disabled "for security reasons". He'd also come into his office in the Office of War and found all his locks changed because "there had been a situation" and a few days later, an official told him they would like him to rally the troops in orbit. He had actually been making plans to go there, but had put them on hold because of his frustration that no one would allow him to see MacArthur.

"That's because he was dead," I said.

"So I understand now. But as soon as that happened, and you escaped, the president's office went offline and no information came out other than that they wanted me to inspect the troops in orbit. I made it this far in my career by taking orders, but I can tell a good order from a bullshit order, and this was one of the latter variety."

I'd given the responsibility of getting the *gamra* document signed to Margarethe, partly because she had helped draft it, and she knew Dekker better than I did.

While the leaders held their talks, Reida and the rest of the team were busy getting any data they could. Within Nations of Earth, it was generally accepted practice to use a dedicated disposable device for meetings like this, but few of the attendees—not even Minke Kluysters—were equally diligent with their passcodes and ID chips. While the visitors were in the meeting, Asha's security people scanned their accommodation and passed information to us. It kind of horrified me to think about the stuff the Reida was getting into, but he had also told me many times that the most interesting material was not the super-secret accounts, but the more mundane stuff because this was what people actually did—not what they merely talked about—and they tended to be much less careful with it.

At this point, Deyu got up and showed us—while standing in the kitchen of the hall—an integrated model of all the places where we now knew the enemy was active. This was a live model that used data from Amarru's database and information obtained—voluntarily or otherwise—from all the security forces that were here.

Rotterdam was an active area, and so was America Free State. There were also cells in western Russia and adjacent eastern Europe. And Israel. Egypt as well, which was slightly worrying because the launch station for the Nations of Earth's private space transport was still there.

In the middle of the chaotic events where I divided my attention between far too many things, I spotted Dekker signing the *gamra* agreement and handing it to Margarethe. She gave him a wry smile.

I heard Celia Braddock pledging Atlantia's military support.

Minke Kluysters said that the new Exchange would be happy to set up a hub in New York. Oo—er. I'd always assumed it would be in Pretoria.

Too unstable, Minke said.

So things were progressing well until—

Sheydu called in from the door. "Action."

The game was over. The satellite link had been discovered.

CHAPTER THIRTY

WITHIN SECONDS, Reida shut everything down.

The rest of my team, and Asha's guards, and all the security and military people in the entourage of Ezhya and Asha, sprang into action.

We had warned the participants that this might happen, and we were already close to the four hours that Thayu had given us as safe margin.

We had also given them evacuation plans.

The bus took Dekker back out to the point, where the same craft that had brought him here would take him to a locality of his choosing.

Apparently, Margarethe Ollund had offered to put him up in her holiday villa in Norway. They left together, so I presumed this rumour was true.

Sandeep Mookherjee and Gracelyn Sebaya arranged their own transport. They had already called in defensive air teams to test the new cooperation agreements with Asto's military.

"Make absolutely sure that Federza gets that agreement as soon as possible," I said to Amarru as she left the hall.

"Yes. Although it may be a while. The military are not going to want to give away their positions by sending our messages."

Fair enough.

But the agreement with *gamra* would expire soon. It might have expired already.

Minke Kluysters and his family were still in the hall. He told me they would find a place to stay in between here and Auckland and enjoy a few days' holiday. Under the shadow of Asto's military was the safest place to be right now.

He was right, but also selfish. But he'd also said that PanAf forces would be available if needed. PanAf had very little spacefaring capability, and all of it was civilian. But they owned a large fleet of gyro-copters and even more solar planes to get into difficult to reach areas. I told him to keep in contact with Sebaya.

I might have hoped that he held armies of Tamerians in reserve, but the Tamerian program seemed to have come to a halt, after many entities declared they didn't pass the "human" test. Creating people was harder than they thought.

We packed up everything in the community hall.

I entered the back room at my father's house with Asha, where I found all the security personnel huddled around a screen.

They'd spotted drones, and were following their trajectory and that of the Asto military craft to intercept and destroy them. I had no doubt that they would. Once the military knew where the drones were, they never reached their target.

That was a matter for the troops in orbit.

Several members of my team had set up their devices on the floor in the corner of the room. Reida was there, as well as Sheydu, Ynggi, Isharu and Leisha.

They were scrolling through blocks of hexadecimal code.

I asked them, "Did we get enough information from the meeting?"

"There is no such thing as enough information," Sheydu said.

"Useful information, then," I said.

Reida said, "I've sent it all off. The kids are looking at it."

It was night in Athyl, according to my calculations. When this was all over, I should reward those kids for their excellent service.

Now we needed to wait for the results while everyone vacated the community hall and returned to their homes.

The military was also packing up.

I met Asha at the back door, carrying his military satchel. He was, I was disturbed to see, in his dress uniform in desert pink.

He stopped while I was on my way in and he was about to go out.

"Anything to report?" I asked, looking over his uniform. It sported many patches on his chest and shoulders, while the top of his jacket was open and I could see the body armour underneath.

"We've taken down two drones that were on their way here."

"Are there going to be more?"

"We can't tell. It pays to be prepared. You got your agreement and did your talking, but now we need to face the battle. Come back to orbit. You can always continue your data analysis up there. We'll be the first place to restore Exchange connectivity. I'd advise to get out of the way as much as possible."

"I will." My team needed to discuss what to do next, but going back to orbit was definitely an option.

"Also..." He hesitated, which was uncharacteristic for him.

"Yes?"

"There have been occasions... where you rendered an invaluable service to me personally. There is no other way to say this, but without your intervention, especially when we first encountered the Aghyrian ship, I would not have known the joy of seeing my grand-children—No, don't say anything."

He waved away the hand I held up and continued, "It *was* in your brief and you *were* doing your duty, but you were doing your duty faithful to your principles, which is to avoid loss of life. I think that gets lost, sometimes. In the military, we're about destruction and people are killed when you destroy things. It's what we sign up for. The proud Domiri clan has many people who signed up to defend Asto over valuing their own lives. Except that lives are important. Without our lives, we can't enjoy things, like grandchildren."

He gave me such a sincere look that I was at a loss as to how to respond. Yes, he did this sometimes. Come out at you with a deeply emotional response at the gut punch level. What could I possibly say to this?

I opened my mouth—

"No, don't say anything. I wanted to make it clear to you that if ever you're in a perilous situation, I will employ every resource at my disposal to come to your assistance. That's all I wanted you to understand."

"Thank you."

Then he said, "*Iyamichu ata.*"

And I responded, "*Iyamichu ata.*"

Into battle.

"Keep my children safe." He placed a hand on my shoulder and a moment later he was gone, walking over the road to the beach where the dinghy waited to take him and Ezhya back to the aircraft.

I went back into the house. While we were away, Reida and the team started packing up their stuff so that we were ready to move if moving quickly became necessary.

The satellite link was no longer safe at any rate.

We could only wait.

My father made tea while we sat at the table with Fred at our feet, following the movement of Asto's military craft on the screen of a single reader that was not of the type that my team usually used.

We could see how the craft joined, split up, evaded fire, fired at targets—the screen didn't tell us what sort of vehicles they destroyed.

Following warfare at this distance was weirdly detached and also disturbing, like watching someone play a game, but knowing it was real.

Reida commented during the parts where we ran into trouble picking up the signal or interpreting the mess on the screen as they flew through the reach of scrambling beacons.

In the middle of this, bright green text flashed on the screen. *I know where you are.*

Wait.

"How do they know where I am? I've never touched this reader. I haven't even turned on that cheap reader since we left Nations of Earth."

Isharu said, "They must use a different beacon—no, don't turn it off." The latter to Reida.

She took the device to the back room. Reida followed her.

We remained in the kitchen in silence, sipping tea. This was not at all going the way I hoped.

The agreement was signed, but the enemy had stepped up their actions, and the Asto military was going to do something drastic.

Reida's kids in Athyl were working on the data, but there was no guarantee that they would find anything useful.

All my actions amounted to too little, too late. The meeting had been good, but pointless for as long as the enemy still sent drones and they could do so without giving away where they came from.

And we still faced this random person who kept sending me childish messages through some unknown means.

Twice now I'd received a message on a device that they should have been unable to track, unless they possessed a different means of tracking me. The only way I understood this could happen was if I had an implant. And I didn't.

Well, not that I knew.

And inserting an implant was not a big deal, but also not something you could do to a person without them noticing.

Which meant that I would have to have been unconscious. The last time that happened was after the genetic alignment procedures that Lilona had put me through and before that, I'd spent time in the high oxygen chamber in the hospital in Barresh. I couldn't see them having inserted a chip that anyone from Earth could read.

And supposing I had an implant, it had to be a chip that my team couldn't read, and likely I'd been walking around with it for most of my life.

That thought made me feel itchy. All of a sudden, I could feel lumps everywhere under my skin.

Supposing that was the case, then where would this have happened?

On Midway Space Station?

I didn't remember that I'd ever spent time in the hospital there.

On New Taurus? I'd broken my arm when falling off a bike, but that had all been dealt with while I was conscious.

But there *was* that time at Mars University when I'd been bashed after a particularly nasty argument about human space politics.

There were many people at Mars University who didn't agree with the position of Nations of Earth on *gamra*.

I'd been bashed when walking back to my student room. I remembered nothing about the attack and had only woken up in hospital two days later.

Damn.

I ran my hands over all the places where people inserted those chips: in the side of my neck, my arm, behind my ear, at the hairline, but found nothing. I tried to remember what sort of injuries I'd had, but I'd blissfully forgotten about that time.

"Anything wrong?" my father asked.

Thayu had been dozing with Emi asleep on her lap. She now looked up.

"I don't know," I said. And I truly didn't.

If someone had inserted a chip in me, and it looked like they might have, then Mars was where it would have happened. Mars, where they had been about to make GenCode ID chips mandatory.

I got up and went to the back room.

Reida and Isharu had inserted the disposable reader into a scanning cradle.

"I don't think there is anything wrong with it," I said. "It's me. There has to be a chip inside me we've never noticed."

"If that was true, it would solve a lot," Sheydu said.

"How can we find out?"

"We can detect it when it's active. Respond to this message and it might show up. We need to find the most likely place first. The signal is likely very weak."

"Normally, those chips are in your arms or in your neck at the hairline. But if you'd had a rogue chip there, we would have picked it up before. Where would it likely be?"

I thought back to the bashing incident. I'd been told I'd fallen down the stairs and bruised my left upper leg. The bruising had been spectacular.

"It would be here." I pointed.

Reida vacated his chair, and I sat down. He pulled the reader out of the scanning cradle and gave it to me. "Reply something."

I waited until he and Isharu had brought over the ultra-sensitive equipment and sent, *Pavona, Mars.*

Isharu nodded.

She showed me her screen. It said GenCodeID5537487CD.

Well, shit.

Here was me thinking that I didn't have a GenCode chip and having no end of trouble verifying my ID. I'd always thought it was because I had been part of the space settlers. But here was the reason.

The excited talk and activity in the room had brought my father to the door.

"We never gave you that," he said. "I objected to this way of tracking people, even if the administration at Midway was keen for us to have these chips."

"You didn't do this," I said. "I didn't agree with it, either. They inserted it in me after I'd been taken to the hospital at Mars University."

Then another thought: how did this mysterious person know that?

But now something else came on the screen.

A reply.

It said, *You were in first year, I was in third.*

Well, holy crap. We finally had something to start looking.

Now I only needed to go through the publicly accessible list of all students who had started there two years before I did and I'd have the name of my mysterious follower. And hope all the names were public.

Was this a diversion tactic, or would it lead somewhere? We had so little time.

Perhaps the best way to go about this was to forget about the personal connection. Someone who was at Mars University was likely to have been part of the space settler community. There were not that many of those. They were likely to go into the administration of space programs and rarely returned for careers on Earth.

And then it dawned on me that there was one major place where we hadn't really looked for enemy activity.

And the thought was both revealing and a stupendous mistake on our part.

I said, "I have an idea."

And at the same time, Reida got up and jumped to the bank of screens that were still set up. "That's the kids in Athyl reporting back. They found it."

I was too far away to see what scrolled over the screen.

But after the text finished scrolling, he detached the screen and took it to us.

The message was short and consisted only of a set of coordinates.

"Where is that?" Isharu asked.

Yes.

Yes, I knew where it was. I'd just realised. I knew where the enemy's operational centre was.

Reida copied it and fed it into the projector.

The projection of a bright world sprang up with a couple of localities marked, most of them around the equator. The surface was barren and pockmarked with craters.

It was as I had thought.

Selena Base, on the North Pole of the Moon.

Holy crap.

CHAPTER THIRTY-ONE

WE NEEDED to double check that we definitely focused on the right location. I called everyone into the kitchen, including the team members who had been asleep.

Including Deyu who was with the animals outside and Ynggi who'd gone fishing.

Reida and Thayu explained what they had done: collected data from all the data points in Amarru's network and added up the places where more people entered than left. Then they had cross-referenced this with the data they had collected from our guests. In the pocket of Dekker's fluffy dressing gown, they had found a data stick with a gold mine of useful data. But there were gaps.

Knowing that I had a GenCode chip helped, because Reida had found that one of Mookherjee's companions had access to this database and my team could get in with the help of a list of hacked passcodes they skimmed from Minke Kluysters.

So, presuming that the GenCode chips were compulsory in communities that had joined the Independence Force, they plotted the GenCode readings against Amarru's file of movements and found a pattern that people who displayed opinions sympathetic to the Independence Force travelled to Selina Base and vanished there. Sometimes they came back months or years later, but often, they just ceased to exist. A rough calculation showed a deficit of about ten thousand people.

Selina Base had a fairly long history as a mining settlement. I'd been to the Moon but had never visited the base. It was an industrial settlement. I knew little about it other than that its heydays appeared to be in the past.

The signs were good.

"Is this definitely what we've been looking for? Is this their elusive base?" I asked my team members.

Isharu said, "It's our best guess. We could go through all the communication data to see if they're sending messages to the drones, but frankly, that's such a wide scope that the amount of data we'd have to process would take us days to get through."

We all knew. We didn't have days.

The enemy were launching an offensive against the Asto military, and Asha would hit back hard and would first wreak destruction on the sites they thought most likely to harbour enemy bases, with all the loss of innocent life that would entail. The Moon was an exclusively civilian settlement.

A hostile action against civilian bases would also create a major diplomatic crisis.

They would also likely destroy any technology at these locations that would help us pinpoint where else to look for further bases, and the answer to the question of how they made these endless drones appear out of nowhere, and how many people were involved and...

So many questions I wanted answered *before* Asha let loose the power of the military sling. And to be honest, I actually wanted that terrible piece of equipment to stay as far away from Earth as possible, so if these people were at all amenable to negotiations, I wanted to give them that chance, too.

I said, "Right. We're going to have to go there ourselves."

"That seems a little... suicidal," Sheydu said.

But the fact that she no longer vehemently opposed my—sometimes futile—attempts at negotiation and diplomacy showed how much she had changed and how much she had come to know me.

"Asha has assured me that he is prepared to rescue us."

"That's only if everything goes his way. If it doesn't, he may not have a choice but to retaliate."

"We went to save him in a similar situation."

"He wasn't stupid enough to go into an enemy base voluntarily."

"He didn't voluntarily go to the Aghyrian ship?"

She met my eyes and I could see that she realised I was right.

"We're going, because the prize for being successful is potentially great. If we can negotiate, if we can talk to these people and stop unnecessary loss of civilian lives. If we can see their technology... We just have to hope with all our might that we have the right place."

"Yes." Thayu said, one of those heartily agreed definitive yeses. *She* was pretty convinced that we'd found the right place.

"How are we getting there?" I asked.

Sheydu shrugged. "We got enough craft to take us there. It wouldn't take very long."

True. "But we'd be breaking a host of rules so authorities are likely to notice us and come after us."

"Let them try," Sheydu said.

Well, yeah. "I don't want to create any more conflict with parties that are supposed to be friendly."

"We'd established Nations of Earth was compromised."

"The assembly is. The security forces are still going to be sticking to the established rules."

"Let them try to stop us. We go in and out quickly. Just like we've done in the past few days."

It was not quite the same, because we would be extremely visible to all. Much more visible than anything we did on Earth. In fact, I was wondering if this was the reason for having the base on the Moon.

"We'd have lots of backup," Isharu said.

Yes, it was the backup I was afraid of. Secretive military craft that had no business being where they were.

"No," I said. "I don't want to draw anyone's attention to our presence. Let's talk about other options."

"We need to talk about our aim first," Sheydu said.

"Looking at their installations, potentially figuring out how they make the drones appear. Negotiate, if they're inclined. If not, render the base incapable of fulfilling its function. But only as a last resort."

"It will come to that," Sheydu said. "If they wanted to talk, you've given them enough opportunity. Are we all in agreement that we all want to do as much damage to this outfit as possible?"

She gave me a penetrating look.

"After we investigate the place, and we give the inhabitants the option to get out safely, we can destroy the place."

She blew out a breath. "Good. I'll know which explosives to bring."

We talked about the logistics.

To get to the base, we needed equipment and vehicles and a good cover story that would allow us to visit an area of the Moon that had been pretty much abandoned. We studied the network of mining tunnels and the likely places for an underground secret base.

It turned out that the Asto military had some data on this. Because the military believed there was no problem that couldn't be solved with an abundance of data.

They had collected—and filed away—maps of the Moon that included below-surface scans.

When Thayu overlaid the known position of tunnels and the infrared heat scans, it became fairly clear where the concentration of people was likely to be. Selena was listed as a mining exploration base, but had seen little action for the past thirty years.

Current official population: ten.

Yeah, right.

Could you still travel there? Deyu wanted to know.

We checked, and it seemed that public forms of transport would take you quite close, although the bus service to the base had been suspended ten years ago.

We would need our own transport and other gear, and we wouldn't be able to rely on the military. We would have to get that locally.

"Maybe we can pose as a prospecting team," I said.

We couldn't leave anything to chance. We would have to take breathing apparatus, and also an air machine. There was plenty of ice in the craters for making air, so that was not the issue.

The issue was getting the equipment to the surface without attracting attention. Since we didn't know how they were getting their intelligence, we could only go in quickly, hit hard, and hope we could do enough damage so that they couldn't hit back.

We agreed we would send a small advance party through the regular transport network. I wanted at least Thayu, Sheydu, Deyu and Reida, Evi and Telaris. Ynggi had completed his vacuum training and he was keen to come, but he was very visible and it was likely that suit hire companies wouldn't have anything in his size. Veyada was—by his own admission—not a fighter. He'd been part of Ezhya's guards, but every member of those guard associations had hugely differing skills.

Anyu would again look after our communication. She would have to transfer to a military craft that was going to stay close, because the large command ship would be otherwise engaged, and it needed to stay further out. Veyada was going to stay with Anyu, so were Nicha and Ynggi, because we needed a few people to answer questions for us.

We said goodbye to them, and Asha's guards, knowing that this was probably the most dangerous thing, and the most important thing, that I had ever done in my life.

"You always say that," Thayu said.

"But this time it is really true. If we get through this, I'm going to take some of those trips that we have promised the team to take. I am going to help Erith sort out her family's affairs at Damarq, and we will go to Indrahui to help Evi and Telaris and their family."

So we were left alone with just part of my association and the children, who would stay with my father.

In the morning, I first went to see the White Bay community doctor and asked her to cut the chip out of my leg. The procedure was rather more graphic than I bargained for and left me feeling rather ill. The chip was a tiny little pellet no bigger than a mouse dropping. After having bandaged me up, she gave it to me in a paper packet that I put in the pocket of my jacket.

I stumbled back to my father's farm and was met by an equally stiff-legged Fred on the driveway. My leg was sore, and I was still tired from the frantic past few days. I had never felt less prepared to go out to war.

Inside the house, I found everyone busy packing. Thayu was in the spare bathroom drying her hair. She'd dyed it black, like Nicha used to do when I first met him.

I stopped at the door and looked at her, kind of horrified.

"We need to blend in," she said, in reply to my unasked question.

Yes. Of course. But I still hated this.

When we had finished packing, we said goodbye to the children with Erith on the beach. My father took us out in the dinghy around the point.

The sea was getting choppy. It was about to get dark and it was hard to see where other boats—or aircraft—were. An Asto military aircraft was in a special class of invisibility all on its own.

The only reason we could see it was because they told us where to look, and when we came closer, someone opened the door, which made a weird dark rectangle appear on the waves.

Someone walked over the craft's wing—visible only where it touched the water.

The person wore a full military uniform and a second person appeared in the door opening, also in military uniform. So much for my statements that they only wore uniform when they were with other military.

There was much I got wrong about the Asto military.

The first person—a woman, I thought—helped us out of the dinghy, handing all our luggage to the second person. Then we balanced and half-slid over the wing to the craft's entrance.

I waved to my father, although I wasn't sure that he could still see me.

The craft was a very basic model, with seating along the sides and storage racks in the middle.

The light only came on when the door to the craft shut.

The storage racks contained tanks, vacuum suits and packs—containing batteries, I assumed.

The craft took off.

As we flew through the night, the crew distributed suits to us, as well as tanks and power packs. There were also rations of food and supplies for the group as a whole, including a first aid kit and a water purifier.

We were going to split up into smaller teams. I was with Thayu, Deyu, Mereeni and Evi would go together, and Sheydu with Reida and Telaris.

The Lunar travel hub was inside an enclave of Nations of Earth near Cairo, protected by a no-go zone and heavily guarded from the surrounding hostile country.

When we arrived at the space port, it was very early in the morning, having been dropped in a small town outside the city and taken through the checkpoints by someone I assumed to be from the Coldi register. I was too tired by this stage. Days of too little and poor sleep were starting to catch up with me. My leg was still sore.

I had been to the Lunar Travel hub before, as a young boy, excited to go into space for the first time when my father and Erith and I were going to Midway Space Station.

Back then, I would have been far too young and too excited to see the incredibly stark difference between the despair and poverty outside the enclave—where I would have travelled through because the airport was outside the enclave—and the sleek modern world inside.

To be frank, it was obscene.

Had I truly never seen this even as I travelled to Ethiopia to chase Romi Tanaqan?

Had I just become so much more attuned to it after having added Deyu and Reida to my association?

I remembered about the Lunar travel hub that I found it an intimidating and frightening place with guards with guns, and in that respect not that much had changed. It was still an intimidating place, populated by far too many people carrying heavy weapons.

I now understood that they were there to keep desperate refugees and smugglers out. The people in the camps outside the gate. People waiting for an unlikely chance to secure passage across the Mediterranean, people who believed that this would solve all their problems.

Inside the enclave, it was business as usual. There was even very little indication that the drone attacks had disrupted the liftoff schedule.

But twenty years without major investment—years in which Earth had hoped to be able to buy *gamra* equipment—was showing in the dated terminal, the functional but battered shuttles, the worn seats and that distinct *old space craft* smell.

The shuttle that took us to the launch station in orbit was still quite new, but I heard that the old vehicles were still flying if it got busy. Of course, with the drone attacks, the volume of passenger travel had diminished, although I had also heard that placings on the Moon had become coveted because it seemed to be a place fairly safe from attacks. Surely, there was still all the political unrest, but it seemed to be a small price to pay in relation to the other troubles.

Until you found out that even going there compromised your neutrality. Like people put chips in your body when you were unconscious.

They would be tracking us through this thing. They would know we were coming. But I couldn't discard the chip too soon, because they would grow suspicious.

The little packet in my pocket felt heavy. I would have to dispose of it, but I also had to hang onto it for as long as I dared, to leave them in the illusion that I didn't know about it.

CHAPTER THIRTY-TWO

IT WAS RATHER strange to move through this old bit of human space settlement infrastructure in the company of *gamra* people. We were pretending to be regular travellers, so we couldn't discuss any of the old hardware.

But I didn't miss Reida's raised eyebrows at some of the old devices or Sheydu's frowns at outdated security equipment.

It simply surprised me that this old technology still worked.

The structure of the launch station predated Earth's relationship with *gamra*. When Earth fully joined, the space program would become obsolete, and the signs of delayed maintenance manifested everywhere.

Most of the human space program had become a kind of weird anachronism maintained for the sake of stubbornness, a sense of achievement and for those who found this important, independence. Of course, the Independence Force was intertwined with the program, but ironically, it couldn't function independently, because the space program was run and managed and paid for by Nations of Earth.

The authorities kept the lunar settlements as research bases, although whatever research one could do that was not possible in less costly places became ever harder to defend.

People settled on the Moon because of its proximity. Because they didn't have access to the Exchange network and didn't even know about the Exchange way back when the space program started, and the Moon orbited barely two days from Earth. Easy.

Human settlement in space? Tick.

But this sort of space settlement was utterly alien to most of *gamra* except the most secretive arms of the Asto military.

No one at *gamra* would give a celestial body like the Moon more than a few seconds' consideration. Ceren had two small moons. No one had ever set foot on them. Why would they when with the Exchange they could keep looking for habitable worlds?

But not the Earth space program. They colonised the Moon because it was easy to get to and not too far away.

Then they justified spending the effort getting there by trying to find a purpose for the settlements.

Mining had been big in the beginning.

When flying over the surface before coming in to land, I spotted Reida recording and making notes of the old mining facilities. Selena Base would be a similar place.

Large concrete bunkers for ore gathering trucks and equipment. Larger concrete bunkers or a dome for the habitat. The lunar authorities encouraged employees to bring their families to create a feeling of community.

Today, many of those settlements lay abandoned, surrounded by a landscape ravaged through mining, the surface depleted of whatever scarce materials it once held.

Luna City, the first and biggest civilian settlement, however, was still a vibrant and busy place.

I had been here before—when my father briefly held a position here—and it was comforting to see that not all of Earth's space settlement effort had fallen into disrepair. The space port was modern and busy, with no hint of the threat from drone attacks that was so obvious on Earth.

There had been no drone attacks on the Moon bases. I had assumed this was because the drones needed an atmosphere to fly, but the lack of attacks on the Moon could also be interpreted in many other ways.

Like, that the enemy wouldn't attack their own settlements. When we thought they might be based in America Free State, we'd wondered how to justify the attacks there, but now it made sense. Patterson might have asked the invaders to send some drones to communities within their borders whom they considered unsupportive of their point of view. Those attacks would make it look like America Free State was also a victim.

Because at its core, this was the underlying conflict of the war: the people who occupied Earth's space program fighting back at being made obsolete and having their entire lives discarded. To them, *gamra* had done this, and yes, *gamra* actually had. And they'd been unwilling to adapt to change and accept *gamra* as a partner.

This conflict had so many layers.

We were supposed to be tourists in Luna City. We had booked into overnight accommodation in our three groups. I would have preferred to keep going, but we needed to wait for Asha's military backup to manoeuvre into a place from where they could protect us and also, we'd now been going for far too many days with too little rest.

When the shuttle landed, Thayu and I walked to our accommodation separately from the others, pretending not to know them. We dumped our stuff in the modern and airy room and next needed to find something to eat in the domed settlement of Luna City. I took the GenCode chip out of my pocket and put it in the cupboard in the room. For days, I had debated with myself about what to do with it. I'd thought about casually dropping it into someone else's bag, but it would be discovered as soon as that person went through a security checkpoint, and there were many. On the other hand, GenCode ID chips were *not* mandatory, so it was plausible that someone—like me and Thayu—walked through these checkpoints and didn't return a reading. We needed to buy ourselves time, so I decided to leave that chip on the shelf and let the enemy circle the accommodation, thinking we were inside, wondering when to pounce, while we made our final move.

It was quite busy in the streets of the settlement. About two hundred thousand people lived in Luna City these days, a number that had been stable for years. Most of them serviced the space ship building industry, mostly for space mining operations. There were also training facilities, schools, the Lunar Tech University, and the services that serviced the base, like shops and restaurants.

It was a sizeable town, and it was still as I remembered: modern and pleasant.

But while walking through the main thoroughfare close to our accommodation, I found it painfully obvious that there were almost no *gamra* people, and Coldi people in particular, on the streets.

With her dyed hair, Thayu reminded me of Nicha all those years ago, Asian enough to pass as being of Chinese heritage.

The thought that we were back to pretending to be Asian made me feel sick.

I thought we'd left that garbage behind.

Since Thayu and I had entered the settlement as a prospecting party, we visited a mining hire shop to hire a vehicle. This was not as easy as I thought. The rental shops asked for mining company endorsements and permits.

I was doing all the talking, but listening to the people in the businesses and streets, I realised that my accent stood out. If someone was looking, and we should assume that they were, they would easily pick us as non-local.

So I changed my tactic, and used one of my other cover stories, that we were looking for some people who had gone missing, a brother of mine who was last seen in this area and had a penchant for wanting to live independently. I knew this would also attract some attention, but hopefully wouldn't require as much administrative stuff as the prospecting story. By the close of business, we had a truck and an air machine.

On the way back, we found a very nice eating house close to our accommodation, but the clientele were all Earth-based workers, and I didn't feel comfortable staying any longer than necessary because people kept looking at Thayu. So we took the food up to our room.

This was just as well, because in the time we'd been away, a message had arrived from Reida. It contained a large file with registration data for students at Mars University for the year that I had been attacked there.

The list contained over twelve thousand students, not including the staff or university employees. Yikes. It was going to be hard to find my mysterious messenger.

I eliminated students enrolled in unrelated degrees. People like engineers wouldn't lower themselves to do courses in international politics. That still left me with close to four thousand names to check. And I didn't even know what I was looking for. A familiar name. Someone from the enemy camp who had been there with me. Who I remembered as being aggressive.

I eliminated another thousand students from a different campus. It was a blunt elimination, because the two campuses were within the same settlement and students often travelled between the two. But I needed to get this down to a manageable level.

Thayu offered to help, but I didn't know what I was looking for. A familiar name. I couldn't give her a list.

She fell asleep, and I sat in bed next to her, knowing that I should also go to sleep because tomorrow was a very big day, but I couldn't get over my curiosity. I wouldn't be able to sleep, anyway. My brain was just too active.

So I scrolled through list after list of names, occasionally forgetting to read and having to scroll back to the names I last remembered checking.

I came across some familiar names, mostly of fellow students I'd long since relegated to the back of my mind as distant memories. I entertained a large and active circle of friends and a reputation as a shit-stirrer. People who studied journalism liked to hang around me. They were all people from my year. I didn't know terribly many people in older years.

But the lists were too long, even for my curious mind.

I was about to turn the reader off when I spotted another familiar name. And it was of someone I didn't even know was at Mars University.

Joseph Sullivan, son of the head of security at Midway, Don Sullivan, who was a known Independence Force supporter.

Well… that was odd. I'd never noticed Joseph in my classes. He was an older kid at the Midway Space Station school.

Back then, I was ten, and he must have been eleven or twelve. He was a gangly, shy kid, and I felt sorry for him because his father was an authoritarian bully who used to frighten me.

He kept a pet rabbitooh, an artificial creature normally kept in space settlements for meat production. Productive like a rabbit, with quality meat like a kangaroo. They were not particularly suitable as pets, but he owned one anyway, which he hid from his father. It escaped—which was my fault in a weird kind of way. And this episode chasing after this damn escaped pet was the start of my current career when it brought me face to face with Joyelin Akhtari, then Chief Delegate of *gamra*. She was ancient even back then, and my ten-year-old self looked at her and thought the world of her, and I wanted nothing more than to learn about the *gamra* worlds. We used to call it *Union* back then.

Life had a funny way of reconnecting.

The space community was not large. Did this mean that Joseph Sullivan had taken over from his father as the leader of the group of people who wanted to kill Joyelin Akhtari and escape to a newly discovered world with the station's only shuttle?

I'd forgotten about the episode, especially Joseph, because he was a good kid—I thought—or at least he had been back then.

Well, holy crap.

I'd probably come to their attention as a kid and had resurfaced when I came to Mars University. They'd wanted to shut me up. They'd sent thugs to attack me. They'd bugged me. I couldn't be a hundred percent sure I was right, but in my mind I was sure: this was Joseph Sullivan sending me these childish messages, never having gotten over a grudge he'd held since primary school.

Thayu was already fast asleep, so I couldn't tell her about my discovery. She might not care all that much, either. How significant was it that Joseph Sullivan was in the enemy camp? I hadn't interacted with him since leaving Midway. For me, it just put a face to the enemy. I wondered if back then when a discovery I made stopped their plan to steal the shuttle, they had been planning to go to Barresh.

I mulled over all these questions, but eventually fell asleep.

Luna City's days were artificial and when I woke up, light filtered through the window from behind the curtains.

To my surprise, Thayu was already awake and sitting at the little table near the window.

"Anything the matter?" I asked.

"Ha, you're awake."

"Don't get too used to getting up first. That's my job."

She grinned. "Anyu reports that the traffic is busy in orbit and that the rescue and defence ships have retreated a small distance to avoid detection."

"Is that a bad thing?"

"Not really. It just adds a tiny bit of time to the recovery window."

That was security jargon for how long it would take an external rescue team to retrieve us. I was used to working with recovery windows of days, or even non-existent ones, so I couldn't get excited about a few extra minutes.

I told her about my discovery, but lacking my experience, she only said, "Well, these are indeed the people you thought, right?"

Yes, we did, but it was good to have it confirmed, and to put a face on the enemy.

We went to breakfast.

On the way to the eating house, Thayu reported that she heard from the others through Anyu and that they were all in position, and had also hired vehicles. Deyu and Evi were already outside the settlement. Reida, Sheydu and Telaris were staying in a different part of the settlement.

After breakfast, we took our bags, left the accommodation and collected our vehicle and air making machine. The young man in the equipment hire office took pains to read out the entire page with safety tracking protocols and we needed to sign in many places. We got a map with all the areas where we were not supposed to go clearly marked out. Selena Base was in one such restricted area. The truck came with a tracking device.

Well, guess which device would magically stop working as soon as we left the building? In fact, it took Thayu less than five minutes after we left the airlock.

I drove the vehicle over the grey plain. The sun hung low over the horizon and made the grey landscape glitter with brightness.

The landscape was utterly desolate, plain after plain of grey dirt criss-crossed by a tapestry of tracks. The approved road followed a straight line with reflective posts every few steps on both sides. Huge signs declared warnings to stay on the marked roads, that the substrate was unstable and that there were mining tunnels underneath.

Reida's map showed me where to go.

I looked around for the other groups from our team, but didn't see a sign of life. Yet I knew they were there because Thayu was sending them messages.

Asha's ships were in orbit. I couldn't see them either, but Thayu's screen showed the distinctive dots with numbers.

Three military ships were ready and waiting in the next valley.

Since we were pretending to be a tracking team, either prospecting or looking for someone depending on who asked, we stopped a few times to take scans and collect data. Thayu did this, getting into the awkward vacuum suit, clambering out the back through the airlock and walking around in the dust. I realised that this was not familiar terrain for Asto's military. They hid in deep space and didn't send people to places without an atmosphere. In fact, Asha had laughed when I first told him about the Moon and Mars bases. Why would anyone do that? He'd wanted to know.

Thayu sent the data she collected through to the ship, and sitting there by myself, feeling nervous, I had too much time to wonder about whatever they were going to do with it. Did I really want to know the ins and outs of calibrating the amount of force needed to turn this area into the latest Moon crater?

After a while, we came to a low set bunker-like building with a dark maw for an entrance. A variety of tracks lead out to show that many vehicles used to be parked inside this construction. From what I had read, the mining vehicles used to roam the surface and scoop up the dirt and feed it through crushers and turn it into useful things.

They had stopped doing this because not only was it highly destructive, but they had found much more efficient ways of farming rare earths in the asteroid belt. While you could send a robot army over the moon and turn it over, the vehicles still needed fuel, and their efforts needed to be more than compensated for by the proceeds of what they found.

Today, most of those large mining vehicles were gone from the big open-sided hall. A lot of dust had been tracked in, even though there was no air movement on the moon, and I was wondering where it had all come from.

If the hall was in active use, it would be full of trucks.

There were just two trucks inside.

One was a battered up vehicle that looked like it hadn't moved for the past hundred years. It sported a metal attachment to the side, likely something related to mining.

The other had no wheels and looked to have been used for spare parts.

"Wait," Thayu said.

She zoomed in on the intact vehicle's tracks, which cut through all the others. She looked at me, and we both knew what that meant. It had come here recently.

Thayu grabbed her weapon.

I stopped the vehicle, jumped from my seat and handed her the helmet and air tanks that stood behind her, and then grabbed mine.

We both put our helmets on.

As we stood there, the back door of the other vehicle opened and a couple of suited figures came out.

They fanned out around us.

CHAPTER THIRTY-THREE

OH, crap.

I looked at Thayu.

Where were the others? Deyu and Evi, Reida, Mereeni, Sheydu and Telaris? Had they also walked into this trap?

She glanced aside, but I couldn't see where she was looking through the reflective surface of the visor.

She gestured *Don't say anything important.*

I connected my air tank and opened the valves, but left the mouthpiece dangling inside my helmet for the time being.

One of the people outside pointed a weapon at the front of our truck. Another made a gesture *come out.*

There wasn't anything else we could do. This truck carried all we needed to survive. We both got ready to go out the back airlock.

"I'll go first," I said.

"I'm better with weapons."

"They will more easily talk to me."

That argument won her over. We were outnumbered until the other members of our team showed up, and we didn't know when or even whether they would. I'd like to think so.

I cycled through the airlock first and clumsily climbed down the little ladder at the back of the vehicle and stepped into the dust.

Five figures faced me, unrecognisable in their pressure suits.

They waited until Thayu had also come out. Then the figure next to the one with the gun pointed to the side of his helmet.

Turn on the reception? I wasn't sure how to do that. We'd made a point of not using the local network.

But user-friendliness was an extremely important feature of life in space. Apparently, one controlled the display of options inside a helmet with eye movements.

A list of options came up. One was *turn on sound*. I did that.

A scratchy male voice came into my helmet.

"You are trespassing on private land." His accent brought me back to the time I'd lived at Midway Space Station and New Taurus, where people spoke various dialects of Cosla, the space settler variant of Isla.

I stuck to my story. "We are prospectors. We have an issue with our truck that we need to fix and we were looking for a place to camp. This place looks abandoned. The map says it's abandoned."

"Why are you here? The hire company would have told you that this is a restricted area."

"I must have misunderstood. The Nations of Earth convention says that land on non-Earth bodies cannot be bought or sold, so unless this is a restricted area for military purposes, there isn't actually any private land."

"They are wrong. And what does Nations of Earth care, anyway?"

"I'm sorry for interrupting you. If you let us get back into the vehicle, we will go somewhere else."

"No. You're coming with us."

"On what authority?"

"Ours. This is private property."

The people came closer.

We were outnumbered, and I had no doubt that these moon-dwellers were much more experienced in fighting in vacuum suits in low gravity than we were. Besides, we might learn something by talking with them.

I gestured *back down*.

Thayu had probably already figured this out herself.

Two each grabbed my arm and Thayu's arms. They pushed her in front of me in the direction of their vehicle. She entered the airlock with one of the people.

Then it was my turn.

The truck's airlock was bigger than ours and fitted two people at a time when wearing vacuum suits. Even when I stood very close to the person in the airlock with me, all I could see was my own reflection in the visor.

We waited.

The connection in my helmet fell quiet. Was there some sort of shielding in the vehicle?

The airlock hissed, and the inside door opened. The first thing I saw was Thayu, with her helmet off, seated on a bench with two beefy guys standing on either side of her.

The way they allowed her to just sit on the bench—not tied up or secured, like a weak woman—showed me that she had not tried to test their defenses, because it probably wouldn't end so well for them. Also, how they were clearly unaware that it was the Coldi women who tended to be stronger and more dangerous.

The figure who had been in the airlock with me was also a man. He looked similar to the others: broad-shouldered, a perfect example of a male human specimen. He eyed me with a hard face.

Meanwhile, the door to the airlock had closed again and the remaining three people came in.

When they took their helmets off, they were also young men, two with brown hair, one with a short beard and one with blond hair. The beard guy appeared to be the leader, judging by the way the others let him go first.

They spoke to each other in short sentences, but I didn't recognise the language.

Sure, when I'd lived at Midway, the residents spoke a dialect of Cosla—the space variety of Isla—with lots of unusual words. Like they said the word ferrets in place of swearing. I'd found that amusing.

But Cosla and Isla were dialects. This was a different language. It sounded like... Polish or something?

It got rather crowded in the truck with all of us in the cabin.

I glanced at Thayu. She was holding her helmet on her lap and did her best to ignore the men's stares. I copied her by holding my helmet on my lap when I sat at the bench opposite her. I hoped she'd been able to warn the others.

The bearded guy was also the one who had spoken to us, judging by the sound of his voice.

The other four had either come along for the ride as thugs or they couldn't speak with us because they only spoke whatever language they spoke amongst each other.

One of them now got behind the controls of the vehicle, while the others, including the bearded guy, sat on either side of us.

"Now, let's talk again. What were you doing here?" asked the bearded man, while looking at me.

"As I told you, we are private prospectors."

His nostrils flared. "Show me your ID."

"Who are you? Only officials are allowed to ask for that. Are you working for Nations of Earth?"

He ignored the question but jerked his head and said something I didn't catch. One of the men on my bench leaned forward and passed a device over me. I could see the tiny screen from where I sat. A horizontal line tracked across. It vibrated a tiny bit as he moved the device.

He shook his head.

The beard guy barked a response, like he didn't believe what the other man said.

The man showed him the screen.

A brief expression of confusion flickered over his face. He gave one of the other men a disturbed glance.

They had probably expected to see the GenCode ID that was on the chip that I'd left in the drawer in the accommodation.

The men exchanged a few words.

One asked a question, and the leader replied with a resolute tone.

The driver turned on the vehicle. He slowly backed away from our rented vehicle and the broken truck, turned around and steered towards the entrance of the bunker.

I glanced at Thayu, whose keen eyes would observe and remember everything. This was useful information. We had come here because we thought this low building provided an entrance to the underground tunnel system, but these men weren't going to use it for whatever reason. A cave-in, a lack of security, other people living in this area, or just that the base wasn't in this exact location, but further away. We'd find out where it was.

But they might also take us to a deserted plain and toss us out the airlock.

Damn, that was not a helpful thought. Our means of surviving independently were in the truck we were leaving behind.

I hoped someone out there was tracking our progress and would do something when things went wrong.

Although I also very much didn't want the Asto military to get involved. But they would. Asha had said so.

The vehicle left the underground bunker, back into the brightness of the plain.

Reception returned.

The chatter of the normal activities of the moon bases came into my earpiece. Some sort of talkback bulletin and some music going in and out of hearing. It sounded strangely normal.

I looked at the sky, full of bright stars. The sun was hitting the plain side-on, and rocks cast long black shadows across the grey plain.

We followed the same track that had taken us to the bunker, but turned off before we arrived at the main track. The terrain was quite rocky here, and the truck zig-zagged up an incline.

For a moment, I was afraid that we might spot the Asto military aircraft that had landed in the next valley according to Thayu.

But the military had very good invisibility shields. Also, possibly *the next valley* was too literal a description. They'd be a distance away, and we didn't see them.

The truck zig-zagged between jagged rocks and came to the maw of a tunnel wide enough for one vehicle. It was extremely dark, with only the vehicle's headlights showing the way. The walls of the tunnel were made of concrete. It felt like being in a train tunnel.

After a while, the tunnel opened out into an underground chamber where several other vehicles stood.

My reception had again disappeared. Thayu held her head cocked as if she was listening to something.

The driver stopped the vehicle at the entrance to an airlock.

A moving arm came out from the wall and attached a tube to the vehicle. Now I understood the purpose of the strange contraption on the side of the vehicle.

These were old mining trucks, but these people had modified them to their own requirements.

When the connection was complete, the men got up, carrying their helmets, and gestured for me and Thayu to do the same.

So I got up and clambered down the ladder into the tube and then followed the men into a well-lit underground room that held benches and racks with environment suits, tanks and an air fill station.

The room looked well-used and quite old, and even some of the equipment was ancient. I didn't know anyone still used these completely rigid suits with special joints that were still very limited in their movement. Last time I'd seen one of those was in a museum.

A large sign on the wall said *Emergency Way Station* and underneath hung a sign with instructions on how to operate the air machine.

I understood. This was an old emergency shelter that used to be for the surface miners in case they needed to take cover for a solar storm or when they had trouble with their vehicles.

The tunnels had only been added later.

It didn't look like there was an exit to the room other than the airlock where we had come in, but then one of the men unlocked a metal cupboard at the back of the room. Inside was another door with a security panel on the side.

He opened the cover of the panel and typed a code. And... nothing happened.

That was interesting.

He opened a second panel, which contained a communication device. He said something, and a moment later, a blaring voice replied.

This woman still spoke with a heavy accent, but at least I could understand a good portion of her words.

She spoke about resetting the panel. There had been an outage, she said. They were still going through resetting everything.

The man did that, whatever it entailed. Lights on the panel flashed.

The door rolled aside.

Because this room also functioned as solar storm shelter, the door was very thick and heavy and opening it was a slow process.

When the opening was wide enough, the bearded guy stepped through—and fell backwards against one of the other men.

Thayu swung her helmet around and brought it down on his head and then knocked out the guy who had just found out that she was *not* a weak female by swinging her elbow against the side of his head.

That left my minder, whom she took out by swinging the helmet back.

That was three of them out cold on the floor.

"Thanks, Thay'."

She was awesome.

Now where had beard guy gone off to?

The door had stalled, but someone pushed it open from the inside with a huge gloved hand.

Telaris.

Thank the heavens.

Deyu stood behind the bearded guy, her formidable arm around his neck. He tried to scratch her arms, but she wore a thick undersuit.

"Hey, what kind of freak is this?" he squealed when he noticed me.

"This is Deyu. It's not easy to get her annoyed, but once you do, you cannot fight her or hide from her. She is a killing machine. I promise you won't feel anything."

He tried to look over his shoulder. I doubted he had realised that Deyu was female.

Deyu had no idea what I'd just said. She was utterly focused on her task. Keep us safe. Get us out of here alive. She gestured for the man to take off his weapons and his devices.

He protested, and Deyu shut him up by tying his equipment belt over his mouth.

"Now, be quiet. You might want to know that we are the same people who got into Nations of Earth and killed the treacherous lot there."

His eyes were wide.

"Let's go." Sheydu came out of a doorway. "I don't like this place and I want to be out of here before Asha gets too annoyed."

She was followed by Evi and Reida, each carrying a bunch of equipment.

"Suit up first." Reida held a set of survival gear out to Sheydu. She connected leads from the receiver that hung at her waist. She slotted the air tank in the holes in a type of backpack and tied the helmet to her belt.

Then she strapped her weapons over the top. A charge gun on her arm, a smaller gun on her left arm, a heavy duty military weapon on her left leg and her jacket with all her explosive goodies over the top.

All this was done in silence, with a dead serious expression on her face.

Reida handed out the other similar sets of equipment, which we all put on, helping each other with the packs of air tanks. There were not enough clips to thread through the helmets, so some of us used a piece of rope. We had to have both hands free.

Fortunately, the gravity was light, and it was not that uncomfortable to carry this gear.

A few minutes later, we were all ready to go.

Reida had pulled up the map and had, of course, already studied the layout of the place for as far as he could see it. He had been studying it since we had left my father's farm. We had just entered in a different place as we had expected.

He pointed at a section of his map. Yes, I could see that the temperature was much higher in that area. But in between there and where we were lay a section that was very dark and displayed no passages joining up with the section where we wanted to go.

I circled the area on the screen. "What's this?"

He spread his hands.

A shielded area? An area with particularly dense rock? The edges were not clearly defined, as they would be in case of a shield. We would have to pass this area in order to get to the more promising section, where corridors and rooms stood out clearly.

"It doesn't look like there is a way through," I said.

"I'm pretty sure there is. I've seen people use it."

We were all ready. Mereeni had used her skills to tie up the prisoner so that he could walk but not escape. Her technique for keeping people quiet was also something special. She had not only taped his mouth shut, but tied his jaws so tightly together that he could only breathe through his nose.

His eyes held a furious expression.

Reida led us along the corridor and then into a stairwell. He and Deyu went first, followed by Evi, Thayu and I, Mereeni with the prisoner and Telaris and Sheydu bringing up the rear.

Reida would sometimes stop to scan our surroundings for listening equipment, but he was happy with what he found.

Would we just be allowed to walk into this place without being challenged?

Surely they were already watching us, and we were walking into a trap.

At the bottom of the stairwell, we turned left and walked down another corridor, this one roughly hewn out of the rock.

There was a safety station on the side with compressed air bottles, where we refilled our tanks. Not because they were empty, but because we wanted to be as well prepared as possible.

Then Reida held up his hand. He gestured *Quiet* and we all stopped and listened. The only thing I could hear was a kind of humming. I gestured *What is that?* Of course, nobody knew the answer.

Ahead, the rough corridor opened into a chamber, and this was the origin of the sound.

We crept forward along the walls.

Reida held his scanner up, but saw nothing that caused him alarm

A glow of blue-purple light emanated from a bubble-like transparent encasing in the middle of the chamber.

It was so bright that it was hard to look at.

A walkway led around the perimeter of the chamber, one side attached to the rock walls.

We stood at the entrance, unsure of what to do next.

"What is this thing?" Evi said in a low voice.

"Whatever it is, it gives me the creeps. I doubt I want to know what it is. I'm more interested in getting through," Sheydu said.

I walked up to the railing and looked down into the chamber for as far as I could. The bright light inside the glass encasing made it hard.

I couldn't see another way out of here, and dreaded that we had been mistaken and the network of passages didn't link up to the other side at all. Or maybe it once had but had been closed off.

The glass encasing met the surface of the round structure below ground level. The round transparent structure broadened out at this point, disappearing below the ground. A second walkway encircled the chamber below the point where we stood.

This walkway—closer to the transparent case and with railings on both sides—included a platform with a set of three control panels.

What the hell was this thing?

Deyu was recording everything.

Reida leaned against the railing, studying the map.

Sheydu stood next to him, her hands at her sides. She was speaking to him in a low voice, looking more agitated than I knew Sheydu normally to be.

I joined them.

"We're running out of time," Sheydu said. "This is taking too long. We need to get out of here."

Mereeni held our prisoner, who held his head bent back, staring at the ceiling with wide eyes. Sweat made his forehead glisten.

So he was nervous, too, huh? About what?

Being discovered couldn't be it. That would only be beneficial to him.

So he was afraid that he was going to meet the same fate as the others—but he knew we needed his GenCode chip to open the doors —or he was afraid that we'd do something else... like mess with this installation?

Hmmm.

The height difference between our level and the walkway underneath was not that great. I leaned over the railing to look down.

"Could you lower us down there?" I asked Deyu.

"Of course. That's easy. If you want."

The prisoner made a strangled noise.

"What's down there?" I asked in Isla.

Our captive shook his head.

"I want to get your bosses to come out to talk to us. You're telling me that if I mess with those panels down there, someone will come?"

"Hmmmmmmm!" He shook his head again, his eyes wide.

"Then tell your bosses to come here and talk to me right now, to save yourselves. Out there in orbit are some very dangerous ships that know exactly where we are and they now know where you are. I'm here to talk. All I want is to get through past this chamber. That shouldn't be too hard."

He nodded, his eyes still wide.

I gestured to Deyu to remove the gag from his mouth.

The first thing he said was, "I need to send a message."

I held up his device while he told me how to use it.

We let him speak briefly with his superiors, but we made sure that he couldn't touch the device.

Incredibly, Thayu had already found a translation module that let us know the gist of what they spoke about. The language, it declared, was Euro-Russian. He told them he had been captured. He said his captors were bringing him into the den.

The voice on the other end said to proceed, and that they were prepared.

He said something about a threat of alien ships.

The other man said they knew about those ships and were keeping an eye on them.

When the other man signed off, he nodded. "That way."

CHAPTER THIRTY-FOUR

HE LED us along the walkway to the far side of the chamber.

At a section of the rock wall that looked just like any other, he stopped and nodded at the side.

"It's here. I need my hands."

They were still tied up.

I glanced at Sheydu. She nodded. That was another measure of how nervous she was. There was no way she would have allowed us to untie a dangerous prisoner unless she had a very good reason for it.

I warned him. "Understand that the moment you try to pull a trick on us, you will regret it deeply."

He nodded.

Deyu undid the knot.

He put his palm against the rock surface—and an entire section of it folded in and slid aside.

Walking through, I touched the surface. It *felt* like rock.

We ended up in a dimly lit passage that ended in another chamber. This one was much, much bigger than the previous, and the level where we entered was much further off the cavern's floor, a massive cylinder, which was—I realised—a continuation of the big round thing I'd seen in the other chamber.

Wow.

The other chamber was a kind of control and monitoring station for this big underground... thing that was built deep in the moon rock. We could just see the top of it, like the back of a whale in the ocean. Most of it sat under the surface.

Thick pipes ran the length of the chamber, connecting the thing to... other places. Maybe they carried water for cooling.

It reminded me of the time when Ezhya had shown me the military sling.

This had to be something like that. A weapon that generated energy or particles from plasma or antimatter, or through fusion.

How big was this thing under the ground?

I hoped we'd be able to save this thing from destruction.

If not, I hoped we'd be able to figure out what it did and how it worked from what Reida was recording.

As soon as we were in this chamber, our prisoner took off like crazy, clearly not happy to be here. I understood why this area had shown up as dark on the scans. It diverted energy. And people didn't come here when this machine was in operation, something like that.

Boy, I'd never been good at physics, but now I wished I'd paid closer attention.

Asto's military sling was a one-sided Exchange node. Normally, transfer through anpar lines required two connecting nodes. A sling could fling objects randomly into deep space and, if the setting was right, totally obliterate them.

This machine transferred things... into low Earth orbit? Was that why the drones came out of nowhere and didn't appear to be suited to long-distance space travel or to atmosphere entry?

Damn.

We came to the end of the chamber marked by a partial wall. On the other side lay a deep pool, the water dark. A tiny light burned at the very bottom, at least five metres down. The glow appeared sickly green. The surface of the water was showing weird ripples. I'd also seen this on Midway Space Station. Water did this in low gravity, where the smallest movement would create really strange wave patterns in the surface.

I guessed this water was for cooling the machine.

The walkway went along the side and entered another room, this one a workshop.

Long tables stood in rows, with trays that contained little boxes with parts that came from all over the settled worlds. There were

Asto-made parts, and Earth-made parts and Damarcian parts and others I didn't recognise.

Yes, this was a workshop where the drone prototypes were put together.

And then replicated with the machine in the other room?

I glanced over my shoulder. Reida and Deyu and Sheydu were recording everything.

On the far side of the workshop, we came to a closed door.

"We're here, as I promised," the prisoner said. "This door is open."

Heh, yeah, and he thought we were going to fall into that trap.

Sheydu took the big gun from her leg bracket. Telaris unstrapped the rocket launcher.

There was a small moment's silence in which she said, "Prepare."

And then Thayu said, "Action."

Both Telaris and Sheydu fired at the door, which blew outwards. The prisoner made a grab for the weapon on Deyu's arm. She swung and whacked him with her elbow so hard that he flew across the room and slammed into the wall.

Reida said, "This way."

We ran across the workshop to another door. Shots rang out behind us as the people who had been waiting on the other side responded to my team's distraction and came into the workshop looking for us.

Reida had located another door in the corner of the workshop that led into a storage area. At the end was a lift for goods. He was really good with his maps.

We just fitted into the lift with all of us and our gear.

Reida closed the door and then fired at the control panel to destroy it and block the lift.

Deyu lifted him to the ceiling, where he pushed a hatch aside.

"Come, climb up." He held his hand down and pulled the members of my team up. First Thayu, then Mereeni. In the case of Telaris, this wasn't easy, because he was not only very big, but carried a lot of awkward stuff that he had to pass to us first.

As I was helping to push him through the opening, a heavy thud on the metal door made the lift cubicle shake.

Male voices shouted outside.

"Quick!" someone whispered from above.

I held my hand up. Deyu pulled me up, and then Sheydu was the last. We pushed the hatch back, even if only that it was crowded on top of the lift and it provided space for someone to stand.

While we stood there, two heavy *foomp* sounds in close succession shook the ground.

"What was that?" Mereeni asked, her voice alarmed.

"I don't think we want to know," Sheydu said. "Come on, hurry up."

Up in the dark lift shaft, Reida was already climbing the ropes to the next floor. He reached a narrow platform next to the closed doors and waited there.

Telaris joined him and then Deyu, and then the ledge was full.

Sheydu threw Reida a little packet, which he unfurled into a net with sticky pads. Reida stuck two of the pads to the wall and threw the other side of the net to Thayu next to me at the top of the lift ropes. She attached the remaining pads to each other, so the ensemble formed a rudimentary and very wobbly bridge-ladder.

The rest of us climbed as far as we could.

The low gravity meant that the net held us all.

Meanwhile, Reida wrenched open the lift door.

In quick succession, we all scrambled out of the lift shaft, with Sheydu pulling up the ladder. A shattering crash sounded downstairs, like something destructive hitting the lift doors.

We came out into a clean and airy hall. A set of open doors across the smooth floor opened into a large room lit by the glow of many screens. A kind of control centre, with people—as yet unaware of our presence—sitting in front of screens with data flickering over them.

Holy crap. This young man never failed to impress me. Reida had brought us straight to the enemy's nerve centre.

"How did you know this was here?" I asked him in a whisper.

"I didn't. It was luck. I thought there might be something important here, but I didn't know for certain."

"You're too modest."

"Get ready," Sheydu said.

She held her gun in one hand and a packet I assumed was a smoke bomb in the other. The tiny marble that was the fold-up breathing mask hung from a button on her collar.

Mine was in my breast pocket. I also unclipped my weapon.

Deyu ran into the room, followed by Sheydu and Telaris. I followed him, holding my gun with one hand and making sure that my mask was still in my pocket with the other.

One of the workers turned around and gave a shout.

There were about ten people in the room. Some dropped under their desks. One tried to run out, but Deyu grabbed him by the back of his shirt and flung him aside.

Someone shouted on the other side of the room. A man rose between the workstations with a weapon.

Sheydu took care of that with a precision shot.

As usual, when someone discharged a gun, the skin on my arms puckered into goosebumps.

The remaining people huddled on the ground under and around a desk.

Deyu stood next to them, having dragged her victim to them and having dumped him on the ground. He was moving, but not very happy.

I said, "Quick, get a data dump of everything in these machines."

Thayu got to work. She and Telaris could do this incredibly quickly.

We waited, keeping an eye on everyone in the room.

Reida was scrolling through his maps, plotting out a route to the nearest vehicle.

I had to contemplate what to do with the prisoners. We couldn't take them with us, and we couldn't allow them to create trouble for us either.

There were many control screens in the room. One showed a loop of live action from different cameras around the base. Another was a radar screen, showing ships in orbit. It displayed a couple of slowly moving dots against a grainy background. Old radar machines might give this type of inferior quality picture, or alternatively, when there was bad weather. Since the Moon had no weather, the graininess was odd... no, wait. Those specks were all *moving*.

"Reida, look at this," I said in a low voice.

He came over and frowned at the screen.

"Is that...?" he began.

"A drone army? I think so. You know those foomps we heard? That was the machine replicating or whatever it does."

"Oh, fuck."

"You can say that again."

As we stared at the screen, realising the horror, while Thayu and Telaris were still reading data from the computer systems, I became aware of a sound on the other side of the room.

Deyu jumped into alertness.

As she took her attention off the prisoners, one of them tried to run.

Sheydu made short work of him.

I didn't even hear the charge go off, but the goosebumps crawled over my arms.

The man fell in a place where I could only see his feet. They did not move again.

Mereeni said, "Action."

The door had opened on the other side of the room and a group of people was coming through. The first two were heavily armed soldiers.

We ducked behind the workstations.

Thayu was done with her work. She stuffed her equipment in her pack and calmly took her gun out of the arm bracket.

The party had advanced about halfway through the room when Sheydu shouted, "Action!"

Telaris rose and fired the rocket launcher.

It hit both the guards at the front, but just missed the thin and lanky man walking behind them. Two more armed men ran into the room.

One shouted, but I couldn't make out what he said.

The room's workers, most still hiding under the desks, were looking around.

"You stay right where you are," I said to them. "Or you will share the fate of your colleague. I'm serious."

I wasn't sure if they understood.

Telaris had recharged the big gun and was taking aim again.

"Wait," I said to him.

"Come out if you dare and look me in the face, you cowardly alien scum," the tall man called into the room.

I replied, "Believe it or not, we're here to talk and save you. If you believe I am your enemy, you haven't seen your real enemy."

He laughed.

Something about him was familiar.

Yes. I'd come across that name on the list of the students at Mars University.

Joseph Sullivan.

"So it was you sending me those messages through the GenCode chip I didn't know I had and that someone illegally inserted in me when I came to the hospital after having been bashed—by one of your cronies, because you wouldn't lower yourself to do something like that with your own hands?"

While I spoke, I raised myself from between the workstations, but not enough to be completely in the open, so that the two guards who still stood on either side of him couldn't see my charge gun.

"So you were behind this," I said.

He had gotten much older, of course. When I had met him as a ten-year-old, his face was already losing the softness of youth, and his skinny limbs were already lengthening, further hastened by the harsh treatment at the hands of his father.

Time had not been kind to him, and life in space tended to age and wrinkle people's skin at a younger age than normal. He'd been thin and lanky even back then, but now he looked like a hollowed-out husk of a spider, hunched over by growing too fast in low gravity.

"Me and my father and a lot of other people stand up against the alien invaders. If you think we are just random small time actors, you've got that wrong. We are the last remaining organisation that stands for true humanity."

He studied my face. With my transformation, a lot of things had changed about me, but not significantly in the shape of my face.

He laughed. "You thought you had defeated us?"

"I thought nothing. I was ten at the time. What did I know?"

"Even back then, you were already a self-absorbed piece of work. Always meddling in other people's business."

"I did what I thought was right. And in the end, your father helped us against the terrorists."

"That's what you think. We were merely biding our time. That was clearly not a good time with that traitor of that father of yours in the position of station director. That station did not belong to you, even if you acted like it. The director's son. You snivelling lying piece of shit."

His two guards were now standing on either side of him. I had no doubt that there were more of them waiting to be called back behind the door where he had come from.

Sheydu made an impatient noise. That drone army would come in here the moment they ordered it to do so.

"Look, I'm trying to save all of our lives. There are Asto military ships in orbit that are very, very nervous and are going to deploy their firepower soon. We are not here assisting them. We are here trying to save you from them. Because I get a lot more satisfaction from seeing you and your leaders humiliated and convicted in a courtroom than I get from killing you, which any member of my team would do in a heartbeat, if I gave the order. I want the entire world to know who you are and I want the self-absorbed reasons that you use to justify subjecting your home planet to this kind of treatment spelled out in all the news channels."

"Are you trying to get us to surrender? Don't you know that we never surrender?"

He raised his arms and pointed a weapon at me.

"I've been looking forward to this moment for a very long time. It's payback time."

His muscles stiffened, but before he could fire, several white sizzling beams hit him at the same time. He fell sideways.

Before I could run over to see, an alarm started blaring in the room.

A red light was flashing on one of the screens.

It said across the screen in big letters, *perimeter broken. Take cover and defensive action now.*

This was it. Asha had ordered the ships to go in and destroy the place.

I called, "Quick, get out of here, any way we can. Anyone here can come with us if they want. Those ships are going to blow this place to bits."

CHAPTER THIRTY-FIVE

IT WAS a mark of the fear or level of brainwashing that people had undergone that no one dared put up their hand to come with us. It was a mark of their sense of fate that none of them tried to stop or attack us, even as Sheydu took one of her secret packages out of her backpack, slapped it onto the control panel of a workstation and activated it with her reader.

A special new type of explosive they called a powered bomb that used power connections to expand its reach. An explosion here in the control room would be felt and noticed across the entire base.

Sheydu called, "Quick, go, before this thing goes off."

The last I saw when running after Thayu out of the room was the workers crouch around the body of their leader.

Joseph Sullivan.

Shy, awkward, gangly Joseph Sullivan. I'd barely wondered what had happened to him after we parted ways. And he'd spent much of his life wanting to get back at me. He was truly part of another world.

But we definitely weren't going to hang around while the bots turned on their own base and Sheydu's explosive and the Asto military ships did the rest.

According to Reida, the quickest way out of the underground tunnels was ahead of us, not around the back way where we had come in.

Also, he noticed that the operation of the underground machine had triggered warnings about the tunnels we had passed. I wondered if that was why our first prisoner had been so nervous. When someone operated the machine, those passages became unsafe.

Damn it, the trail of death we had left behind was disturbing, and there could be more still to come.

I liked to think one stopped being human when you no longer worried about this. I'd gone in to *save* these people, and now we faced all-out war.

When the entire team had made it to the door, Sheydu grabbed one of her famous smoke bombs and tossed it into the opening. The projectile bounced on the hard floor and disappeared in between the workstations.

It exploded with a loud *pop*.

The sound was followed by muffled coughs and then the sound of people running.

Unlike at Nations of Earth, these people weren't amateurs. They didn't swear or blunder into an exposed position.

We put on our breathing masks while making our way down the hallway. It was hard to see for all the smoke. I followed Telaris, and Thayu was behind me. Reida at the front knew where we were going, I hoped. We ran down the corridor and into a stairwell and then up a level into another passage. Despite the low gravity, running was heavy work. The suit limited mobility, and the backpack with the air tank bumped against the back of my legs. The helmet swung around, hitting my side.

Even though Deyu carried a local communication hub, reception between us in the team was patchy.

It didn't help that an alarm was blaring inside this passage, alternating a wailing tone with a loud male voice warning for people to make their way to safe stations.

A figure came running out of a doorway, saw us, and bolted in the other direction. Someone from my party, I thought it was Sheydu, fired and hit him in the back. We walked past his body a few moments later.

The passage ended in a T intersection. Reida said to take the passage to the right. He stopped briefly around the corner to show us the layout of the base, so that if we became separated, we would at least have a clue where to go.

We ran past several open doors to workshops and computer stations. I hoped that someone on the team was still recording this and that the recordings were going to be clear enough for us to see the purpose of all these rooms. After we got out of here, of course.

We ran into another stairwell going up, but when the door had slammed at the bottom, a loud bang echoed at the top of the staircase, and something flew into the railing with a metallic *ting*.

Reida stopped. "They're shooting live bullets."

Nobody at *gamra* used bullets, and certainly not inside a closed atmosphere facility. Many of the Nations of Earth weapons didn't even use bullets anymore.

We all stood along the sides of the stairwell, weapons at the ready.

The earpiece inside the helmet crackled. The only sound that came through it was the breathing from my team members from having run in their awkward suits.

It wasn't far to the top, and Reida had said that from there, we needed to cross a hall to get outside. Presumably, there was also an airlock involved. There might be vehicles, or were the military pilots going to come this close to the base?

I checked to make sure that my helmet still hung on my belt. I manoeuvred the air hoses inside my suit so that I could easily reach them if I had to put them on in a hurry.

From where I stood, underneath the halfway landing, I couldn't see what was happening at the top of the stairs. Reida and Telaris were at the top, and Sheydu was right behind them. Deyu, our top fighter, stood behind me. I thought Nicha was also up there, because I couldn't see him. Mereeni, too. She was highly trained in these kinds of fights in underground passages.

The door at the top squeaked when it opened.

Someone shouted and then there was a bright flash. My skin felt cold.

Deyu, behind me, pointed up.

I followed Thayu further up the stairs.

A loud bang echoed in the stairwell, followed by two more flashing discharges, and a person fell over the balustrade onto the steps. Evi just managed to step out of the way.

The man wore a uniform with an Independence Force logo. His neck bent at an odd angle and he did not get up.

"Come up here now," Reida shouted.

I followed Thayu up the stairs.

The door at the top was open, and a body lay halfway across it. We had to step over it to get into the larger hall, where it was busy, panicked and noisy. Alarms blared, people sped to vehicles. Trucks mainly, of the type that had brought us here. But there were also two space craft.

Reida pushed the body into the stairwell and closed the door.

Sheydu was putting on her helmet.

We all did the same.

Sheydu said inside my earpiece, "The military is closing in. We have one chance of getting out of here. Contact our rescue team."

Reida said that he would.

We split into small groups to cross the hall unnoticed, each of us taking a different path.

On the way, Reida stopped to try to break into different vehicles, but it seemed you needed some kind of code to get in.

The GenCode ID. Which I had left in the hotel room so as not to be discovered.

Well, dammit.

He *could* hack the locks, he said, but it would take time we didn't have, and our normal solution—to fry the lock by firing at it—would not keep the cabin airtight.

A lot of people and vehicles were moving up to the large airlock.

"I suggest you just break into one of these trucks," Sheydu said in my earpiece.

Reida said, "The ships are so close I can hear them. They know that we're here. If we can get outside, they will come and pick us up."

"That's risky if we have no vehicle."

"How likely is it that we'll quickly get out of this scramble?"

Sheydu didn't reply to that.

Someone shouted on the other side of the hall.

Deyu said, "They've discovered the mess we left on the stairs."

"Time to get out of here quickly," Sheydu said.

It was very hard to run in the cumbersome suit, and the helmet made it difficult to see where I was going. I hadn't turned on the air supply to conserve air. It got hot inside the helmet and because I hadn't sealed it—because I wouldn't be able to breathe, it bumped up and down as I ran. Then it started to fog up.

I tried to lift the front of the helmet back up, so at least I could see properly.

"Keep running. I'll open the airlock. Get your helmets on," Telaris yelled.

He dropped into a crouch and aimed his weapon straight at the airlock door.

We ran past him. I was following Thayu as close as I could.

A white hot beam shot over our heads, and hit the metal door once, and then again for the outside airlock door.

I stopped to jam my helmet shut. Deyu behind me turned on my air tanks. The fog inside cleared in an instant.

A spray of dust and small items flew through the hall as the atmosphere blew out.

A blaring siren was cut off into silence as the air necessary for sound to travel vented. The force knocked me off my feet.

Deyu behind me grabbed the back of my air tank and pulled me up.

We ran.

We ran out through the broken airlock, and through the second door, still smouldering, we ran into some kind of underground parking lot, up a ramp that was slippery through a coating of fine dust, and then into the moon landscape.

The glaring sun shone into my helmet. Even with the visor down, it was impossible to see much. It was also getting hot inside the suit, but I ran.

Garbled voices blared in my helmet. Voices yelling, and people giving commands. This was not the sound of panic. It was the sound of soldiers going into battle.

We ran up a low hill and stopped on the other side.

"There," Reida said, and he pointed at a couple of bright specks in the sky. One detached itself from the group. Was it closer and coming in our direction?

Sheydu was looking in the other direction, scanning the opening of the base, where people were cutting a way through the broken remains of the airlock so that vehicles could get through.

As we watched, a flash of light and dust exploded into the sky. The *foomp* travelled through the ground to our feet a moment later.

"They're still replicating drones," Deyu said.

"Yup. There are millions of the things out there," Reida said.

"But what about your explosives?" Deyu asked.

Sheydu checked her reader. "Not long now. But we really want to be out of here before it goes off."

The few specks in the sky became brighter. There were two that appeared closer than the others.

"Is that them?" I asked.

"Our rescue team," Reida said.

"What's that glittering behind them?"

"I don't see any glittering."

"There." I pointed, but the effect was gone again.

Then I realised. "It's from the sunlight reflecting off the sides of drones. How far are they from the craft?"

Nobody knew. It was impossible to guess. The Asto military's data was good, but didn't update immediately.

Damn. Was this all going to end in grief?

"Thayu?"

If this was the end, I wanted to be with her. She stood behind me. I leaned back. She put her gloved hand on my shoulder.

"Watch," Sheydu said.

The two craft split up. One of them continued ahead. The second rose steeply into the sky, looped around, and dropped into a dizzying dive for the surface. A terrifying cloud of glittering objects followed it.

"Those drones are programmed to follow movement," Reida said, to no one in particular.

It was true, because most of the drone cloud had abandoned the second craft that had kept its course. This craft now turned around in a wide loop.

The other one still plummeted towards the ground.

I watched on in horror.

"What's he doing? Is he a drone, too?" This would not end happily.

I could see the craft clearly, without magnification. It was one of the fighters from the big hall in the orbiting command ship, those craft I'd seen while hanging in their positions along the wall.

Damn, was Asha sacrificing these craft—

No. It pulled into an evasive manoeuvre and veered to the side. The craft's nose turned up. A cloud of dust exploded from the surface, hitting two approaching vehicles. The craft used the downward jets *and* the main engine.

There was no sound on the Moon but I could swear I heard the roar of the engine.

It missed the ground—by less than a few metres.

The pursuing drones were not powerful enough to stop their descent. They crashed into the grey plain. They crashed into the building. Tens, hundreds of them. Explosions rocked the ground.

Dust exploded into the air.

Holy crap.

"Come on!" Mereeni called.

The second craft came to a hovering standstill not far from us.

The door opened.

A figure in a military pressure suit stood in the entrance.

We ran. Mereni first, and then Evi and Deyu, and I followed Thayu, grabbing the hand held out to me, falling unceremoniously on the floor.

But then Sheydu said, "Where is Telaris?"

The grey plain looked deserted.

Then Reida said, "There." He pointed.

Telaris was still about fifty metres away from the craft, limping towards us, hunched over, clutching his side with one hand while holding onto the rocket launcher with the other.

"Quick, get him!" I called.

I jumped back into the dust. Deyu and Thayu and Evi came as well.

We ran to him. Deyu and Evii heaved him up. I grabbed hold of the rocket launcher, but the strap was tangled in his gear, so we carried him across the dust in a tight group.

An object that looked like a fragment of an air tank landed in the dust next to me. And then a piece of pipe, and fragments of concrete.

"Quick!" Sheydu yelled.

We ran the remaining distance, heaved Telaris into the entrance. The people who grabbed him dragged me along with him until I freed myself from the rocket launcher's strap.

I half-fell into a seat, dragged the weapon with me and shoved it in the space underneath the bench and secured the netting.

The door wasn't closed yet—and I hadn't found my safety harness—when the craft took off. The force pinned me in the seat.

Two military crew were frantically trying to shut the door. Both of them were secured by tethers to the craft's ceiling. But the force of our movement made it hard. Hanging onto a seat opposite me, Deyu took a sticky pad out of her pocket, unreeled the rope, flung the thing at the ceiling and went to help the crew.

Finally, the door shut.

Mereeni and Evi had wormed off Telaris' helmet. His face was slick with sweat.

"Where did they hit you?" Mereeni asked.

"It was falling debris," he said. "Knocked me flat. I think it punctured my suit and it auto-fixed."

"We'll have a look when we can."

"Thank you... I'm all right... for now."

Meanwhile, Sheydu was watching something on her screen. A clock counting down. Eight... Seven... Six.... Five.... Four... Three... Two.... One...

I watched her screen, which showed an image of the base from outside.

For a while, nothing happened, and then the ground burst open. Chunks of rock flew into the air. A cloud of dust exploded outwards as the base's atmosphere vented.

But the dust did not fall back down. It shimmered and coalesced into bigger shapes, and even bigger shapes, that moved and followed each other.

The ship's navigator said, "We've unleashed the entire drone army."

"Holy crap," Sheydu said, staring at the screen.

Ships from the military fleet were firing at the drones.

But there were too many of them.

The ship's navigator was talking to someone through her earpiece.

"We're going to beat a path through the swarm," Reida said. He sat closer to the pilot and could better hear their communications.

"Hang on, strap in," said the pilot. "It's going to be rough."

The next moment, I was pushed hard into my seat as the craft shot forward. The floor vibrated with the power of the engine. Reida lost his grip on a little connector that he would use for linking devices. It flew across the cabin into the back wall with a sharp *thwack*. He swore under his breath.

The thing flew back again when we made a sharp turn.

The force of the acceleration made it impossible for me to lift my head. On the forward view screen, light objects whizzed past us at ridiculous speed. We were ridiculously close to far too many drones. There was... another craft in front of us?

Really?

I had to close my eyes because certainly, we were going to collide with something?

I heard a soft *pop*. That was it. We'd hit something and would fly out of control into the oncoming swarm for them to obliterate us.

But no, we kept flying.

There was another pop and another one.

Someone was firing the rockets. Was that our ship? No, it was the craft in front of us. Our pilot was... not doing very much. Just following.

And still we accelerated. Slaved to the fighter in front, which was guiding us in and clearing the way.

We zigzagged in between the bright dots that were coming for us. The slight lag between our craft's manoeuvres and the display on the screen was dizzying.

Even Sheydu's expression was distinctly uncomfortable.

The drones passed so close that the screen couldn't handle the scene rendering. Sometimes it appeared we flew right through them. Debris exploded into space before us. The craft jumped and twisted.

Somewhere during this crazy, white-knuckled ride, I must have passed out through too much acceleration.

When I opened my eyes, we were in weightlessness. On the viewscreen, I spotted the familiar outside of the command ship, where we had spent three months waiting.

The wide docking doors were open. Our pilot eased our craft inside and landed in one of the marked spots on the floor.

The door opened, and someone shouted inside, "Good one. Now get yourself strapped in. We are leaving."

We all scrambled. I felt sweaty and shaky.

We pulled ourselves into the hall. Meanwhile, the other fighter craft came in. The one that had cleared the way for us. First, by letting the drones crash into the ground, and then by creating a path through the swarm. I had to remind myself to thank that pilot.

We floated in weightlessness to a room with safety netting and holdfast stations. Several people were already there. I recognised some familiar faces.

Veyada, Nicha, Isharu, Anyu.

Where were Ynggi and Zyana? Had Leisha made it back yet? Yes, I could see my familiar craft.

The ship crew were the last ones to come into the safety station. These types of military ships always had at least four or five crew on board. They would include a pilot, navigator, and an engineer, and one or two people for operating the weapons. You could recognise the pilots because they wore headsets and always wore a pressure device that looked like an octopus when it was unplugged.

They were Coldi military personnel. I nodded to them, recognising the pilot and navigator of our craft, and they acknowledged me with similar nods. They were military people. Getting overly emotional would be unbecoming.

The second pilot, the one with the deathly skills, was still wearing a helmet. This person was much shorter than the typical Coldi military officer.

He lifted the helmet off.

Ynggi.

He grinned.

I gaped.

What the—

And also, a lot of stuff started making sense.

"I didn't know that you could fly."

"Let's get strapped up first," he said, utterly professional.

So we strapped in just when the ship started moving with a jerk that felt too powerful for a craft of the size.

"So you learned to fly. Was that what all the tests and training were about?"

All those tests the military had put us through in the months that we'd hung in orbit, when they decided to leave me where I was because I clearly had no military value, but they had seen something in Ynggi.

Ynggi grinned. "They discovered, yet again, because it's well known, that Pengali people have an extraordinary sense of space, they have very quick reflexes, and they don't pass out as quickly as most other people at high acceleration."

Yes, quite a few of the larger courier craft based in Barresh used Pengali pilots for those reasons. An infallible sense of space that didn't as easily become disoriented in three-dimensional navigation.

"What happened to the enemy?"

"The base is completely destroyed," Nicha said. "The fighters are mopping up drones, but there won't be any more because the machine used to create them blew a giant hole in the ground."

"It re-arranged the map of this useless piece of rock," Sheydu said. "We've added a new crater." She looked pleased with herself. She loved explosives, and it wasn't often that she got to use them to their fullest potential.

"I'm going to suggest to Dekker that it be named after us," Mereeni said.

"So where are we going now?" I asked.

Thayu "said, We're going to rejoin the rest of the fleet. They're waiting further out. My father has handed orbital command back to Gracelyn Sebaya."

No doubt the fallout from the destruction would take months to settle, both literally and figuratively.

Also, the Independence Force and their sympathisers had their fingers in almost every organisation of power on Earth, and so we would have to remain vigilant.

CHAPTER THIRTY-SIX

THE DRONE REPLICATOR base of the Independence Force was well and truly destroyed.

I heard this when seated in an official briefing, surrounded by people in pink uniforms, when Asha reported to his troops at the end of this operation.

The military had—as he called it—performed an aggressive sweep of the higher orbit of both Earth and the Moon and had destroyed as many enemy satellites as possible. Prior to the destruction of the base, in between the time he'd received the messages from my team that we knew where it was and the base's destruction, military trackers had traced a couple of links into deep space. They'd be following up on those.

Amarru opened the Exchange for public use.

Apparently, Marin Federza was not happy. We might have secured Dekker's begrudging approval at the eleventh hour, but the document hadn't *reached* the *gamra* assembly before the deadline, which meant Asto's action was technically illegal.

But, to be honest, none of us could worry too much about this. We'd sort it out once we returned to Barresh.

The drone attacks stopped.

Up to twenty percent of Nations of Earth officials resigned in the days following the defeat. According to our contacts, entire departments walked out, especially in the communications sectors.

As a result of this, a flood of stories came out that never made it to publication because they'd been held up by Independence Force censorship.

Stories about corruption and coercion in the sub-top ranks of diplomats. Stories about subverted elections to replace delegates. Concerns raised about integrity of candidates and their loyalty to the principles of Nations of Earth. Those concerns accused certain delegates of wanting to enter the assembly purely to dismantle its powers.

There was also plenty of evidence that certain delegates used court action to stifle criticism of their dealings, and more than a dozen journalists—mostly freelancing individuals—regained their freedom from detention after those cases and their judgements were thrown out.

What was left of the Emergency Council held an urgent meeting to re-establish a working council that met the quorum.

We collated all the data we had collected and Reida sent it all to Margarethe Ollund to give to someone at Nations of Earth she trusted, when all the dust had settled. That someone might be Gracelyn Sebaya, if her career survived the fallout of the conflict.

But we had little to do with all this. We returned briefly to New Zealand to pick up the kids.

The White Bay community had set up scaffolding to re-paint the community hall, and when we visited, a bunch of carpenters were walking around taking measurements to instal a new kitchen.

A projection screen remained in the hall and the townsfolk wandered in and out to follow the news.

That news consisted of a stream of discovery after discovery of corruption, coercion and outright abuse by people sympathetic to the Independence Force.

Locals discussed world and *gamra* politics in a way I'd never seen before. I'd come here many times with at least one Coldi person, but this was the first time they actually seem to have *noticed*. They were also busy talking to two European journalists who had come to investigate this sleepy little town. Was it really true that the first ever official meeting of both political and military leaders of Earth and *gamra* had taken place here? And what was the involvement of the Pretoria Cartel? Had we really linked up with Celia Braddock? So many questions.

There was a sense of vibrancy about the place, a sleepy community that had found its place in the world.

Meanwhile, a huge cleanup forensics operation started at the crater at the former locality of Selena Base. Of course we were also not there to witness it in person, but news channels showed it in curious, and dare I say quite boring, detail. Bulldozers gathering rubble in heaps. People in environment suits sifting through the moon dust. Rows and rows of items of evidence on tables in an underground bunker. Most of those fragments were smaller than my hand. I suspected that the data we had recorded during our run through the base would be more informative than this giant one-hundred-billion-piece jigsaw puzzle that would take many years to solve.

We watched some of these proceedings, seated in the White Bay hall, sipping coffee made by Diana. Her son Brad wanted to know how hard it was to get into the Nations of Earth international relations training, and I spent a good hour discussing his options. Basically, I convinced him it might be easier for him to apply to Amarru, because I could put a good word in for him.

We discussed the future with our team and my father and Erith seated around the table in the kitchen. I had no illusion, as with any other enemy group we encountered, that the Independence Force would quietly disappear and never give us grief again.

Life didn't work like that. But when they came back, they would hopefully find a strong Earth-*gamra* bond.

A few days later, Simon Dekker made an official appearance from the Nations of Earth compound. He stood on the steps of the building that housed the president's office. I assumed he didn't record from the office because it was still a mess.

He announced his immediate resignation and called an election. The position of interim president went to Gracelyn Sebaya.

I asked Asha whether they continued to detect further activity from out of the system.

There was some, he said, but it wasn't on par with the activity he already measured from the Tamer Collective. The Independence Force was not terribly big, but they had demonstrated the capacity to create dangerous technology, and needed to be closely watched.

"They need to be included in some sort of political body," I told him.

"Probably." And after a brief silence, he added, "That's your job."

I guessed it was.

Asha's people combed over the hours and hours of footage that we had recorded in the base. They concluded that the underground machine was a particle injector that used either fusion or dark matter to replicate weaponry and to direct it precisely where they wanted it.

An anonymous source also sent me a long manifesto that included a playbook for how the Independence Force would take over the governments of Earth and drive the aliens away.

Both the tone and language reminded me of when I lived with these people at Midway Space Station. Even when I was a kid, they came across to me as frightened of people who weren't like them.

But time after time we had seen that small groups could form formidable enemies if they set their minds to it.

We needed to continue to be vigilant, and we needed to engage these people in discussions.

As Asha said, that was my job, so I started thinking about a few trips I had been putting off for a long time.

On Evi and Telaris' world of Indrahui, unrest had brewed for many, many generations. Wars had been fought, and nothing had ever come to a resolution that *gamra* found respectable enough to upgrade Indrahui's status from provisional remember to full member. Indrahui was also trying to be part of the Tamer Collective, but I wasn't sure how well that was going.

The Tamer Collective itself could be useful because it could undertake the commercial functions that the Exchange was struggling to cope with.

I heard some rumours that Minke Kluysters grew impatient with the slow progress of the Tamer Collective. Strong whispers suggested that his wife was going to run for president of Nations of Earth in the same way Fiona Davidson—Robert Davidson's wife—had done before her. I was doubtful she would win, but one of these days, someone from PanAf would take the position and would add a whole level of complexity to the already complex situation.

There were lots of frameworks to be set up, lots of things to do.

"You should come to visit and you can play with Emi however much you like," I said to my father when we were sitting by the fire on the last night of our visit.

I was looking forward to going home, because by now we had been away for over four months and I dreaded to think of what would have happened at home in the intervening time. The rainforest in Ynggi's room might have taken over the apartment.

My father nodded. "Poor old Fred probably has a few more months left in him. When he passes to the dog beach in the sky, we will think about it."

Fred lay on the floor on his rug. It would probably be the last time I saw him.

I knelt on the rug and scratched his head. He looked up at me with baleful brown eyes. Poor old Fred.

I looked at Erith, and could still see the hesitation in her eyes. There was a story there, a story about Damarq, a nasty situation that would come to the fore at an inopportune time, and that I would have to deal with.

There was plenty still to do, but for now, we were going home.

Thanks for Reading

THANK you for reading *Ambassador 12: The Unfolding Army*. As the author of this book, I would hugely appreciate it if you could return to where you purchased it and write a short review. Thanks so much!

Buy my books from my online store and get specials, bundles and editions not available on mainstream stores.

Never again miss a new release and get four books free if you sign up for my newsletter.

ABOUT THE AUTHOR

Patty Jansen lives in Sydney, Australia, where she spends most of her time writing Science Fiction and Fantasy.

Her career started in earnest when her story *This Peaceful State of War* placed first in the second quarter of the Writers of the Future contest and was published in their 27th anthology. She has also sold fiction to genre magazines such as Analog Science Fiction and Fact, Redstone SF and Aurealis, before making the move to independent publishing.

Patty has written over fifty novels in both Science Fiction and Fantasy, including the *Icefire Trilogy* and the *Ambassador* series.

pattyjansen.com

BOOKS BY PATTY JANSEN

For a complete list of books, scan the image below with your phone.